Acclaim for Ayelet Waldman's

Love and Other Impossible Pursuits

"Quick and graceful. . . . Through her vivid descriptions, Manhattan, especially Central Park, comes beautifully alive." —*The Seattle Times*

"Waldman achieves . . . a smart and finally affecting portrayal of a woman working her way out of her own grandiose self-image into something like real love. . . . *Love and Other Impossible Pursuits* is . . . strongest at its most satirical . . . [and] offers . . . the chance for Waldman to make her case beyond the boundaries of mere likeability."

—*New York* magazine

"Incisive . . . well paced, cleanly written, [and] moving."

—*Los Angeles Times*

"Masterful. . . . Gratifying. . . . Impressively astute."

—*Rocky Mountain News*

"Poignant. . . . Astute. . . . Waldman tells [the story] with a wittiness and pace that never slacken." —*The Independent* (London)

"*Love and Other Impossible Pursuits* is the most riveting and sharply rendered novel I've read in years. Ayelet Waldman writes the language of grief with virtuosic fluency. Piercing, provocative, and unflinchingly honest, she makes us rapt participants in her protagonist's struggle with the most painful complications of marriage and motherhood. Once you begin this book, there will be no putting it down. Once you've finished, you will never forget it."

—Julie Orringer, author of *How to Breathe Underwater*

"I had a great time reading *Love and Other Impossible Pursuits*, which I did in one sitting. . . . I thought the heroine was a great accomplishment in that she's impossible, but one likes her. And William (her stepson) is a triumph." —Diane Johnson, author of *Le Divorce*

"A deft and enthralling work. Trapped in the agonies of love, Emilia chants her rage in the shockingly funny and grief-stricken voice of a woman on the edge. An astonishing character, a beautiful novel. If you are not moved to tears, then your heart is carved from wood."

—Andrew Sean Greer, author of *The Confessions of Max Tivoli*

"I read this book in one sitting while lying on my favorite couch. And I'll read it again on a future road trip. And I'll read it for the third time in the bathtub. Ayelet Waldman is that good."

—Sherman Alexie, author of *Ten Little Indians*

Ayelet Waldman

Love

and Other Impossible Pursuits

Ayelet Waldman is the author of *Daughter's Keeper* and of the Mommy-Track mystery series. Her writing has appeared in *The New York Times*, *The Believer*, *Elle*, and other publications. She and her husband, the novelist Michael Chabon, live in Berkeley, California, with their four children.

www.ayeletwaldman.com

Also by Ayelet Waldman

Daughter's Keeper

and Other Impossible Pursuits

Ayelet Waldman

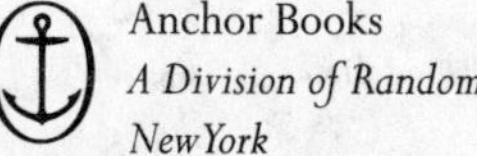

Anchor Books
A Division of Random House, Inc.
New York

FIRST ANCHOR BOOKS EDITION, JANUARY 2007

The Library of Congress has cataloged the Doubleday edition as follows:
Waldman, Ayelet.
Love and other impossible pursuits / Ayelet Waldman.—1st ed.
p. cm.
1. Married women—Fiction. 2. Infants—Death—Fiction.
3. Stepfamilies—Fiction. 4. Grief—Fiction. I. Title.
PS3573.A42124L69 2006
813'.54—dc22 2004063546

Anchor ISBN: 978-1-4000-9513-1

Book design by Donna Sinisgalli

www.anchorbooks.com

Printed in the United States of America
10 9 8 7 6 5 4 3 2

To my parents,
Ricki and Leonard Waldman

Chapter 1

Usually, if I duck my head and walk briskly, I can make it past the playground at West Eighty-first Street. I start preparing in the elevator, my eyes on the long brass arrow as it ticks down from the seventh, sixth, fifth, fourth floor. Sometimes the elevator stops and one of my neighbors gets on, and I have no choice but to crack the carapace of my solitude, and pretend civility. If it's one of the younger ones, the guitar player with the brush of red hair and the peeling skin, say, or the movie executive in the rumpled jeans and the buttery leather coat, it's enough to muster a polite nod of the head. The older ones require more. The steel-haired women in the self-consciously bohemian dresses, folds of purple peeping from under the hems of black wool capes, demand conversation about the weather, or the spot of wear on the Oriental carpet runner in the lobby, or the front page of the arts section. That is quite nearly too much to bear, because don't they see that I am busy? Don't they realize that obsessive self-pity is an all-consuming activity that leaves no room for conversation? Don't they know that the entrance to the park lies right next to the Eighty-first Street playground and that if I am not completely prepared, if I do not clear my mind, stop my ears to all sounds other than my own breathing, it is entirely possible—likely even—that instead of striding boldly past the playground with my eyes on the bare gray branches of the trees, I will collapse outside the playground gate, the shrill voices of the children keening in my skull? Don't they understand, these ladies with their petitions and their dead banker husbands and bulky Tod's purses, that if I let them distract me with talk of Republicans stealing elections or whether Mrs. Katz from 2B saw Anthony the new doorman asleep behind the desk last Tuesday night, I will not make it past the playground to the refuge of the park beyond? Don't they get that the barbaric assault of their voices, the impatient thumping of their Lucite canes as they wait insistently for my mumbled replies, will prevent me from getting to the only place in the entire city where I am able to approximate serenity? They will force me instead to trudge along the Seventy-ninth Street Transverse, pressed against the grimy stone walls, inhaling exhaust fumes from crosstown buses all the way to the East Side. Or worse, they will force me to take a cab.

Today, thank God, the elevator is empty all the way to the lobby.

"Have a nice walk, Mrs. Woolf," Ivan says as he holds the door open for me.

That started the day after our wedding. The first few times I tried to explain that I was still Ms. Greenleaf. I know Ivan understood. He's not an idiot. But he merely smiled, nodded, and said, "Of course, Ms. Greenleaf," and then greeted me with a "Good morning, Mrs. Woolf," the next day. At least it was better than when I'd first moved in with Jack. Then I had muttered something like, "Oh, no, please call me Emilia." Ivan hadn't even bothered to smile and nod. He had stared at me from behind his thick black glasses, shaken his head as if he were my fifth-grade teacher and I'd disappointed him by forgetting my homework or, worse, using foul language in class. "No, Ms. Greenleaf," he had said. That was all. Not "I couldn't," or "I wouldn't feel right." Just, "No." Because of course he would never call someone in the building by her first name; it was appalling to have suggested it at all.

Today I smile, nod, and walk out the door and across the street to the park.

February is the longest month of the year.

Winter has been on us for so very long and spring seems like it might never come. The sky is gray and thick with clouds, the kind of clouds that menace the city, threatening not Christmas postcard snow, or a downpour of cold clean rain, but bitter needles that immediately melt the snow, so that it feels like what is coming down from the sky is actually yellow-gray slush. The sidewalks are banked by mounds of black-fringed snow and every step off the curb is a game of Russian roulette which might end with glacial black water sloshing around your ankle, soaking your sock and shoe. Normally I hunker down; I build fires in the fireplace, wrap myself in chenille throws and wool socks, reread Jane Austen, and will the short, dark days to creep by more quickly. This year, however, I long to embrace the unrelenting grimness of New York in February. This year I *need* February. Even now, at the end of January, it is as if the city has noticed my dejection and proceeded to prove its commiseration. The trees in the park seem particularly bare; they poke at the dreary sky with lifeless branches that have lost not just their leaves but the very hope of leaves. The grass has turned brown and been kicked away, leaving a mire covered by a scrim of dog-shit-spotted ice. The Bridle Path and the path along the Reservoir are muddy and have buckled in places, gnarled roots and knots marring the once smooth surfaces and tripping up the fleece-clad runners.

But the Diana Ross Playground is full of children. New York children will play outside in all weather, except the most inclement, their nannies and mothers desperate to escape the confines of even the most spacious apartments. On the dreariest winter day, when the swings are wet enough to soak water-repellent snow pants right through, when the expensive, cushiony ground cover is frozen to a bone-breaking hardness, when the last bit of metal left in the meticulously childproofed playground is cold enough to cause a plump pink tongue to stick fast to it, until an unflappable Dominican nanny pours the last inch of a Starbucks mocha over the joined bit of flesh and teeter-totter, the kids are there, screaming their little-kid screams and laughing their little-kid laughs. I quicken my step until I am galumphing along at an ungainly jog, my extra weight pounding into my widened hips, my bones aching with every jarring thump of heel to path.

I allow myself to slow to a gasping walk as soon as the children's voices fade into the background hum of the rest of the park. In the summer Central Park sounds like the countryside—or a version of the countryside where birdsong competes with the hiss of skateboard wheels on cement and with the flutes of Peruvian buskers playing Andean melodies as interpreted by Simon and Garfunkel. In the spring, when the cherry trees are in full blush and the hillocks around Sheep Meadow are covered in yellow daffodils, it is easy to love Central Park. In the summer, when the Shakespeare Garden is a tangle of blossoms and wedding ceremonies and you cannot walk two feet without stumbling over a bank of asters or a dog playing Frisbee, loving Central Park is a breeze. In the winter, though, the pigeons fly under the naked elms, keeping close to where the conscientious, lonely old ladies with their paper bags of bread crusts congregate on the snow-dampened benches of the Mall. In the winter, the park is left to those of us whose love is most true, those of us who don't need swags and fringes of wisteria, those of us for whom snow-heavy black locust trees, mud-covered hills, and the sound of the wind creaking through bare branches are enough. I have always understood that it is in the escape provided by these 843 acres that real beauty lies. The pastel Mardi Gras of spring and summer and the brilliant burnt reds and oranges of autumn are just foofaraw.

I cut north to the trail along the Reservoir. There is one more playground in my path, but it is far enough away that I can keep my eyes averted from the Lincoln Log play structure and the red-and-yellow slide. It is late for the mommies with jogging strollers, and if my luck holds I will miss them entirely. Last Wednesday I left a couple of hours early, to meet a friend who had decided that a morning of shoe shopping would bounce me out of my despondency, would turn me back into someone whose company she enjoyed. Mindy did not, of course, say that. Mindy said that her husband had given her a pair of Manolo Blahniks for her birthday in the size she had led him to believe that she wore, and she needed to see if the store carried the shoe in a ten and a half.

On that day, I came upon a whole row of new mothers crouched down in back of their strollers, their postpartum-padded behinds thrust out, their hands gripping the handles as they rose up to their toes and then squatted back down, cooing all the while to their well-bundled infants who squawked, laughed, or slept in $750 strollers, Bugaboo Frogs just like the one parked in the hallway outside our apartment, next to the spindly table with the silk orchids. The blue denim Bugaboo that kicks me in the gut every time I stand waiting for the elevator. They squatted and rose in unison, this group of mommies, and none of them said a word when I stopped in front of them and grunted as if I'd been punched. They looked at me, and then back at each other, but no one spoke, not when I started to cry, and not when I turned and ran, back along the path, past the first playground and then the second, and then back out onto Central Park West.

Today I am lucky. The mommies have stayed in, or are sharing a post-workout latte. I don't see one until I am on the Bridle Path on the East Side. She runs by me so fast that I barely have time to register the taut balls of her calves pumping in shiny pink running pants, her ears covered in matching fur earmuffs. The babies in her double jogging stroller are tiny purple mounds, pink noses, and then gone. Too fast to cause me anything but a momentary blaze of pain.

At Ninetieth Street, having made it safely and sanely across the park, I look at my watch. Shit. I am late, again, with only five minutes to make it up to Ninety-second and then all the way across to Lex. I quicken my pace, pinching my waist against the stitch in my side. The tails of my long coat flap against my legs, and with my other hand I do my best to hold the coat closed. I can button it now, but it looks dreadful, my thick torso straining against the buttons, causing the fabric to gape. While I'm not vain enough to buy a new winter coat—I will not spend hundreds of dollars on a piece of clothing I am bound and determined not to need a month from now—I am sufficiently self-conscious to leave the coat open, counting on a thick scarf to keep out the bitter damp.

It is not until I run around the white fence barriers and the cement planters, show my ID card at the security desk, pass through the metal detector, and am shifting from foot to foot in front of the bank of elevators that I remember that I have set my watch forward fifteen minutes for this very reason, so I will not be late again, so that Carolyn will not have yet another reason to call Jack and berate him for my capricious negligence, my disregard for her and all she holds sacred. I feel myself deflate, as if the only thing keeping me buoyant was my agitation and anxiety. By the time the elevator arrives I am tiny, I am shrunken to the size of a mouse, I am the smallest person in the 92nd Street Y.

A claque of women follows me into the elevator. Two are pregnant; one holds a baby strapped to her chest in a black leather Baby Björn infant carrier. The last pushes a Bugaboo stroller identical to the one parked outside my apartment. Because of course the irony is that for all my expertise as the preeminent cartographer of a childfree Central Park, my very destination is into the belly of the beast. My goal, my journey's end, is the 92nd Street Y Nursery School.

All this fecundity would have stopped me dead in my tracks had I stumbled upon it in the park. Central Park is my refuge, and its invasion by the baby brigade enrages and devastates me. At the preschool, however, I am used to a certain quality and quantity of misery. I have never been anything but uncomfortable and unhappy here. To be reduced to tears in the elevator by the milk-drunk flush of an infant's cheek is pretty much par for the course.

The women in the elevator acknowledge my presence with the barest nod, precisely the nod I give those of my neighbors who permit me this coldness. I respond in kind and affix my eyes to the lighted buttons over the elevator door, clocking our progress up through the building to the sixth floor.

The hallway of the preschool is decorated, as always, in brilliantly colored children's artwork that changes with every Jewish holiday. Now it is Tu B'Shevat that we are celebrating, and the children have painted various kinds of trees. The hallway trumpets the school's celebrated student-teacher ratio. It evidences sure and patient guidance, a wellspring of inventive and carefully educated creativity, and an art supply budget rivaling that of the School of Visual Arts. I scan the paintings, looking to see if William has done one. He is an adept artist for his age, is William. He has inherited his mother's agile and delicate fingers. He draws mostly seascapes: fish and octopi, multi-fanged sharks and moray eels. His latest is displayed outside his classroom. William, it turns out, is the only child who has failed to honor the birthday of the trees. At first I think his picture is nothing more than a huge scribble of red crayon, but when I lean in to take a closer look I see that on the bottom of the page William has drawn a rainbow-colored parrot fish. The parrot fish is lying on its side because a swordfish has torn a hole in its belly. The red overlying the scene is blood spurting from the fish's wounds. Perhaps the picture is meant to be an allegory, and the parrot fish to symbolize the Jewish people should they fail to recognize their connection to the land. But I doubt it.

I gather William's coat and hat from his hook and wait for the door to the Red Room to open. William is Red this year. Last year he was Blue, and Orange the year before. Orange was his favorite, as he never tires of telling us. It is, apparently, a more interesting color. Many of William's favorite things are orange. Not oranges. Nothing that prosaic. It's not that William is opposed to fruit. He likes a nice kumquat, especially in preserves. But the things he enjoys that are orange include paella spiced with saffron, Monarch butterflies, the Orangemen of Northern Ireland and of Syracuse University, and especially traffic cones. William likes to talk about this kind of thing. He also likes to discuss the similarities and differences between the various dromaeosaurids, especially *Dromaeosaurus* and *Velociraptor*, what his daemon would be (a cat like Will Parry's, of course), and whether or not Pluto should really have been reclassified as part of the Kuiper belt of objects. (Williams thinks not. William thinks Pluto was robbed. William thinks having been a planet since its discovery by Clyde Tombaugh on February 18, 1930, Pluto deserves to stay a planet.) William is five years old, and sometimes sounds like a very small sixty-two-year-old man. Everyone finds these utterances of his very charming. His precocity is, by all accounts, enchanting.

Everyone but me. I find William insufferable.

What kind of a person feels this way about an innocent child, even a child who corrects your pronunciation of the word "travois," one who accurately estimates your body mass index while you are halfway through a piece of chocolate cheesecake, one who rebuffs your attempts to please him with a knowing and dismissive smirk more suited to an acne-faced adolescent than a plump-cheeked preschooler? I am the adult and so I should be able to love this child despite his peculiarities, and despite my own guilt for having wrecked his home.

I unzip William's insulated lunch box and dump the half-eaten contents into the trash can, holding my breath against the lunch-box smell—part sour milk, part plastic. I realize, a moment too late, that the mothers are watching me. One of them is bound to report back to Carolyn that I have thrown away the remains of lunch without taking careful note of what William has left uneaten. Another demerit. More evidence of my untrustworthiness. Without meaning to, I catch the eye of the mother with the baby carrier. I blush, but she does not. She turns away and lays her cheek against the top of her baby's head. I can feel the baby's soft skin under my own cheek, the wisp of hair against my lips, the feathery pulse beneath the thin bones of her skull. I blink and turn to make a thorough study of William's bloody drawing.

By now the hall is crowded with nannies and mothers. The doors to the classrooms open and a teacher peeks her head out. "Is Nora's nanny here?" She sends a fat redheaded girl out into the hall. Down the corridors outside the Blue, Green, Yellow, Purple, Orange, Red rooms a kind of choreography of welcome is taking place. One by one the children tumble out, yelping greetings at the women waiting for them. The women kneel simultaneously, scooping children in their arms. Then it is William's turn to be released. He stands in the doorway of the Red Room, waiting patiently while a triple-scoop chocolate ice-cream cone of a woman hugs a tiny freckled girl to her chest. The nanny's hair is like a replica of her body in miniature, a tower that trembles as she lifts the little girl in her arms. William ducks under his classmate's wagging feet and walks up to me. I lean over and hug him with one awkward arm. He stiffens, then seems to resign himself to my embrace.

"You're here today?" he says.

"It's Wednesday."

"So it is."

What kind of five-year-old says, "So it is?"

"Come on," I say. "Let's go." I need to escape the press of small bodies. I can smell them—the sour milky tang of their sweat, the strawberry fragrance of their shampoo. They eddy about my legs in a quicksand of sticky hands and pink cheeks. The sound of miniature rubber-soled sneakers squeaking across the floor is worse than nails on a chalkboard. I trip over a Spider-Man lunch box and kick a pair of aqua Shearling boots across the hall. Their heads are at my waist, and my fingers long to slide through their soft hair, to twirl their ringlets. I remind myself of the note that came home in William's lunch box last month. They all probably have lice.

"William, let's go," I repeat, my voice louder than I had intended. Two of the mothers look at me, eyebrows raised, mouths twisted into disapproving frowns. "We're running late," I mutter, shrugging my shoulders, as if this is an explanation, as if this will prevent the phone call to Carolyn. Not just irresponsible. Abusive, too.

William allows himself to be zipped into his coat. I tie the strings of his hat tightly under his chin.

"Where are your mittens?"

He pulls them out of his pockets and I tug them onto his limp hands. His left thumb stays with the rest of his hand, refusing to go where it belongs, and for a few seconds I tried to twist the mitten around and stuff the thumb in correctly. Finally, I just give up.

"All set," I say, smiling falsely.

William gives me a baleful look and sets off toward the elevator. By the time I pick up the booster seat that his mother has left in the broom closet outside the classroom, he is waiting for me, watching the elevator doors close.

"We missed it," he says.

"I'll bet you ten bucks there'll be another one."

I never meant to feel this way about this child. My assumption was that I would love him. I love the father so very much; it seemed inevitable that I would adore the child. I longed for William to love me. Jack finally allowed me to meet William after we had been seeing each other for six months, a few weeks before we moved in together. He might have introduced us earlier, but he had determined, for a while, to leave the decision of timing up to Carolyn, to give her the sense of controlling that, if nothing else. Jack had taken matters into his own hands only when it became clear that, if the choice were left to her, William would live out his life in blissful ignorance of the woman who had come to share his father's bed. That was one of the last conversations between Jack and his ex-wife to which I was not privy, and thus I have no idea what it cost Jack to insist on the Saturday morning that he, William, and I spent at the Central Park Zoo.

I approached my first meeting with the son with far more trepidation than I had my first date with the father. It was so important, this first moment we would lay eyes on each other. I played it and replayed it in my mind as I rode the subway uptown. It was September, but it felt more like August, muggy and hot, one of those Indian summer days where it's such an oven on the subway platform that the air is hard to breathe, as if every molecule is weighted down with something extra—some kind of liquefied dust that sticks to your lungs and the inside of your nostrils. I took the train from my apartment in Stuyvesant Town, and when the doors opened at Fifty-ninth Street, just two, too brief stops in cool, dry, air-conditioned air, it was almost more than I could do to get to my feet and leave the car.

Jack and William were waiting for me at the entrance to the zoo. Jack had William up on his shoulders, and even at three years old, William's legs dangled down halfway to Jack's waist. Jack is a handsome man, compact and well built, like my father. He hovers somewhere between five foot six and five foot seven, depending on his mood. He is optimistic and cheerful, and when he is happy seems much taller. On the rare occasions when he succumbs to depression, he shrinks, sort of folding in on himself, as if he is willing himself to disappear. Jack once said that one of the very first things that attracted him to me is that, while I am small, I never disappear. On the contrary, I seem always to be doing what I can to be visible. Jack has never seen me doing my mouse act at William's preschool.

Jack's mother is a Syrian Jew, and he looks like her side of the family. He has a straight, sharp nose with delicate nostrils, his hair is very dark, nearly black, and his eyes have navy blue irises. It is a color that manages to look piercing and deep and velvety soft all at the same time. This is not an eye color I have ever seen before, and from the moment I first saw it I have wondered if it is unique to him, or if it will be reproduced in his children.

William's eyes are just plain, everyday blue.

Jack is a runner and a mountain climber and though he is small, perhaps *because* he is small, he is very strong. His muscles are flat and hard, and his waist is slim. He looks wonderful in a suit, and possesses a casual, almost instinctive grace and elegance. For instance, although he cares little about clothes, he never wears ventless, double-breasted jackets. He says that they make him look like a midget. Weeks before we met, when I had just graduated from law school and had gone shopping for a life for which I possessed no wardrobe, among the pile of marked-down suits and dresses I bought was a black, double-breasted Tahari coatdress. After Jack explained his philosophy of double-breasted jackets, I could never again wear that dress without feeling like I was auditioning for the part of a munchkin in *The Wizard of Oz*. I donated the dress to a charity that supplies clothing to women trying to make the transition from welfare to work.

As I waded through the sluggish heat toward my lover and his son I saw Jack grab William's feet and tip backward, making as if to dump the boy off his shoulders. I could hear William's squeal of delight all the way down the path as he grabbed fistfuls of his father's hair and struggled to right himself. If it had not been so terribly hot I might have turned and run back down the path, across six blocks, and down to the chill of the subway train. They looked so happy, this father and son, standing underneath the Delacorte Clock outside the zoo. They looked so happy, and all they needed was a mother to complete the perfect picture of familial bliss. The mother, however, was in her apartment at 1010 Fifth Avenue, on the corner of Eighty-second Street, maybe soaking a tissue with her tears, maybe prescribing herself double doses of Ativan or Xanax. The mother was maybe combing through old photographs and letters, trying to find some clue to the betrayal that had laid waste to the perfect triangle that had once been her family. The mother was gone, and in her place was me, a hopeful smile plastered to my lips, a crumpled FAO Schwarz bag stuck to my sweaty palm, trying to bribe this small boy to forget that I had thoroughly and comprehensively ruined his life.

Falling in love with Jack was so easy that I had assumed that falling in love with his son would be just as effortless. I did not imagine that the boy would be equally infatuated with me; I am not that foolish. I presumed that I would have to win him over, that slowly, over the weeks and months, even the years, the force of my affection would topple his reserve, would chip away at his suspicion and resentment. He would learn to care for me, would find one day that my love had insinuated itself into his life and heart. He was, after all, a very small boy, only three years old. Soon he would not remember a time when I was not part of his life. While he might not love me as a mother, he would look upon me as a beloved aunt, a confidant, a trusted friend. And he would be my buddy, my co-conspirator, my practice baby. I love children and I always have. As a teenager, I had been a sought-after babysitter, a well-loved (and well-tipped) camp counselor. Here, finally, was a child whose right to my devotion was unimpeachable. This was the child of my beloved. How could I help but love him?

When he finally noticed me, Jack swung William down off his shoulders. He was so nervous that his voice actually cracked. "Look, Will. Here's Emilia!"

Had William flung himself to the ground, his legs and arms windmilling in a tantrum, it would have been easier for me to handle. Had he scowled at me, or turned his back to me, or even kicked me, I would have given Jack an understanding wink and led the way through the gates of the zoo. Had he burst into tears and begged to go home to his mama, I would have reassured my boyfriend with a sympathetic, discreet pat of the hand, and sent them on their way.

Instead, William reached one long-fingered, limp hand toward me. "Pleased to meet you," he said. I smiled uncomfortably and took his hand in mine. His fingers were cool and slightly damp, the nails evenly trimmed, not chewed.

"Pleased to meet you, too," I said. "I brought you something." I handed him the bag. He opened it and pulled out the plush dinosaur I had bought him. Jack had told me that William was obsessed with dinosaurs, that his favorite place was the Museum of Natural History.

The three-year-old boy held the stuffed dinosaur at arm's length. "Theropods only have three toes," he said.

I looked at the smiling creature with the tiny dangling forelegs. It was green, with blue velvet polka dots. "I guess it's not terribly realistic," I said.

"It's fine. Thank you." William handed the stuffed dinosaur to his father, who tucked it under his arm and smiled at me apologetically.

Now it was finally time for that rueful wink, but somehow I just didn't have it in me.

"It's almost ten thirty," Jack said. "We don't want to miss the penguin feeding." He led the way into the zoo.

Chapter 2

It is always next to impossible to flag down a cab outside of the 92nd Street Y when I am with William. I never have these problems when I am here for a lecture, or on the rare mornings when I have to drop William off at school, so I know it is not the location that prevents the cabbies from stopping. It is the goddamn booster seat. It is the fact that they know it is going to take me an extra few minutes to wrestle it into the backseat, wrestle the kid into it, and wrestle it back out again once we arrive at our destination. I feel like I should carry a sign that says, "I promise I'll make it worth your while." Or maybe one that says, "Look, I don't like this any better than you do. His mother insists on it, and I swear to God I'll give you an extra five bucks, so please will you just stop and pick us the hell up? Please?"

A sympathetic or desperate Sikh in a pale blue turban pulls over and I wrench open the door and throw William's lunch box and my purse inside. William's booster seat is the kind that has a five-point harness and has to be installed in the car using the seat belt. Once, a while ago, when William first graduated from a car seat, I showed Jack a picture on the Web of a booster seat that was designed to raise a child up and allow him to be buckled using the shoulder strap alone. That seat would have saved me the three minutes on either end of the trip home from school and who knows how many dirty looks from cabbies. When Jack brought it up with Carolyn you would have thought I had suggested strapping William to the front bumper.

Once I get the seat installed I turn to William. "Okay, up you go."

William pretends to be very busy staring at a stiffened turd partially embedded in a crust of snow.

"Come on, William."

"I wonder at what temperature poop freezes?"

"William!"

"Since poop is hot, it will freeze more quickly than a Popsicle, did you know that? Hot water freezes more quickly than cold. Most people think that cold water will freeze faster because it's closer to the temperature of freezing, but it's not true. Hot water freezes faster."

"It's not fair to keep the driver waiting." I am getting ready to lose it. In about two seconds I am going to pick this kid up and pitch him headfirst into the cab.

"It's because of evaporation. Hot water evaporates faster."

"Get in the cab, William."

William sighs. "I don't want to sit in a baby seat," he says.

"I said get in the cab!"

"I don't want to sit in a baby seat," he repeats, this time more loudly, as if he is trying on one of the other children's tantrums. After all, he's seen it work for them. He's watched their mothers capitulate to their demands, no matter how outlandish—anything, anything, just please stop that screaming.

"It's not a baby seat," I say, through gritted teeth. I can feel my jaw starting to ache. It is not William's fault that I suffer from temporomandibular dysfunction. I have had it since before I even met his father. It began in law school, when I would prepare for exams by sitting curled up on an ugly butcher-block chair in the Radcliffe library, subsisting on Diet Coke and Raisinettes, and endlessly grinding my teeth. Now that I think about it, I believe the chair's nubbly tweed upholstery was orange.

It is certainly because of William, however, that I had to begin wearing a mouth guard. I am not crazy; I know he didn't consciously impose this on me, although I imagine that if he were not five years old with (I certainly hope) little understanding of what it is his father and I do in our high sleigh bed, William certainly would have willed on me the bit of yellowish-tinged plastic that I have to snap out of my mouth and leave on the nightstand in a pool of slick and vaguely evil-smelling saliva whenever I want to give his father a blow job.

"It is not a baby seat," I say again.

The cabbie beeps the horn, and William and I both jump.

"Oh dear," William says and lifts up his foot. He has stepped through the frozen crust of the dog shit to its soft and disgusting center.

"Goddamn it, William," I say. I say to the cabbie, "I'm sorry," and grabbing William's leg, I scrape his foot against the sidewalk, rubbing off as much of the shit as I can. Then I pick him up and put him in his booster seat. I buckle him in and run around to the other side of the cab. As I fling open the door, I hear the blare of a car horn.

"What the fuck, lady!" someone screams. "Are you trying to get killed?"

I look over my shoulder at the car that has just missed ripping the door out of my hands. I shrug, either apologetically or carelessly, you choose, and slide into the cab, slamming the door behind me. The Sikh cabbie is looking at me in the rearview mirror. His eyes are very sad. He, like my doorman, like my husband, like everyone it seems, is disappointed in me.

"Central Park West and Eighty-first Street," I say.

As we drive across the park, the cab warms up and I unwind my scarf from around my neck. William and I don't talk. We never do. He looks out his window and I look out mine. A faint but foul odor begins to tickle my nostrils and I wrinkle my nose. The dog shit on William's shoe has begun to defrost.

Chapter 3

In the Olivia books, it doesn't matter if the little white pig is not at all sleepy. She still has to take a nap. William, however, is under no such compulsion. His mother has decreed that since William's imagination is so "activated," since he is so bright, so creative, so highly intelligent, he is in need of constant stimulation and thus cannot be compelled to sleep during the day. I cannot help but believe that Carolyn could have issued such an edict only because it is never she who has to stimulate William's activated little self. Whenever William is not in Jack's or my care, he is with his nanny, Sonia. Sonia's days off are identical to the custody arrangement—every Wednesday and every other weekend. Only then does she retreat to the bowels of Queens and drink slivovitz or play the single-stringed gusle, or is a Croatian gangster's gun moll or does whatever it is that recent immigrants from Dalmatia do on their days off from catering to the needs and whims of overprivileged five-year-olds on the Upper East Side. Actually, I know virtually nothing about Sonia other than the name of the region in Croatia where she is from, and the fact that she once told Jack that one of her grandfathers was Jewish before the war. I don't know what that means, "Jewish before the war." I don't know how long Sonia has been in America. I don't know where she lives when she is not in the little room off the kitchen that I once glimpsed, when I was looking for the bathroom during a firm dinner in the days before Carolyn threw Jack out, before I fucked Jack in the black Aeron chair behind the desk in his office at Friedman, Taft, Mayberry and Stein, the desk Carolyn chose for him when he made partner and was given a corner office and the money to decorate it.

Sonia takes care of William every day after school, except Wednesday, and I take care of William on Wednesdays, and thus Carolyn has no idea how hard it is to entertain her child for an entire afternoon. I understand from looking her up on UrbanBaby.com that Dr. Carolyn Soule is one of the few obstetricians in the city of New York, perhaps the only one, who does not have other doctors take call for her, who always performs her own deliveries, be they in the middle of the night, on weekends, or on Christmas morning, on any day of the year, in fact, except during the three weeks every August that she spends at her family's house on Nantucket. This makes her a very desirable and comforting doctor, and a somewhat less desirable and comforting wife. Though I didn't get that last judgment off UrbanBaby.com. Presumably on the occasional weekends that she is not working, when she is not called to the hospital to deliver a baby or to monitor a high-risk patient, Carolyn is faced with hour after hour of William's company. Perhaps she has more resources than I. Perhaps she is as excited as her son by the project of reading the dictionary cover to cover and debating the merits of each individual definition. Perhaps she finds it as perplexing as he does that we have come to use the word "morning" for the period of time between sunrise and noon rather than the more aptly named "forenoon." Perhaps mother and son keep matching magnifying glasses in the kitchen drawer to read the contents of every food packet, searching for the dreaded molecules of wheat, lactose, and, God forbid, partially hydrogenated vegetable oil. Carolyn *must* love it, or else she endures no more than half an hour of it at a stretch before calling in Sonia, because otherwise she would never have banned the reliable salvation of the television.

I rarely complain about these afternoons, because, after all, isn't the weakness my own? Wouldn't a better stepmother have figured out a series of fascinating ways to pass the time, perhaps constructing a mathematically accurate replica of the Hoover Dam from sugar cubes or starting a breeding program for genetically modified fruit flies with an eye both to finding a cure for color blindness and teaching them how to ride teeny-weeny bicycles? I occasionally whine to my mother, who makes me swear that I will never breathe a word of my dissatisfaction to Jack. I grumble, but I trust her. My mother was herself a stepmother. She is my model of a stepmother, in fact, not because of her success in the endeavor but rather because of her catastrophic, her epic, her operatic failure. My older sisters hated my mother from the moment they met her, years after their own mother had abandoned them to my father's incompetent and grudging care. My mother was a young wife bursting with devotion for the forsaken, motherless waifs, the neglected daughters of the much older man who had swept her off her feet and convinced her to drop out of college and marry him. Despite the fact that my mother proceeded to devote her life to taking care of Lucy and Allison, aged eight and ten, driving them to band practice and skating lessons, making their dentist appointments, packing their lunches, washing their clothes, affixing their perfect spelling tests and SAT results to the door of the fridge, they never changed their minds about her. They never stopped despising her, and they never stopped telling her so.

They were, in fact, so relieved when my parents divorced after almost thirty bitter years that they were even willing to acknowledge their own role in the disaster that was my parents' marriage. Lucy said to me, "It can't have been easy for your mom, taking care of two kids who never wanted her around." Then she asked if my mother had gained a lot of weight since the divorce and wondered if I'd met our father's new girlfriend yet, who was, Lucy said, "Just fabulous. And beautiful. Really thin." And then she laughed.

So when my mother says I shouldn't let Jack know that spending time with William makes me so tired that I feel a headache forming deep in the center of my skull, I listen. I allow myself the ludicrous fantasy that each day will be the day that William and I will magically connect, that this is the day we will find ourselves speaking the same language. My other fantasy involves hiring some pleasant young Columbia student to hang out with William in the afternoons while I go to the movies. When I was working full time William went to his mother's apartment with Sonia on Wednesdays and Jack picked him up after work. But then I quit my job, and we changed the schedule, giving Sonia a free day. It doesn't seem fair to take Sonia's day off away from her just because I find amusing her charge to be unbearably difficult. Especially since I am determined that Jack will never know of my grotesque and unacceptable inability to love his child.

"Do you know what eBay is?" William says, interrupting my thoughts. As usual, we are having a snack instead of a nap. William is swirling his spoon around in his bowl of nonfat, dairy-free sorbet.

William is lactose intolerant, according to his mother. He drinks soy milk, and eats Tofutti and dairy-free sorbet.

"Yes," I say, vaguely.

"My friend Bailey's dad sells things on eBay."

"Hmm."

"Bailey says his dad takes all their old stuff and sells it on eBay. Everything they don't want anymore. Like Bailey's old bike, and his dad's skis from when he was in college."

I nod, but I am not paying much attention.

"Emilia?"

"Yes, William."

"Bailey's dad makes a lot of money on eBay. A lot."

"Good for Bailey's dad."

"Do you ever go to eBay?"

I sigh and look at him. "No, not really."

"Maybe you should."

"Or I could just ask Bailey's dad. I'm sure he'd sell me a pair of old skis if I needed them."

William wrinkles his brow. "No, no. I mean, you should *sell* stuff. To make money, like Bailey's dad. Don't you have any old stuff?"

"We could sell your dad's skis. Or just one of them. How about that? One Völkl ski. Two years old. And one pole."

William shakes his head. "That's silly. Nobody would buy one ski. We should sell the baby's stuff."

I do not answer. I sit on the other side of the kitchen table and clutch my coffee cup so tightly that I cannot believe it doesn't shatter beneath my fingers.

"We can sell the crib," he says. "The crib cost one thousand three hundred and eleven dollars." William likes to know what things cost. "So if we sold it on eBay we would get two thousand dollars. Or maybe even ten thousand dollars."

"No, we wouldn't," I say.

"That's how eBay works," he says, patiently. "You take all the stuff you don't need anymore and people give you lots of money for it."

I stare at the top of William's head. He has Carolyn's pale brown hair, but while hers hangs in a preternaturally shiny sheath to her shoulders, swinging smoothly, with never a split end or ragged edge, his is full of cowlicks, standing up on one part of his head, flattened on the other. The hair is fine, and you can see the yellow crust of his scalp through the greasy strands. William has something called cradle cap, Jack says, or rather Carolyn says, and we must rub baby oil into his head every night and brush it with a soft-bristled brush before using a fine-toothed comb to gently lift off the flakes. When Jack refers to this condition, I must clamp my lips together to keep from pointing out that the child is far too old for a cradle, and that as far as I can tell he has nothing more nor less than a bad case of dandruff.

I say, "We could not get ten thousand dollars for the crib on eBay."

"We can sell the stroller, too. I bet we would get five thousand dollars for the stroller."

"William, that's not the way eBay works. It's not magic. People have to want something in order to bid on it. Nobody is going to bid thousands of dollars for . . . for a stroller they can buy brand new for eight hundred and seventy-five." My jaw is clenched so tight the pain is traveling up behind my ears, along my temples and tying itself into a knot at the top of my head.

"Bailey's dad says . . ."

"You're just misunderstanding Bailey's dad. Or Bailey's misunderstanding him."

William scowls. "You don't even know Bailey. Or his dad."

"I don't want to talk about selling the baby's things, William."

"But that's what eBay's *for*. You're supposed to sell stuff you don't need. You don't need the stuffies or the baby clothes or the diapers. That dumb American Girl doll you bought is still in the box. You should sell that stupid Samantha on eBay."

And now it is too much for me. "Shut up, William. Just shut up." I get up from the table. My chair clatters to the floor. I stare at it, already feeling guilty, already resentful of the guilt. It sometimes seems like William is Carolyn's little mouthpiece, her surrogate goad. He prods and pokes until I satisfy their low expectations, until I prove once again that I am a terrible person. I tell myself that he is not trying to trap me, not trying to force me to reveal my failings and my flaws. He is only a little boy. And yet Carolyn and I have both vested in him so much more power than any small boy should have.

I leave the chair lying on the floor and William sitting at the table and walk out of the room. I stop in the doorway of the little bedroom down the hall, the one intended, when the building was built, as a maid's room. It is moss green with a border of pale pink roses. I painted it myself, so the edges are ragged, almost frayed. If you look very closely you can see that the row of roses is crooked, that it staggers down across the wall and around the room so that when the roses reach the left of the double window they are a full inch-and-a-half lower than when they began on the right. This bothers me very much and I wish I could redo it, or that I had paid someone to do it correctly.

I lean against the doorjamb, and press my fingers into the soft flesh of my belly. I feel for my uterus, wondering if it is still swollen and engorged. I palpate the loose jelly roll that was once my waist and dig my index and middle finger into the place right below my belly button. It hurts, and for that I am grateful. I would hate to think that everything had gone back to normal, that it had all been erased or blotted out, that the only evidence of what had happened was a crooked stencil on a poorly painted wall.

I keep my eyes on the stenciled border, and I do not look at the rest of the room. I do not look at thc ridiculously overpriced crib, with the pink bedding—fat, overblown roses on one side, gingham checks on the reverse. I do not look at the changing table, the neat stacks of infant diapers, the baby-wipes warmer with the cord wound around it like a dead snake, the pots of diaper rash ointment and baby lotion. I do not look at the antique carpet with the Arts and Crafts pattern, in a shade of pink that the rug dealer told me was so rare that he had never seen it before. I do not look at the glider rocker, with its cream-colored leather seat and matching footrest, special ordered by my mother as a baby present. My father gave us a $5,000 savings bond. I wonder what one does with a savings bond in the name of someone who no longer exists?

It is only when I lick my lips and taste salt that I realize I have been crying hard enough to make my nose run. I wipe my face on my sleeve and head back to the kitchen. I must convince William not to tell his mother that I have once again proved myself to be a wicked stepmother, that I have said shut up to him, that I have let him see me cry.

Chapter 4

Jack was the first married man I ever dated. I believe that women who date married men are cruel and irresponsible, and that they betray their sisters. Worse, I believe that they are fools. If they think that the married men whom they are seducing will be faithful to them, then they are deluding themselves. A man who cheats on one wife will surely cheat on another. Fidelity is a personality trait; it is not case specific. It is a matter of character, not of circumstance.

The commencement of my relationship with Jack was the most typical of stories. I was a young associate at the law firm where he is a partner. He was my boss. We first kissed on a business trip, outside the door of my hotel room, on the third floor of the Claremont Hotel in Oakland, California. The first time we made love was, as I've said before, in his office. I was thirty years old when we first began seeing each other; he was struggling to come to terms with his impending fortieth birthday. I am Jack's red Porsche.

It's all very trite and seedy, sordid and humiliating, except that I love him. I love him so much that while I know other people feel this kind of love, I cannot imagine that it is possible that they continue with their daily lives without stopping strangers on the street and declaring the magnificence of their lovers. I love him so much that I am in a state of constant terror that something will happen to him—I want to wrap him in cotton batting and put him in my pocket where I know he will be safe. I only feel totally secure with him before my eyes, in no danger of dying in a plane crash, or getting hit by a taxicab, or having a bowling ball fall from the roof of a building to crush his skull. I love him so much that I want to swallow him, to start with his curled pinkie toes and work my way up to the whorls of his small and high-set ears.

I never knew that it was possible to feel this way. I thought I was in love before. There was an Israeli who worked for Moshe's Moving whom I was convinced I ought to marry. There was a guy in my orientation group in law school whom I probably would have married but for his conviction that marrying a white woman would ruin his chances of being elected to public office (he and his mocha-colored wife just moved to Washington, D.C., representatives of the Nineteenth Congressional District of New York). There were others, so many that nowadays, when sluttiness has come back into fashion, I am a veritable trendsetter. But I never before felt anything remotely akin to what I have felt for Jack from the moment I first saw him. I loved him for two years before he noticed me, and for another year before he allowed himself to touch me.

I saw Jack on my very first day at Friedman, Taft, Mayberry and Stein. I was being led down the hall by the recruitment coordinator, on my way to the office I was to share with another first-year associate, a languid, heavy-lidded young graduate of Yale who gave the impression of not caring very much about his work at the firm, who took long lunches and left early, but who would become the youngest person ever to make partner, after structuring a series of telecommunications acquisition deals that left opposing counsel reeling at his unexpected avarice and mendacity. I followed the recruitment coordinator, staring at her heels, which bulged over the back of her mules. Her shoes were too small, and she snapped them against her feet when she walked. I was doing my best to seem bright-eyed and eager, not to appear ungrateful for my job with its six-figure income. I did not want to let on just how depressed this place made me, the gracious wood-paneled lobby, the grim-faced cheer of the receptionists, the long hallways, a crossword puzzle of square offices just barely larger than a cubicle, all with the doors propped open to better permit the sleek-suited attorneys to exhibit their industry to their falsely benevolent taskmasters.

I had formulated no clear plan about my future when I started law school, and even as the three years drew to a close my ambitions grew no less muddled. To this day I am not sure why I became an attorney, other than because my father is one, although that might as soon have given me reason to avoid the law as drawn me to it. It is not that my father has ever expressed dissatisfaction with his career. On the contrary, he is absolutely content with his professional life. He practices real estate law in New Jersey, near the town where I grew up, in a firm with offices right off Route 17. My father was once the president of the New Jersey Bar Association. It is not any discontentment on his part that might have repelled me, but rather the fact that when I was a child the only thing guaranteed to lay my insomniac brain to rest was a discussion with my father about one of his deals. Further motivation for choosing another career is the fact that my sister, Allison, is an attorney in the appellate division of Legal Aid in Manhattan. They say she will soon be appointed to the judiciary. They, meaning Allison and my father.

I did not go to law school immediately after graduating from college, as did both Allison and my father. After a few years of travel and the sort of vaguely artistic jobs that college graduates with little ambition and less talent find when they first move to New York City, I took the LSAT. I took it on a lark, I suppose, or perhaps because I was sick of living in an apartment where I could turn on the coffeemaker in the kitchen without rising from the pullout sofa in the living room where I slept. To be honest, I don't really remember why I took the LSAT. But I did very well—better than Allison—and after that law school seemed inevitable. I started out with the vague purpose of doing public interest law, but criminal law was the only thing that interested me in the slightest and I was afraid of following in the aggressively competent footsteps of my older sister. In the fall of my third year at law school, when I was interviewing for jobs, I decided that if my work was doomed to be monotonous, it might as well be lucrative. Thus I found myself at Friedman Taft, following the swishing behind of the recruiting coordinator in the ill-fitting shoes.

She lost her mule outside Jack's office. I'm not sure how it happened, but somehow she kicked it off, and then tripped over it. I was walking too close behind her and when she stumbled I nearly came down on top of her. I righted myself by grabbing onto the pedestal of a carved wooden sculpture of a naked woman that was displayed in the hallway. The sculpture rocked back and forth, and for a moment I was worried that we would both, the wooden woman and I, come crashing down on top of the recruiting coordinator. We didn't. The sculpture held fast to its plinth, and I found my balance and stayed on my feet. I was immediately sorry that I had. A handsome man was crouched beside the recruiting coordinator, her foot in his hands.

"Does it hurt when I squeeze?" he said. The muscles of his back strained against the soft white fabric of his shirt. I could see them flex as he lifted her foot gently in the palm of his hand. I felt a nearly insurmountable urge to kneel down behind him and press my body against his, cleave my breasts and belly to his back, slide my fingers around his waist.

"Ooh," the recruiting coordinator murmured, wincing. The faker.

"I think it's probably sprained," he said.

He laid her foot tenderly on the floor, blew his forelock out of his eyes—he was going through a floppy-hair phase back then—and reached around her waist. He hoisted her to her feet and half led, half carried her into his office. "Marilyn," he called out. "Will you see what you can do about finding some ice?"

His secretary, whose desk was in the hallway outside his office, got to her feet.

She turned to me. "Was Frances taking you somewhere before the tragic loss of her shoe?" She didn't seem in a particular hurry to get the ice.

"Yes. She was showing me to my new office."

"I think you'll be on your own for a while. What's your name?"

"Emilia Greenleaf. I'm a new associate."

"What number office are you in?"

I looked down at the folder in my hand. On the page with my code number and my telephone extension and e-mail address was an office number. "Eighteen eighteen," I said.

"Double life," she said.

"Excuse me?"

"The numbers. That's what they mean." She looked at me appraisingly. "You *are* Jewish, aren't you?"

"Yes."

"I'm Marilyn Nudelman."

"I'm not religious or anything."

She shrugged her shoulders. "Come, I'll show you to your office."

Marilyn is still Jack's secretary, and while she danced the hora at my wedding, while she is satisfied that at least I am more Jewish than Carolyn Soule, twelfth-generation descendant of the *Mayflower*, still she does not consider me Jewish enough. This is clear from the presents she sends me—a Hebrew calendar every year before Rosh Hashanah, a box of fruit jells at Passover, a little mesh bag of gold coins at Hanukkah. Each gift is accompanied by a little explanatory note, as if she really believes I do not understand the significance of gelt or wheat-free candy. There is something passive-aggressive about all this gift giving, but I am certainly up to the challenge. I buy lavish presents for Jack to give to Marilyn—cashmere sweaters from Saks, a Coach briefcase and matching purse, gift certificates for a day of beauty treatments at Elizabeth Arden. Then I insist that he give them to her on Christmas Eve.

This gentle battle will likely continue forever, or certainly until Marilyn retires. It began on the evening Jack first succumbed to the signals I had been sending him for three years, ever since he failed to notice that I was standing behind shoeless Frances Defarge in the hallway in front of his office.

It was late in the afternoon, around six o'clock. I had prepared a brief for Jack in support of a motion to recuse a Texas judge who had not once but twice referred to Jack as his client's "Jew York lawyer." This was not the first assignment Jack had given me in the three years

I had worked at Friedman Taft. There had been a few minor research projects over the past year, memos a first-year associate might well have been assigned, but I had leaped at the chance to work with Jack. This brief was finally an opportunity for me to show off a little. I was good at briefs. I had learned while still in law school that style, though it could not entirely substitute for adequate research and a sophisticated grasp of the law, could make the difference between a winning argument and one that put the judges to sleep. This brief was not meant to persuade the Texas judge. The man probably had a hard time every morning deciding which robe to wear, his black or his white, and to him I, too, would be just another shyster from Jew York. I wrote the brief for the appellate court, and I wrote it for Jack. It was lucid, it was incisive, it sliced and diced the bigoted judge and left him bleeding and burning on a cross of relevant precedent. And it was funny.

I sat in a chair in front of Jack's desk and watched him read. At first his face was blank, but as he kept reading a small smile played on the corner of his lips. Jack's lips are very red, he looks like he's wearing plum-colored lipstick, except in the height of winter, when they get chapped from skiing and are covered in flakes of white peeling skin. His upper lip is curled at the edges, and his smile begins on the right-hand side. His lip fluttered in a half smile, once, then again. By the time he'd reached the end he was laughing.

"This is very good," he said.

"Thanks."

"Judge Gibbs is going to burst a blood vessel when he reads this."

I have very pale, freckled skin and I blush easily, but not prettily. I mottle. Knowing that I am blushing makes me self-conscious about how bad I look, and so I grow ever redder until, often, someone asks if I am in need of medical attention. Jack watched his words of praise have their effect on me. His eyes flicked to the V of my shirt. I had on a white cotton blouse that day, its collar starched into stiff wings on either side of my neck. This left my throat bare, an effect which that morning had struck me as demurely sexy. Now it served as a wide-open canvas for the most startling pyrotechnics of my cardiovascular system.

"I mean that in the best possible way," Jack said.

"I know," I said.

He studied my throat, and something about his face shifted; it was as if he began to glow. Now I know that he was blushing, too, but in those days, I was not well versed enough in the topography of his skin to understand what the variations of color and tone meant. He has his mother's olive complexion, and when he blushes he does not turn red like I do. Instead, his face takes on a subcutaneous, burnished, coppery hue. It is a subtle change, and at first one senses only that he has become even more beautiful, more alive, more vibrant. Jack shines when he is embarrassed or ashamed.

"I have just a few notes," he said.

Jack spread the pages of the brief out on the black credenza against the far wall of his office. The credenza is ever so slightly too low for comfort, and when I went to look at his notes, I ended up bent over a bit at the waist. The tabletop was wood, varnished to a high shine, and as we stood side by side our reflections were clear, almost as if we were looking into a mirror. I could see inside my shirt. One of my breasts had fallen forward and swelled outside of the molded cup of my bra, bared almost to the nipple. Jack stood to my left and a little behind me, his left hand pushing the pages aside, one by one, his right shoved into his pocket. I know now, because he told me, that he was doing his best to camouflage his erection.

I was wearing a black miniskirt, not so short that it was unseemly, but neither so long that it would pass the scrutiny of the headmistress of a Catholic school. Underneath I wore stockings and a garter belt. Had it been July or August, I might have claimed that I wore this outmoded style of lingerie because it was hot, and because wearing panty hose in the summer in New York is an invitation to a yeast infection. This was, in fact, the reason that I owned the garter belt. But it was March. The first crocuses were just beginning to peek through the remains of the last snowfall. I wore a garter belt and stockings because I had fantasized about seducing Jack. I had dressed for the fantasy, but had not planned for it. I had not imagined I would work up the nerve.

I bent low over the table and reworked a sentence he had marked. While I agreed that my phrasing had been awkward, I thought his correction even more so. I leaned my cheek on my left hand, scribbled a better sentence than the one he had written, and crossed out a line in the next paragraph that now seemed redundant. At that point, I realized that my skirt had ridden up, that the black straps of my garter belt were surely visible, cutting into the flesh on the backs of my thighs, that the tops of my stockings were sagging just enough to leave bare an few inches of soft, white skin. I paused, the pen hovering over the paper. I could hear the hiss of Jack's breath coming from his nose. Before I could stop myself, before I could even think through the ramifications of what I was doing, I stepped one foot ever so slightly away from the other, parting my legs, and then I leaned gently backward, until I felt the wool of his trouser leg brush against my thigh.

Jack pressed back. It was like junior high school, like a Friday night dance, bumping and grinding against the hopeless boner of a pimple-faced boy who knows with a desperate certainly that he will never, not in a million years, get laid. Except that there was no bumping and grinding, just soft, insistent pressure. And except that I would have fucked Jack in a second, right there, with the door open for everyone to see.

I turned to the hallway and standing in the doorway, her hand on the doorknob, was Marilyn. Our eyes met, and then she shut the door with a firm click of the latch.

I felt a gut-wrenching stab of guilt. I felt like I had pursued Jack, tracked him, shot him, and heaved him over my shoulder, with no thought at all for his wife and child. But that's not true. I thought about them. I thought about them all the time. I felt guilty and miserable, and I hated myself for wanting so wildly and urgently to take him away from them, not just because I knew it was a bad thing to pursue a married man but because I knew precisely how Carolyn and William felt. I knew what it meant to have the man around whom you have built your life betray you, discard you, and find a younger, more appetizing object of his desire.

When my sister Lucy informed me of my father's many infidelities, she was revealing nothing I did not already know. In fact, there are secrets about my father that would bring my sister to her knees with horror if she knew them. I was the one who held my mother's hair back from her face while she vomited her despair into the pale blue toilet of the master bathroom in the house where I grew up. I sat in the waiting room of my mother's gynecologist—the same doctor who had, ten years earlier, given me a prescription for Zovirax, along with a lecture about sexual responsibility—while my mother lay on his examining table and tried to explain, without crying, why a fifty-three-year-old woman who had only slept with one man in her entire life needed an HIV test. Only I—not my sisters, not my parents' friends, not my grandmother, not, I presume, my father's law partners—know that my father did not leave my mother. *She* threw *him* out after discovering that he had been spending as much as $50,000 a year supporting a Russian stripper. No one knows but me, and my father has no idea that I know. I have kept my knowledge a secret from him, and revealed his secret to no one, not even Jack, to whom I have told everything else. My father's secret has been safe with me despite what it has cost me. Every time I see my husband and my father together, I feel soiled, as if my father's filth has been rubbed off on me by my complicit silence. I don't know why I haven't told Jack. I don't know if it's because I am afraid he will be disgusted with me and with my father, or if I am more afraid that he will not be, that the behavior that I find so horrifying will strike my beloved as normal.

I worry that this is something men do. Maybe there is a vast secret underworld about which the wives and daughters know nothing. Maybe the men are all there, in the clip joints of New Jersey, watching as some girl barely out of her teens, a faint blush of acne staining her buttocks pale pink, spreads wide her spindly thighs clad in nothing but a poorly laundered polyester G-string. Maybe all men sit in dark rooms, fingers itching to explore the plump bodies of girls younger than their daughters. Maybe it's perfectly normal to slip hundred-dollar bills into the fists of fat pimps with gold chains digging into the flesh of their necks and then check into third-rate hotel rooms for an hour or two, paying extra to leave the condom in its wrapper, paying even more to do things the wives and daughters could never even imagine.

Or maybe my father is just a fucking psycho. I vote for that. It helps me to keep from hating him, thinking he's crazy. It helps me to have some kind of relationship with him, after he left my mother wretched and alone in a five-bedroom, mock-Tudor house, crying into a wine spritzer, asking me if I thought he would have been faithful if she had not gained so much weight over the years. It helps me to love my husband to think that only men suffering from my father's mental illness—sexual compulsion, sexual obsession, surely there is some heading in the DSM-IV under which to file my father—would engage in this kind of behavior.

So, yes, I've seen betrayal and its cost. When I stood, bent over Jack's credenza, his erection pushing against my ass, even before I saw my self-loathing reflected in Marilyn's eyes, some part of me felt miserable and sorry for what I was doing to Carolyn and William. Mostly, though, I was just so happy, so filled with joy at the palpable evidence of Jack's fervor, that I pushed away the idea of the devastation I wrought on his wife and child. I was the atom bomb of desire, and they were Hiroshima and Nagasaki. I could not spare time for mercy. I had a war to win.

Chapter 5

When Jack comes home, William is building a Mega Bionicle in his bedroom. William has already pointed out to me, twice, that the recommended age range on the box of this elaborately violent-looking Lego is seven to twelve years, and I have expressed astonishment and admiration for his prowess and also informed him that nobody likes a braggart. I am in the kitchen unpacking tonight's dinner from the foil and cardboard to-go containers in which it arrived. Once again, one of the containers is poorly sealed and a slick of curry sauce from the tiger shrimp covers the bottom of the plastic bag. The oil has separated from the coconut milk and little clots of congealed peanut sauce stick to my fingers. By the time I realize I am doing a veritable Lady Macbeth at the kitchen sink, I have used nearly half a bottle of dishwashing liquid scrubbing my hands clean.

My mother taught me how to cook. She is a natural in the kitchen. She started as a girl adding piquant spices to the family brisket and exploring alternative methods of poaching the carp that swam in the clawfoot tub every Friday, and progressed quickly to butter-infused French dishes learned from Julia Child. Two of my most prized books are ragged paperback editions of Elizabeth David's *French Provincial Cooking* and *Italian Food* that my mother presented to me when I left for college. She hated the idea of my being forced to subsist on dorm food when she'd brought me up on a diet of coq au vin de Bourgogne and saltimbocca alla Romana. Despite having been raised, like most Jewish girls of her generation, on a steady diet of boiled chicken and kasha, and despite raising her own family in the culinary wasteland of the 1970s, my mother never in her life cooked a green bean to a gray paste or began a recipe with a packet of onion soup mix or lemon Jell-O. Every cooked vegetable she placed on her table gave a little against the teeth before snapping, unless it was supposed to melt on your tongue, in which case it did so with style. She grew her own herbs and greens and would drive hours to find a good tomato or a rumored cache of morel mushrooms. Had she never married she might have become one of those revolutionary chefs who, in the latter part of the century, transformed the American palate. Certainly she could have opened her own restaurant, if she had been young enough after the divorce to withstand the vigors of a professional kitchen. Or so I like to imagine. She says she would have gone back to school and finished her master's in library science.

I've never quite reached her level of artistry, but the first meal I cooked for Jack was a revelation to him. His apartment was still almost entirely unfurnished and I had to bring my own pots and pans. I made a chilled soup of yellow tomatoes with peppers, cucumber, and basil; veal meatballs with artichokes, green olives, and sage; and a simple arugula and fig salad. I baked a Meyer lemon cake for dessert. I did it all before his eyes, bustling around the kitchen wrapped in a long white apron with my hair piled on my head. He sat on his kitchen counter and opened his mouth obediently for me to pop in bits of balsamic vinegar–soaked bread, olives, ends of crisp vegetables, spoonfuls of whipped cream. I was the witch in the forest, and Jack was my willing Hansel. Except he never grew fat and the only man-eating that was planned was of the figurative variety.

I have not cooked a meal in months now. I still shop as if I am planning on it. I go to Fairway every few days and fill up a basket with plump vegetables, soft ripe cheeses, deep-red wild salmon, organic roasting hens. I would like to feed Jack. I want to delight his tongue and fill his belly with a meal that I know will make him happy. But I cannot seem to bring myself to face my beautifully seasoned iron pans, my Le Creuset roasters, the Piazza cookware my mother brought back for me from a recent cooking-school vacation she took to a North Carolina resort. And so the greens wilt, the filets and chops go pale and start to stink. Every two weeks the cleaning service comes and throws out the rancid contents of the fridge.

After Jack turns his key in the lock and pushes open the apartment door, he pauses, and I know he is holding his head up, sniffing to see if the air is redolent of tarragon and thyme, a reduction of butter and white wine, the tang of lemon zest. Or, once again, of princess prawns from Empire Szechwan.

"Hey sweetie," Jack says, coming into the kitchen. "Can I give you a hand with dinner?"

"I've got it under control," I say as I lift my face to be kissed.

"What did you two do today?"

"Oh, you know, built a cold fusion reactor out of rubber bands and swizzle sticks."

Jack laughs perfunctorily and I remind myself to stop joking about William's precocity.

There is a pounding in the hall and William barrels into the kitchen, skidding across the floor and flinging himself headlong into his father. He buries his face in Jack's belly and rubs it madly back and forth, shouting, "Daddy, daddy, daddy! I missed you so much!"

"I missed you, too, Will-man," Jack says, and lifts William into his arms. I know this is a heartwarming sight. I know I should clasp my hands together and smile benignly at my boys.

"What's for dinner?" Jack says to me.

"Thai," I say.

"Great," he says, and I wish he wouldn't. I wish he would say, Goddamn it, Emilia, I've been working all day, would it kill you to cook me a meal? I wish he would ask me what it is I do with myself while he is clocking billable hours. But he is far too kind, too considerate of me and of my broken heart. It's not fair of me to wish he knew that his kindness makes it that much easier for me to be so appallingly self-indulgent.

"Emilia told me to shut up," William says.

Jack puts William down and looks from one of us to the other. "What's going on?"

I turn back to the bag of takeout, finish pulling out the foil trays with the paper tops. "Ask him," I say.

Jack crouches down next to his son. "William?"

"I was teaching Emilia about eBay, Daddy. And she said shut up."

"William suggested that we sell the baby's things on eBay," I say. "The stroller. The crib. The American Girl doll."

"What?" Jack says. "William, what's going on here?" He is doing his best not to raise his voice, and his suppressed anger makes me very happy. And immediately guilty for being so mean, so immature, that I am pleased to foment conflict between this little boy and his father.

"We don't have to sell *that* stuff," William says. "Any stuff we don't use is okay. We could sell, like, my old Mega Blocks. Because I don't use those anymore."

Jack pushes his hand through his hair. "Sweetie pie, what's the deal with eBay?"

"He wanted to sell the baby's things!" I say. "He wanted to take all the baby's clothes, and her toys, and auction them off on eBay."

Jack lays a hand on my arm. "Just give me a second, okay?" He turns back to William. "Will-man? Did you really want to sell the baby's things?"

I cannot believe that this has somehow turned into a refereed squabble, that Jack is doubting me.

William's eyelashes are wet with unshed, glycerin tears. "I wanted to do eBay and I was trying to think of stuff we aren't using. I thought since the baby's dead she's not going to use her stuff. I didn't mean to make Emilia so mad."

Jack looks up at me. I can feel the heat in my face.

"Emilia's not mad," Jack says.

"Yes, she is."

"No, sweetie. She's not."

Yes, I am.

"Emilia's just so sad about the baby that it's hard for her to talk about selling the baby's things. You're right, we'll never use the baby's things, but we're not going to sell them on eBay."

"I'm sorry, Daddy." William lets loose with his tears now and buries his face in Jack's belly.

"It's okay, sweetie," Jack says, lifting him in his arms. "It's okay, my little man. I know you didn't mean to hurt anybody's feelings."

"I didn't. I didn't mean to hurt anybody's feelings," he wails. "I just wanted to do eBay."

"I know, and Emilia knows, too, don't you, Emilia? She's sorry, too, sweetie." Jack looks at me over the top of William's head, and gives a little half smile of encouragement or pleading.

Yes I'm sorry, of course I'm sorry. I'm sorry about so many things. I'm sorry that your son seems able to pierce my heart with unerring accuracy. I'm sorry I am unable to rise above it, to recognize that he is a child and I am an adult. I am sorry that the baby died and left me an angry and guilt-ridden mess, unable to laugh at the thought of making a killing selling Bugaboo Frogs on eBay. You have no idea how sorry I am, Jack. Would you love me if you knew everything I had to be sorry about?

I pull out a stack of three shamrock-green Fiestaware plates. "Who wants a squeeze of lime on his pad Thai?" I say.

Chapter 6

At night, in bed, Jack says, "William doesn't realize what he's saying."

"I know."

"He's just trying to figure out how to deal with all this."

"I know."

"He's misses her, too."

I do not reply. Instead I repeat her name in my mind. I chose it when I was a few weeks pregnant, before I had even shared the news with Jack. Jack was telling me about his grandmother, his father's mother, who had left Marseille for the United States when she was a small girl but had persisted in speaking with a thick French accent until the day she died. While he told me about her, he tied a Prada scarf around my neck, one he said his grandmother would have loved; although never wealthy, she had an eye for couture and loved bright colors. We had eaten an expensive lunch at Nobu, and had taken a nice long walk to Barneys. It was the anniversary of the first time we made love, and while we had flirted with the idea of celebrating by reprising our acrobatics in the Aeron chair, we decided to save Marilyn's delicate sensibilities and buy each other lavish gifts instead. There was a dark brown leather jacket in a garment bag hanging from Jack's finger, one that was going to take a good chunk of my next paycheck, and for my part I had to move three or four black bags out of the way so that Jack could expertly knot the length of emerald green silk around my throat.

"We should name the baby after your grandmother," I said, as I admired myself in the mirror.

"Hmm?" Jack said, as though he hadn't heard.

"I mean, if we ever have a baby."

Jack caught my fingers in his hand and squeezed them. "We'll have a baby, Em. Some day. Just not right now, okay, sweetie?"

I didn't say anything.

"My divorce isn't even final yet. William has barely begun to adjust to the idea of us living together. And you're only thirty-one; hardly more than a baby yourself."

What I wish I had done was laugh musically, trace a long fingernail down his cheek, and sing out, "Ah well, my love, too late! You're going to be a papa!" *Esprit de l'escalier*. Instead, I burst into a flood of gasping tears that left a shining snail's trail across the Prada scarf, which Jack paid for in cash so that we would not have to wait for his credit card to be processed, before he hustled me out of the store.

Eight months later, our daughter was born.

She was a perfectly healthy baby, and her birth was, according to the doula, easy and uneventful. I have my own opinions about that. Those of my girlfriends who have survived long labors (one in particular takes every opportunity to bemoan, with irritating braggadocio, her forty-four hours in hell) have little sympathy for this part of my maternal experience. (They are, however, so crippled with sympathy for the rest of it that most of them cannot even bring themselves to call me on the telephone. Instead, they send supportive, vaguely cryptic e-mails that never mention the baby's name or even refer to her, but merely ask how I'm doing, and hope I'm "bearing up" or "feeling better." Honestly, who can blame them? It's not like I'd be so eager to call someone suffering from a melancholy sufficiently bleak and contagious that it could infect a person through the fiber-optic wires. If the roles were reversed would I have done any more than send a basket of fruit and a sympathetic but not too schmaltzy condolence card? Probably not.) My labor was a mere nine hours long. We'd planned to spend the better part in our apartment, in the bathtub, or bouncing on the big purple exercise ball that Felicia, the doula, provided us. But we ended up in the hospital instead. I had been so placid in the face of the handful of freezing ice they gave us to simulate the pain of labor while we practiced our breathing in birth-preparation class. I could breathe through my nose and out through my mouth, visualizing the petals of the lotus blossom hovering above my head. But as soon as the first real contraction hit, I began wailing and hyperventilating.

Off we went to the hospital, with Ivan's best wishes to Mr. and Mrs. Woolf, and a fond reminder to dress the little one warm on the way home, because November is always colder than it feels. On the cab ride through the park I put my head in Jack's lap. He tapped his fingertips gently around my eyes, the way he does when I have a headache.

"Kiss me," I said.

He leaned over and pressed his lips against mine. They were a little bit chapped; he had gone skiing once because he knew he wouldn't get to go much for the rest of the season. I licked the rough skin on his lower lip. He kissed me again. Just then a contraction started, and I tried to pull away, but Jack didn't let me. He kissed me through the contraction, moving his tongue against mine, probing and licking my mouth until I could not tell if the ache swirling around my belly was pleasure or pain.

Our baby was born at New York-Presbyterian Hospital on York Avenue, even though if I'd had my way she would have been born at Mount Sinai. The obstetrician who delivered her was named Dr. Fletcher Brewster (not Dr. Brewster Fletcher, as it erroneously says on UrbanBaby.com) and he is the first non-Jewish doctor who has ever touched any part of my body, intimate or otherwise, except for a Nepalese dentist who fixed a tooth I broke tripping over a severed cow foot on a street in Kathmandu. While I am neither biased against non-Jewish physicians nor a Jewish chauvinist like my father, I am convinced, superstitiously, and surely erroneously, that if my doctor had been named Abramowitz or Cohen, if I had given birth at Mount Sinai, if I had not been touched by those goyish hands in that goyish hospital, my daughter would be alive today.

Dr. Carolyn Soule, however, has her obstetrical practice at Mount Sinai Hospital.

Now, lying in bed next to Jack, I say the baby's name, silently. I mouth it, but without breath so Jack will not hear.

Isabel.

Jack sighs. "William is sad, too," he says again.

"I know."

Jack folds his hands behind his head and stares up at the ceiling. I count the gray hairs over his left ear. Sometimes I do this out loud and while he pretends only to be pretending to get angry; I don't think he likes it very much. It reminds him that he is nine years older than I am.

"Em," Jack says, his voice soft and husky.

"I know," I say.

"You know what?"

"I know we have to clean out her room."

Jack doesn't say anything. He long ago stopped wondering how it is that I sometimes appear to be reading his mind, how I know what he is thinking or feeling even before he knows it himself. I have explained to him that it is because he is my *bashert*, my intended. I knew it from the first moment I saw him. There is a Jewish legend, a Midrash, that before you are born an angel takes you on a tour of your life and shows you the person whom you are meant to marry. Then the angel strikes you on your philtrum, leaving that subtle channel in the skin between the nose and mouth, and makes you forget what you have seen. But not entirely. There remains a vestige, enough to evoke a jolt of recognition if you are lucky enough to stumble across your *bashert* during the course of your life. When I saw Jack kneeling on the carpet with Frances Defarge's foot in his hand, I knew he was my *bashert*. I recognized him.

"I can't pack it away yet," I say.

"That's all right," Jack says.

He slips his arm underneath my neck and I rub my cheek against the smooth cotton of his pajama sleeve. Jack only wears pajamas when William is sleeping at our house. I don't. I tried to, at first, but during the night I would twist and turn, tied up in the knots of my nightclothes. I would always end up shucking them off in my sleep. Now I drape a nightgown over the end of the bed, and when William calls out in his sleep or comes into our room, I grab it and slip it over my head.

"I'm not making a shrine or anything," I say.

"I know, Em."

"It's just . . . not yet."

"Okay."

"I'm sorry I said shut up."

Jack changes the subject. "What did you do today, before William got home?"

I shrug my shoulders. "Nothing really. Read the paper. Talked to my dad."

"How is Old Man Greenleaf?" Jack says. That is what they call each other, Jack and my father. Old Man Greenleaf and Old Man Woolf. It began, I suppose, because my father was so angry at first about my relationship with Jack, so horrified by the age difference. The irony of this coming from a man who married a woman fourteen years younger than himself, and then cheated on her with a girl who was probably not much more than twenty-one, at first seemed lost on my father. When I pointed out the former (but not the latter, keeping my promise and my tongue) he grudgingly admitted that I had a point, although he then reminded me that his and my mother's marriage had ended in divorce, so perhaps I should derive a lesson from that. I reminded him that the marriage had lasted for thirty years, and once again managed to refrain from bringing up the stripper. Then he met Jack, and immediately took to him. He teased Jack, calling him "old man." The affection was mutual, and Jack returned the joke. Thus, Old Man Greenleaf and Old Man Woolf. They kid each other, they poke fun, they laugh at each other's jokes and puns. I am grateful for this relationship, although I spend much of the time we are in my father's company thinking about what my husband would say if he knew that Old Man Greenleaf tucked most of his ready cash into the tasseled underwear of a gyrating stripper.

"Old Man Greenleaf's fine," I say. "He and Lucy had an argument."

"About what?"

"I don't know; I wasn't really listening. I'm sure Lucy did something bitchy." I know I am ungenerous with my sisters, Lucy in particular, but I've never forgiven them for their treatment of my mother. They were so horrible for so many years that I don't know if I could muster forgiveness even were they to apologize, although as it would never occur to either of them that they have behaved in a manner at all deserving of contrition, I will never have to confront this possibility. Still, it would be nice if they would one day regret their behavior and say they are sorry, not to me but to my mother.

It occurs to me, suddenly, that I have not sent Lucy a thank-you note for the set of engraved Tiffany baby silverware and Curious George dishes that she sent. What is the etiquette on such occasions? Does one send a note? And if so, what does it say? Thank you for the gift; so sorry the baby will never use it? Does one return the gift? What if the giver has taken great care to make clear that the gift is an expensive one by shopping at a store that adds a premium for the pleasure of its pale blue box and white ribbon? Perhaps I should write to Miss Manners. Surely I am not the first to confront this issue. Tomorrow I will surf the Web sites where the mothers of dead babies congregate. Perhaps someone has posted an answer to this very question.

Usually I try to avoid these Web sites as well as the various support groups around the city. The company of other bereaved mothers does not comfort me. It just makes me more depressed. As does the company of nonbereaved mothers. Other than Jack, I can only tolerate people who have never been or will never be parents, like my friend Simon, gay and avowedly single. Jack tried, once, to convince me to attend a meeting of a support group for parents who had survived "pregnancy and infant loss." I referred him to an article in the *Times* that quoted studies showing how most people who suffer the loss of a loved one neither need nor benefit from participation in a bereavement group or from grief counseling.

"Have you talked to your mom?" Jack says now.

I nod. That goes without saying. I talk to my mother every day, sometimes a few times a day, more when she is worried about me, as she always is, since Isabel died. I have become my mother's current cause, and I am quite frankly worried about the state of the Bergen County Food Bank and the Glen Rock Neighborhood Association.

Jack leans over and turns off his light. He creeps his hand tentatively across the bed and rests it on my hip, tracing a line with his pinky finger along the joint where the skin is loose and papery soft from pregnancy.

I stiffen. "Do you mind if I read?" I say. "I'm not tired yet."

"No, not at all." His disappointment is so obvious that it's almost funny. He looks like a five-year-old who opened a Christmas present hoping for a laser gun and found a book instead.

Poor Jack. I think he assumed, when he married a woman nearly ten years his junior, that his life would be one long letter to *Penthouse* Forum. And, for more than a year and a half, his nights were bacchanals of the kind of lovemaking that leaves you limp, damp, and sweaty, with stuff in the corners of your mouth and under your fingernails. He probably thought it would last forever. He probably thought he would have to start popping Viagra just to keep up. Instead, it's been two and a half months since I've allowed him to touch me in any way other than the merely affectionate. Two and a half months since the day that Isabel was born.

I read my book, a novel about young New Yorkers whose lives flame out in a fabulous blaze of restaurants, gallery openings, sado-masochistic clubs, and methamphetamine. This is the only kind of book I can stand to read lately: no babies, not even of the possibility of reproduction. Once I am sure that Jack is asleep I wait a few minutes, my finger marking my place in my book. Then I fold down the corner of the page, settle the book on my nightstand without making a sound, and quietly, so quietly, open the small drawer where I keep the most intimate, secret items of our marriage. Condoms, lubricant, a blue vibrator with a silver ball tip. The tweezers I use to pluck the hairs between Jack's eyebrows and the ones that grow around my nipples. A joint hidden in a box of matches. An envelope of photographs.

The week before I gave birth, I bought Jack a digital camera. He had been teasing me for months about shooting the birth on video, about how he'd zoom in between my legs just when I was expelling the contents of my colon prior to pushing out the baby's head. I told him I knew these were empty threats—Carolyn got the camcorder in the divorce. She also got the still camera, however, and the only camera I had, a manual-focus Nikon F3, was far too complicated for Jack to figure out. In the end, he didn't even take that many pictures, not as many as I wish he had, not as many as he would have, had he known that photographs would be all we would have left of our baby.

There are exactly seventeen photographs extant of Isabel Greenleaf Woolf. Jack must have uploaded them before she died and ordered prints from an online photo-delivery service. One day they arrived in the mail and I took them without telling him.

The first is of her face, purple with effort, eyes closed, cheeks ballooned and dimpled, a smear of vernix over one eye. The rest of her is still inside me. Right after he took this photograph, Jack handed the camera to Felicia and knelt down next to Dr. Brewster. He spread his hands on top of the doctor's, as instructed, and caught Isabel in his outstretched palms. When she felt the cold air and her father's warm touch my daughter let loose a wrenching cry, but as soon as Dr. Brewster toweled her off and put her on my belly, she stopped. Felicia insisted that they allow the baby to nurse for a few minutes before taking her away to be weighed and measured, and Isabel latched on as if she had been nursing all her life, or as if she had been waiting impatiently inside me for the chance to get her mouth on the breast that she considered her own personal property.

There are two photographs of Isabel being weighed, on one of which you can read the digital scale—seven pounds, nine ounces. A nice, solid weight. Average. Perfect. There is a photograph of Dr. Brewster holding her, and another of her in the arms of one of the nurses. There is one of her with Felicia. There is one blurry photograph of Jack and a second nurse giving Isabel her first bath, an hour or so after she was born. There is a clearer photograph of Jack holding her in the hospital room. His smile is so broad that his cheekbones are pushed far up to the corners of his face. One of Isabel's eyes is open and the other closed, and you can just barely see my swollen foot in its pale green, acrylic hospital sock in the right-hand corner of the frame. This is the only photograph we have of the three of us together.

There are three photographs of Isabel and me in my hospital bed. My hair is lank and unwashed, pressed flat against my head. My face is round and my skin is puffed taut. My whole body looks pneumatic, like it was attached to a compressed-air tank and pumped until it was quite near to bursting. Isabel, on the other hand, is pretty cute, for a newborn. Her cheeks are plump and her head is covered by a fuzz of soft dark hair that curls over the tops of her ears. Jack tells me that

William had exactly this kind of hair, and that it all fell out by the time he was two months old.

Isabel has Jack's mouth, exactly, a tiny plum-colored kiss of a mouth. Her eyes are round, not lashless slits like those of some babies. They are navy blue. I know they are. Jack and Felicia said it was hard to tell, that babies eyes change, but I would know that color anywhere.

The rest of the photographs are of Isabel on her first and only day at home. Isabel in her Moses basket, asleep. Isabel propped on an upholstered pillow on the couch. Isabel on her changing table without a diaper, her bare rear end covered in black, sticky goo that I am wiping away while making a disgusted face, my tongue stuck out, my eyes crossed. Isabel on her changing table with a new diaper, clean and fresh and wearing a too-big onesie. Isabel on the sheepskin mat someone gave us at my baby shower. Isabel lying on our bed, a tiny form on a vast white expanse, looking, premonitorily, like a negligible dot, too small to last very long in such an empty space.

I am staring at this photograph, feeling my throat constrict and the tears gather, when I realize that Jack is no longer asleep. He lies still, but I can feel a pulse of energy coming from him. I slide my eyes to his face. His eyes are open, and watching me. The photographs spill from my hand onto the coverlet, the one of Isabel, lost in our bed, landing on top of the pile.

"I hate that one," Jack says. "I can't even bear to look at it."

He reaches across and sifts through the pile of photographs. He pulls out one of the hospital pictures of Isabel and me. We are in profile, looking into each other's faces. I am holding her with my thumbs under her arms, her head supported by the four fingers of each of my hands and her bottom resting in the crooks of my elbows. We have identical double chins. "This is my favorite," Jack says. "And the one with you changing her diaper. I have both of those framed on my desk at work."

"You have pictures at work of Isabel?"

"Yes."

"I didn't know that. You didn't tell me that."

"You didn't ask."

I take the photograph back from him and look at it again. "I look fat."

"You look like you just had a baby."

That, of course, makes me cry. I am not trying to force Jack to spring into action, but he does. He sits up and hugs me, nestles my head against his chest.

"Why aren't you mad at me?" I blubber. His pajama top is unbuttoned and I wipe my nose on the hairs on his chest.

"For what?"

I push my face into his chest.

"For what, Emilia? Why should I be mad at you?"

"For . . . for stealing the pictures."

"I just ordered another set and had them delivered to the office."

I lift my head. "But weren't you mad at me for not telling you that I had them? For hiding them in my drawer?"

Jack pulls a tissue out of the box on his nightstand and wipes at the mucus I have left smeared across his chest. "Of course I'm not mad."

"Why not? You should be."

"You sound like you want me to be angry at you."

I press my cheek back against him. He is so warm and the hairs on his chest tickle my skin.

Jack kisses the top of my head. "Do you want to choose one or two of the pictures for me to enlarge? We can get a couple of nice frames and put them up somewhere. Maybe in here. Or in the living room."

"God no," I say. "I mean, not yet. I'm not ready for that, yet."

His sigh is almost imperceptible.

"It's not that I won't ever want her picture up. Just, you know. Not yet."

"Okay."

"For now I need them to be private. Mine, not anyone else's." It takes a moment for me to realize what I have said. "And yours, too. Of course yours."

"Of course."

I pick up the little stack of photographs once more and leaf through them until I reach the one of Jack and Isabel with my foot in the corner. "Do you like this one?" I ask.

"Not much," he says. "She's got that Popeye the Sailor Man, one-eye-open-one-eye-closed thing going on."

"You look nice, though." I trace a finger over his smile. "You look happy."

"I *was* happy. The day Isabel was born and the day William was born were the two happiest days of my life."

I say, "I was happy, too."

"I know, Em. I know you were."

It takes us a long time to fall asleep.

Chapter 7

The next day I talk Simon into playing hooky from work and coming with me to the movies. I can tell he really hasn't the time for this kind of foolishness, that he's got serious, adult things to take care of, real work to do. Simon is a labor lawyer, but only while he waits for the ACLU to hire him. He applies, year after year, for every opening they have, even those in the reproductive rights project. Meanwhile he will likely make partner at his union-side labor firm, even though he hates the work. Simon is smart, diligent, and not easily distracted. His devotion to a job he despises is the reason I am forced to play the dead-baby card.

"That's not fair, Emilia," he says.

"Tell me about it," I say. "It's at the Angelika, it's Cambodian, and it's three and a half hours long. I'll buy you a double espresso."

We are the only people at the theater at eleven in the morning, despite the fact that this morose exercise in Far Eastern tedium has been nominated for an Oscar. The movie is so gloomy that Simon begins to supply alternative subtitles.

"Oh lordy, lordy," he pretends to read in a thick Southern accent.

Simon often affects to be from Alabama or Mississippi. He grew up in Great Neck. "It is so hard to keep my hair clean in these filthy killing fields!"

I feel a giggle tickle the back of my throat for the first time in a long while.

"You there, with the gun! Yoo-hoo! Do you have conditioner? A little Paul Mitchell? Some curling balm? I have never seen less body, or more bodies, if you know what I mean."

Now I laugh out loud. The female character in the film stumbles along next to a river, driven forward by a bayonet-wielding soldier. Simon keeps up his commentary. "I swear, as God is my witness, I will never go this long without a wash and set again!"

I poke him in the side and say, "Oh my God, will you stop! This is genocide we're watching here." By now I am laughing so hard I have to pee.

"No, girlfriend, this is a bad movie we're watching here," Simon says, and then he is silent. I look up at the screen. The woman has fallen into the water. She rises to the surface, water streaming from her hair into her eyes. She is surrounded by the corpses of infants. They bob in the water, naked, their eyes open and lifeless. She bats them away, screaming, howling, wailing with terror and revulsion.

"Fuck," Simon says. "Let's get out of here."

"No."

"Emilia, come on. You don't need to see this."

I argue with him. I remind him that we have never walked out on a movie before, no matter how awful. We've been to every implacably dull Asian movie ever to flicker on the screens in the city of New York. I list them for him: *Raise the Red Lantern. The Scent of Green Papaya. Raise the Green Papaya. The Scent of Red Lantern II*. We have gone to see dreadful movies on purpose and stayed to the bitter end, through the credits, even. We can't leave; it's a matter of pride.

Simon puts his arm around me and heaves me to my feet. "Up we go, lady," he says, and leads me out of the theater.

In the lobby we put on our coats and scarves. Simon has a new winter coat, long and black. It balloons when he swings it around to put it over his shoulders and he looks unusually debonair. All of Simon's clothes are black, gray, or white. His apartment is entirely gray. Simon explains the monotony of his palette by telling people that he is color-blind. He is not. He is a gay man with no sense of style. Simon is tall, and a bit cadaverous. His eyes bulge from his head, as though he has a thyroid condition, although he doesn't. His hair is receding and he keeps what is left cropped so short that the lines of his skull are clearly visible. Still, he is handsome, in a lugubrious way.

"Well, what now?" I say.

"Shoe shopping?"

"Why does everybody want to take me fucking shoe shopping?" I ask. "Mindy insisted I go with her to Manolo Blahnik. Why are you all under the impression that shoes are what's going to make me feel better?"

"Because you like shoes."

"Yes, well, I like sushi, but nobody imagines a California roll is going to solve all my problems. And I like Jane Austen, but nobody imagines rereading *Pride and Prejudice* will make me recover from the loss of my baby."

"You like *me*, and I imagine *I* will help you recover from the loss of your baby."

Simon is not looking at me when he says this. He is looking down while he wraps his plaid scarf twice around his neck and into the collar of his coat. He does not see my eyes well with tears, or if he does, he does not say anything. Maybe that's because his own eyes are filled with tears. I slip my hand into his pocket and say, "Okay, fine. Shoe shopping.

"At least shoes are better than Mindy's other idea," I say as we are walking uptown to our favorite shoe store.

"What's that?"

"A Walk to Remember," I say, shuddering.

"A walk to what?"

Unlike me, Mindy has wholeheartedly embraced the grief community, both virtual and actual. She is trying to get pregnant, and has had three miscarriages in two years. She sees a grief counselor, and is an active poster on not one but two infertility Web sites. Sometimes I think my certain derision is the only thing that keeps Mindy from creating a blog devoted to her struggles with infertility, complete with violin concertos and clip art of winged cherubs. She had sucked me into this latest madness of hers by playing expertly on my feelings about the babies in Central Park.

"What you really need to do," Mindy said, "is be in the park with other people like us."

"People like us?"

"People who've experienced our kind of loss. So you can take back the park from the smug mommies."

Mindy's plan for "taking back the park" involves a group stroll. This yearly event is usually conducted during October, a month given the dubious honor, by none other than Ronald Reagan, of being named National Pregnancy and Infant Loss Awareness Month. An entire month devoted to the memory of babies lost through miscarriage, ectopic pregnancy, still birth, and newborn death. Lucky October.

This year, we are fortunate enough to be treated to a second group walk, to commemorate the son of the founder of the New York walk.

"Are we celebrating her ectopic pregnancy?" I asked.

"Don't be a bitch, Emilia," Mindy said. "She's lost two babies to a genetic kidney disease. The older of them died eight years ago, on February 29. We're honoring him with a special walk because it's leap year."

I was suitably chastened, and sufficiently embarrassed to consent to accompany Mindy and the other grieving walkers.

"It will be healing," Mindy said.

"I doubt it," I replied.

"Do you want me to come?" Simon says now, gamely.

"God, no."

At the shoe store, I buy a pair of red leather boots that I doubt I will ever wear. Simon buys a pair of white patent leather bucks that I *know* he will not wear. He only buys them because the salesman is wearing the same ones, and tells Simon how cute they are and how gorgeous they look on Simon's long, elegant feet. I wait for the salesman to drag out the old saw about the connection between foot and penis size, but he doesn't have to. He is giving Simon a foot job, massaging the arch of his foot, rubbing his heel. When the salesman goes in the back to get a larger size I say, "I'm not sure Jack's grandmother would have approved of white shoes after Labor Day."

"Jack's grandmother?"

"Isabel, the style maven."

Simon frowns, his eyebrows drawn together like pigeon's wings. He looks like a sad circus clown and it makes me want to kick him. "The one you named the baby for," he says.

"Yes," I say, and I leave it at that. I have a cruel and entirely unacceptable urge to tell Simon that the only reason the salesman is being so nice to him is for the commission. I do not, because not only is Simon my best friend but he is slowly becoming my only friend. I cannot let myself drive him away, too. I will have nothing to do with my friends who have babies, or my friends who are pregnant. Even Mindy is hard for me to be around. She thinks we are members of the same sorority of pain, that we are sisters in grief, that together we will sit and make bitter faces at the smug mothers passing with their strollers and swelling bellies. But when I am with Mindy I am afraid every minute that I will tell her she has no fucking idea, that a curl of flesh and DNA floating in a toilet bowl full of blood is not a baby, and that feeling the remnants of a pregnancy run down your legs is nothing, nothing like holding your dead child in your arms. This comment would not, I imagine, do much for our friendship.

Simon is the only friend I have who I am fairly confident will never have children and thus I cannot alienate him, even if he does sometimes react with a false-looking frown of sadness when I mention Isabel's name. Plus, he loves me, and he cries for Isabel. He is, I think, the only person not related to her by blood who does that. It's not his fault that his sadness isn't expressed in precisely the way I would like. It is my fault for expecting it to be.

I am quiet at lunch, and Simon has to do most of the talking, which is not normally the way it is with us. Normally we banter back and forth. Normally it is the Emilia Greenleaf and Simon Fargo Hour, and we are a team, each other's devoted audience. That is the way it has always been, since the day we met in our first year of law school, at a study group that a few other students in our section were forming. I did not last in the study group—they were far too earnest and serious for me. Simon did, and for the rest of the year he generously slipped me the study group's shared outlines, violating not only the rules of the group but an actual written contract that one of the more neurotic members drew up after learning about offer and acceptance in contracts class.

Simon picks at his Caesar salad. I eat all of mine, and then order sweet potato fries.

"I am dreading this weekend," Simon says.

"Why?"

"Another bachelor party. You'd think being gay would absolve me from attending these horrible events, but apparently not. Every time one of my college roommates gets married, I am expected to spend an evening drinking tequila shooters and watching some poor Russian girl spin around a pole. And honestly, Emilia, you would not believe how *naked* these girls are. If I had a speculum and a couple of Q-tips I could do a residency in gynecology."

I think I am going to throw up my Caesar salad. The waitress brings my sweet potato fries and I stare at them. They look like a pile of shorn hair. Shriveled. Dead.

"I don't understand why these places aren't busted," Simon says. "It's not like it's hidden. I mean the girls are giving blow jobs right in the clubs. They even try to give them to me, for Christ's sake. You have never seen anything sadder than me trying to explain the word 'homosexual' to some teenage farm girl from Moldavia. I end up paying more *not* to get blown."

I cannot reply. I cannot say anything. I have in my mind the image of my father and the Russian stripper he claimed he was in love with. The girl in Plainfield, New Jersey, whom he visited every Monday morning for nearly a year, the girl for whose company he withdrew $1,000 every Monday morning at precisely nine o'clock from the drive-through window of the Citizens First National Bank. If I had not sold my mother on the fun of online banking she never would have noticed these transactions. She still might have missed them but for their regularity and the sheer quantity of cash. As the numbers downloaded with a cheerful chirp and ping, linked and synced from their account into her Quicken program, my mother grew more and more befuddled. Finally, a Luddite at heart, she resorted to paper and dug out their old bank statements, reading them for the first time in her life. She finally understood why, with a fancy lawyer husband, president of the bar association, two-time Northern New Jersey Real Estate Lawyer of the Year, she never seemed to have enough money for things like the cruises her friends took every year, the personal trainer that she had always wanted to help her lose weight, a nicer car than the Honda Accord she'd been driving forever. At first she assumed my father was gambling. She confronted him with the bank statements and begged him to go to Gamblers Anonymous. My mother told me the fight lasted long into the night, that it was almost dawn before he finally confessed. He didn't spend it on horses and cards. He never went to Atlantic City. The money was for Oksana.

In my mind she has a high round forehead, kinked hair drawn into a bun, bee-stung lips. My father told my mother she is only a few years younger than me, but I imagine her much younger, a teenager almost. I've managed to strip her of the ice skates, but the outfit remains, tarted up for purposes of fantasy, no pale pink bodysuit underneath to simulate flesh, but rather actual skin peeking through shredded spangled miniskirt and thong. When I imagine them together, my father and his Russian whore, what I see them doing is some kind of pornographic paired triple lutz. I suppose that if the girl's name had been Nadia or Olga, my fantasies would have involved back handsprings and the uneven parallel bars. The most pathetic thing about it all was that my father claimed Oksana loved him. He told my mother that this girl thought that he was special, that she didn't think of him as a client but rather as her lover, her boyfriend, the man she would marry if only she could. He told this to my mother as the sun rose on a crisp autumn day, the trees a riot of color, the air redolent with the coming winter. Then he went to work, and my mother called me. I took the bus from Port Authority and I was there in a little over an hour, so that I could hold her hair while she vomited. I helped her pack his bags, and I crossed my arms and stared her down when she tried to change her mind.

"We've been married for thirty years," she said. She was standing in her bedroom holding a stack of wool sweaters in her hand. Her housedress was buttoned wrong, one end sticking up by her ear, and her small, narrow feet, blue-veined and pink-polished, were bare.

"Twenty-nine," I said.

"Almost thirty."

"And how much of that time was he cheating on you?"

"I don't know." She put the sweaters into a suitcase, layering tissue paper between them.

I pulled the paper out, crumpled it into a ball, and threw it in the trash can. I pulled open my father's underwear drawer and, holding my breath, dumped the contents into a carryall.

"He says this Russian girl loves him."

"Yeah, right," I said. "And were there other Russian girls? Did they love him too?"

I stood over my mother while she sent my father an e-mail telling him where his belongings would be, and then I drove the suitcases to a Ramada Inn on Route 17, not too far from his office. I took a room in his name, putting the charge on my mother's credit card and forging the signature I had perfected in high school. When I got back to the house she was standing in the front hall, still in her housedress.

"I don't know if I can do this, Emilia," she said.

I stood in the doorway, the keys jingling in my hand. "I will never forgive you if you take him back, Mom."

My mother stared at me, her face spongy and pale. "Oh," she said.

She swayed on her feet and I saw that this was too much to bear. I saw, too, what she would never say: that no matter what I felt, no matter what I imagined, my father's betrayal had been of her, not of me.

"I'm so sorry," I said, and rushed across the room. I wrapped my arms around her and she sagged against me, soft and moist, as if desperation was leaking from her, dampening her skin and clothes. "I had no right to say that." And I had no right, of course. But it is true that I never would have forgiven her, and she knew that as well as I did.

Now, sitting in a Soho café across from Simon, I cannot get an image out of my head. It is of my father and a young Russian stripper. I see his naked back, skin loose and gray, pocked with brown birthmarks. I see her smooth and unlined face over his shoulder, bored and anxious as she watches the clock above the door; she will be punished if he takes too long. I know I have a very active and vivid imagination, torqued and twisted by too much television, a steady diet of gothic novels, and an Electra complex worthy of twenty years on Freud's couch. I also know that, like my friend Simon, my father is a sensitive man. How can he possibly live with himself?

"Emilia?" Simon says.

"Excuse me?"

"Did you hear what I said?"

"No, I'm sorry."

"I was telling you about the lap-dancing sixteen-year-olds."

"I think I'm going to be sick."

"I know. It's totally disgusting. And meanwhile, what are the cops doing with themselves? What's the FBI up to? Busting medical marijuana users. Making the world safe from all those little old ladies with ovarian cancer growing reefer in their backyards. And let's not forget the time and money the Justice Department is spending writing amicus briefs in favor of the so-called partial birth abortion ban." He makes little quotation marks around the phrase with his fingers. "Gotta make sure those women with the hydrocephalic babies get the jail time they deserve. We live in one fucked up country, you know that?"

Simon's voice has gotten louder. He is normally a fairly sedate person whose wit is of the sardonic kind, spoken under the breath rather than aloud. But when he is angry about some injustice, when he has a political point to make, Simon can climb up on a soap box with the best of them. I allow him to go on, hoping that his highly vocal outrage will camouflage my quiet. It is mysterious to me why I have not told Simon about my father. It is almost easier to understand why I have kept the secret from Jack. Jack, after all, must see my father on a regular basis, must interact with him and pretend affection. Simon has met my father only a few times, and those meetings did not go well. Although my father would never admit to it, although he would, in fact, shake his fist in the face of anyone who accused him of it, my father, longtime donor to the Democratic Party, onetime member of the Young Communist League, sexual sybarite, is a homophobe. Only my father seemed to require an explanation for why my cousin Seth, who lived one town over from us in Fair Lawn and whom we saw frequently throughout my childhood, wore eyeliner and leather hip-huggers to nearly every family occasion. When my aunt Irene finally explained, in language you would use with a simpleminded child, that Seth "liked boys better than girls," the blood drained from my father's face and his silver tongue cleaved to the roof of his mouth. I have never seen him hug his nephew since then, and on the few occasions when he and Simon have met, he has managed somehow to avoid shaking Simon's hand. Simon would be only too glad to hear a story this vile about my father, and I do not understand why I cannot bring myself to tell him. Why do I feel such loyalty for a man who seems entirely unfamiliar with the concept?

The man sitting opposite me, however, knows nothing except loyalty. For ten years he has been my most stalwart companion, sticking by me even in the past few months when I have been so unpleasant. And, worse, so *boring*.

"Simon," I say. "Simon, I have something to tell you."

"What?" He grimaces, reacting to the urgency in my voice.

"You are my best friend, Simon, and I love you."

"And?"

"And? And nothing. That's what I wanted to tell you."

"That's all? I know you love me, girlfriend. I love you, too." He takes one of my sweet potato fries, dips it in aioli, and stuffs it in his mouth.

"I don't deserve you. You're a better friend than I deserve."

"Oh please. How many bad boyfriends have you saved me from?" He shudders. "Did you or did you not step in and terrify that horrible Christopher until he turned over all my stuff? And where was I? Cowering in the elevator, punching the 'open' button."

"He was not a good boyfriend."

"Exactly! And you bullied your way into his apartment and got me back my two pairs of black Hanro boxer briefs, my good Diesel jeans, and my toothbrush. You even managed to get a bottle of shampoo that wasn't even mine! I love that shampoo, by the way. I still use that same brand. Bumble and Bumble. It is so fucking expensive, it's like a dollar fifty per hair folicle."

I won't let him distract me. "You've been so wonderful to me, ever since Isabel died."

"Are we going to get all maudlin now? Because if we are, then I'm going to need dessert. There's only so much drama I can stand without dessert. They're supposed to have incredible pie here."

"You don't even *like* pie. You and William are the only two people in the known universe who don't like pie."

"How *is* dear little William? What's he up to? Studying for his SATs? Applying to medical school?"

Simon is faking this snide disregard for my benefit. He actually *likes* William. When he visits they invariably end up wrapped in an animated discussion of their shared appreciation for Philip Pullman or closeted in William's room hunched over some elaborate Lego model of the universe. I have a feeling that Simon sees reflected in William something of the child he once was, awkward and precocious, far more comfortable with adults than with children his own age, an outsider able to explain the shifting orbits of the moons of Saturn but unable to ask another child to join him on the jungle gym.

"He's in fine form." I tell Simon about the eBay fiasco.

"Oh God," he says. "You poor thing. What a nightmare." He sips his sparkling water. "I'll bet he was just looking to earn some money. I was always trying to find ways to get money when I was a kid."

"He doesn't need any money. His mother gives him everything he wants."

"Still. It's the *money*. The fact of it. I used to make my grandmother give me my birthday money in singles so I could have more of it. More bills. I just liked having them. I'd spread them out on my bed and roll around on them."

"He's too little for that," I say sourly.

"William? He's not too little for anything. Girlfriend, that stepson of yours is older than we are."

Chapter 8

It is Wednesday again and today it is raining, and while that will make the pickup from preschool even more unpleasant, I will be able to walk through an empty park. My first visits to Central Park, with my father when I was a little girl, had a quality of dream-like isolation. I don't mean to imply any sort of bucolic seclusion—in the early eighties the park was a neglected place. Turtle Pond was filled with beer cans, and were there sheep in Sheep Meadow they would have been forced to subsist on dust rather than grass. But my father's middle age was permeated with a nostalgic longing for the park's paths and playing fields, and so visits there were something of a pilgrimage, no matter how seedy and rundown it had become. He grew up on the Upper West Side, in a family that could afford to retreat to the Catskills only for one month of the year. For the rest of the summer, Central Park was his playground. Every six months or so, when we had an hour or two to kill between waiting on line for our half-price theater tickets and the start of our Sunday matinee, my father would decide that we should spend the time not in Bloomingdale's or the Gotham Book Mart but in the park. My mother did not enjoy these excursions; she was afraid of muggers and of the young men who would call out "Loose joints, smoke, shake" as we passed. She was probably not unreasonable in her fears; the park was a much more dangerous place back then, and those young men were likely making their sales pitches to intimidate rather than because they imagined that the prosperous-looking white man, with his fur-clad wife and young daughters in white tights and Mary Janes, was there to buy some pot. But I loved walking through the park with my father. He pointed out the fields where he used to play baseball with his brothers and their friends. He dug with the toe of one pointed shoe at the base of a tree because he thought he remembered that that was where Bobby Finkelman had buried a 1946 Canadian silver dollar.

Once, when I was about ten years old and it was just the two of us—I can't remember why my mother had decided not to join us, perhaps she had a cold, perhaps she and my father had had an argument, perhaps she just wasn't interested in seeing *Dreamgirls*—my father took me up to the Harlem Meer. It was a daring adventure. The gray ski threatened rain, and the old boathouse was a burned-out hulk, stinking of urine and splashed with graffiti. I had never been to Harlem before, and imagined it as a dark and scary place, filled with dark and scary people. My father refused even to notice my trepidation. He led me around the Meer, pointing out the bluffs of schist and the different types of trees growing on the high slopes. He smiled broadly at the few people we passed, even the drunk old men slugging wine from bottles wrapped in crumpled paper bags, in what I now recognize as the self-conscious expansiveness of the uncomfortable limousine liberal. Back then I thought him no less than an emissary of racial equality and, once I overcame my apprehension enough to see beyond the vandalism, of the wild beauty of the north-most corner of the park.

When I moved to New York City I began exploring the park on my own. It was just beginning its slow transformation from an urban wilderness full of homeless people pushing shopping carts and young black men in thick gold necklaces pushing crack, to a pastoral wilderness full of middle-aged white women spotting yellow warblers through expensive binoculars and elderly black men trolling for large-mouth bass. There was still something brave and pioneering about my willingness to hike on my own through the more isolated parts of the park, like the Ravine that stretches from Lasker Rink down to the Pool. Now, in the days after the tenure of Rudy Giuliani, for whom none of us good liberals will admit to having voted but for whom we cannot help but hold a certain grudging admiration as we make our way through a virtually crime-free city, even the Ramble is overrun. Once only men bent on anonymous, alfresco encounters would wander the paths, especially out to the Point, where they ignored the birds in favor of more earth-tied distractions. Nowadays, though, it's a free-for-all. The men are still there, God knows (one particularly sybaritic soul upon whom I've happened more than once brings along a folding chair; not for him the discomfort of a rocky path or log), but they've been joined by hordes of tourists, lunching office workers, ambling senior citizens, and groups of schoolchildren with laminated checklists of tree species. Still, in the winter, in the rain, I am lucky enough to find some solitude.

I am not alone in the elevator, but my companions are too entranced by each other's company even to greet me. I stare straight ahead and pretend not to notice that the guitar player has his hand down the back of his companion's jeans, although her yellow rain slicker is bunched up around her waist and she is giggling. When we arrive at the lobby he pinches her on the behind before he pulls his hand free. I have been so busy pretending not to look at them that I have not done any preparation in anticipation of crossing the park. However, the rain is coming down in sharp, cold needles and even hardy New York children will not be out in this kind of weather.

Ivan opens his umbrella over my head and steps outside to whistle a cab down for me. He frowns when I tell him I will walk, and then he tells me he has a spare umbrella inside. I show him the capacious hood of my long raincoat. I lift one of my legs in its knee-high rubber boot. The boots have leopard spots and are very cheerful and cute. I quite nearly left them in the hall closet—it seemed odious to wear something that contrasted so sharply with the mood I have managed to sustain for this long—but not even I am sufficiently self-indulgent to ruin a perfectly good pair of shoes just to prove to myself that I really am as wretched as all that. Besides, with these boots on I will be able to satisfy a longtime urge to march across the park in the rain without heeding path or road; I will be able to ford the Ramble, squelch my way through the mud, the woods, and the bog. Once, a couple years ago, I stumbled across a little wooden structure while walking through the Ramble and I want to slog around and find it again.

I walk the paths to the Lake, and somewhere around the Azalea Pond I try to go off-road and bushwhack. The Ramble is cut through with paths, and at first it is hard to imagine myself as at all intrepid. In the winter, however, they do not plow the small trails, nor do they do much in the way of clearing away what the wind brings down, so I finally manage to get lost. The dried and withered winter underbrush crackles beneath my feet despite the damp, and I cannot see very far ahead of me. I cannot even hear the traffic that usually rumbles in the background, because the sound of the pounding rain drowns out everything else. I am blessedly alone; I might be in the Adirondack Mountains or on some secluded part of the Appalachian Trail. I climb over a boulder, holding on to the mossy and cold rock, carefully placing the toes of my boots so they will not slip.

Suddenly, out of the corner of my eye, I see something moving on the other side of the boulder. I am already up and over the top, and I try to scramble back the way I came, but I cannot get purchase on the slippery stone. I end up sitting down hard, a sharp pain in my tailbone. A man wearing two black garbage bags, one over his body with holes cut out for his arms, and the other like a hood with a hole cut out for his face, unfolds himself from the ground and rears up over me, his face twisted in rage, his mouth open in a snarl to reveal yellowed and broken teeth and a long bluish tongue.

I scream, thinking immediately of the serial murderer who raped and bludgeoned the Central Park jogger, crushing her skull, and leaving her no future other than a best-selling memoir about her struggle to relearn how to read and walk, and the lifelong guilt of having played a role in the decade-long incarceration of a group of innocent teenagers. The ugly man stares at me, dark eyes in an ashy face, his cracked and torn lips working. He looks at my leopard boots and steps backward, growling in his throat. I try to scramble back but I instead fall forward, off the rock, landing in a ball at his feet.

He howls and throws his hands out toward me. His nails are long and ragged, black with dirt.

Most people assume that they have reservoirs of courage, untapped nerve that they can draw upon in order to spring forth in acts of bravery, should they ever be faced with a situation demanding it. No one ever believes him- or herself to be capable of true, deep cowardice. In the abstract everyone is Miep Gies, smuggling food and notebooks to Anne Frank up in the annex behind the cupboard in the Dutch Opekta Company. Courage is, in large part, a form of self-aggrandizement; the only times I have ever been brave in my life have stemmed from narcissism, a desire to make myself *appear* courageous, to define myself for others as a person of valor, to have a story to tell that will put me squarely in the camp of the Mieps and the partisans. Like the time I rushed to the defense of a woman whom I saw being punched by her husband outside a restaurant on Eighth Avenue. I ordered my cab to stop, opened the door, and invited her inside all in a flush of some thoughtless exhilaration. Courage is impulsive; it is narcissism tempered with nihilism. It is not that the courageous do not realize or understand the extent of the danger they face. They make a conscious decision not to care.

I leap to my feet, and shout, "Fuck off!" as loud as I can.

The man screams and spins away, crashing through the woods.

I slide down the rock and hit the ground. I get to my feet and run, too, in the opposite direction. Breaking through a thick tangle of brush, I find myself on the back side of Balanced Rock, a massive boulder upended atop a slab of schist. I leap down the four-foot drop, and run as fast as I can along the familiar path to the rear of the Loeb Boathouse. Once I am out of the lonely woods, I bend over and put my hands on my knees, nearly crying with relief. Then I run toward East Drive and up in the direction of the Seventy-ninth Street Transverse, trying to put as much space between myself and the man as possible. By the time I reach Fifth Avenue, my fear has been replaced by anger. How dare he have sought shelter in *my* refuge? How dare he have frightened me so badly that I was thwarted in my goal of an hour of solitude? How dare he have evicted me from my park? I am furious with that filthy, crazy man, and I am furious with Central Park, too. The Angel of the Waters has proved herself a treacherous and disloyal guardian, sheltering crazed homeless men with the same benign grace she extends to me. Why is it that loving something provides so little protection from betrayal?

Chapter 9

Waiting in the hallway outside of the Red Room is a woman I do not recognize. I haven't seen her before, but I am confident she is not a nanny. She is definitely a mother. It is always possible to distinguish between the mothers and the women whose love is a function of employment. It is not that the mothers are obviously more devoted to their children; on the contrary. I have seen many nannies who love their charges with an openheartedness, a ferocity, so obvious that it worries me. When the object of such devotion can be withheld at another's will, due to economic forces or even due to sheer selfishness or ill-temper, it is frightening. But what distinguishes the mothers from the nannies at these preschools is not love for the children; it is an intersection of class and age, with a soupçon of confidence. Some of the nannies are obviously so—black women from the islands caring for blond-haired girls named Kendall, Cade, or Amity. But the 92nd Street Y, despite the fact that it is Jewish, celebrates "diversity," and that means there are one or two cocoa-skinned children. No one would ever confuse the mothers of those children, however, with a nanny. There is an apartheid in the hallway that makes it easy to note the difference. At this preschool, at least, the nannies are more neatly dressed than the mothers who, with the exception of the lawyers or investment bankers, generally adopt an "artsy," dressed-down appearance—crumpled comfort at a four-figure price. Also, while the mothers look harried and overwhelmed, the nannies seem competent and in control; some even appear bored. Although each group seems to enjoy its own company, the nannies' laughter is more muted. The mothers' voices ring out loudly; even when they hush one another they do so at full volume. The nannies are quieter; they greet each other fondly and with obvious pleasure, but softly, so as not to disturb.

This new mother is young, closer to my age than the others. She stands a bit apart like I do, although as I watch she shifts almost imperceptibly closer to the mothers. She catches my eye and smiles.

"Hi," she says.

I am so taken aback by being spoken to that I stammer before returning her greeting. There is one other stepmother in the Red Room, but she has never dared show her scarlet-lettered self. I am the only one who comes to school to pick up her husband's child, and the women, all of whom have known Carolyn since Orange Room days, have joined forces and frosted me out. They will not speak to me; they shrink from me; they pull their children away from me as if touching me will give them some kind of disease, as if infidelity is contagious.

"We're new," the woman says. "I'm Adik Brennan. Frida's mom? We've just moved here from LA."

"Oh," I say, struck dumb. I glance at the mothers to see if one will come forward to escort Adik into their circle, to correct her in her misapprehension that I am someone with whom she is permitted to speak.

"I'm Emilia." Loath to ruin this opportunity, I don't identify my relationship with William.

"With an *A*?"

"No, an *E*."

"That's unusual. Although I should talk, right?"

"Right, er, no. I mean . . ."

"I can't believe this weather," she says. "I actually called a car service just to come and pick Frida up. There was no way I was even going to try to get a cab in this."

"Your daughter's name is Frida?" I say.

"With just an *i*," she says. "Like Kahlo. I know, you're probably thinking that Kahlo's been totally commodified and trivialized. I mean, at this point she almost symbolizes lightweight feminism. And it's certainly true that the art world has moved way beyond identity politics."

"Um," I say.

"But I really loved Frida Kahlo when I was starting out. Like every other female art student. And I still reference her in my work, although my painting is nonobjective." When she says the word "painting" she mimes quotation marks with her fingers. "Nowadays I source a pretty wide range of artists. Do you know John Currin's work, or the photographer Philip-Lorca diCorcia?"

"I saw *Frida*," I say. "It was pretty awful." Then I blush.

"The movie? I didn't see it," Adik says. "I'm not that interested in film. Linear narrative is just really hard for me to follow."

Someone touches me on the elbow and I jump. It is William's nanny, Sonia. She is wearing a black, knee-length coat and high, patent-leather boots. Her face is carefully made-up with dramatic blue eye shadow and dark lipstick. I have never seen her look like this.

Usually she is scrubbed clean and her hair, rather than sprayed into today's stiff curls, is held back in a simple headband or elastic.

"It's your day off," I say, confused. "I'm supposed to pick William up today, aren't I?" Could I possibly have mistaken the day?

"Dr. Soule tells me to give this to you." She hands me a pharmacy bag. Inside is a bottle of pink medicine. "For the ears."

"Why didn't she just put it in his backpack this morning?"

"She gives me directions. They are very specific." Sonia's English is good. She has a large vocabulary and her sentence construction is usually almost perfect, unlike some of the Eastern European cabdrivers I've had, or the men who work in the bagel store near Stuyvesant Town where I used to buy breakfast every morning before I moved in with Jack. She only knows the present tense, however. I have never heard her use any other. Neither has Jack and while I've only met her a few times, he has spent hundreds, even thousands of hours in her company. Sonia has been William's nanny since the day, when he was six weeks old, that Carolyn went back to work.

"But it's your day off," I repeat. "She made you work on your day off."

Sonia's face is very broad, flat, with Slavic features that hint at pillaging ancestors thundering on shaggy ponies across steppes and forests. She blinks her almond-shaped eyes and a sneer of contempt flits across her wide mouth so quickly that I am not sure it was really there. Perhaps I imagined it. Perhaps she does not actually scorn my blatant attempt to suck up to her, to convince her that we two, Sonia and I, are on the same side, that we are alike in our victimization at the hands of the powerful Dr. Soule.

I remind myself, for the millionth time, that I am the one who hurt Carolyn, and any anger she expresses, any venom she spews, any mortar shell she lobs across the park from her apartment on Fifth Avenue to ours on West Eighty-first Street, is entirely justified. Still, it pisses me off that she feels she must send an emissary with specific instructions on how to administer a spoonful of antibiotic.

"Three times a day he takes this. With food. And keep cold. But not in the fridge."

"How am I supposed to keep it cold if it's not in the fridge?"

Sonia shrugs her shoulders.

"Dr. Soule says also when Mr. Woolf drops off William this time, William's clothes are clean and fold, not shove in the backpack."

"Okay, now that is *not* fair. First of all, it's ridiculous to make us return his outfit every Thursday morning, instead of letting us send it back over the weekend, and second of all, his clothes weren't shoved, I had just pulled them out of the dryer and maybe I folded them too quickly or something . . ."

Sonia holds up her hand. "Ms. Greenleaf, I am only messenger here. I am not Dr. Soule; is not my message. Please do not yell at me."

"I'm not yelling."

"It is very embarrassing for you yelling at me in public."

Sonia is younger than I am, perhaps in her late twenties, but she makes me feel like a badly behaved child.

"I'm sorry," I say softly. "I just . . . I'm sorry."

She nods. "I look at William. Then I go to my day off. Don't forget, three times a day. Cold, but no fridge."

"Got it," I say. "Cold, but no fridge. And folded, not shoved."

She nods.

We both look over to the door to the Red Room. It is still closed. The mothers have gathered closer to the door, Adik among them. I smile at her, but she turns away. Someone must have told her about me. Or perhaps she overheard my conversation with Sonia and figured it out on her own. At any rate, Adik and I will not be discussing nonobjective art or linear narrative again.

Chapter 10

There is no catching a cab in front of the preschool. Not with the rain, and William and me already sopping, and the goddamn booster seat in its clear vinyl cover advertising our status as nightmare fares. I do my best for a while, hopping in and out of the street, trying to avoid the sheets of muddy water sprayed up by the passing cars. I wave madly at the cabs, even those that have their lights turned off or their off-duty lights on. Finally I say to William, "Let's try Park Avenue. Maybe we'll be luckier there. At least they'll be going in both directions."

We head west, our heads bowed against the rain. William wears the most subdued rain gear I have ever seen on a child. The other children wear bright yellow raincoats, fuchsia oilskins, purple slickers. His raincoat is military green and buckles up the front. However, at least it is lined with goose down and is very warm. I shiver in my thin raincoat. Even with my thick woolen sweater and silk long underwear I am freezing. William's boots, also dull green, are plain old rain boots and I am afraid his feet are as cold as mine. When we get to Park Avenue there are cabs going in both directions, but none are for hire. I curse myself for having failed to bring an umbrella. I imagine the telephone conversation in which Carolyn screams at Jack because I have caused William to catch cold by forcing him to stand in the freezing rain with no umbrella. Worse, I imagine Jack and Carolyn huddled over William's comatose body, the suck of the respirator forcing his pneumonia-damaged lungs to expand and contract. Barely controlled panic over their desperately ill child draws them together and they fall into each other's arms. They cling to each other. How could they have allowed this to happen? How could they have failed to protect their child and their marriage? They promise a lifetime of renewed troth and fidelity, if only William will get well.

We are facing the northbound traffic and I lead us downtown, trying to move ahead of the other waterlogged taxi hunters. We are standing at the corner of Ninetieth and Park when I have had enough.

"We're taking the bus," I say.

"The bus?" William says.

"Please don't tell me you've never taken the bus."

"I've taken the bus."

"Thank God."

"Just not in the winter. Not during flu season. My mother prefers that I not use public transportation during the winter months."

I shift the booster seat to my other hip and glare at him. "Your mother wouldn't want you to stand here in the pouring rain."

"You should have called daddy's car service."

Of course I should have called a car service. Even a five-year-old child knows that. The idea, however, had never occurred to me. I am not the kind of New Yorker who uses a car service. I am the kind of New Yorker who either rides the subway or takes cabs. I don't even ride the bus, except in and out of New Jersey.

"It's only four blocks. It's a five-minute walk to the bus stop."

"The crosstown bus is at Eighty-sixth Street," William says.

"Right. Come on."

"Emilia?"

"What, William?"

"Le Pain Quotidien is at Madison and Eighty-fifth."

"Le what?"

"Le Pain Quotidien. My favorite café. Sonia takes me quite often. It's at Madison and Eighty-fifth."

"And?"

"As far as we know, it is the only café in the city that has dairy-free cupcakes."

"William, it is pouring rain; we are both drenched to the skin, and I am not taking you out for dairy-free cupcakes."

William does not cry, but his nose turns a shade of red more intense than rain and cold could produce. He pokes out his lower lip and suddenly he looks like the little boy that he is. I feel terrible. I am horrid, an unspeakably wretched bitch. Of course he wants a cupcake. When did I turn into the kind of person who would take a cupcake away from a child?

"If you promise," I say, "that you won't give me a hard time about getting on the bus."

The right side of William's mouth lifts, and then he is grinning. We run as fast as we can to Eighty-fifth Street and over to Madison, William's booster seat and lunch box bumping along between us.

The café is meant to evoke the French countryside. The floors are made of wide oak planks, waxed warm and buttery smooth. The walls are plastered sienna brown and in the middle of the room there is a huge rustic table where pairs of mothers and children and nannies and their charges huddle, blowing the steam off hot chocolate and coffee drinks served in bowls of heavy white porcelain. I recognize a couple of the women; their children are at the 92nd Street Y Nursery School, although not in the Red Room. At one end of the community table sit two women with strollers covered in plastic sheeting. I try not to look into the strollers, try not to gauge the ages of their babies relative to the age that Isabel would have been. Instead I lead William over to the other end of the table. When the waitress comes, I order an espresso, and for William a hot chocolate made with soy milk. Then William asks for a dairy-free cupcake, explaining to the waitress that he is lactose intolerant, which means he has a milk allergy, which means that he will get both a stomachache and a rash from drinking milk or eating butter.

When I was first dating Jack, before I was well-enough versed in the various permutations of the supposed milk allergy, I gave William a piece of lemon ricotta cake. He happily consumed it to absolutely no ill effects. I have never been able to say anything about this telltale piece of cake, however, have never been able to trot it out to prove that William's lactose intolerance exists only in his and Carolyn's minds, because back then, once I realized my mistake, I told William it was *tofu* lemon cake and I don't want him to know, even two years later, that I lied. The waitress is still waiting so I order myself a cupcake, too.

"Dairy-free?"

"No, regular. Strawberry."

William does not lick the frosting off his cupcake like a normal child would. Like I do. He takes careful, even bites in a circle, peeling off the pleated paper cup as he goes. When a crumb lands on the table he licks his finger and dabs it up.

The cupcake I have ordered for myself is yellow cake with pink frosting, and it is the best cupcake I have ever eaten in my life. I lick the strawberry frosting very slowly, trying to be Zen about it, so mindful of the flavor, of the buttery texture of the frosting on my tongue, that there will be no room in my consciousness for the woman who is now breast-feeding her baby at the other end of the table.

William, hopelessly mired in his rational, left-brain, Western approach to cupcake eating, finishes long before I do, and turns his deadpan gaze to consider my cupcake. Something about it seems to be troubling him.

"They do not make dairy-free cupcakes with pink icing," he says.

"That's too bad," I say.

"Only vanilla and chocolate."

"Maybe it's never occurred to them to make pink, dairy-free cupcakes. Perhaps you could leave a note for the baker. I have a pen. Would you like to borrow it?"

"Perhaps," William says. He licks his lips and looks longingly at my cupcake. The intensity of his analysis sours my pleasure, breaks the meditative focus of my attention.

"Would you like a bite of my cupcake?"

"Yes," he says. "Only I'm lactose intolerant."

"I know you're lactose intolerant, William. The waitress knows you're lactose intolerant. The girl behind the bakery counter knows you're lactose intolerant. Everyone in the café knows you're lactose intolerant. But it won't kill you to have a bite of cupcake. It probably won't even hurt you."

"Perhaps just a *small* bite," William says.

I hand him my cupcake. I have licked off much of the frosting on one side, and William carefully turns it around so that he can take his bite from an unlicked part. He bites carefully, holding the cupcake with two hands and taking a single nibble—a cartoon mouse cherishing a nugget of cheese. Then he hands the cupcake back to me.

"Thank you," he says.

"You're welcome."

"It's very good."

"It is."

"I think it is even better than my dairy-free cupcake."

"Really?"

"Oh the dairy-free cupcakes are good. They are very good. It's just, yours might be better. Perhaps a little bit better. Because of the strawberry." His face grows very grave. "Or the butter."

"Gotta love that butter."

William sighs.

The nursing baby at the end of the table burps loudly, and his mother laughs. I swallow, wondering how it is that one moment I can be having a surprisingly pleasant conversation about cupcakes, and the next I can be on the verge of dissolving into tears.

William is looking at the baby. "How old is that baby, I wonder," he says loudly.

"He's four months old," the baby's mother says.

"He looks older," William says. "Is he big for his age?"

The mother laughs and gives me one of those your-kid-is-so-delightfully-precocious looks. I try to smile, but I can't.

"He's pretty big," she says.

William sips his hot chocolate thoughtfully. Then he says, "Emilia, did you know that Isabel wasn't really a person?"

"What?" I whisper, because if I do not whisper, I will scream.

"She was never really a person. That's what it says in the Jewish law. In the Jewish law, a baby doesn't become a real person until it is eight days old. Isabel was only two days old when she died. So that means she wasn't a person. Not in the Jewish law."

"Where did you hear that?"

He licks the rim of his cup. "My mother. I told her I was a *little* sad about Isabel, but not as sad as if I had known her for a long time. Not like if she had time to be my real little sister. And my mom told me about how in the Jewish law she wasn't even a real person. So I don't have to feel bad about not being *so* sad."

This is coming from Carolyn, I tell myself. Not from him. But I cannot stop myself.

"Isabel was a person," I say. "She was every bit as much of a person as you are."

William seems unperturbed by my vehemence, by my shaking voice, by the saliva that sprays from my lips and flecks across the scarred top of the oak table.

"*I* didn't say it. It's the Jewish law. My mother said she was surprised they let us have a funeral."

Isabel is buried in the Linden Hill Cemetery, out in Queens, in a corner set aside for others like her, others whose plots take up so little room that two or even three can fit in a space meant for one adult. We buried Isabel four days after she died, a longer delay than that dictated by the Jewish law on which William and Carolyn are apparently such authorities, but there was a backlog at the New York City morgue, and when a healthy infant dies for no apparent reason, an autopsy must be performed, whatever the Jewish law says about defiling the human body and the imperative of immediate burial.

I wore sunglasses to the funeral. The sun was very bright and my eyes hurt from crying. I had been crying pretty much nonstop for four days at that point, and had not been outdoors at all. I had kept the curtains and shades in the apartment drawn, and the harsh light of the midmorning Queens sun started a migraine creeping up the back of my neck. The cars carried us very near to the gravesite—we needed to walk only a little way. Everyone was there: my parents, my sisters and their husbands and children, Jack's mother, our friends, colleagues from work. There were dozens of people crowded around the tiny hole that had been cut in the earth and blanketed with rolls of bright green sod. As the service went on, people kept arriving, and I jumped every time I heard a car door slam.

The service was conducted by the rabbi who married us, and I wondered who had called her. I hadn't given a thought to the question of who would officiate. My outfit, yes—I had managed to spare five minutes to choose the plain black knee-length skirt and sweater. But it hadn't occurred to me to wonder who would lead kaddish over our daughter's grave.

Jack had managed to hold off his tears until the Town Car rolled through the cemetery gates. Before that he had, by and large, been too busy in his role of comforter of the bereaved mother and footman to her grief to spare much time for his own sorrow. My mourning devoured everything. It was so all-encompassing that it left little room for Jack to grieve. He had to catch his sadness where he could, around the edges of my own. For the past four days he had rocked me in his arms, fed me sleeping pills and Valium, bought me boxes and boxes of the softest tissues, sat next to me while I toyed with the meals my mother and his had prepared. Now, on that stony green hillside in Ridgewood, Queens, Jack's agony overtook him, and he began to cry.

Jack's tears were not manly. They were not reluctant drops wrung from stoic eyes. His tears came in torrents, sending great shudders through his frame. By the time we had crossed the stretch of grass from the car and sat in the folding chairs next to the empty little rectangle in the earth Jack was bawling. When they began to lower the plain white coffin with the gold-painted handles, so small, so light I felt as if I could have effortlessly picked it up in my arms and held it to my chest, he was wailing. The force of his grief, the massive candor of it, was making the people around us—our friends and family, his partners and employees—uneasy. The women started to cry and the men shifted awkwardly from foot to foot. And then something strange happened. His weeping drew a flow of milk from my swollen and aching breasts. Milk dripped through the layers of nursing pads, trickled through my bra, painted circles of pointless damp on the wool of my black turtleneck sweater.

When I didn't think I could stand it for another minute, when I was sure I was going to have to turn and bolt, William ran up and wrapped himself around his father's legs.

"Daddy," William said. "Daddy, don't cry. Don't cry."

"Oh God," Jack said. He picked William up and rocked back and forth, holding the boy close to him. "Daddy is so sad, Will. Daddy is so, so sad."

William said, "Don't be sad, Daddy. Because I love you. I love you so much."

"Only the most Orthodox rabbis think that a two-day-old baby isn't a person," I tell William now, trying to be patient because I remember how he ran to comfort his father. "We're Reform. Reform Jews know that babies are people from the moment they are born."

William ponders this as he drains his cup of cocoa.

"I think I am Orthodox," he says.

"You are *not*," I say. I feel a frightening urge to hit him. "You aren't even really *Jewish*. Your mother has to be Jewish for you to be a Jew. Your mother is Episcopalian."

"I am half Episcopalian and half Orthodox Jew."

"Let's go," I say.

Outside, the rain has stopped. I raise my hand and a cab pulls over instantly. My Orthodox Jewish Episcopalian stepson's God has given us an authentic miracle.

I open the cab door and start to unzip the booster from its cover.

"I don't want to sit in a baby seat," William says.

"It's not a baby seat." I realize with a sense of great liberation that I don't care if this child sits in his goddamned booster. I don't care if he is protected by a five-point harness or if he careens around the backseat of the cab like a Lotto ball in a rotating drum.

"Pop the trunk," I tell the driver. Then I go and throw the booster seat in, alongside an old NY Giants stadium blanket and a box of traffic flares.

"Get in," I tell William.

His eyes widen.

"Get in!"

"With no booster?"

"What, all of a sudden you want your booster?"

"No, no!"

William is so happy during the cab ride that he can barely contain himself. He sits backward on the seat, on his knees, looking out the rear window. He provides color commentary—now we are passing a maple tree, now there is a woman with a large gray dog, perhaps it's a Russian wolfhound, or perhaps a Scottish deerhound. Meanwhile I am sitting with my lips clamped shut, trying to keep myself from shouting to the driver to pull over so that I can make William safe and secure, protected in his booster seat, where he belongs.

When we pull up in front of our building and Ivan opens the door, William vaults out of the taxicab.

"I don't need my booster seat anymore!" he announces to Ivan.

"Well, that's very nice, young man," Ivan says, tousling William's hair with one gloved hand.

When we are alone in the elevator I say, "William, if you tell *anyone* I let you ride without a booster seat, I will put you back in it. I will make you ride in your booster until you are thirty years old."

"You can't," William says. "It's six or sixty. Six years old or sixty pounds."

"It's six *and* sixty," I say. "And you are very skinny. It will be a long time before you weigh sixty pounds. It will be *years*."

William thinks this over. While I am unlocking the door to our apartment he says, with a faint, conspiratorial smile, "I won't tell anyone."

Chapter 11

Carolyn calls the next evening. I know it is her as soon as the phone rings, because it is ten o'clock and she is the only person who would call us this late at night, except for Simon, and it is Thursday night and on Thursday nights Simon volunteers for hospice. (Although Simon is a very altruistic person, he does not do this out of the goodness of his heart—he does it to meet men. Not dying men; he's not that fucked up. He is just convinced that if he volunteers long enough, at some point an attractive gay son will turn to him for comfort in his grief.) Jack is taking a shower when the telephone rings, and at first I intend to let the answering machine pick up, but I hate the messages Carolyn leaves. There will be the beep, and she will pause for a long moment before she speaks, and then she will say, with no preamble, and without identifying herself, "Jack, call me immediately." Of course we recognize her voice, but would it kill her to say, "This is Carolyn"? I understand that it pains her to acknowledge my presence in her ex-husband's home, but the fact that she behaves as if he is the only one who owns the machine on which she leaves her messages bothers me. What I hate the most, however, is that it never *is* urgent. The immediacy of his return call is never justified by whatever supposed crisis precipitated it.

"Fuck it," I say to myself, and pick up the phone on the third ring.

"Hello," I say. There is the usual pause.

"I'd like to speak to Jack, please." Her voice is so frosty, so *mean*. On UrbanBaby.com, the women all talk about how warm she is, how comforting, how gentle yet assured her manner in the delivery room. I wonder, not for the first time, if there is more than one obstetrician named Carolyn Soule in the city of New York.

"How are you, Carolyn?" I say.

"How am I? How do you think I am? I'm dealing with the fallout of your abusive behavior. So I would not say that I'm very well."

That little weasel ratted me out.

"I'd hardly call it abusive."

"Oh, wouldn't you? You don't think it's abusive to give a child a respiratory infection?"

"I'll get Jack."

"Wait a minute. I'm not done. I don't know what you're playing at, but I hope someday you have a child and a stranger walks him around the city in the pouring rain. Maybe then you'll have an inkling of what I'm going through right now. Maybe you'll understand what it means to see your child suffer."

The urge is almost overwhelming. I could so easily do it. I could tell her that she is right, I do not understand what it means to see my child suffer, because Isabel died in her sleep. I could so easily tell this awful woman that I would give anything to have my child back long enough to send her out into the street in the pouring rain in a drab green raincoat and a pair of rubber boots. It would feel wonderful to make Carolyn guilty and uncomfortable, to do to her what she has done to me every single time we have spoken over the last two years. But I'm so relieved that it's just the rain she's angry about, that she does not seem to know about the booster seat, not to mention the lactose-laden cupcake, that I merely say, "I'm sorry," and take the phone to the bathroom. Jack has turned off the shower and is standing on the bath mat, toweling himself off. I hand him the receiver.

"It's Carolyn," I say.

He holds the phone in one hand and his towel in the other. I stay in the bathroom and draw a picture in the condensation on the mirror while I listen to his side of the conversation.

"Hey," Jack says.

I can hear her voice, shrill and angry, but I cannot make out the words. I draw a circle, two eyes, a nose, and an angry frown. Then I draw squiggles for hair standing straight up on top of the stick figure's head. I try to draw a stethoscope, but it doesn't come off right.

I look at Jack. "I forgot my umbrella," I whisper.

He sighs.

I turn back to my drawing and cast a critical eye. There is not much my limited skill can do to improve it, so instead I take Jack's towel, fold it in half, and hang it on the towel rod.

"I think you're overreacting," Jack says into the phone.

I move behind him and look over his shoulder into the mirror. Bits of Jack are reflected back at me in the lines where my angry Carolyn face has rubbed away the condensation.

"We both know it's a petri dish at the preschool, Carolyn. You're a doctor. You know that he caught a cold from one of the other kids, not from being out in the rain."

I reach over his shoulder and draw a line on the right side of the mirror. Chalk one up for my husband.

"Yes, I'll talk to her about it. But I'm sure it won't happen again."

I erase the line with the edge of my palm.

Jack is silent for a while. Then he says, "I think you're misinterpreting that."

"What?" I mouth.

He shakes his head. "Well, then *he's* misinterpreting it. And what's the point, anyway? It's over, it already happened. And at the time you agreed that he could go. The shrink agreed that he could go. You called him and he said it would be good for William, that it would be part of the healing process."

"What?" I say again.

He holds his hand up, shushing me. I look down the length of his body. His penis is loose and flaccid after his shower, his testicles dangling. I take his penis in my hand, squeezing gently. He grabs my wrist and shakes his head.

I leave him in the bathroom and go lie down on the bed. He follows and sits next to me, still talking to Carolyn. They talk for nearly twenty minutes, and by the time the conversation is over, I have figured out what is going on. William came home after his night with us with the sniffles, and, between sneezing and wiping his nose on the furniture, told his mother that he and I had talked about newborn babies and funerals. He was upset, or more likely Carolyn decided that he was upset, and she called his therapist. Dr. Allerton agreed with her that, in retrospect, William's attendance at Isabel's funeral had been traumatic, that it had upset his fragile equilibrium, the equilibrium already cast into turmoil by his parents' divorce. Carolyn is furious at Jack, and at me, for having forced William to witness Isabel's interment in the ground of the Linden Hill Cemetery, between the bodies of Flora Marley Moscowitz born August 17, 1984, died October 1, 1984, and

Sebastian Jacob Hillman Baum taken from us on the day of his birth 6 Elul 5759.

On the morning of Isabel's death, Carolyn was remarkable. She was empathetic and caring. She was everything the women on UrbanBaby.com said she could be. When Jack first called to tell her about Isabel, she wept. She said she was so sorry; she said she could not imagine how awful we felt; she even told him to give me her condolences. It was Carolyn who broke the news to William, and by all accounts she did it well—simply, seriously, leaving him plenty of room to express whatever were his feelings.

The phone calls began that very evening. What was the *quality* of my grief, Carolyn wanted to know. Because William's therapist was concerned that he not be exposed to any level of emotion *inappropriate* in its intensity. I missed this call because at the time I was lying on my bed, sandwiched between Simon and Mindy, trying to stop screaming into my pillow. But my father was in the kitchen, eavesdropping, and he heard what Jack was too exhausted, too wrung out, too despairing to conceal. Afterward, over a tumbler filled to sloshing with scotch, Jack recounted Carolyn's side of the conversation to my father and, in a rare moment of détente, my father whispered it all to my mother, and she told me, cursing Carolyn's brutal selfishness in a furious whisper while she collected used tissues from the floor next to my bed and threw them into a plastic garbage bag.

I don't know how many times Carolyn called over the next few days, but I do know that every once in a while, I would stumble through the apartment looking for Jack, and find him in the kitchen, or in his office, slumped in a chair, curled around the telephone, absentmindedly rubbing his eyes as he listened to the berating squawk on the other end of the line. There were protracted debates over what the teachers would tell the other children at school, whether William should have his regular Friday piano lesson, whether he could go to a birthday party on the morning of the funeral, whether he should attend the funeral at all, whether he would be allowed to sit shivah, whether Jack would owe Carolyn a weekend because we were, after all, out of turn. I didn't actually care if William came to the funeral or to the shivah, and I came close, once, to telling Jack that.

We were sitting in the living room, and I was huddled on the couch, warming my hands on a cup of tea without drinking it. There were fewer people in the apartment than there had been over the past few days, since Isabel's death. My father had gone to check in at the office, my sisters were home tending to their children. Jack's mother had returned to her hotel to take a nap. Mindy was home with Daniel. Only Simon was there, and my mother.

Jack walked by the living room, carrying the phone, and raised his eyebrows to me, as if to ask how I was, if the pain was overwhelming or only horribly acute.

"Jack," I said.

He pointed to the telephone receiver.

"Jack!" I said more loudly. "Tell her it doesn't *matter*."

"Emilia, honey. Don't," my mother said.

"Hold on a minute," Jack said, and covered the mouthpiece with his hand. "What is it, sweetie? Do you need something? Can I get you something?"

"Don't," my mother breathed, so softly only I could hear her.

I narrowed my red and swollen eyes at Jack.

"Sweetie?" he said.

I closed my eyes. "Never mind. Just. You know. Finish up, if you can."

He nodded. "I'll only be another minute."

Tonight, by the time he hangs up the phone, Jack looks beaten, all the vigor of his showered and roughly toweled body gone. He sits on the edge of the bed, slumped and slack-jawed. Carolyn has somehow managed to reduce him to a preview of his elderly self. It is as if, in disgust at his grasping for youth in the body of a younger woman, she has conjured a mannequin. She has made Jack into the voodoo doll of her revulsion, has bent him so that his very body now personifies the fundamental absurdity of our relationship. She has turned him into an old man.

I grab him around the waist and haul him back down on the bed next to me, hugging him, curling my body around his. I like how it feels to be clothed when he is naked. I feel powerful somehow, strong, even dangerous. I push him onto his back and climb on top of him, straddling his thighs, pressing the hard seam of my jeans against his penis. I rock slightly and feel him shift underneath my crotch.

He settles his hands on my waist. "*Now* you're horny, Emilia?"

"No." I push against him hard enough to hurt. He winces.

"Do me a favor, honey," he says. "When it's raining, take a cab."

"I *tried* to take a cab. Do you think I enjoy being out in the rain with a five-year-old boy? I couldn't *find* a cab."

"So call the car service."

"Funny, that's just what William said."

Jack laughs. "He's a smart kid."

I am not laughing. "It's not any easier to get a car service on a rainy day than it is to get a cab. Anyway, you know what, Jack? If you don't like how I pick William up from preschool, you can pick him up yourself."

"You know I can't pick him up. I have to work."

Was there a subtle stress on that "I"? Was there a criticism implied?

"Fuck you," I say.

"What? What did I say?"

"I'm going back to work. I just need a little time."

"Emilia, why are you jumping all over me? I didn't say anything about you working or not. I don't care if you ever go back to work. All I said is that I can't pick William up because *I* have to work. But if you don't want to pick him up anymore, we can send him home with Sonia, like we used to."

I can taste the delicious flavor of the words in my mouth: Yes, let's do that. Let's do that, because I don't want to be with him anymore.

I can taste those words, and I have an awful feeling that Jack can see me rolling them in my mouth.

"Of course I want to keep picking him up," I say. "I just forgot my goddamn umbrella. Jesus."

The muscle in the corner of Jack's jaw works. He is trying very hard to remain calm. "His therapist is worried about him."

"So Carolyn says."

"She's not a *liar*, Emilia. Carolyn is fucked up in lots of ways, but she's compulsively honest."

I wonder if kissing him right now will be too obvious. I wonder if the naked manipulation, the needy jealousy, expressed by a kiss at this moment will be so unattractive that it will outweigh Jack's pleasure at finally feeling my tongue. I kiss him lightly on the lips. I keep my tongue in my own mouth.

His jaw relaxes and for a moment his lips soften under mine. Then he says, "Dr. Allerton thinks Will might have post-traumatic stress disorder."

"William does not have post-traumatic stress disorder."

Jack rubs his eyes with his fist. "Oh Jesus. Oh Jesus. Poor Will."

"He's fine, Jack. Will's fine." This is the first time I've used this nickname in years. When I first met William, I tried on Jack's nickname for him, the way one tries on an unlikely outfit in a favorite boutique, or an unusual pair of shoes. *Who knows, maybe these powder blue clogs will suit me. Maybe I've been a silver strappy-sandal kind of girl all along, but have been too conservative, too cowardly to find out.* I used the nickname "Will" once or twice, but it did not fit him when it came from my mouth. I went back to calling him William, our relationship as formal as a pair of staid black pumps.

"I'm so sorry, Em. I'm sorry I keep losing my shit like this," Jack says, wiping his eyes. He rolls me off of him and tucks me under his arm.

"You don't keep losing your shit. When have you *ever* lost your shit?"

He doesn't answer. I get up and get undressed, tossing my clothes on the little French armchair in the corner of the room.

I slide under the sheets and turn to face him. He presses his lips into my hair, which has been, ever since he has known me, a brilliant, natural-looking shade of pumpkin red. It is the color Allison's hair was before she went gray, and I have heard that it is the precise hair color of her mother, my father's first wife. My older sisters were four and six years old when their mother divorced my father and not very much older when she abandoned them entirely. As I am not sure that a child can be trusted to recollect color with any real accuracy, particularly when the person at issue is one around whom the emotions are so fraught, I don't know if my hair is really the same color as Annabeth Giskin's. The only pictures of this woman from my sisters' childhood are in black and white, and by the time Annabeth contacted them again, when her daughters were in their thirties, her hair had long since turned white. At any rate, I have the skin and freckles of a redhead, and I envied Allison her russet curls until I realized that they could be mine with a little help from Bumble and Bumble. And so I am a redhead, and while the absurdity of constructing an entire personality around a hair color that comes out of a bottle does not escape me, still I found myself not a little surprised when Isabel arrived with such dark hair.

I slide my hand along Jack's belly and he moans, but not with pleasure.

He stops my hand with his and says, "Sweetie, I can't believe I'm saying this, but I don't think I can, not tonight. I'm just so freaked out about William. I'm sorry. Is that okay?"

I rest my hand under his palm, on his abdomen, and press gently, feeling for any hint of flab. "Sure," I say, and I am relieved, but only for a moment. After three months in a sexual desert, he is rejecting my advances? After three months of surreptitiously beating off in the shower when he thinks I'm not paying attention, he is pushing away my hand? This is the first time in the not quite two years we have been together that Jack has ever said no to sex. From the very beginning, sex has been one of the most important loci of our relationship, the fulcrum on which everything is balanced. This does not mean our love is any less profound, any less real than that of couples for whom physical passion is unimportant. Abelard and Heloise were not content to exist as platonic companions, reading the Bible to one another and composing poetry. On the contrary. They ravished one another's virginal bodies, defying their sovereigns, risking excommunication, and ultimately sacrificing their testicles to lust—well, his testicles anyway.

So too with Jack and me. Except for the virginal part. And the castration. And the excommunication. Although if William succeeds in his conversion to Orthodox Jewry, he may yet convince his fellows in Crown Heights to toss us from the fold as punishment for having ruined his life.

This emphasis on the sexual between Jack and me undoubtedly has something to do with the fact that Carolyn refused to make love with Jack. Even before William was born, she held him at arm's length, denying him access to the long, golden body for which his assimilated Jewish libido ached. They were married two years before William was born, and together for two years before that, and in those four years Jack swears he can remember, because there were so few of them, every incidence of lovemaking. He remembers none after William's birth, because there were none. They never had sex again, once she became pregnant.

Jack has told me that Carolyn despised it when he asked for sex, despised *him*. She said it made him seem pathetic. When I asked him why she refused to make love, he said that after the baby, she was exhausted, drained by work and caring for William. And before? Before, Jack told me, she simply found him repellent. She loved him, Jack said, but something about his body repulsed her. Once she had confessed that it was his small stature. He was like a squirrel, she said, scurrying over her body.

When Jack told me all this so long ago, when we first began having an affair, in the days when I used to interrogate him constantly about his marriage in my quest to consume the details of his life, become the repository of his every intimate secret, and also rationalize our betrayal, I licked his body from his ankles to the crown of his head. I lifted myself onto him, wrapped my arms around his neck, and whispered in his ear that he was the most beautiful man I had ever seen, that he was strong, and powerful, and so sexy that it made me wet just to see his name on the firm letterhead. Only afterward, when we were lying, sweaty and spent on the naked bed, the hotel pillows and blankets thrown to the floor, did I ask him why he had ever married her, this woman who had never desired him.

He thought about it for a moment, then shrugged. "We were in love," he said.

Now I lie next to him, my hand resting on his belly, inches above his flaccid penis. I am terrified that I have become like Carolyn, cold to sex, unmoved by my husband, uninterested in the passion that once meant everything to me. Worse, I am terrified that this woman who desired my husband so little has now managed to make him desire *me* not at all.

"Jack?"

"What."

"I promise I won't take him out in the rain again."

"Okay. Thank you."

"I promise I'll call a car service and I promise I'll never forget my umbrella again."

"Thanks."

"In fact, I'll buy us little matching plastic rain bonnets, and coats, too. The kind that fold up and fit in your purse. William and I will wear them whenever there's even a chance of showers."

He smiles perfunctorily.

"Would you like me to get you one, too? I think you'd look smashing in a little rain bonnet."

"Sure, Em. Get me a rain bonnet."

I kiss him gently and dart my tongue between his lips. Then I say, "I'll try to be good, Jack, I promise."

"I know you will," he says, and nestles me into the crook of his arm.

Chapter 12

Every other weekend, when we have William with us, Jack does not go into the office. Jack is compulsive about structuring his filings, his conference calls, his hearings and depositions, so that he will be free at five o'clock on the alternate Friday evenings when he must pick William up. But this Friday evening, at the hour when he is supposed to be standing awkwardly in the hallway of his old apartment at 1010 Fifth Avenue, making sure William has packed everything he needs into his stegosaurus backpack, Jack is at George Bush International Airport, in Houston.

"I don't understand," I tell him. "You're in *Texas*. How can you possibly be snowed in?"

"I'm not snowed in. The *plane* is snowed in. In Denver. And I can't get on another one until tomorrow morning. You'll have to pick Will up."

I am in a cab, heading downtown through the park on my way to meet Simon and Mindy for a movie. They had demanded my presence at dinner, but dinner requires conversation, and my jaw feels too tight to talk. Plus, there were two pregnant women comparing belly-button protrusions in front of the imported cheese case at Fairway this afternoon, so naturally I have been crying. I need to be in the dark.

"What do you mean 'pick William up'? I'm not allowed to pick William up. I'm not allowed in her apartment. I'm not allowed in the lobby of her building. I'm barely allowed on Fifth Avenue."

"You don't have to go up. Just tell the doorman you're there for William. She'll send him down."

"She will not. She'll totally freak out. I'm the abusive shrew who gave him a respiratory infection, remember?"

"You won't even see her. It's not even five o'clock. Anyway, I left a message for her explaining what happened."

"Like that'll help. Tell Sonia to bring him to our house."

"I've been trying to reach Sonia and Carolyn all afternoon. You're just going to have to go over there, Emilia."

"Did you leave a message on her service?"

"Of course I did. Many. She hasn't called me back."

"But I'm on my way to the movies." This doesn't deserve a reply and does not get one. I make one final craven attempt.

"How about if *I* keep trying Sonia? Or Carolyn? I'm sure I'll reach one of them at some point."

"Em, I'm stuck in fucking Houston, okay? I will get home as soon as I can. First thing in the morning. By ten. Or noon at the latest. Can you do me this one favor? Can you just please go pick William up at Carolyn's and bring him home? You can even turn on a DVD for him if you want. Order *Microcosmos* from Video to Go."

"William isn't allowed to watch television. Watching television gives children attention deficit disorder and makes them prone to violence."

"Emilia. Please." This is as close to angry as Jack has come since Isabel died. It excites me. I have finally tried his unceasing patience. I have finally disturbed his imperturbable, loving concern.

"I'm sorry," I say. "I'll pick him up. Of course I'll pick him up."

"Please don't be late."

I can hear the echo of Carolyn's harping voice in his request.

"I'm on my way right now."

"I love you, Em."

"Change of plan," I say to the cabdriver. "I need to go back uptown. To the East Side. Fifth and Eighty-second."

Only when I hang up the phone do I realize that this means that Jack will not be home tonight or tomorrow morning. How will I face an entire morning with William? Or, worse, another night alone in my bed? I now take two Ambien before I go to sleep, and I'm worried that that's too much, or not enough. I cannot risk waking up in the middle of the night or, worse, in the half-light of the guilt-edged dawn. Dawn is when Isabel died. No, that's not true. Dawn is when I realized that Isabel was dead.

I look out of the windows of the cab at the dark trees of the park, and think back to the one night in which we were a family in our own home. After the excitement of bringing the baby home from the hospital, we decided to go to bed early. I took a shower while Jack rocked Isabel in the glider, and as I stood under the hot stream, my breasts, which were aching, the nipples sore, the bottoms and sides tender and bruised, began to harden. By the time I stepped out of the water they were massive—round and cumbersome, like bowling balls covered by a thin scrim of flesh. The nipples were as long and as fat as my thumbs.

"I think my milk's come in," I called to Jack. "And it hurts!"

I put on the white lawn nightgown with the nursing slits that

Allison had given me and went into Isabel's room. Jack had slipped his pinky in between the baby's lips. He smiled at me. There were crinkles around his velvet eyes and he pursed his lips in perfect imitation of the baby's. "Good, because this girl is hungry," he said. "She wants her mama, right now." On Felicia's instructions we had not permitted the hospital to give Isabel any bottles. She had not had so much as a sip of sugar water since she was born. Every mouthful she had taken was from my breasts. Pure, golden colostrum.

I took her from Jack and brought her back to our bedroom. I shucked my nightgown, got into bed, and positioned her according to the lactation handout Felicia had given me, ready for more of the same easy nursing that we had experienced in the hospital. We were a perfect "nursing pair," Isabel and I, so at ease, so natural and flawless, that Felicia had photographed us for her lactation support album. Now Isabel bumped her lips against my protruding nipple, struggled to fit my drumlike areola into her mouth, and began to wail. For the next three hours I passed her from breast to breast, leafed through *The Breastfeeding Bible* and *The Nursing Mother's Companion*, hand expressed milk to soften my breast tissue, left tearful phone messages on Felicia's answering machine and on La Leche League's hotline, took hot showers and pressed warm compresses and ice packs against my breasts. Isabel continued to do battle with the engorged spheres that had once provided a trickle of warm comfort and now did nothing but torture her. They had become strong and forbidding, breasts on which to bang your face and cry, not to snuggle against and hug, not to latch on to happily and nurse. By eleven I was crying harder than the baby, and by one, Jack was on the phone offering a lactation consultant referred by La Leche $1,000 to come to our apartment that very minute. She promised to be there first thing in the morning, and suggested a hot bath.

At one forty-five, after a bath in which my milk and tears fogged the water, Isabel latched on. She was still nursing ten minutes later, and Jack said, "I think you can lean back."

"Be quiet," I whispered.

We were sitting on the edge of the bed. I was hunched over, with Isabel cradled high in my left arm. With my right hand I pushed my breast away from her tiny nostrils. Her lips were flanged out and she sucked rhythmically, with a little catch at the end of each gulp and a click as she swallowed. We stayed there, immobile, for nearly twenty minutes. Then, out of nowhere, she arched away from the breast and began to scream. I whipped her around to the other side and repeated the position in reverse, this time with my right arm bearing her weight. She settled in with a grunt and began her happy clicks. After a few minutes I shifted slowly back toward the headboard, stopping whenever I felt her shift or stir.

"Do you want a pillow under your arm?" Jack whispered.

I shook my head. Very slowly I leaned back until I was half-lying down, Isabel beside me, curled in the crook of my arm, her weight resting on the mattress. I kept my breast away from her nose with my left hand, which meant I was tipped over, my left elbow in the air.

"Are you sure?"

"I'm fine," I whispered. "Turn off the light. I think she's asleep."

When we woke, three hours had passed. Isabel lay just as she had, in my right arm, nestled close to my body. My left arm was draped over my waist. Isabel had fallen away from my breast and her mouth was partly open. In the dim light from the windows I could just barely see the tip of her tongue protruding from one side, curled like a small, pink shrimp. She was ice cold. I pulled the down comforter up toward her chin and rubbed one of her hands between my own. It was stiff and waxy. It rolled in my palms. I reared up in the bed and took her chin between my thumb and forefinger. I bent low over her mouth. Then I began screaming. I know this can't possibly be true, but I remember hovering high over our bed, close to the ceiling, watching myself scream, watching Jack struggle to the surface of his thick sleep, knock his lamp over, reach across me to turn on the lamp on my nightstand. I remember him on all fours on the bed, his mouth wide over Isabel's mouth and nose, pumping air into her lungs while I kneeled next to them, hands on my cheeks, my fingernails digging into the skin under my eyes, my mouth open in a shriek I could not hear.

Jack groped for the phone with one hand while he kept breathing into Isabel's still mouth. He dialed 911 and pushed the phone at me. I do not remember what I said. I cannot believe that I was sufficiently articulate, but somehow they understood. I think Ivan let them into the apartment; I'm not sure. There were many of them, in different uniforms. Police officers, paramedics. I have a memory that there were even firemen. They pushed us off our bed with large, competent hands, and hovered over our baby. One of them leaned forward with a knee against the mattress, and I stared at the bottom of his thick-soled shoe. There was a piece of pink chewing gum stuck deep in the tread.

He stood up, the paramedic who had stepped in gum, and said to us, "I'm so sorry, but I'm afraid she's gone."

I went up to the ceiling again. I looked down on myself and I thought, with a kind of dispassionate, nearly analytical curiosity, I wonder when I put my nightgown on? And look, how interesting, when one has had her body pierced by an unbearable pain, one does, in fact, fall to the ground. I looked at myself lying on the bedroom carpet, my nightgown twisted around my legs. On Jack's face was an expression—eyebrows knit, mouth pinched in a puzzled frown. It was an expression that I would remember many times in the months to come, one that we would even talk about on those rare occasions when we could bear to remember that gray dawn. When Jack recalled that expression, which sometimes he claimed that he could and other times said that he had no idea of what I was talking about, he would say that it had been the face of a man bewildered, unable to comprehend the chain of circumstances that had led to this impossible outcome. I always said that I believed him, that of course he was bewildered. But to me it was unmistakably a look of accusation—a look that said, How could you let this happen? Or even, Emilia, what have you done?

From my perch high above the room, I watched Jack fall to his knees and pull me onto his lap. I saw his lips forming my name, over and over again.

I could not hear a sound.

Chapter 13

The Upper East Side doorman's livery is more splendid than Ivan's, the fabric of his greatcoat stiffer, the double rows of brass buttons more highly polished, the gold braid looped more times around the wings of his shoulder pads. I wonder if Ivan wishes for a position worthy of this resplendence. Perhaps he has résumés on file at all these buildings, and is just waiting for the summons that will call him up to duty on the more elegant side of the park.

Carolyn's doorman holds opens the taxicab door and I step out. I don't walk up to the large front doors; I trudge. I dread entering this building, even though I know Carolyn is most likely to be at work. The thought of stepping foot onto the territory she has marked with her sour spray makes my bowels clench.

Halfway up the walkway the doorman taps me on the shoulder. "Miss," he says. "Are you looking for William?"

Ivan doesn't have a prayer, I'm afraid. He has no lilting Irish brogue to recommend him.

"Excuse me?" I say.

"Are you here to pick up young William Woolf?"

"Um, yes."

"William and Sonia are waiting for you at the Three Bears Playground. At Seventy-ninth Street. Just south of the museum."

"They're *what*?" It's dark and cold, and the sun is setting. I look at my watch. It's five minutes to five.

"They're waiting for you at the playground. It's just four blocks down Fifth Avenue."

"Why aren't they waiting here in the lobby?"

The doorman shrugs, steps between me and the building's entrance, and I realize that he is not going to let me inside. I wonder who told him that I am a potential danger, a hazard to the elegant palace he guards in his nutcracker suit? Suddenly, and only because I am refused entry, I *want* to go into the building, and I consider making a break for it, bolting past him and bursting into the lobby, grabbing a frond from a potted palm or a Chinese takeout menu as evidence of my successful transgression. Instead I thank him and hurry down the block.

I cross the street, a foolish decision it turns out, because I am forced to dodge the crowds of tourists in front of the Met. As I am dancing an impatient pas de deux with a group of teenagers who for some reason waited until they reached the curb to don their coats and scarves, it occurs to me that you can pretty much guarantee that someone wearing a Rebel Rebel T-shirt isn't one. I finally push by them.

"It's five o'clock," William says. He is sitting on a bench next to Sonia, his stegosaurus backpack on his lap and his booster seat in its cover at his feet. "The playground closes at five. It's against the law to come here now. They could arrest us."

The image of William being hauled away in handcuffs is so satisfyingly ridiculous that I almost smile. "They don't arrest people for staying in the park after five," I say.

"They do so."

"First of all, William, there was nothing I could do. My taxi dropped me off at your building, where, incidentally, I was expecting to pick you up. I got here as fast as I could; I can only run so fast. Second of all, look around you. This playground is full of kids. None of them look like they're being arrested to me."

I wave my arm to illustrate my point. The Three Bears Playground is one of the most pathetic in Central Park. It has the statue of the Three Bears and an old-fashioned, malevolent-looking jungle gym on a padded surface. There's a big sand circle with a metal slide, and a ladder to nowhere. The children playing here do not appear to be criminals, but neither do they appear to be having much fun.

"You should have taken a car service. A car service would have waited," William says.

I sigh. "William, not everybody has a car service at his beck and call. Not everybody can afford to just flit around the city in a Town Car."

Sonia gazes at some distant point behind my head. She remains bland-faced, although her disgust is as obvious as if she had curled her lip. Sonia knows, as do I, as does William, that we can afford to keep a car service on retainer; we can afford to flit freely from Town Car to Town Car. Jack is a partner at the fifth-largest law firm in the city, one of the largest and wealthiest law firms in the United States. He is a young partner, true, but still his draw is probably three times my father's.

Who am I kidding? The fraudulence of my carefully contrived parsimony is obvious even to a five-year-old. While my parents would have had more disposable income if my father had not spent the bulk of his days in the throes of a sexual compulsion, I have never experienced a moment's want in my entire life. Sharing a one-bedroom apartment in the East Village with two other girls and eating ramen noodles for supper three nights a week because I was too mediocre a waitress to sustain employment for longer than two months at a time does not count as deprivation. I can tell by Sonia's carefully composed expression that she *has* experienced deprivation. I do not know if she has ever gone to bed hungry, but I am sure that whatever troubles led her to travel four thousand miles to stand at dusk in the bitter cold of this miserable playground were more serious than having her cell phone service cut off or watching the salesgirl at Otto Tootsi Plohound cut up her credit card while she awaited the results of the LSAT.

"Go play," I say to William.

"What?"

"You're in a playground. Go play."

"I don't want to play. It's too cold. And it's *dark*."

"You won't be cold once you start playing. Look, none of the other kids are cold. They're all too busy playing."

There are more children in the playground than I would have expected this late, and there is a desperate edge to their play, as if they are frantically squeezing the last few moments out of the gray light of the day. William sighs as though I am sending him to haul coal from the bowels of a West Virginia mine, not climb a Fifth Avenue spiral jungle gym. He hands his backpack to Sonia and, shoving his hands into the pockets of his coat and scuffing his boots in the dirt, makes his way over to the outskirts of the crowd of children, resolute in his determination to have a miserable time.

I sit down in the spot he has vacated. His narrow behind has warmed more of the bench than I would have thought possible.

"I hate playgrounds," I say.

"Pardon?" Sonia says. She is in the process of getting to her feet but pauses as I speak.

"Playgrounds. I hate them. Now. I mean, since Isabel died. Isabel was our baby."

Sonia sits back down. "I know Isabel is your daughter's name."

I think I will buy her a grammar textbook so that she can learn more verb tenses.

She interlaces her gloved fingers. Her gloves are very beautiful, fawn-colored leather, with fur lining. Not rabbit, even. Mink, or sheared beaver. The pads of the fingers are darkened and the seams are frayed, however, and I think the gloves must be hand-me-downs from Carolyn.

It takes Sonia a moment to speak, and when she does I sense that she has made a deliberate decision to stay and converse with me, to engage in a discussion beyond that which is absolutely necessary or required by basic rules of civility. She says, "Why do you now hate the playground?"

I exhale loudly and wave in the direction of the play structure and swings, just barely visible in the gloom. "All the children. Especially the babies. They make me miss Isabel."

"The babies make you sad."

"Not just sad. I feel . . ." I pause and look at a woman holding a baby on her hip and bundling a little boy into one side of a double stroller. The baby is wearing a quilted snowsuit, so thick her legs stick out like little sausages. She flaps her arms wildly and her mother jiggles her up and down while she straps in her older child. "I feel angry," I say.

"You feel angry when you see babies?"

"Yeah. You know. It's like, why are those babies alive. When my baby is dead?" I look at the round face of the snowsuit-clad baby. Her cheeks are very red, chapped by the cold. "But I don't hate the babies. I hate their mothers."

"William!" Sonia calls. "Give the toy back to the little boy."

On the other side of the huge sandbox I can just barely make out William crouched down next to a small boy, no more than two years old. The boy is sitting helplessly while William does something to his yellow bulldozer.

"He's probably fixing it," I say to Sonia.

"He knows he does not touch other children's toys," she says. "William!"

William sets the bulldozer down and stands up. He pats the little boy on the head and moves to a different part of the playground.

"I think always people are sad and angry when something terrible happens," Sonia says.

"Probably," I say.

"I think you have another baby and then you are not hating the mothers. Because you are now a mother, and you don't hate yourself. You don't want your new baby to die."

This, I think, is as much as I will confide in Sonia, more than I have confided in most people. A few people know I am this angry. Mindy knows how I feel about the mothers, because she feels the same way as I do. I once told Jack about wishing that another baby had been taken in Isabel's place. What I have said to no one is that I cannot imagine having another baby. I don't want another baby, precisely because Sonia is wrong. I *would* want my new baby to die—if I could somehow get Isabel in return. If such a grotesque bargain were possible, if there were some pitchfork-wielding Satan I could barter with, I would bear and murder a thousand children, if doing so would bring Isabel back.

I look up to find William standing in front of me. "The sign says the playground closes at dusk. It's *way* past dusk," he says.

"All right," I say. "We'd better go."

"Goodbye, William. I see you on Monday. Give me a kiss." Sonia plants a kiss on his cheek, which he accepts far more graciously than he does those I offer. I fear William may be more sensitive than I give him credit for. He knows Sonia's fondness, while stern in character, is heartfelt and thus he responds warmly to it. I fear he perceives the grudging quality of my affection and that is why he stiffens under my embrace. Or else he just likes Sonia better than he likes me.

William shrugs his backpack onto his shoulders and we watch Sonia walk quickly out of the park. We trail after her. She turns up Fifth Avenue.

"Where's Sonia going?" I ask.

"To get her suitcase. She doesn't like to bring bags to the park, because then she has to watch them all the time and she can't play with me."

"But she was just dropping you off. There wasn't time to play."

"We figured you would be late."

"You know, William," I say as I wait for the light to change and release a new flow of cars in our direction, "I wasn't really late. I came as soon as your daddy called me. And you weren't playing. You were sitting on a bench."

"I'm hungry," William says.

He will not give an inch, this child. "How about ice cream?" I say. "How about ice-cream sundaes for supper? With hot fudge? Have you ever been to Serendipity? It's the best. They have sundaes the size of your head at Serendipity. And frozen hot chocolate."

William shakes his head. "I'm lactose intolerant."

"Oh, dear," I say. "I must have forgotten."

"That means I have a dairy allergy. Ice cream is a dairy product. I could get very ill from eating ice cream."

"Oh well. I guess we'll just go home and see what's in the fridge. Maybe there's some leftover Chinese or something."

A cab pulls over and I open the door and toss in the booster seat. William ducks under my arm and climbs in. Before I tell the cabbie where we are going, William turns to me, an unusual look on his face.

"Emilia, do you think Serendipity might serve dairy-free ice cream?" he says. "Do you think they might have a kind of sundae with no milk?"

I realize that the unusual expression on his face, the one that I do not recognize, is hope.

"I don't know," I say. I disgust myself. I am so mean, and William is just a little boy. But I will be well punished for my cruelty. There is not a single place in the entire city of New York where there are more babies, toddlers, and children than standing in line outside of Serendipity 3 sweetshop on a Friday evening at five thirty. And there is no way in hell they serve dairy-free ice cream.

"Sixtieth, between Second and Third," I say to the driver.

"We have rainbow sherbet," the waitress says.

"That has dairy. Sherbet has dairy." William is close to panic. He is kneeling on the cushion of his scrolled metal seat, his elbows on the fancy Victorian table, his hands spread out on the sticky menu. We waited almost an hour in the cold for this table and William is desperate. He spent that hour discussing the relative merits of dairy-free frozen hot chocolate and dairy-free ice-cream sundaes while I did my yoga breathing and tried not to stare at the families in line with us. I was tremendously relieved when the hostess's announcement that strollers were not allowed into the restaurant caused the family in line behind us to take their four-month-old baby girl in her jogger and roll away to more hospitable climes. Everything about that child felt too close to Isabel; I could not bear her proximity. I am sure William noticed neither the announcement nor my relief; he was consumed by a highly audible debate with himself over whether his failure to move his bowels that day was too likely an indication of constipation to risk the consumption of the bananas in a banana split.

"I guess I'll have sorbet," William says, close to tears. "Do you have sorbet?"

"He'll have a frozen hot chocolate," I say. "And a banana split. Extra nuts."

"I can't, Emilia. I'm lactose intolerant. I could get very ill." His face is pale and drawn. He looks very ill right now.

Now is the time to tell him that he is *not* lactose intolerant, that he once ate a huge piece of ricotta cake just fine, that his grandmother, Jack's mother, routinely fills the phyllo pie she feeds him with Muenster and Gruyère and then lies and says it's soy cheese. She doesn't buy this milk allergy any more than I do. But I'm not brave. Instead I say, "Serendipity has Lactaid. You know, that medicine you take for lactose intolerance? They sprinkle it on their frozen hot chocolate. And on their sundaes." I turn to the waitress, a middle-aged woman in a frilled apron. "Don't you have Lactaid powder? I know it costs extra, but I don't mind. I'm willing to spend the money."

The waitress shakes her head uncertainly and I smile at her, willing her to go along with this, to accept my dubious authority, to help me trick this boy into risking an imaginary stomachache for the sake of an hour of bliss. Because whatever William thinks, I am certain that the pleasures of hot fudge, ice cream, whipped cream, and butterscotch outweigh the unlikely perils of his fictional ailments.

"My mother is not convinced that Lactaid works very well," William says.

"Trust me," I say.

The impossibility of this request weighs very heavily on his narrow little shoulders.

"What kind of ice cream?" the waitress asks.

"William?"

"Um, chocolate?" he says.

"You get three flavors." She taps her pad with an impatient pencil.

"Chocolate, chocolate chip, and cookie dough," I say. "How does that sound?"

William nods.

I say to the waitress, "Please instruct the chef to grind up the Lactaid extra fine, so the ice cream doesn't taste gritty."

"Right," she says. "And for you?"

"I'll have a hot fudge sundae with chocolate chip mint. And a café latte. Low-fat milk."

After the waitress leaves William says, "Why do you bother to put low-fat milk in your coffee, if you're going to have ice cream and whipped cream?"

William eats all of his frozen hot chocolate and almost all the banana split. He licks both the bowl and the back of his spoon, uses his fingers to scrape fudge from the pleats of the glass dish, and sucks melted ice cream through his straw with the force of a Hepavac. He bends so low over the tall, fluted glass that he fogs it with the breath from his nose. I realize that this is the first time I have ever spent so long in William's company without hearing him speak. An hour with William is generally akin to sitting through a college lecture from a very short professor. Now, other than the nasal whistle of his breath, the slurping of liquid through the straw, and the lapping of his tongue against the long metal spoon, William is absolutely quiet. I have, for the first time, a sense of well-being in his presence. I eat my sundae and drink my coffee and watch him drip fudge and caramel onto his orange pique shirt. In the end, his concern for his bowels wins out over his gluttony and he leaves the bananas sitting in a pool of melted ice cream in the bottom of the crescent-shaped bowl. He graciously offers them to me, but I decline, equally graciously.

When he is finished, when his cheeks are slick with cream and sauces of various hues and his belly sticks out like a small, round drum, we leave. As we stand on the corner, waiting for a cab, William slips his hand into mine. My palm goes stiff and my fingers tremble. I realize that I have pulled mittens onto his hands, I have scrubbed them clean, I have put Band-Aids on them, but I have never held them. I grip his small, soft fingers firmly in my own.

"That was excellent," William says.

"That was another secret," I say. "Like the booster seat."

He looks up and gives me a sly wink. "Deal."

Chapter 14

The next morning, as soon as Jack arrives home from the airport, we are back in a cab on the way to Allison's for my niece's birthday party. I like my niece and nephew, but I generally avoid spending time in the company of my sister and her family. While Allison's brand of judgment is not as hard to endure as Lucy's—she is more earnest and well meaning—the fact that she lives her ideals with a religious devotion can be tiresome. She is also arrogant, and though Jack reminds me that this is a Greenleaf family trait, I am convinced that Allison's failure to inherit from my father the self-deprecating sense of humor that I cultivate so assiduously makes her more insufferable than I. At least I hope that's true. What is the point of all this self-loathing if not to temper an otherwise repugnant egotism?

William has never been to my sister's house in Carroll Gardens. More astonishing, he makes the unlikely claim never to have even once set foot in the borough of Lundy's restaurant, the Charlotte Russe, and the long-lost, accursed, but still beloved and mourned Dodgers. As we leave Manhattan I tell him that a person who has never walked across the Brooklyn Bridge can hardly claim to be a New Yorker.

"Brooklyn is not really New York," he says. He is sitting between Jack and me in the backseat of the taxicab, showing absolutely no ill effects from his evening of lactose debauchery. He is in his booster seat, which he allowed himself to be buckled into with nary a protest, to my grateful surprise. He seems to have taken our bargain seriously.

Jack says, "I know about two and a half million people who would take issue with that statement, my man."

"But when people say, 'New York,' they mean Manhattan. If they mean Brooklyn, then they have to say, 'Brooklyn.' Also Queens, or the Bronx, or Staten Island, or New Jersey."

"New Jersey is not a borough of New York," I say.

"I know that, Emilia," William says. "I am not a stupid baby. I know there are only five boroughs of New York. But sometimes *you* say you're from New York. And you're really from New Jersey. New York means Manhattan. Not Brooklyn. And definitely not New Jersey."

Jack sputters, swallowing his laughter, and points out the window.

"Look," he says. "If you look behind you, you can see where the towers used to be."

"I can't look behind me because of my booster seat," William says. Then he gives me a knowing glance. "But that's okay, because I am happy to ride in my booster seat. It's very safe. Six and sixty, that's the rule."

"Sixty," I say. "You'll probably be in high school by then, but whatever."

William giggles.

"What are you two laughing about?" Jack sees William and me sharing a joke, the weight that has crushed him for more than two years suddenly takes wing from his back and flutters out the windows of the cab, and he floats two inches above the plastic upholstery.

I lean across William and rub my nose against Jack's face. "It's private," I say and kiss the rough stubble of his unshaven cheek.

Jack's smile is so wide that the creases in his cheek are hard under my lips.

Allison's kitchen table is crowded with dozens of bagels, glazed pottery bowls of cream cheese, heavy platters of pink lox, plates mounded with flaked whitefish. There are tomatoes, red onions, and capers. There are multicolored pastas, spreads, and casseroles that I don't recognize, that I expect were provided by various of the dark-skinned families milling around the living room. Allison's stable of friends is always meticulously assorted and multihued.

She exchanges our coats for plates and pushes us in the direction of the buffet. "You must try the coconut rice with chicken," she says. "Marybeth Babalalu made it and it's just delicious." Allison points to a sallow-faced white woman wearing a calf-length wrap of black, green, and yellow kente cloth with a pattern of diamonds and arrows. Another piece of kente cloth is wrapped around her hair. It leans, a precariously tall tower, slightly off-kilter at the crown of her head. Her husband, who has purple-black skin and a small pink scar under one eye that is the precise hue of his plump lower lip, is wearing pressed Chinos and a white button-down shirt.

"William, you're gigantic!" Allison says. "Get some food and then go downstairs to the basement. Emma is down there with all the other kids."

Allison's daughter, Emma, is nine years old. She is in the third grade at the Carroll School. It is, of course, a public school, PS 58. Lennon, Allison's son, is graduating this year from Stuyvesant High. My sister agonized for some time about Lennon's decision to apply to a magnet high school. Allison is an opponent of tracking; she believes it stigmatizes those not blessed with a certain, easily quantifiable intelligence, that it unfairly benefits the middle and upper classes. Lennon, however, wanted very much to commute with his circle of friends across the river, and his scores on the admissions test were among the highest in the city. His father, not usually given to interfering with the decisions of the not-yet-but-sure-to-be-appointed-any-day-now Judge Greenleaf, took the boy's side. Allison will not face the same crisis with Emma. Poor Emma is learning delayed, and struggles with even the simplest of school assignments. At Passover last year, after the third glass of wine, and in a rare moment of maternal insecurity, even despair, Allison told me that she worries that the girl will never learn to read, that her disabilities will prove to be permanent, that she might never be able to function in even the most basic of academic environments.

My sister has clearly determined to do battle with her fear. She is the room parent of Emma's classroom, and most of the adults at this birthday party are, like Marybeth and Olatunji Babalalu, the parents of Emma's classmates. Lucy is not here. Her youngest has a hockey game in Lancaster, Pennsylvania, this weekend, and she has gone along as a chaperone. Allison tells me that Lucy has high hopes for the hockey coach, the divorced father of two of the boys on the team. Over the years since her divorce Lucy has worked her way through two soccer coaches, an SAT tutor, and an earth sciences teacher.

William does not want to go downstairs with the rest of the kids. He stands next to Jack and me eating pita triangles and peculiarly bright-colored humus while Jack makes small talk with Allison's husband, Ben. I like Ben, although he reminds me of an egg. He is round and bald, and his skin is smooth and speckled. He has an egglike personality, too. It is hard to latch on to Ben, hard to feel close to him or to figure out whether what you are saying is having any effect on him. Allison says that his clients, particularly the young African American men, adore him, that they find him to be a kindred spirit. While it is hard for me to believe that a sixteen-year-old black kid whose wrinkled, baggy pants are slung so low that they hobble him could possibly have much in common with Ben, I am willing to give my brother-in-law the benefit of the doubt.

"How's work?" Ben asks Jack.

"Fine," Jack says. He never discusses his work with my sister and her husband. This is not because he is ashamed of being a commercial litigator. Jack does not accept Allison's view of him as a tool of the corporate establishment. I should not criticize my sister. As I have said, she personifies her principles. She has been a public-interest lawyer, representing only the indigent, ever since she graduated from law school. Before that she spent a year with the Peace Corps in Burkina Faso, digging wells. Allison's family eats organic food, some of which they grow in their garden; her thermostat is set to sixty-two degrees; and she does not drive a car. I cannot quibble with the way my sister lives her life, but her look of disdain when Jack first described his work made me want to slam her face into a platter of cold noodles with sesame sauce. My father had invited Lucy, Allison, and Ben out for Chinese food to meet the man I was moving in with, the man I had told my father I intended to marry as soon as his divorce became final. While I think Jack expected a certain amount of suspicion from my family, he had probably assumed it would be because of the age difference, or because he was married when we met. He did not imagine that it would be because my sister views any attorney who does not devote his or her life to battling on behalf of the underprivileged, myself and my father included, as having sold his or her soul to the devil. I should have warned him, but I was so enraptured that it had never occurred to me that anyone else would think Jack was anything other than perfect.

Allison greeted Jack's description of his latest case, an acquisition soured into a lawsuit, with a sneer and a sharp exhalation of disgust.

I said, "Why is it that the only people who find the earning of money to be morally reprehensible are the ones who grew up with plenty of it?"

"Em, hush," Jack said.

"No, honey, it's okay," I said. "Allison, you are so fucking sanctimonious. Well, guess what? Jack didn't have a childhood like ours. He didn't grow up in a nice big house in New Jersey. He didn't have horseback riding lessons." For a brief period, when she was about twelve, Allison had wanted to be a jockey. "Jack grew up in Yonkers, in a three-family house that his father lost to the IRS when Jack was in his sophomore year of high school. He went to SUNY New Paltz, because that's where he could go to college for free, and he got a full ride to Columbia Law School. He has about two hundred Syrian cousins he sends money to, he bought both his mother and his sister houses in Boston, and he pays more child support than any other divorced father in the city of New York. So give him a break, Allison. Just give him a fucking break."

Jack stared at his plate, combing his chopsticks through his pile of rice.

"The work we do is an expression of the world we want," Allison said.

"Girls, enough," my father said. He was sitting across the table from me, and over the top of the lazy Susan heaped with soy sauce, mustard bottles, and brimming platters of food, I could see his hands outstretched beseechingly. "This is a family dinner, not a political debate."

"Everything is a political debate with Allison," I said. "And if you dare say 'the personal is political,' " I said to her, "I will reach across this table and dump the kung pao shrimp down the neck of your shirt."

Everyone laughed, pretending that I had made a joke, and for the rest of the meal we acted as if nothing had happened, as if I had not just humiliated my boyfriend by trotting out his working-class credentials like a badge of honor, a trump card in the never-ending game of Greenleaf family one-upmanship. Jack doesn't talk about his work with any of them now, except my father, and only when the others are not there.

Jack says, "How about you, Ben? Any good cases, lately?"

"Rape case. You probably read about it in the paper. The victim allegedly had her finger cut off."

"William, it's time to go downstairs and play with the other kids," Allison calls out from across the room. "The upstairs is grown-ups only now." Allison has magical powers; she can overhear with particular detail and accuracy any conversation that happens within the walls of her house. It must be very frustrating to be her child.

"I don't want to go downstairs," William says.

"Go on, Will," Jack says. "The kids are all down there. You'll have fun."

Lennon picks his way across the room, clearly sent over by his mother.

"Hey, William," he says. "Do you remember me?"

"Yes," William says. "Lennon, like John Lennon."

"Right on, man. You're an awfully little dude to know about John Lennon."

"My father takes me to Strawberry Fields sometimes."

"That's cool!"

"I don't like the Beatles."

"Maybe you haven't listened to the right songs. Has anyone ever played you 'Imagine'?" Lennon winks at me. He is trying very hard, this good-natured boy. "It's awesome." Lennon sings, "*Imagine all the people, living for today* . . ." in a surprisingly pretty voice.

William says, " 'Imagine' is not a Beatles song. John Lennon wrote it all by himself."

"Go downstairs with Lennon," I say. "If you don't have fun, you can come back up."

William closes his eyes, clamps his lips in a thin line, and then nods. He follows Lennon through the arched doorway and we watch their retreating backs. They are separated by a mere twelve years, these two, and yet they could be different species. Lennon is huge, six foot three or four, and if his father is an egg, then he is the hatchling, all knobby knees and splayed paddles for feet, his feather-soft hair defying its armor of bright blue gel, his arms like long wings, flapping at his sides as if he is so surprised by their size that he cannot control their jerking movements. While Lennon, who is so much older, still seems unformed, slightly blurred around the edges by growth and change, there is a rigid, finished quality about William's tiny form, as if this is the size he has always been, the way he has always looked, and the way he intends to remain for the rest of his life.

After William's descent into the perilous bowels of the rumpus room, Ben tells us about his trial, about his borderline-retarded client, about the victim who Ben believes accidentally severed her own index finger while chopping chicken parts. He tells this story with his usual bland impassivity, as if he is recounting a dull and pointless Mets game played long after the team has given up hope of winning the pennant. I wonder if Ben sheds this laconic style when he is in front of a jury, or if it is this very mildness that convinces them so often to acquit his clients.

"Ben," Allison calls across the room, "I need you to make a quick Grand Union run."

He pushes his glasses back on his egg face with one finger and nods distractedly, continuing his story about his thwarted attempts to convince the judge to authorize funds for an expert on self-mutilation.

"*Now*, hon," she says.

He snaps to attention.

"You forgot Rice Dream," she says reproachfully.

"Rice Dream?" he says.

"For the kids who can't eat ice cream."

"Don't trouble yourself on William's behalf," Jack says. "He'll be fine with just birthday cake. He's used to it."

"Don't be silly," Allison says in her booming voice. "We have other children with lactose issues. I have a spelt alternative for the children with wheat allergies and I want a rice-milk alternative for the children with dairy allergies. Ben, you have to leave right now if we're going to cut the cake by twelve thirty."

Ben makes for the door. As he is wrapping a long purple muffler around his short neck he says to Jack, "I don't suppose you'd like to join me? Take a walk to the market? It's just a few blocks."

"Sure," Jack says.

I am about to follow when Allison says, "Emilia, come meet Lizbet. Her daughter Fiona is William's age. Lizbet and her partner, Angela, live on the Upper West Side, too."

Jack winks at me from across the room and makes his escape. I trudge over to be introduced to a slightly younger version of my sister. Lizbet has Allison's frizzle of gray hair and her earnest and pietistic expression.

"Lizbet's signed Fiona up for PS 87," Allison says.

"We're hoping to get into the dual-language program," Lizbet says. "By eighth grade the children are completely bilingual. Have you signed William up for kindergarten yet? Or will he be going to . . ." Here she pauses and purses her lips around the words, as though they are too sour to be spoken without making a face. "To private school?"

"It's really not up to us," I say. "William's mother would never in a million years let him near a public school."

"It's such a shame," Allison says in a pained voice, as if she is very sorry for William. And for me. "William is a sweet boy, but I think it's already possible to see in him the effects of an overly sheltered upbringing. When a child grows up surrounded only by people of his own race and socioeconomic class, he cannot be expected to be sensitive to difference."

"Oh for God's sake, Allison. He goes to the 92nd Street Y preschool," I say. "He's got black and Asian kids in his class. Diversity is one of their *things*."

"Experiencing rich people of all colors is not experiencing diversity."

"Not everyone there is rich."

"You're rich."

"Not really," I say. But of course we are rich. Certainly richer than the other people in this house. Certainly richer than I ever expected to be.

Olatunji Babalalu, who is listening to the conversation, reassures me. "Private schools can be wonderful. I myself attended the Bishop Pertteerson Comprehensive Secondary School, in Mbosi."

I am saved from replying by a loud pounding from the stairs leading up from the basement. Lennon appears, red-faced and sweaty. "Emilia!" he shouts. "You better get downstairs right now!"

"What happened? Is William okay?" I run across the room, dodging around the dining-room table and nearly toppling a woman in an apple-green sari.

I take the stairs two at a time, Lennon on my heels. At the bottom, on the garden level that my sister has turned into a playroom complete with beanbag chairs, ugly peach carpeting, and an ancient stereo system, but devoid, of course, of television, video, or anything else that might pollute her children's pristine minds, I find a dozen or so children huddled together under a banner that says, FELIZ COMPLEAÑOS, EMMA.

"Where is he?" I shout. "Where's William?"

My niece, who is sucking on the end of one her red braids, points to a foam sofa. "He's hiding behind the couch."

I grab one end of the sofa and heave, expecting to need all my strength to budge the thing, but it is so flimsy it flies away from the wall and halfway across the room, toward the group of children. They scatter, squealing.

William is lying on the floor curled in a ball, his head buried under his folded arms. I can tell immediately what has happened; it is horribly obvious. The smell is overpowering.

"Oh no, William," I say. "Did you poop in your pants?"

He scrambles into a tighter knot.

"We were playing statue tag," Lennon says. He has come up beside me and is obviously trying not to breath through his nose. His voice has a nasal twang. "He was tagged and I think he was just afraid to move or something. I guess it sort of hit him suddenly because one minute he was totally fine and the next he just . . . I dunno. Did it."

I kneel down next to William and, doing my best not to gag from the stench, reach out a tentative hand. "William? Hey, William? Are you okay?"

His groan is muffled by his arms.

"Oh, William. Why didn't you just tell Lennon you needed to go to the bathroom?" I know even before he starts to sob that I should not have said this, but I am out of my depth here. I don't know how to deal with this kind of accident or with William's humiliation.

"William? Let's go get you some clean clothes, okay? Okay, honey?"

"Go away!"

I bend over to pick him up, but I pause, my hands hovering above his khaki pants where a dark foul-smelling stain is spreading.

"Leave me alone!" he screams. "I want my mommy. I want my mommy right now."

Of course he does, of course he wants Carolyn. She would know what to do. He is born to her, she speaks his language, she does not need to counterfeit a mother's response. My skills of interpretation and deciphering, barely competent when things go smoothly, fail miserably when William is so humiliated and in such pain. When he really needs a mother, a fake one is not good enough.

"Your mom's not here, honey," I whisper.

"Daddy!" he cries.

"Daddy had to go out for a minute. To get Rice Dream." Oh no. I realize that this is my fault. It was the ice cream. He has had a horrible attack of diarrhea because of the ice cream. "There's only me, William. I'm the only one here. But I can help you, honey. I can help you."

"I don't want you! You're not my mommy! I want my mommy! I want my mommy right now!" He lunges away from me, bicycling his legs, kicking as hard as he can. One of his feet lands directly in my stomach. I grunt and fall to my knees, bent over the pain in my belly.

"William, please," I say. "Honey, just come with me. You've got poop in your pants and you've got to change your clothes."

"I hate you!" William yells. "I hate you!"

"Why don't you let me give it a shot?" Allison says gently. I had not even noticed her but now realize that she must have come down after me and been watching this all along, she and the rest of the assembled company. She eases me out of the way. She kneels down next to William and, stroking his hair, bends over and whispers in his ear. At first he shakes his head and continues to cry, but after a few minutes he begins to calm down. Finally, with a ragged, trembling inhalation, he unwinds himself from his tight knot and gets to his feet. Allison gives him her hand and they make their slow way out from behind the couch. William keeps his eyes firmly averted from mine. He clings to her as they climb the stairs. I follow close on their heels.

Once we are upstairs Allison turns to me and says, "I'm going to take him up and give him a quick bath. Why don't you stay here? We won't be a minute."

"It's okay," I say. "I can take care of it."

"No!" William says, leaning against my sister. "I don't want Emilia. I want you!"

"I've got this under control," Allison says. She steers William toward the stairs to the second floor. "Emilia, would you be a peach and get the cake ready for me? The candles are in the drawer next to the stove."

While they are climbing the stairs she catches my eye and mouths, "Don't worry." Easy for her to say.

By now the other guests have resumed their party small talk, although there is a self-conscious quality to the attention they are not paying me. One woman gives me a sympathetic smile, but the rest avert their eyes.

While I am arranging the candles on the cake, nine to celebrate the years of Emma's life and one to grow on, Jack and Ben return. I am girding myself to tell Jack what has happened when I hear his light tread running up the stairs. I know I shouldn't be relieved at having avoided the task of recounting William's shame and rage, but I am.

I take the decorated cake out to the dining room and place it in the center of the table. A few minutes later Allison comes downstairs, holding William's clothes in a tight bundle.

"I'll take those," I say.

"Let me put them in a bag."

I follow her into the kitchen. She deposits the clothing into a plastic grocery bag and ties a tight knot. She hands it to me and washes her hands.

"Is he okay?" I ask.

"He's fine. Just freaked out. He had diarrhea. He was terribly embarrassed and the other children didn't help him any by laughing at him. Emma is going to be writing him a nice long letter of apology."

"She doesn't have to do that."

"She most certainly does."

I swing the bag on my finger for a moment. "It's my fault he has diarrhea. He's lactose intolerant and I made him eat ice cream."

"Why would you do that?"

"Because I didn't think he was really allergic. I thought it was just Carolyn's craziness. Go ahead. Tell me I'm a terrible person."

She sighs impatiently. "You're not a terrible person, Emilia. You're immature and self-centered, but you're not a terrible person."

"Gee, thanks."

"What? You want me to lie to you?"

"No. You're right." I wrinkle my nose. The stink of William's clothes is coming through the plastic bag. "He hates me."

"He doesn't hate you."

"He said he hates me."

"He doesn't really hate you. He's a sad and confused little kid. That's all. Children his age do not feel things like hate. That's an adult emotion."

"I know. I know you're right." She's wrong, though. I think she underestimates William. I think he is fully capable of all sorts of adult emotions, including hatred.

"Come," Allison says, pushing me out of the kitchen door. "It's time for birthday cake."

When we are riding across the Brooklyn Bridge, William's voice creases the thick silence in the cab. "I hate Brooklyn," he says. It is the first thing he has said since he and Jack came downstairs after his bath. Under his winter coat he is wearing a pair of Emma's overalls, rolled up at the ankles, and a plain white T-shirt.

Neither of us replies.

"I can see where the twin towers used to be," he says.

"Good," Jack says.

William stares at the empty space in the skyline.

"Emma is nine," he says. "That's almost two times as old as I am. Two times five is ten. And nine is one less than ten."

"Yes, that's right."

"And she can't even read!"

"Okay, Will," Jack says. "I know you're upset and embarrassed, but you don't need to say mean things about Emma."

"I'm only five and I can read chapter books."

"William!" Jack says. "I said that's enough."

"She's stupid. She's a stupid girl."

"William!"

"She's not stupid, William," I say. "She's just got problems reading."

"What's the difference?" he says.

Jack strokes William's cheek with his palm. "Be quiet, Will," he says.

Chapter 15

When we get home, there is a message waiting from Simon. Since I stood them up the night before, will I come to a matinee with him and Mindy today? I immediately call back and take them up on their invitation. I cannot bear the thought of the rest of the day in William's reproachful presence. To Jack I say that it is clear he and his son need some time alone. I try not to let on how relieved I am at his lack of objection.

After the movie, Simon, Mindy, and I end up in a restaurant on East Sixth Street, eating Indian food. Simon is pretending to be here under protest. He calls this block "diarrhea row" and picks at his vindaloo, muttering about how the Indian joints all share a single kitchen, one that has been condemned by the health department.

I have had enough talk of diarrhea to last me a good long while. "That is an old joke, Simon. That is a bridge-and-tunnel joke. See that man?" I point to a heavyset man whose dark hair creeps over his head and down the back of his collar like moss on a log. "That man made that very same joke tonight, on his way through the Holland Tunnel."

"Don't be such a snob, Emilia," Simon says. "You're from New Jersey."

"Yes, I'm from New Jersey, but I embrace New York. I embrace Bombay Palace. I eat my chicken tikka masala with gusto and do not complain about a few cockroaches and the odd case of salmonella."

Simon rolls his eyes but I can tell that he is happy. I saw him and Mindy briefly clasp hands as we walked over from the movie theater, after I announced I was hungry and that I was in the mood for Indian food.

Mindy spears the last piece of tough, stringy chicken breast. "Did you know that tikka masala isn't really Indian at all? It was created by Indians in England because their customers couldn't handle the subtle flavors and spices of real Indian cuisine. It has ketchup in it. Or tomato soup. I can't remember which."

I sop up the remains of the sauce with a piece of burned nan. "Tikka masala is made with tomato paste," I say. "And spiced with cardamom, tumeric, cumin, nutmeg, and, I think, mace. And if it was invented by Indians, then it's Indian, no matter who it was invented *for*. That's like saying pizza isn't really Italian. I hate that. I've been to Italy. In Italy, people are constantly gobbling pizza. And pasta. Like it's supposed to mean anything that Marco Polo stole the noodle from the Chinese. Chow fun is Chinese. Pasta is Italian. End of story."

The pleasure with which Simon and Mindy greet my ill-tempered diatribe about the origins of different foods is so great that I am surprised they do not leap to their feet, join hands, and dance the hora around our table. They think that Emilia, famously opinionated, cheerfully bitter, neurotically invested in their perception of her as sharply, wickedly funny, is back. They do not realize that I will do anything, make witty and scintillating conversation until their eyes glaze over with exhaustion, juggle plates full of biryani and lamb roganjosh, pretend that the picture of the god Ganesh over the cash register is not exactly like the one silk-screened on the tiny T-shirt I bought for Isabel when I was just six months pregnant, at the Gupta Spices and Saree Center in Park Slope near Mindy's house, I will do anything, anything at all, if only they will stay out with me tonight, keep me away from that apartment, keep me away from that boy whose prodigious talents include making me feel like a terrible person, and reminding me that not only am I not his mother but I am nobody's mother at all. I will do anything to stay away from the place where he is alive and she is nothing but a frozen memory, stiff and cold, her tongue curled out of the corner of her mouth, her breath forever stilled in her chest.

"I think we should go dancing," Mindy says.

Simon says, "Don't be ridiculous," and kicks her under the table. His legs are so long that his knee bangs the table when he kicks her and a bowl of purple sauce spills onto the glass-covered surface.

"Subtle," I say, and put my napkin on top of the spill to keep it from spreading. The napkins are pink, made of some remarkable polyester that repels water. "I think dancing is a great idea. Let's go dancing."

Simon shakes his head. "You don't really want to go dancing, Emilia."

"Yes, I do. Dancing is exactly what I want to do."

"We can't," he says, and looks meaningfully at Mindy. She opens her eyes in a parody of innocence and flutters her thickly mascaraed eyelashes.

"Sure we can," I say.

"We're not dressed for it."

"Don't be an idiot. You're wearing jeans and a black T-shirt. If you stood in front of your closet for four hours that's precisely what you'd come up with. I, number one, don't care what I look like, and number two, have a T-shirt on under my sweater in case I get hot. Mindy is dressed, as usual, like she's trying to get laid. By the way," I say to her, "what was Daniel's reaction to the red leather miniskirt? Didn't he think you were a tad overdressed for the movies?"

She shrugs.

"We look fine," I say. "We look amazing. We're on fire. Let's go dancing."

Simon crosses his arms over his chest. He shakes his head and gives Mindy a sullen, angry look.

"What?" I say.

Mindy twists the paper wrapper from her straw around her finger, cutting off the circulation. Her finger grows red at the tip and white near where the rope of paper binds it. A small smile plays at the corners of her mouth.

"What's going on?" I say.

"We can't go dancing, Emilia," Simon says, his voice very tender, like a mother speaking to her baby, like he spoke to me in the days right after Isabel died.

"Why not?" I say.

"Because Mindy's pregnant."

"Oh," I say. What kind of person begrudges her friend this joy? What kind of person denies her friend the right to feel a moment of bliss after two years of frustrated longing? What kind of person can barely keep herself from reminding her friend that three times before the friend has allowed herself happiness only to find it smeared in her underpants, spilled on the bathroom floor, scraped into a hospital garbage pail?

I say, "Does this mean I don't have to go with you to that Walk to Remember?"

"No, you don't have to go with me to the Walk to Remember," she says. "I mean, I thought I was going to go anyway, and I still might go next October. But I don't think I want to go this month. I've been feeling a little superstitious about it. I don't want to *plan* on going."

"Good," I say, "because I never wanted to go."

"You made that pretty clear."

"Anyway, no dancing tonight," I say.

"But I do want to go dancing," Mindy says. "I've done the bed-rest thing. I've done the no-exercising, no-climbing-stairs, no-running, no-walking thing. Even when I lie on my bed, perfectly still, I lose the baby. This time I'm going to try a different approach. I'm going to try the dancing thing. I'm going to try the pound-the-floor-until-you-sweat, spin-around-until-you're-dizzy, rock-and-roll-until-you-drop thing, and see what the fuck happens. Who knows, maybe this one will stick."

Simon and I look at each other. Simon shakes his head but lifts his hands in defeat. "Misstress Formika is at Opaline tonight," he says. "You haven't lived until you've been seen at Area 10009."

Opaline is a cavern with a pulsing electro beat, the neon needles of pastel strobes whisking across gyrating bodies, dark with flashes of brilliant light. Go-go dancers on the bar—boys, with one lone woman in tasseled pasties and leopard-skin pants. A flash of ass in cutout chaps, an oiled chest in a wife-beater torn by grasping hands. The boys on the dance floor suck us into their midst, not seeming to notice that Mindy and I are two of the only women in the room other than the go-go dancer and a few slick-haired and dark-lipsticked lesbians sprawled on the banquets.

We dance together, the three of us, to the Felix Da Housecat mix of "The 15th" by Fischerspooner. Mindy and I sandwich Simon between our grinding hips like a sausage in a too-small bun until he is spun away by a man with a mane of soot-black hair, a man all hairdo, nipple ring, and, I fear, an eye for loneliness, for self-delusion, for Simon's willingness to loosen his belt in the back hall of an East Village club in exchange for nothing more than a scribbled telephone number which will likely prove to be that of a Korean grocery store on West Fifty-seventh Street. Mindy and I dance alone until she puts her hands on her hips and shouts to me, "I'm exhausted. I'm going to get a drink of water."

I nod and start to follow but she pushes me back. "No, you stay. You're having fun," she yells.

I keep on dancing alone, whirling in a circle, but without my friends next to me I am aware of the heat, and of missing Jack. I spin more slowly and wish I were home in bed spending my evening as I usually do, lying next to my husband, thinking about my daughter, and feeling sorry for myself. It's not that I really enjoy those evenings at home. On the contrary, they are miserable and tedious. However, there is a certain pleasure to that familiar pain, the kind of pleasure one takes in picking a firm, well-grown scab, or poking a tongue into a canker sore and tasting the metallic twinge. The desolation I feel on the dance floor at Opaline is unfamiliar—I do not recognize this ache and thus I do not like it one bit.

I feel hands on my shoulders and turn to see a man dancing behind me, his hips swaying in rhythm with mine. He looks younger than me, maybe twenty-five or twenty-six. He is handsome, slim, and sharp-nosed with sleepy eyes and narrow lips. His nylon trucker hat is poison green and cocked to one side. He snaps his teeth at me and I laugh. He is quite clearly gay; straight men do not wear tight Christina Aguilera T-shirts and pants cut so low that their public hair peeps from above the open button at the waist. He slides his hands up the sides of my body and then lifts them between our faces, waving his fingers like a Thai dancer. His rings sparkle in the flashing strobes. I lift my arms like he does and we are dancing together, mirroring each other's movements, our arms, legs, and hips gyrating in unison. We dance exactly alike, our hips swing in the same rhythm, our legs lift from the floor at the same moment and rise to the same height. We are fluid. We are exquisite. We are a perfect pair, the king and queen of the dance floor. We are like ice dancers; we should be at the Ice Capades. My partner takes my hands in his. His body undulates like a snake's as he moves me closer to him. Our knees touch, then our hips, our groins, our bellies. My breasts against his chest, my lips against his collarbone. I open my mouth and press my tongue against the hollow of his throat. His skin is salty and sharp, bitter almost. I feel his pulse against my tongue and the sensation moves through my body, down my neck, along my breasts, through my belly, into my groin. I melt, my knees buckle, and he catches me in his arms.

"Rrr-oww," he yowls. "You are one hot little kitty cat!"

I laugh, as if I too was joking, as if I was not just knocked off my feet by a wave of gut-twisting desire for a strange gay man in an ugly T-shirt. I wave goodbye and duck through the crowd, searching for

Mindy and Simon. I do not know what is wrong with me, but I must get out of here before something happens.

Jack has left the small beaded lamp in the front hall lit for me, and by this dim bulb I drop my coat and bag and make my way to the bedroom. He is asleep, of course; it is past midnight and he must wake up early and take William to school on his way to the office. I strip off my sweaty clothes and stuff them deep into the laundry hamper. Then I climb into bed.

Jack used to joke that I seduced him under false pretenses, that because our first real sexual contact was a blow job, he was misled into believing that I was an aficionado of oral sex, that it would be a routine part of our lovemaking. "You tricked me," he would say.

I used to think this was funny. Tonight I am determined to reprise that first time. I must have sex with my husband, because I wanted to fuck that gay boy at Opaline. But I cannot bear to have Jack inside me. My belly contracts and twists at the idea. It closes tight. I can't do that yet. But I can do this.

When Jack wakes to find himself in my mouth, he is so grateful that his navy blue eyes, the eyes I love so much, fill with tears. After he is done, he holds my head in his hands, smoothing the hair from my temples, and tells me that he loves me. Then he moves me onto my back and begins to give me fluttery kisses down toward my navel.

"It's okay," I say.

"I want to."

"No."

"But what about you?"

"I'm fine. I'm good."

He rests his cheek on my belly.

"Allison called. Three other kids came down with whatever William had. She thinks it was the rainbow-pesto hummus. She said she's very sorry."

I am so relieved it was not the ice cream. "Rainbow-pesto hummus. It would have killed her to order pizza?" I say.

He laughs softly and the puff of air from his mouth raises goose bumps on my stomach. I wriggle. "Are you sure you don't want me to make you come?" he says.

"Definitely. I'm fine."

He kisses me again, but does not insist.

I stare into the dark room, his head heavy on my belly, and remember the beginning. After that first brush in his office, after Marilyn closed the door and left us bent over the credenza in an attitude of animal sex, we moved apart and finished editing. Ever the conscientious associate, I took the marked-up pages and returned to my office where I meticulously rewrote the brief to Jack's specifications.

We did not see each other for two weeks, until he called my extension late on a Tuesday evening. I had been avoiding him, had been keeping away from the seventeenth floor altogether, printing entire cases out from Westlaw rather than go to the library to pull a volume off the shelf. I had pushed too far, I thought. After years of patiently tracking my *bashert* like a red-tailed hawk tracks a prairie dog, with a sharp and forbearing eye from a full mile's distance, I had lost it all by striking too soon, moving too close, pressing myself where I wasn't wanted.

"Hi," I said into the phone, a little gasp in my voice, like a thirteen-year-old on her first telephone call with a boy.

"Hi," he said. "Um. You're working late."

"I have a lot to do." I wasn't working. I was shopping online while I waited for Simon to call and say he was done for the day so we could go out for sushi.

"Oh."

"Do you have something you need me to do?"

"Not if you're busy."

"I lied. I'm surfing the Web. I'm not working at all. What do you need?"

Jack laughed. "I need someone to help me prepare for a discovery production. It's not very glamorous. It's pretty awful, in fact. There's a warehouse full of old hard drives and handwritten documents. Notes and sketches. Junk, really. I need an associate to help me go through it all."

"I'll come by your office and pick up the pleadings and the document requests. Is tomorrow okay, or should I come now? And where am I going? Is it local, or am I going to need to book travel?"

"It's in Emeryville, California. Do you know where that is? Outside of San Francisco, near Oakland. And you won't be going alone. You'll be with me. You can read the papers on the plane. That is, if you can leave tomorrow morning."

"*You're* preparing for a document production?" Partners almost never sift through dust-filled bins of papers and files. That kind of scut work is left to those lower on the totem pole.

"It's an important client. Marilyn made reservations for us. She'll e-mail you your ticket."

"You already booked my plane ticket?"

There was no sound on the line, no buzz of static, no hum of empty air.

"JFK or LaGuardia?" I asked.

It was March, and in the Bay Area it was the height of spring. The Japanese cherry trees had already shed their pink blossoms and were covered with red leaves. It was the plum trees' and the dogwoods' turn to flower and they were doing so riotously, shaming the tulips, the daffodils, and the paperwhites with their hysterical efflorescence. Our hotel sat regally atop the hills of Oakland, a sprawling Victorian Stick–style mansion, a white wedding cake with blue frosted edges, a turret, and rows of pruned and scentless roses. Jack and I arrived at the hotel just as the sun began to set, after a long day of business class and the deciphering of scrawled documents under too-bright fluorescent lights. We ate our dinner on a small terrace overlooking the lights of San Francisco. The night was cool but there was a heat lamp next to our table so we took a long time over our meal, our conversation alternately animated—we shared childhood memories, favorite books, office gossip—and strained. Sometimes our voices would just fade away as one or the other of us remembered that this trip was or could become illicit. We were in a hotel, far from home, and it had been clear from the moment we had arrived at the warehouse in Emeryville that this was not and had never been a two-attorney job. Jack had brought me across the country under false pretenses, and I had come hoping that that was so.

When it was no longer possible to sit at the table, when we had ordered and eaten a plate of gourmet ice-cream sandwiches that neither of us wanted, when we'd each had a second cup of coffee, when

Jack had looked over the digestif menu and considered and rejected a glass of Fernet Branca, we left the restaurant. We stepped into the elevator and I pushed the button for the third floor. We stood silently in the small, wood-paneled box, did not talk as we walked down the long hall. We had left our suitcases with the bellman while we ate, and now they bumped along behind us, the muffled squeak of their wheels on the carpet the only sound in the hallway. I looked down at the little folder in my hand, and then at the numbers on the doors as we passed them. When we reached the door to my room, I stopped.

"Well, this is me," I said. "Where's your room?"

"On the spa level," Jack said.

"But that's the floor below the lobby."

"I know."

He leaned forward and kissed me. I let go of the handle of my suitcase and opened my lips to his. Jack planted his hands on the wall on either side of my head and pressed his mouth to mine, licking and nibbling, sucking my lower lip into his mouth, traveling his tongue over my teeth and gums, tasting me. Swallowing me. We kissed and kissed, standing in the hall outside my hotel room. I wanted him so much; I was delirious with wanting him and with happiness at finally feeling his mouth against mine.

After a while, Jack pulled away and said, "Okay, enough now. Is that okay? I don't think I can do anything else right now."

"As long as you don't say that you're married and you've never done this before and you're afraid of hurting your wife."

"I'm married. I've never done this before. And I'm afraid of hurting my wife."

"That's what they all say."

The next morning Jack received a call that the plaintiffs had tentatively accepted our client's settlement offer. The case was no more. We were at the airport an hour early for our flight, and Jack arranged for me to join him in the American Airlines Admiral's Club. We settled in abutting armchairs with our individual copies of *The New York Times* and mugs of coffee. While I was scanning the headlines I felt Jack's eyes on me. I looked up.

"Jesus Christ," he whispered. "You're so beautiful."

I smiled and looked back down at my paper.

A few minutes later he stood up. "I'll be back in a minute," he said.

I watched him cross the room and then I leaped to my feet. When I reached the restroom there was a man in an expensive four-button suit coming out of the door, shaking his hands dry.

"How many people are in there?" I asked.

"Excuse me?"

"In the men's room. How many guys are inside?"

"Just one," he said.

I winked at him and ducked through the door. Jack stood at the urinal, his legs planted slightly apart, his hips jutting forward. When he saw me, he opened his mouth in astonishment. I walked across the room, grabbed him by the belt, and dragged him into the last stall at the end of the row.

If they had looked under the half door, our fellow admirals might have seen my legs, in flared jeans and high-heel boots, crouching on the floor. Some would surely have objected to the presence of two people in a single bathroom stall. Others might have enjoyed the vicarious thrill; they might have lurked next to the sinks, washing their hands for far longer then necessary. But no one came into the men's room of the Admiral's Club in those few minutes. Or perhaps they did; I didn't notice. I was far too busy listening to Jack whisper my name to listen for the sound of men's dress shoes clicking across the tile floor.

Chapter 16

I *spent* the Wednesday after the Brooklyn birthday party debacle with my mother in New Jersey, leaving Jack to take the afternoon off work to be with William. The next weekend was Carolyn's. I have tried not to think about the boy at all during these last ten days. When he does cross my mind the guilt I feel for having failed once again to rise to the simplest occasion of mothering makes my own stomach hurt. I remind myself that at least I'm off the hook for Serendipity.

William seems to have forgotten what happened and is his usual self when I pick him up the following week at preschool. His greeting is no more nor less stiff and uncomfortable than usual, and neither is mine.

As he gets ready to leave I watch the other children. One, a small girl wearing very pink gloves and a spangled ice-skating dress, spins on one foot while her nanny tries to stuff her into a fluffy white coat. She is graceful and delicate, a pixie child. She bends her back nimbly, nearly touching her toe with her dangling ponytail. If she were my companion for the afternoon instead of William, I would take her ice-skating.

I love to skate. I'm not especially talented, nor was I ever a competitive skater. I left that to my sister Lucy. She had practice three afternoons a week, and when I was a little girl I had no choice but to ride along with her and my mother. At some point my mother got tired of my whining and began renting me skates, and I would circle the rink during the hour of Lucy's lesson. There was something about the speed, the smoothness of the glide, and the sound of my blades slicing along the ice that entranced me. When I got to high school I even tried out for the girl's hockey team. I might have made it, too, but I am just over five foot two, and light-footedness could not make up for that fact when a six-foot monster of a girl with linebacker shoulders came barreling across the ice with a hockey stick in her hand.

While William is bending over to strap the Velcro on his boot, he stumbles and falls on his behind. He pulls himself to his feet and drags on his coat, but he is stepping on one of the sleeves so he manages to trip himself up once again. Maybe the reason this child is so clumsy, so unlike the supple little girl with the pink gloves and white coat, is because no one has bothered to try to make him any different. Jack has not taken him skiing since the divorce, and I'm sure Carolyn's accepted activities are all of the cerebral variety.

"Hey," I say, hauling him up. "Want to go ice-skating?"

"What?"

"Let's go to Wollman Rink. It shouldn't be very crowded on a weekday afternoon."

"I don't know how to skate."

"It's easy," I say.

The dancing girl says, "I know how to skate. I skate all the time."

"See," I say. "Skating is great."

She says, "My father is a skater. He won a silver medal in the Olympics."

One of the mothers laughs. "Kendall, your daddy is a banker. He owns a bank. He's not an Olympic skater."

"No, she's not kidding," another mother says. "Misha was an Olympic figure skater. He really did win a silver medal. At Innsbruck. That's how Colette met him. She was a skater, too. But not in the Olympics or anything. In Ohio."

"Oh my God!" the first mother says. "Kendall, you are a very lucky little girl."

"Come on, William," I say. "You're never going to win that silver medal if we don't start training today."

William is horrified by the failure of the rink to provide helmets.

"Rollerbladers need helmets," he says. "And ice is just as hard as asphalt. Harder."

"Ice is not as hard as asphalt," I say, lacing up my skates. There is a knot in the middle of my lace and I have to yank it through the hole.

"Yes, it is. Much harder. Asphalt is actually quite soft. Softer than concrete. That's why my mother runs on the street instead of on the sidewalk. Sidewalks give you shin splits. My mother knows that kind of thing because she's a doctor."

"Why don't you just put your skates on?"

"I don't think I should skate if I don't have a helmet. Skating is like rollerblading and you're not supposed to rollerblade without a helmet. And pads. You're supposed to have kneepads, elbow pads, and wrist pads. The wrist pads are the most important because you catch yourself with your wrists when you fall."

"The park is full of rollerbladers who don't wear helmets or pads."

"Well that's very stupid. My pediatrician's office has pictures of kids on their Rollerblades with their helmets and pads. They have pictures of kids on bikes, too. My picture is there, from when I got my tricycle when I turned three, two years ago. In the picture, I'm wearing my blue helmet. I also have a red helmet. If you really want to go ice-skating we can go home and get one of my helmets."

"We're not going to get one of your helmets. Do you see anyone else wearing a helmet, William? No. You do not. No one wears a helmet when they skate. Now stop wiggling so I can put your skates on."

While I am lacing William's boots tightly, wrapping the strings around his ankles, he stares around the rink, his brow furrowed, as if evaluating it.

"It looks bigger than 33,000 square feet," he says.

"Oh, it does not." I frown. "How do you know how big Wollman Rink is?"

"It says so in my book."

"What book?"

"My Central Park book."

"Which book? The one I gave you?"

He shrugs. Last year, on his birthday, to the mountain of toys, stuffed animals, puzzles, models, and various dinosaur books that Jack chose for William over the course of what must have been hours of concentrated shopping, I added a reference book about Central Park. I bought the book on a whim one day, as I passed the Dairy, where the children of New York once went to receive fresh, clean milk and where now tourists can buy sweatshirts advertising the park's baseball leagues, mugs decorated with miniature park maps, Beanie Babies wearing I ♥ NY T-shirts, and books about the park. I had gone into the souvenir shop because I wanted to see what it looked like; I'd never been inside the refurbished Dairy. The book, part photo essay, part reference book, caught my eye not initially as a gift for William but because what I know about the park I have gleaned almost accidentally, from inscriptions on the bases of monuments and archways or from pamphlets I've picked up in my meanderings. I leafed through the volume and found a sepia-toned photograph of a camel hitched to a lawn mower.

Even though the book was quite clearly beyond the ken of a small boy, I knew that it would be replete with the kind of factoids that delight William. I figured we would just look at the pictures and read the captions. I bought it, wrapped it in a map of the park, and added it to the heap of gifts. That year William was much more interested in a building set made of magnetic rods and balls. He looked at the book just long enough to express his thanks, and then tossed it aside.

"It's a pretty cool book, isn't it?" I said. "Did you see that picture of the camel mowing Sheep Meadow?"

"No," he says.

"Oh. Well, what else did the book tell you about Wollman Rink?"

"Nothing."

As we make our slow way around the wooden barrier at the side of the rink a small boy whizzes by us, singing a loud song as he skates. He is wearing a helmet. And wrist guards.

"This is very scary, Emilia," William says. He is holding on to the side of the rink with both hands, his ankles falling in toward one another so far that the knobs graze the ice. His feet look like daisies that have been bent at the stem, right below the flower.

"It isn't scary. It really isn't. Just let go of the wall."

"You can't say what's scary to me. Only I know when I'm scared. You're not scared because you know how to skate. And that boy's not scared because his mother brought his helmet." This last is said in a wail.

I pry William's hands off the wall and skate backward very slowly, pulling him with me. At first he jerks along the ice, his feet moving spastically, as if he is trying to catapult himself back to the comfort of the side of the rink. Suddenly he seems to give up. He puts his skates side by side and bends slightly at the waist and I continue to skate backward, facing him. I risk a smile.

"See?" I say. "This isn't so awful."

"Maybe not for you," he says.

I imagine spinning into a sudden spread eagle, faster and faster, until the rink is a blur, the only thing in focus is William's face, whirling at the end of my outstretched hands. Then I will snap my hands out of his and he will pinwheel across the ice.

We make another slow circuit and I return William to the side of the rink. "I'm going to go around once by myself," I say. "You just hold on to the wall and go slow. You'll be fine."

I skate away and begin to circle the rink, skating faster and faster as I go around. I am suddenly aware of a form at my side. I turn and see a boy, maybe seventeen. He is very handsome, with dark curly hair, red cheeks, and a chipped front tooth. He is a boy who would never have looked my way when I was his age.

"Race you!" he says.

I bend low to the ground and begin swinging my arms back and forth. This boy has no idea what he is getting himself into. I will leave him gasping in my wake. I will leave him eating a mouthful of ice shavings, even if he is wearing hockey skates and I am laced into pale green plastic figure skates that are a size too big.

My beautiful boy and I skate twice around the rink, and he beats me. I am not all that, it turns out. Still, I give him a run for his money, and he is panting when we glide to a stop, our hands resting on our knees.

"You're pretty fast," he says.

"You're faster," I tell him, and then I see William fall flat on his ass on the other side of the rink. I tear across the ice, but I am tired from my race and by the time I get there he is crying.

I skate up behind him and try to lift him around his waist, but before I know it I am on the ground next to him. "Shit," I say.

"I fell!" he says.

"Me too."

I try to get up, but I slip again and fall back down. William grabs me, and we are like a Marx Brothers routine, falling all over ourselves on the ice.

"I've fallen and I can't get up!" I say, and I start to laugh. William does not get the reference. How can he? He is only five, and he is not allowed to watch television. But he surprises me by giving a sort of pathetic giggle. I can't help but admire this. He doesn't want to be here, somewhere inside he can probably tell that I brought him here knowing he would be a terrible skater, and still he tries to laugh at my lame joke. How does he know how vain I am about my sense of humor, and why does he care? Or does he? Maybe it's just funny to a child whenever a grown-up falls down.

I manage to get to my feet and haul him to his. "Are you okay?" I say. "Did you break anything?"

"I don't think so. Unless I have a hairline fracture."

"Do you want to get off the ice, or do you want to try to make it around again?"

William looks longingly at the exit and then at the little boy in the helmet who is now skating backward, still singing to himself. "Could you show me how to do it?" he says. "Not just drag me around?"

"Sure," I say. "Of course."

For the next fifteen minutes, William and I skate in tiny little circles in the middle of the rink. He falls, three times, but rises grimly and gamely to try again. I show him how to put his feet together and slide one out and away, to propel himself slowly along. Finally, he feels confident enough to try a lap.

"But holding hands," he says.

"Definitely holding hands."

It takes a very long time, and we do it the long way, on the outer edge of the rink, but we make it all the way around. William skates almost exclusively with his right foot, as though his left is paralyzed, a wooden foot strapped into a figure skate. Still, he skates.

"You did great," I say as I push him in front of me to the exit. "Way better than I did my first time."

He stumbles out onto the rubber mat. "This feels weird. It feels weird to walk."

"It always feels weird to walk after you've been on the ice."

He wobbles and catches my arm. I hold him steady.

"Did you know," he says, "that before there was Wollman Rink, people used to skate on the Lake, and one part was called Ladies Pond. Only ladies were allowed to skate there. No men allowed."

"Did you learn that from your book?"

"Yup."

I smile and take his hand.

As we are standing in line to return our skates William says, "Emilia?"

"Yes?"

"I think today should be another secret. Because of the no helmet. And because I got my jeans all wet. My mother hates when I get my clothes wet."

"I got my jeans wet, too."

He nods. "So do we have a deal? Skating is our secret?"

I feel a sudden welling of gratitude and affection and I wonder if he realizes that I am the person this silence will protect, not him.

"Deal," I say.

Chapter 17

Last night at parent-teacher conferences, William's teacher exploded all of my contemptuously low expectations. Now I have nothing but nice things to say about Sharlene. I am in love with Sharlene, the South African preschool teacher with the guts to stand up to Dr. Carolyn Soule.

Jack and Carolyn had rescheduled this conference twice, once because of a preterm delivery of twins and once because Jack was stuck in traffic in the Lincoln Tunnel coming home from a deposition. Calendaring this parent-teacher conference was more difficult than scheduling a capital murder trial, and involved a far greater number of tense and angry telephone calls. I suggested to Jack that he meet with the teacher on his own, but the school has a policy of joint conferences, except where the parental relationship is so degraded that it would be too uncomfortable for the teacher. Jack and Carolyn's bitter civility does not, apparently, qualify.

According to Jack, Carolyn and he were sitting on small chairs on either side of an octagonal table, listening to Sharlene discuss William's sophisticated manipulation of multicolored number pegs, when Carolyn glanced over the teacher's head and saw one of William's drawings hanging from a clothesline.

"What's that?" she said, pointing. I can see her finger stretched out, long and trembling. I imagine that Carolyn's nails are perfectly formed, oblong, and pale, clean from all the pre- and post-surgical scrubbing. I'm sure she does not wear polish.

"Aren't they lovely?" Sharlene said. "We've been doing a unit on family structures. The children all drew pictures of their families. Let me show you William's. It's really quite remarkable."

She unpinned the picture from the line and brought it over. William had drawn himself in the middle of the page, wearing a red cap. Next to William, on one side, stood Carolyn. He had drawn her the same size as himself. He had colored in her straight brown hair and given her a very long carrot-shaped nose. Jack stood on the other side, also the same size as William. He wore a red cap, just like William's. On the other side of Jack was a smaller figure, round, with red hair. William had drawn me. Hovering in the air above me was a figure rendered in the pale orangey-pink color they used to call "flesh." The figure was drawn so lightly that it was almost invisible. It was a baby, with wings.

"He drew his little sister as an angel," Sharlene said. "It nearly broke my heart when I saw that."

Carolyn took the drawing from Sharlene's hands and stared at it. Her able hands, sure and still when slicing through skin, fat, abdominal wall and uterus, shook so violently that the piece of construction paper flapped back and forth above her clenched fingers. The paper began to crinkle and crease under her grip and Sharlene reached out tentatively.

"Dr. Soule? Carolyn?" the teacher said.

Carolyn inhaled and then, with a sudden, smooth confidence, as if her hands had abruptly returned to their customary competence, she tore the drawing down the middle.

Sharlene gasped and snatched the paper back. It was torn nearly all the way through, held together by a sad, frayed inch at the bottom.

"How dare you!" Sharlene said, her voice shaking.

Carolyn looked away.

"How dare you!" Sharlene repeated. "This is William's drawing. It belongs to him, not to you. And this is my classroom. I will not allow you to destroy things in my classroom!" The force of the young woman's words, the strength of her defense of the integrity of her student and of her domain, were marred by the tears that gathered in her eyes.

"May I?" Jack said gently. He held out his hand.

Sharlene looked uncertain.

"Please," he said.

Sharlene passed him the torn drawing. He held it in his hand for a moment and then took it over to the supply table in the back of the room. He laid it flat on the table and taped it carefully on both sides, smoothing the edges of the tape so that they were as invisible as possible. Then he hung the drawing back up on the line with the others.

"So William likes the number pegs, does he?" Jack said, as he sat back down in the miniature chair.

Carolyn did not speak for the rest of the conference. She sat hunched over, the smooth waterfall of her hair concealing her eyes. When they were outside the classroom, putting on their coats, Jack said to her, "I'd like to pick William up early this weekend, if you don't mind. Right after school instead of at your place at five."

"Why?"

"Someone gave me a pair of tickets to *The Lion King* for Friday night and I thought I'd make a day of it with him."

"He's already seen *The Lion King*," Carolyn said.

"He won't mind seeing it again."

Carolyn seemed about to protest but swallowed and shrugged her shoulders.

"So I'll pick him up here tomorrow," Jack said.

"We hear from schools tomorrow."

"Great. Call me and let me know where he's going. I'll tell him."

Carolyn smoothed the beaver collar of her wool coat. "I'd like to tell him myself. William and I went through the whole process together. I was with him at the ERB. I was with him at all his interviews. I think I should be the one who tells him."

"Fine. You tell him."

"Because William and I chose Collegiate together. We made that decision together, and when he gets in, we're going to celebrate together. It really should be me who tells him."

"I said that's fine."

"Well, it's just that he knows the letters are coming tomorrow. He'll be waiting to find out."

"Carolyn, I'm picking up William from preschool tomorrow. I'm taking him to *The Lion King* tomorrow night. Then he's spending the rest of the weekend with me. If you want him to know what kindergarten he's going to tomorrow, then I will tell him. Otherwise, you can wait and tell him on Monday." Jack did not inform his ex-wife that as she had behaved like a spoiled child, as she had tried to destroy the drawing her son had painstakingly made of his fractured family, she had, at least temporarily, lost her right to make any kind of demand. But that is what the steel undertone to his voice meant and, to her credit, Carolyn understood.

"Fine," she said.

Of course, I have no idea if that's how any of it happened. Jack's recounting was informative but included none of the emotional detail. All that is my own, and I wonder if Jack really did stand so gently unyielding in the face of Carolyn's rage.

Today I am meeting Jack and William at the Y so that I can see the picture William drew of Isabel. The three of us will spend the afternoon together before they go off to enjoy their hackneyed Broadway extravaganza. I have no interest in seeing *The Lion King*.

I am a little late, and Jack already has William bundled into his coat.

"Just give me a sec," I say. "I want to run into the Red Room and see the picture."

"Jack!" The voice is shrill and raised to a shout so loud that for a moment it silences the after-school hubbub in the hallway. Carolyn is pushing her way through the crowd. I have not seen her in almost three years, since long before Jack and I were together. The only time I ever saw Carolyn, in fact, was at her and Jack's apartment, when they hosted a Christmas dinner for the litigation department. She looks older now; her face is drawn and lined. Yet I am surprised at how beautiful she is. I had forgotten that Carolyn is so much prettier than I am.

"Jack," she says again. She grabs the sleeve of his coat. "We have to talk, right now. Right now!"

Jack eases his arm out from her white-fingered grasp. "Calm down," he says.

"Now, Jack. Now!"

"Okay," he says, a note of appeasement in his voice. "Emilia, will you take William into his classroom for a minute? Carolyn, I don't know if you've ever met Emilia."

"We met at your Christmas party," I say. "Three years ago."

"Not here." Carolyn is looking wildly around the hallway. Some of the other mothers are staring at her. One or two even look as if they want to come over, to ask her what's wrong, if they can help, but there is something about her frenzy that is sending a very clear message to everyone to stay away.

"Fine, let's go," Jack says.

I want to see the drawing of Isabel, that is what I came here for, but I follow them to the elevator. I will be back on Wednesday. I can see it then.

We are silent all the way down to the street. Carolyn sets off at a brisk walk and we have no choice but to follow her. When we have left the Y and the other preschool mothers far behind, Carolyn stops. Jack is holding William's hand, the strap of the boy's lunch box looped over his shoulder, the booster seat tucked under his arm.

"He didn't get in," Carolyn says, looking over her shoulder as if to make sure no one is listening.

"What?" Jack says.

"Collegiate!" she says through gritted teeth. "He didn't get into Collegiate."

"Oh," Jack says.

"Oh? Oh? Is that all you can say? He didn't get into Collegiate! He didn't get into Collegiate, or Dalton, or Trinity. He didn't even get into the UN International School! He got wait-listed at Riverdale Country, a school I only applied to because you insisted, because you spent your childhood in Yonkers staring at Riverdale kids on the train and wishing you were one of them. Well he got wait-listed; he didn't get in. The only school he got into was Ethical Culture!"

"Ethical Culture is a terrific school," Jack says.

"It is *not* a terrific school," Carolyn spits. "It is a mediocre school. It is second-rate. I cannot believe we didn't get into a first-tier school. This is a disaster, Jack. This is a disaster, and the fact that you don't recognize what a disaster this is makes you even more of an idiot than I thought."

"Carolyn, it's not second-rate."

"Hey Jack," I say. "I'm going to take William and meet you at home."

Jack nods. Carolyn is too busy excoriating her ex-husband to notice when I grab her son's hand and flag down a cab. She is so wrapped in her vitriol that she does not see that her boy's face is ashen and he is wheezing. She does not even notice that I have left the booster seat behind.

"Are you okay?" I ask when we are in the taxi.

"No," William says.

"Can you please drop us off as close as possible to Belvedere Castle?" I say to the cabbie.

William is wheezing so hard when we climb up the steep spiral staircase in Belvedere Castle that by the time we reach the top terrace

I am convinced that he has developed asthma. I hand him one of the green discovery kit backpacks I picked up at the park ranger's desk on the bottom floor.

"What's yours got in it?" I say.

He shrugs.

I unzip my backpack and find a beat-up *Peterson Field Guide* with the cover torn off, a handful of random markers and colored pencils, and a clipboard with a few pieces of scrap paper.

"Look. Some kid left his picture." I show William the drawing of the bright red bird clipped to the clipboard. The bird's feet are so out of proportion to the rest of its body that it looks like it is wearing mukluks.

"No wonder the kid left it," I say. "This drawing sucks. What it is supposed to be? A cardinal wearing ski boots? You should draw something, William. You're a million times better at drawing than this kid is."

A smile twitches at the corner of his mouth, but he tamps it down.

I pull a small pair of surprisingly good quality binoculars out of the backpack. "Get your binoculars and let's look for hawks," I say. "Hawks are raptors, just like those velociraptors you like so much. Central Park is full of them. Hawks, not velociraptors. Do you know anything about hawks?"

"No," he says.

I open his backpack and hand him his binoculars. He takes them but does not lift them to his eyes. I look through my binoculars, focusing first on Turtle Pond directly below the castle and then on the tops of trees and on the gray sky. I scan the sky for raptors, but I can't find any. I wonder if I'm just not looking in the right places. When I am tired of looking for hawks I focus on the people in the strip of grass next to Turtle Pond. I see a fat man in a brown down jacket sitting on the grass. He has taped up a tear on his sleeve with silver duct tape and he is picking his nose. I turn to point out the nose-picker to William. William is standing next to me, his binoculars dangling from their cord.

"Come on, this is fun," I say.

He inhales raggedly.

"Don't you want to tell me something about Belvedere Castle? Like who built it or when?"

I try something else. "Did you know that there is a pair of red-tailed hawks that live right near you? Their names are Pale Male and Lola and they nest on a ledge of an apartment building on Fifth Avenue."

He kicks his toe against the wall, evincing no interest in these birds and their extravagant taste in real estate. He is either too upset or does not care about raptors that are not extinct.

"William, it's not the end of the world. Ethical Culture is a really great school. I know lots of people who went to Ethical Culture and loved it."

"Collegiate is the best school."

"No, it's not. Collegiate is snooty. And it's for boys. Who would want to go to an all-boy school?"

"If you go to Collegiate, you can go to Harvard."

"First of all, not everyone from Collegiate goes to Harvard. In fact, the vast majority of Collegiate kids don't go to Harvard. I happen to have met plenty of Collegiate graduates who are so stupid they would be lucky to get into Bergen Community College." I don't mention that I've actually slept with a few of these. "Second of all, there are plenty of kids from Ethical Culture who go to Harvard. Third of all, you are five years old. Why the hell do you care about going to Harvard?"

"You went to Harvard."

"Yeah, and look at me now."

William takes this rejoinder a little more seriously than I would like.

"William, your dad went to SUNY. And he's doing great. It just doesn't make that much of a difference where you go to college. And it certainly doesn't make any difference where you go to kindergarten. All that matters is that you like school. And you love school. You *love* it. You are the king of the number pegs. Sharlene says so."

"You don't understand."

"Yeah, I do. You're bummed out because you had your heart set on wearing one of those dopey little Collegiate beanies. But you'll get over it, I promise. And so will your mom."

"They don't wear beanies. They wear jackets and ties."

"Well that's even worse. Can you imagine? Wearing a tie every day? Gross."

"I like ties."

I rest my binoculars on the stone castle wall and crouch down until I am at his eye level. He is staring at his binoculars, fiddling with the cord and trying hard not to cry. "Dude," I say. "It doesn't matter. It really doesn't matter."

His whisper is hoarse and creaky. "My mom is mad at me."

I am about to reassure him that she isn't, but this child is not stupid. He knows anger when he sees it. Carolyn is furious, and he feels her rage spilling over onto him.

"When grown-ups want something, and they don't get it, sometimes they sort of freak out," I say. "They get mad at everything and everybody. Your mom is mostly mad at Collegiate. And she's mad at your dad. I think it only *feels* like she's mad at you because she's so mad at everybody else."

William still does not look at me. I put one awkward arm around him and pull him close. For a moment he sags against me, resting his head on my shoulder. Then, suddenly, as if realizing what he has done, he pulls away.

"You don't understand," he says. "You don't understand about Collegiate because you're not sophisticated. You're from New Jersey, and you're not sophisticated, like me and my mom are."

I get to my feet and grab him around the waist. I hoist him up and turn to the chest-high stone wall. Far below us is the rocky outcropping on which the castle is built.

"Look through your binoculars, William."

He kicks his heels against my legs, panicking. "Don't drop me!"

"I'm not going to drop you. Just sit up here and look through your binoculars." I balance him on the wall, holding him tightly around his waist.

He lifts his binoculars to his eyes.

"Can you see?" I ask. I show him how to focus on the vast expanse of park stretching before us. "Now look at those buildings. That's the Upper West Side. That's where we live, and that's where Collegiate is."

"It's on Seventy-eighth and Broadway," he says.

"Right. Look on the other side." I move his binoculars to the east. "That's the Upper East Side. That's where you and your mom live." I point him north now. "Now see how far north you can see? If it weren't such a crappy day maybe you'd be able to see all the way to Riverdale."

He turns the focus dial intently, beginning to enjoy it now, despite himself.

"It's a really big city, William. It's a huge city, and Collegiate is one tiny, little dot. It's a tiny, little, meaningless dot. It's a huge city, and you're going to have a huge life, and I promise you, I *promise* you, Collegiate means nothing. No matter what happens, no matter how mad and sad anybody gets, you've just got to remember how big everything is, and how far you can see. Okay?"

He sweeps his binoculars back and forth, but does not reply.

"Okay?" I repeat.

"I can't see anything," he says.

I drop him to the ground, take his binoculars, and head down the winding stairs. William clomps along behind me, his expensive French lace-up boots scraping against the stone steps. As I am returning the binoculars to the desk, I glance at the wall of notices. Weekly naturalists' tours of the park will resume on April 1, volunteers are being sought for next year's migratory waterfowl count, and there will be a special Walk to Remember on the last night of February. Those interested are encouraged to sign up online or by phone. Why require a sign-up, I wonder? So that the organizers can verify the sincerity of claims of loss? Do they check hospital records, death certificates? Or perhaps they are maintaining some highly particularized mailing list to sell at inflated prices to specialized businesses: the manufacturers of two-ply superabsorbent facial tissue, of waterproof mascara, of miniature funeral urns.

"I know all about the hawks," William says. He has come up behind me. "Pale Male lives at 927 Fifth Avenue, at Seventy-fourth Street. In Central Park there are sharp-shinned hawks and broad-tailed hawks and ospreys and kestrels and falcons. I know all about them, Emilia."

"Good for you, William. Come on, let's go home."

Chapter 18

When Jack walks into the apartment he is carrying two grocery bags and William and I have been waiting for him for almost an hour. William rushes his father, pinning him against the still-open front door. Jack sets the bags down and kneels. "I am so proud of you," he says, whereupon William bursts into tears. Jack ignores him. "Ethical Culture is a great place."

"I didn't get into Collegiate," William wails.

"Sweetheart, Will-man, it doesn't matter. You are going to have a terrific time at Ethical Culture. You'll make lots of friends. You'll love it. And now I don't want to hear any more about this school stuff, okay? It's just not that important, Will. You're going to a great school, and that's it."

Jack stands up and lifts Will in one arm. He tries to pick up the grocery bags with his other hand but I take them away from him.

"What's all this?" I say.

"I didn't feel like eating takeout," he says. "I'm going to make kibbe." He walks into the kitchen and lowers William into a chair. "Will, you want to help me make kibbe just like Grandma makes?"

"You're going to make kibbe?" I say, following him with the grocery bags.

"Sure."

"Since when do you know how to make kibbe?"

"I've seen my mother make it about a thousand times. I should be able to figure it out." Jack starts unloading the grocery bags. He puts a lump of meat in butcher paper on the table, a bag of pine nuts, a tall bottle of olive oil. I pick up the olive oil. It is organic, from California, and cost $32.

I say, "Watching someone cook and cooking yourself are two very different things."

"You watched my mother make it exactly once before you made it yourself," Jack says.

"I know how to cook. You don't."

"I know how to cook."

"Scrambled eggs is not cooking. Pasta with store-bought pesto is not cooking."

Jack whips the tabletop with a bundle of parsley, scattering tiny sprigs of green. William looks up, his eyes wide. "Goddamn it, Emilia," Jack says. "I don't feel like choking down another meal of miserable Chinese takeout. I don't want Thai food or salad from the deli. I'm making kibbe, if I have to spend three hours on the goddamn phone with my goddamn mother having her talk me through the whole goddamn recipe."

"I'll make it," I say. I unwrap the package of meat and dump it into a bowl. I dip my fingers into the cold softness of the ground lamb and squeeze a fistful. It spurts between my knuckles and only then do I remember that I have forgotten to wash my hands.

"I'm sorry," Jack says.

"No, I'm sorry," I say.

"You forgot to wash your hands," says William.

While I chop onions, I think about Jack's mother, Tmima. Before Isabel was born she was pleasant to me, but formal, even stiff. At our wedding she had worn a face so long, so drooped with mourning, that my grandmother had gone to comfort her, assuming that, like herself, the ceremony had made Tmima long for her dead husband, miss her own days as a young bride. Tmima had shaken her head and said to my grandmother, "Where I come from, we do not divorce."

My grandmother could not believe that what my mother-in-law was grieving was the loss of the first wife, the shiksa. "But Emilia's *Jewish*!" she had insisted, over and over again.

Tmima shook her weary head and said, "No one. Not ever. The husband, he would take a second wife before he would divorce, like the Arabs. I heard of men who did this, sometimes, outside the city. But now, these children, they divorce without even considering their poor babies."

"Pah!" my grandmother said, and stomped off. What could you say to a woman who would rather her son had chosen polygamy over a second marriage and joint legal custody?

I did my best to win my mother-in-law over. I watched her carefully while she prepared meals of pickled cauliflower and slow-cooked chicken, and then foolishly served them to her when she visited us, realizing only when it was too late that she resented my intrusion into her culinary realm. When I figured this out, I called and begged her to send a package of the little sugared date cookies Jack loves so much, claiming that no matter how often I tried I could not get them to come out right. In fact, my mahmoul are better than hers. I use butter, not margarine, in the dough, and instead of having a faintly dusty texture, like hers do, mine melt in your mouth. She also puts too many almonds in the filling.

It turns out, however, that all I needed to do to earn my mother-in-law's undying love was to lose my daughter. When Isabel died, Tmima dropped everything. Literally. Jack's sister told me that she dropped her carpet sweeper, walked into her bedroom, packed her suitcase, and took a cab to the airport. When she came into our apartment she walked right by Jack and folded me into her soft, powdery, cinnamon-scented arms. She held me while I cried my wretched and guilty tears and said, "I know, my daughter. I know. Before we left Syria, I watched my little sister die of diphtheria. And before Jack, I had a baby born too soon. I know what it means to lose a child."

"You lost a baby?" Jack said. "I didn't know that. You never told me that."

"There's a lot you don't know," Tmima said. She only went to comfort her son when she was sure I had exhausted my tears.

"I'm happy to make kibbe for you," I say now. "I'm sorry it's been so long since I cooked."

"It's okay, sweetie," Jack says. "It's not like it's your job to cook for me."

"Emilia doesn't have a job," William says.

"I'm taking a leave of absence," I say, frying the onions and the lamb together. Jack has forgotten the pomegranate molasses and the sumac. I doubt he even knows the recipe calls for them. I doubt he even knows that such things exist.

"I'm taking a leave of absence from this kitchen," William says, cracking himself up. He scrambles down off his chair and runs out of the room, slipping on the wood floor in his socks. I can hear him hooting all the way down the hall.

"Well, today was certainly a drama," I say.

"She has done such a number on him about this school thing," Jack says. He gets a bottle of wine out of the pantry and pulls two glasses down from the cupboard.

"Your ex-wife is a head case."

"I'm worried about him. I really am. It's like nothing else matters except getting into Collegiate."

"Don't worry about William, William is going to be fine," I say. "Worry about Carolyn. Carolyn is going to be institutionalized. She's going to be carted off to Bellevue. They probably have a special ward for the parents of children who don't get into their first-choice kindergarten."

Jack hands me my wine and takes a slug of his own. He finishes half the glass, leaving a purple mustache across his upper lip. I sip, rolling the wine on my tongue. I can't stand the taste of alcohol, would never drink except that I like very much the sensation of being drunk. I like erasing my emotions, or at least the memory of them.

"She has a lot riding on this," Jack says.

I toast pine nuts in a small pan, tossing them over and over so that they brown evenly. Then I pull out my food processor. It is dusty. As I take my apron from the hook where it has hung for months, stiffened into permanent pleats, the string around the neck bent where it pressed against the hook, I say, "What does she have riding on kindergarten? Whether William gets into Harvard? Don't worry about it. He's going to skip college altogether and just head straight to MIT for a postdoc in nuclear physics."

Jack finishes his glass of wine and pours himself another. He waves the bottle at me but I shake my head. "Carolyn was counting on the sibling preference," he says. "She's pregnant, and she's worried that the next one won't be as bright as William. She thought William was her ace in the hole, and now she's convinced she'll be trapped at Ethical Culture and then at Fieldston. She's afraid she'll never be able to move over to Collegiate or to one of her other first choices."

I am reaching for the iron skillet of sizzling lamb and onion and my pot holder drops to the floor as I grab the iron handle. I scream and run to the sink. I hold my throbbing palm under the cold water and cry.

"Jesus Christ," Jack says, hovering over me. "Do we need to go to the emergency room? Sweetie, how bad is the burn? Let me see." He pulls my hand out of the water and turns it over, searching for the blistering welt. There is a faint blush of red across my palm. He puts my hand back under the stream. "You'd better hold it under the water," he says.

"She's pregnant? How can she be pregnant?" I am sobbing. I wipe my nose with the back of the hand that isn't burned, and then wipe the snot on my jeans. "She's not even married! And she's forty-three years old! How can she possibly be pregnant?"

"She's forty-two. And she's been seeing someone since the summer."

"She has not. William would have told us. He can't keep a secret." But I know he can. He keeps my secrets just fine.

"William doesn't know about the baby. She's been waiting until she passes the three-month mark to tell him."

"How pregnant is she? Two months? Two and a half?"

Jack turns off the water and wraps my hand in a towel. "Why do you care about this, Emilia? She's just about three months. She told me that when we lost Isabel it made her realize that she wanted another child. She got pregnant right away."

I wrench my hand out of his. "She got pregnant because of Isabel? Your ex-wife got pregnant because my baby died?" I am screaming now and my harsh voice reverberates around the kitchen, ringing off the copper-backed pans hanging from their hooks.

"You don't get to be upset about this, Emilia," Jack shouts back. "If anyone gets to be upset, it's me, and I'm not going to be. I'm just not. I've decided it's a good thing she's pregnant. It's a *nice* thing. Carolyn said she was so touched by our loss, by how much I loved Isabel, by how devastated I was, that it made her realize that she wanted that kind of love in her life again. You should feel good about it. *I* do. I feel good about it."

"You're lying," I scream. "You do *not* feel good about it. You're jealous and you're furious, just like I am."

"No I'm not," he says. "It comforts me that something good came out of Isabel's death, that she didn't die in vain."

"That is *not* why Isabel died. Isabel didn't die so that Carolyn could have another baby. Goddamn you, you fucking son a bitch, that is not why she died. That is not a good enough reason!"

I run out of the kitchen, past William who is standing in the hallway, his hands balled up in fists and pressed into his cheeks. I grab my coat, shove my feet into my clogs, and slam out the door. I push the button for the elevator, but it does not come fast enough. I run down the stairs, through the lobby, and out into the miserable gray of a February afternoon.

Chapter 19

It is dark by the time I get to my mother's house, even though it is only five o'clock. I walk down the driveway and let myself in the back. My mother is standing in the kitchen, unloading the dishwasher, and she gives a little scream when I open the door.

"Emilia," she says. "My God, you scared the life out of me."

"Hi," I say. Then I start to cry.

There is a photograph in our family room of my mother when she was a girl. It used to hang in my grandmother's house, but when she died my mother took it and put it on the wall over our television, with the other family pictures. She did not change the frame, however, so unlike those other pictures it is not in a Lucite box. The black-and-white picture of my mother riding on a Shetland pony is in a gilded wood frame, the kind that has once again become fashionable. My mother's family was not the pony-owning kind, and neither was she a typical horse-loving girl, although she did try to claim this affinity when Allison was going through her jockey phase. My mother sat on the pony for the purpose of this photograph only, as evidenced by her smocked white dress, black Mary Janes, and folded white socks—

hardly riding clothes. My mother was only about seven years old when this picture was taken, but she had already acquired the worried smile and the faintly servile expression that I have spent so much of my life trying to charm, shake, and wipe off of her plump and pretty face.

"Honey bun!" my mother says, and hugs me. We are exactly the same height so I must bend over to bury my face in her soft and springy bosom. We waddle together, hugging, across the kitchen to the old sofa under the bay window. Sofas in my mother's house have always followed a migratory pattern. A sofa begins its life in the living room, then, once it is too worn for company, it moves to the family room. When it is really beat all to hell it lives out its final days in the kitchen. This last one has been here since before my parents' divorce, and when we sink into it I think that it is probably the last kitchen sofa my mother will own. A single woman does not wear out a sofa like a family of five. A single woman probably can't wear out a sofa at all.

I tell my mother about Carolyn and she comforts me, using all the right words. My mother knows that I need her to hate Carolyn, and while my mother has never hated anyone—not her stepdaughters, not the husband who left her for a lap dancer—she pretends to hate Jack's ex-wife for my sake.

My mother says, "She's just trying to manipulate him. I'm surprised at Jack, I really am. I would think he'd see right through this."

"He never sees through anything. It's like she's got him in some kind of perpetual mind fuck."

My mother hugs me tightly, but she does not say anything. She does not even nod her head. She's too smart for this. She knows that in a little while I will stop crying, that in a few hours I will remember that Jack does, in fact, usually see through his wife's games and manipulations, and that it is only around the issue of his son that he is sometimes blind to the point of foolishness. She knows that it is far better not to be on record as having criticized him.

"Is she getting married, at least?" my mother asks. "I always used to pray that Annabeth would get married and be happy. Just so that I would not have to *think* about her anymore."

"I don't know," I say. I've been hoping for the same thing; that Carolyn would fall in love and marry, that all her jealousy and bitterness would be swept away by a new and thrilling passion, and that my guilt could thus follow suit. How typical of this woman to torture me with a baby but begrudge me the relief her marriage would have provided.

After a while I realize that I am no longer crying—I am making noises like a person who is in tears, but my eyes are dry. I sit up.

"Well," I say. "I'm hungry."

"Shall I make us dinner?" my mother says. "I was going to broil some salmon. I can run up to the market and get another filet or two."

"Do you still have that crepe pan you bought me in high school? We can make salmon crepes, then we'd just need the one filet. And we can make dessert crepes, too. I saw some Nutella in the pantry last week."

I put a Joni Mitchell CD on the stereo. I bought my mother both the CD and the stereo for her first birthday after the divorce. My father left her all the furniture in the house, every photograph, including the ones of his own children, even the TV set. But he took the Bang & Olufson sound system.

My mother and I listen to Joni Mitchell bemoan the paving of paradise while we mix crepe batter, doing our best to sing along. We cook well together. Long ago I graduated from sous chef to equal partner in the kitchen, but today I let my mother order me around. I dip the pan in batter when I am told to, I allow her to slide the pancake off the Teflon with a twist of the rubber spatula, her motions still smooth and practiced even though we have not made crepes since 1992. She stirs up a simple tarragon sauce for the salmon and we each eat three crepes. When it is time for dessert I leave her with the crepe maker while I drive to the market and buy a pint of whipping cream and some salted hazelnuts. When I get home I whip the cream with just a pinch or two of sugar, crush the nuts, and we eat dessert with our fingers, smearing Nutella down our chins and smiling at each other with chocolate-covered teeth.

While we are loading the dishwasher my mother says, "It puts a terrible strain on a marriage, dealing with an ex-wife."

"No kidding."

"Sometimes I wonder if your father's and my problems didn't have an awful lot to do with Annabeth."

I pause while I'm wiping off the crepe maker. "Your problems had an awful lot to do with Daddy being an asshole."

She doesn't reply for a moment; instead she takes her time rinsing the suds out of the sink. "She used to write letters to the girls, telling them she was going to take them for the day, or for Christmas vacation. It would break my heart to see them get so excited, packing their little overnight bags. More often than not she wouldn't even come to pick them up, or she'd just take them for a couple of hours when she'd promised them a whole week. The girls would be so sad. Lucy would cry for days, and Allison would get that horrible little scowl, you remember the one, with her chin all thrust out?"

"Yes."

"The last time Annabeth saw them," my mother says, turning around and leaning against the kitchen sink while she dries her plump hands on a dish towel, "when you were about three or four years old, she had them all worked up over a trip to California, to Disneyland. I told your father to speak to them, to warn them that she'd probably back out, like she had before, but he wouldn't. He claimed that not even Annabeth would be so cruel as to renege on a promise like Disneyland. Well, of course, when the big day came, she was nowhere to be found. A few days later she came by with one of her boyfriends and took the girls up to the Catskill Game Farm for the afternoon."

I pause while I am pushing the chairs neatly under the kitchen table, the legs squeaking across the tile floor. "I remember that. I remember when they went to the Catskill Game Farm. I was so jealous."

"You remember that? Really? You were so little."

"They brought home water pistols. And Allison got a stuffed pink frog."

"Did she? I don't recall. What I remember is that the next day at breakfast the girls were even more obnoxious than usual. It got so bad that I tried to send Allison to her room, but she kicked up a fuss, shouting about how she wasn't going to listen to me, not after I'd refused to let her and Lucy go to Disneyland with their mother."

"What?" I sit on the table, drawing my knees up under my chin. My mother so rarely tells these stories about my older sisters, about how badly they treated her, how poorly behaved they were. Neither does she complain overmuch about her predecessor; even now that she has joined her in my father's past. This is a rare and unaccustomed treat.

"Annabeth had told them that it was *my* fault, that she had been planning on the trip, but that I had canceled it."

"She did not."

"She did."

"Oh my God! What a bitch. And they believed her?"

"Of course they believed her. Or at least they decided to believe her. The alternative, that their mother was lying to them, would have been intolerable."

"What did you do? Did you tell them the truth? Did you make Daddy tell them the truth?"

"Oh, we tried, but it didn't do much good." My mother gives a funny little half smile. "Still, I got my own back."

"What do you mean? What did you do?"

The back of my mother's head is reflected in the window over the kitchen sink. The collar of her pink blouse is folded up and now she smoothes it down. "Well, you know my old mink coat with the sable collar and cuffs?"

"Of course. I'm counting on inheriting that one day."

"Would you like to know where I got it?"

"Tell me," I say, a trill of excitement in my voice.

She leans forward conspiratorially, as though Annabeth Giskin herself might be lurking nearby and eavesdropping on our conversation. "A few months after the Disneyland fiasco, in the autumn, I got a rather strange telephone call from a pleasant older gentleman who owned a fur storage vault in Paramus. He had called Daddy's office first, but had asked for Mrs. Greenleaf. The receptionist, a new girl, gave him the home number. The man from the fur storage vault was calling all his customers to let them know that he was going out of business. Poor thing, his son, who was in business with him, had died, of leukemia, I think. He just didn't have the heart to continue. He and his wife were retiring to Florida."

"And?"

"And he asked me to pick up my mink-and-sable coat."

"And?"

"And I did. Paying, by the way, nearly six years in back storage fees, which cost me a pretty penny, I'll have you know." She gives the kitchen a once-over with a practiced eye and then begins to head out the door.

"So?" I say, insistently.

She pauses and smiles over her shoulder. "It's a nice coat, don't you think?"

"It's a beautiful coat, Mom. I mean, you know, if you don't mind the whole massacre of small mammals thing."

"So that's how I punished Annabeth."

"Wait a second. It was *her* coat?"

She winks.

"Oh my *God*! You stole her sable coat!"

"I did not steal it. The woman left it in storage for years without even bothering to pay the fees. I merely redeemed it. And it's not sable. It's mink, with a sable collar and cuffs."

I am giggling now, agog with newfound respect for my mother's audacity. This is a woman who never asserts her dominion over anything, who spends her life making sure other people are happy, comfortable, well fed. Her life is a constant bustle of organizing others' needs and desires—the precise brand of ibuprofen they prefer, a Primaloft pillow if they are allergic to down, violin lessons if they show an inclination toward the musical, a basket containing chocolate chip muffins, a gift certificate for the dry cleaner, and a bouquet of pink and yellow gerbera daisies if they are newly moved to the neighborhood. This is the very first time I have ever heard of her taking something for herself, and it is a calf-length mink-and-sable coat.

"Wait a second," I say. "Didn't Daddy notice that you were wearing his ex-wife's fur?"

"No," she says, flicking off the lights in the kitchen and leading me up the stairs. "Funnily enough, he never did. I always imagined that he probably recalled buying the fur, but simply forgot which wife he bought it for."

As my mother is tucking me into bed I say, "I don't think I've had such a nice night since Isabel died."

She kisses me on the forehead. "You know, sweetie, I'd like a photograph of Isabel, if you've got one."

I stiffen under my worn comforter and dig my toes into the bed, feeling the quilted bumps of the mattress. To distract her from the picture I cannot yet give her, I tell my mother about the Walk to Remember.

"Mindy asked me to go with her, before she got pregnant."

"Hmm." She smoothes my hair away from my face.

"I am so relieved that she isn't making me go."

"Are you?"

"The whole thing smacks of vacant sentiment. Wandering around Central Park at dusk with a bunch of other families whose babies have died. It's ridiculous."

"Why ridiculous, Emilia? Don't you think it might be comforting to be in the company of people who understand what you're going through?"

"Grief counseling doesn't help."

"Well, this is hardly grief counseling, now is it? You'd just be walking in the park with other women and other families. It would be a kind of memorial to Isabel. It sounds lovely to me. It sounds very healing."

I close my eyes under my mother's warm hand. She knows, I think, that despite my artfully contrived cynicism, it sounds lovely to me, too. To walk in the park with a group of people to whom no explanation is necessary, no excuses required. A group of women hollowed in the same way. To walk through the cold park, as the winter sky darkens and the branches are sketched black against the gray drifting clouds. To say Isabel's name with the name of so many other small gone things. It does sound lovely. It does sound healing.

"If I decide to go, will you come with me?" I say.

"Is that okay? Are grandparents invited?"

"I'm sure they are. I'm sure everyone is invited."

"I'd love to go then. I'd be honored."

"If I decide to go."

"If you decide to go."

Chapter 20

In the morning, I call Jack on his cell phone. He and William are walking along Eighty-first Street toward Amsterdam Avenue. They are meeting friends for brunch at Sarabeth's. Scott and Ivy were friends of Carolyn and Jack's. Couple friends. The one time Jack and I tried to socialize with them was a complete disaster. Over the course of a single evening, Ivy made me recite my age in a dozen different ways. She asked me what year I graduated from high school, when I was at Harvard, if I was old enough to have voted against the first President Bush, if I was too young to have watched *Laverne and Shirley* in its first run. She and Scott exchanged meaningful glances over comments of mine that I had thought would be innocuous, and when either of them mentioned Carolyn's name they apologized profusely. Since that dinner Jack has played squash with Scott a few times and gone skiing with him once. I think they have lunch occasionally. I don't think Jack's ever taken William to see them, although I imagine William and Carolyn are regulars at Scott and Ivy's apartment in the Apthorpe. Now, when I am gone, Jack and William are jumping at the chance to hang out with Scott and Ivy.

"I'm going to stay here in New Jersey for a couple of days," I say.

"A couple of *days*?" Jack says.

"Yeah."

"But you don't have any clothes."

That's not quite true. I found an old pair of underwear in my dresser. They are high-cut bikinis and look absurd with my low-rise jeans, but they are mine. Or were, in high school. I am wearing a Harvard Women's Law Association sweatshirt that I gave my father. When I found it in my mother's drawer this morning I said, "I cannot believe Daddy left this. I gave this to him. It was a present." Still making excuses for him, my mother had murmured something about his expanding girth. When I was in college and law school I would buy my father aggressively feminist T-shirts and sweatshirts as a joke to which only I understood the punch line. He gamely wore a black T-shirt embroidered with a mountain crest and the words ANNAPURNA: A WOMAN'S PLACE and one that said AMHERST LBQ—LESBIAN, BISEXUAL, QUESTIONING AND PROUD. The only gift he ever turned down was a tank top I picked up at a pro-choice march on Washington. I argued with him, but my father refused even to go for a jog with the words BUSH, OUT OF MINE emblazoned across his chest.

Somehow my mother and I had forgotten to pack these shirts when she first threw him out, and when he had come to the house to retrieve the rest of his belongings he had not bothered with them, leaving them in the bottom drawer of the dresser that had once been his and that now was filled with my mother's off-season clothes.

Now I tell Jack, "I've got some old stuff here, and I can pick up anything I need."

I wait for Jack to apologize for fighting with me. I think he is waiting for the same thing, because he doesn't say anything.

"Well, I'd better go," I say. "See you in couple of days."

"Come home, Emilia," Jack says.

"I will," I say. "I haven't left. I'm just in Glen Rock, visiting my mother."

"Come home."

"I will."

My mother and I spend the day shopping. We go to Lord & Taylor, and I try to convince her not to buy another navy blue cardigan, or at least to buy one in cashmere rather than wool blend. She tells me that I have developed expensive tastes, and then when she sees that this upsets me she tries to buy the cashmere cardigan. I do not let her. I tell her it doesn't look good on her, that it makes her look fat. Then I buy it for her.

We go to the movies that night, in the next town over. My mother refers, sotto voce, to the people who live in this town as "the yuppies." My mother always adopts these phrases eight or nine years after they have passed from the zeitgeist. We are in the car when she says this and I tell her she doesn't need to whisper; I promise that no one can hear her. My mother apologizes and this makes me feel so awful that I criticize her parallel parking. "Just pull into a spot," I say. "Or let me do it. Pull over, and let me do it."

My mother does not point out that I am a terrible driver, much worse than she is. She does not remind me that I failed my driving test twice, once because I could not parallel park, and that I have been in four car accidents, ranging from a fender bender in the parking lot of my apartment building in Cambridge to a major pile up on Route 4. The latter was not my fault. The other guy was drunk, and it is a miracle that nobody got hurt. The cop who called to tell my parents about the accident and to reassure them that I was unharmed, albeit hysterical and threatening to sue both the drunk and the city of Paramus, suggested to my father that he consider sending me to a defensive driving course. Or to anger management classes. Now my mother actually pulls the car over, ready to let me park it for her, but a space opens up and she noses in.

We share a popcorn, a package of Twizzlers, some Raisinettes, and a large Diet Coke. The movie is a romantic comedy, and it makes me so depressed that I want to scream. I chose this movie because I knew it would have no babies in it, the actors were all too young to play parents, but sitting in the theater, two rows behind us, is a couple with an infant. Since when, I would like to ask them, is it considered acceptable to impose one's squalling brat on an entire theater of paying customers, all of whom are seeking an escape from the real world, some of whom have surely paid money for a babysitter to watch their own children? But in fact, this baby is incredibly quiet and had I not turned around to see if the theater was sold out, I would never have noticed him. He does not make a peep. I make more noise than he does, shifting in my seat and blowing my nose.

"Are you all right?" says my mother. "Do you need another tissue?"

"I'm fine," I say. I stare at the screen and tell myself I am crying because I am so worried that the main characters of the movie will never realize that the antipathy they think they feel is really an undercurrent of irresistible sexual tension.

After the movie is finally finished, after I have forced my mother to wait for the credits to roll and the baby to leave, we get up. My mother gathers the wrappers and boxes from our candy and soda, as well as those left behind by our neighbors.

"You don't have to do that, Mom. They pay people to do that. They'll sweep the whole place up after we leave."

"You saw the little dancing boxes, Emilia."

"They don't really expect anybody to pay attention to the little dancing boxes. Everybody throws their candy wrappers on the floor in the movies."

"I don't, and neither should you. It's rude."

I sigh. She's right. It is rude.

While we are walking down the street to the car I feel something different about my mother. Her tread is somehow lighter than it has been. I am lethargic and heavy-footed but she is downright effervescent. Walking next to her, I feel like a child holding on to a helium balloon.

"What's with you?" I say.

"Hmm?"

"You seem happy."

"Do I?" my mother smiles to herself.

"Yes, you do." I didn't mean to sound so grouchy. I try again. "You seem really happy." Not much of an improvement.

"Oh, I'm not. I mean," she laughs, "I'm neither happy nor unhappy. I'm just myself. I liked that movie, though. Didn't you?"

"No."

"Oh sweetie." She rubs my arm and then squeezes it. "You'll feel better soon. It'll take time, but you'll feel better."

"Why did you like the movie so much? It was a romance. I would have thought it would make you sad." We have arrived at the car and I hold out my hand for the keys. She tosses them to me, lightly. She is springy, like one of her special holiday sponge cakes. "Wait a second, have you met someone? Are you dating someone? Do you have a *boyfriend*?" My mother has not been on a single date since I helped her throw my father out of the house. She has slept alone for four years.

"No, I haven't met anyone," she says. She gets into the car and slams the door behind her.

I open the driver's side. I turn on the engine but do not pull out of the parking space. "So if you haven't met anyone why are you behaving so strangely? Why did that movie put you into such a good mood?"

"Oh Emilia!" my mother says. She is bursting with news. I realize suddenly that she has been like this all weekend, that underneath her patient concern there has been a little sizzle of excitement. "Emilia, you're not going to believe this, but your father and I spent some time together on Thursday evening." There is something embarrassingly girlish about her laugh, it tinkles, twitters almost. "I guess you could say your father and I went out on our first date."

"Did you fuck him?" I say. "Did you fuck on your first date, Mom, or did Dad kiss you good night and then go pick up a hooker?"

The thing about a helium balloon is that once you have driven a pin into the bright rubber, you cannot reinflate it and send it back up in the air to hover cheerfully above your head. Once it is popped, it can never be repaired.

My mother is quiet. She holds her hands in her lap, palms up. I can see her soft belly resting on her thighs through her heavy winter everyday coat, the full-length, quilted down coat she has been wearing for as long as I can remember.

"Mom."

"It's okay, Emilia," she says. "I know you didn't mean it." She reaches her hand across the bucket seats and cups my cheek. I press her hand between my cheek and my shoulder and rub back and forth, like a cat.

"Mom," I say. "It's just . . . I love Dad but he . . . he hasn't changed. What makes you think he's changed?"

"Oh, I don't think he's changed," my mother says. She shakes her head ruefully. "There are things you don't understand, sweetie. Things about your dad and me, about our relationship, that you don't know."

"Well then tell me. Help me understand why you would take him back after what he did to you."

"I haven't taken him back. We haven't gotten anywhere close to that. We went on one date." She takes her hand away from me and starts playing with her gloves. "It's only been one date. So far."

I pull the car out of the parking space and start heading up the block. The street is full of restaurants, and despite the fact that it is almost ten o'clock and we are in the suburbs, the sidewalks are crowded. "Wasn't it hard not to think about what he did to you? I mean, didn't you keep thinking about how he cheated on you?"

My mother bites her lip. She is looking straight ahead, out the front window. "We talked about it. We talked about it all. Everything. He told me about everything he used to do. He . . . he showed me."

"He *showed* you?"

My mother shakes her head. "You don't understand, Emilia. I don't understand myself, but hearing about it was . . . well, it was very exciting. Your father and I . . . well, that part of our relationship was always good, and even after the divorce I always had feelings for him. Hearing about it was . . . I don't know . . . It was very exciting. It made me very excited. Sexually."

And that's as much as I can take. I make a sharp right, ignoring the four-way stop sign. I pull over at the taxi stand in front of the train station and jam the car into park. I heave open the car door and, ignoring my mother's cries, run across the pavement and jump into the back of a cab.

"Manhattan," I say. "The Upper West Side."

Chapter 21

The first time Jack and I have sex—full-on sexual intercourse—after Isabel's death is also the first time I've ever faked an orgasm. This is surprisingly easy to do. A few well-timed gasps, a shiver, some rhythmic vaginal clenching, and Jack is deceived. Afterward I wait for him to thank me, but he is under the impression that we made love; he is unaware that I did him a favor.

But of course, why should he be? I've never done anything like this before. More important, this has never been the context of our sexual relationship, not from its inception. Before Isabel's death, I was voracious in bed and there was no reason to doubt the veracity of my passion. The same was not always true of Jack. From the first time we made love, in Jack's office, the night after we came home from San Francisco, there was always a tiny hesitation on his part, before his capitulation to the frenzied insistence of desire. I did not force myself on him. On the contrary, it was Jack who booked the hotel rooms, Jack who lifted me onto his office chair, Jack who tangled his fingers in the hair at the nape of my neck when he passed me in the firm's library. But there was always a second when his velvet eyes clouded over before we made love, when I caught my breath and waited for him to remember that he was married, that he had a little boy, that what he was doing was wrong.

He broke up with me after three and a half months, when we had made love twenty-seven times. Twenty-eight, if you count the Admiral's Club, but I'm not sure a blow job in a public restroom really counts as making love. We were eating pizza at Two Boots in the East Village, which used to be one of my favorite restaurants. Jack and I only ate out in the East Village and occasionally in Chelsea, two neighborhoods in which we were guaranteed never to run into Carolyn or anyone she knew.

I had burned my tongue on my first bite of blackened chicken pizza and was cooling it by trying to stick it into the neck of my bottle of Dos Equis. Jack wasn't eating.

"Aren't you hungry?" I said. Then my hands started to shake. "Don't. Please don't. I love you."

"I know."

"You love me. You know you love me. You love me too much never to see me again."

"I'll see you. I'll see you every day at work."

"That will make it worse. It will drive you crazy." I wasn't trying to hide my sobbing. I cried big, fat, hiccupping tears, letting them slide all over my face and down my chin.

"Emilia, I have a child. I can't do this to Will. It's not fair. You don't understand what it's like when you have a child." Jack's face was very pale under his deep summer tan.

"Did you lose your right to be happy when you had a child?"

"I lost my right to be selfish."

"Why did you marry her?" I cried. "Why didn't you wait for me? You knew I was coming. You should have waited."

Jack did not tell me that I sounded like a crazy person. Instead he got up and came over to my side of the table. He started kissing my cheeks, rubbing away my tears with his lips. Then he put some money down on the table and led me outside. It was an unbearably hot night, even though it was only the beginning of July, too early for such thick and sluggish humidity to have settled so firmly over the city. We walked over to First Avenue and Jack flagged down a cab and put me in it. He told the driver my address—only a dozen or so blocks uptown—and shut the door. I watched him through the rear window, a small man in a suit, looking overdressed and ridiculous standing among the pierced and leather-clad art-scene pretenders of a Friday night in the East Village.

That night Jack confessed to Carolyn. He told her that he had had an affair but that it was all over. She threw him out. Three nights later I slept with him in his room at the Carnegie Suites on West Fifty-eighth Street.

Tonight Jack does not mention our fight, or the ugly things I screamed at him. He is so glad that I have come home that he does not ask why. He does not even ask why we are having sex, and I wonder if he thinks it is a substitute for making up.

Before Jack falls sleep he tells me that he is dropping William off tomorrow evening. Jack has had to tell Carolyn that William overheard him talking about her pregnancy, and she wants the boy back early, to formally give him the news.

The next morning Jack is distracted at breakfast. I have been trying to tell him about the Walk to Remember, and why I think I have decided that we should go, but he isn't paying much attention to me.

"What's wrong?" I say.

"Nothing."

"What?"

He pushes the newspaper across the table to me. "Here, I'm done with the magazine and the book review. Would you be really pissed off if I dropped by the office this morning? Just for half an hour. An hour, max. I've had some people working on a discovery motion all weekend and I'd like to show my face."

"It can't wait until tomorrow?"

"I just want to check in, so they don't think I'm off playing golf all weekend while they slave over the brief. I won't stay very long. I'll take Will if you like."

"I don't want to go to your office," William says. "Your office is even less fun than Mommy's office. At least where Mommy works there are models of people's insides."

"It's fine," I say. "He can hang out with me. I need to get out, anyway. I feel like I'm going kind of crazy cooped up in here."

Jack raises his eyebrows but does not say that I have only been home since eleven last night; I have hardly been cooped up.

"What do you think of this walk thing?" I say. "This memorial walk? Do you think we should do it?"

"I don't know, Em," Jack says. He finishes the dregs of his coffee and pushes his chair back. "You've never wanted to do anything like this before."

"Well, that's sort of the whole point."

"What do you think you're going to get out of it?"

This question, phrased so baldly, stops me short. I am about to tell Jack what I have told my mother, about the healing properties of the companionship, even for just one evening, of those who have undergone similar experiences. But Jack knows how I feel about support groups; he has heard me deride their supposed merits too many times. He will not accept an about-face. Neither will Mindy's claim that the walk will allow me to take back the park make much of an impression on him. After all, he knows how often I retreat to the park, despite the omnipresence of children and mothers. Jack knows me too well to accept such facile explanations.

What I realize only when I try to explain it to Jack is that I hope that this walk, for all its maudlin, syrupy language of honoring lost babies, will do something about the stasis of my life, will act as some kind of gentle shock to liberate me from the catalepsy which has frozen my limbs and thoughts since the night of Isabel's death. This deathless yet furious torpor has got to end; it is too *boring* to continue. Perhaps this might catapult me into a new, less tedious stage of grief.

"Can I come?" William asks, when I am done explaining my hopes for the end of entropy.

"It's not for kids, Will," Jack says.

"No, it is," I say. "I mean, it's for families. I think he should come. I think it would great. It makes sense for all of us to be there, together, don't you see? So we can sort of start over together. The three of us, and Isabel, too, in a way. Her memory. It's like a whole new beginning. Or an end. Or something. But we all should be there. You, and me, and William, too."

Jack looks from William to me, and I can see that the boy and I are once again seducing him with our hopeful faces, the possibility of repair and reconciliation.

"Are you sure about this?" he says.

"Absolutely."

"Even at night Central Park is one of the safest parts of the city, Daddy," William says. "Last year there were only 127 crimes in the whole park, and no murders."

Jack laughs. "I don't really have a lot of safety concerns, Mr. Man, but I'm reassured that murder is not going to be an issue."

"The thing is," William says, "I would really like to see the park at night. I've never even seen any of the luminaires lit up, except when they sometimes forget to turn them off during the day."

"The walk is in the afternoon," I say. "It ends at dusk."

"That's all right," William says. "I still want to go."

Later, I ask William what he wants to do today, where he wants to go.

"Let's go to the park," he says.

"Are you sure?" I am eager to go, but don't want him to feel like he has to go to the park, because that is where he knows I want to be.

"Yeah."

On our way out of the apartment I remind William to go to the bathroom. He informs me not only that he does not have to go but that because he is a boy, there are no impediments to him simply peeing against a tree should the need arise.

"Because I have a penis," he says. "You should go, though. You don't have a penis."

"Thanks for the anatomy lesson." While I am in the bathroom the telephone rings. "Just let the machine get it," I call, but William has already picked up the phone. I cannot hear him, but I know how he's answered it. He has an impeccable phone manner; he'd make an ideal receptionist. He always says, "Woolf residence, this is William speaking." Jack tells me that when William answers the phone at his mother's house, he gives the same greeting, smoothly substituting her name for Jack's. I'm sure he never confuses the two. William is far too careful for that.

"Who was it?" I ask when I'm done.

"Nono." William has used this name when referring to my father from the very first day that they met, which was a few weeks before our wedding. My father introduced himself thus, and because the word was unfamiliar and had no familial connotations or weight to the boy, he adopted it easily. "Nono" is a Ladino word, the language spoken by the Jews in the part of Bulgaria from where my father's grandparents came. My father makes all his grandchildren call him Nono, probably because it would make him feel like an old geezer to hear the word grandpa shouted in his direction.

"What did he want?" I say.

"Nothing. I told him we were going to the park. He said we should go to the Ross Pinetum. Most of the trees in the pinetum are coniferous."

"Well, they would be, wouldn't they? It's a *pine*-etum. Not a deciduetum."

"Deciduetum is not a word." William frowns suspiciously. "Is it?"

"No."

"Nono says to go there, because the trees will be nice and green."

I hand William his coat and pull mine closed. It seems to button somewhat less hideously. I still look lumpy and sausage-like, but not enough to justify braving the weather with insufficient protection.

"Do we have to go there?" he says. "Do we have to go to the pinetum?"

"Of course not." I don't want to go anywhere my father suggested, because last night with my mother has reminded me how very angry at my father I am.

"Because it's right next to our house," William says. "I want to explore. I want to go to the Ramble. Don't you think that's a much better idea?" He stomps his feet in his thick-soled winter boots.

"It's an excellent idea. We can be explorers. I'll be Christopher Columbus. Who do you want to be?"

"Christopher Columbus?" He shakes his head, but his disgust has a rueful, playful quality. "That's so boring, Emilia. I'm going to be Coronado. I'm going to search for the Seven Cities of Cibola."

"What are those?" I ask.

His mouth drops open. "You don't know who Coronado is?"

"Well, I mean I've *heard* of him. I'm just not up on those seven cities."

William is so busy telling me about the Spanish conquistador Francisco Vásquez de Coronado and his search for the fabled Seven Cities of Cibola that he passes the Diana Ross Playground without even asking to go inside. Every third step or so he skips, with a kind of shimmy. He also bends down to poke things with a stick he has picked up.

"The Ramble is the perfect place to play explorers," he says.

"I know."

"It's the part of the park that's the most rugged. Most like a wilderness."

"I know."

He pauses, suddenly. "Is the Ramble dangerous?"

I think of the homeless man in the garbage bags, the man who either attacked me or whom I attacked, depending on which of us is more insane.

"Nope," I say. "The park isn't dangerous. People who say the park is dangerous are just stupid."

William pokes at a clump of hardened slush with his stick. "I think there's a dead bird frozen in here," he says.

"Gross," I say.

He prods for a while until it becomes obvious that what is underneath the ice is just a clot of dirt and leaves.

"My mother says that the man who paid for the Delacorte Clock got mugged right in the park."

"Does she?" It is typical that Carolyn, who to my knowledge has never set foot in Central Park, would know that George Delacorte, one of Central Park's great philanthropists, was mugged, at the age of ninety-two, in a pedestrian tunnel near the very clock he endowed. Carolyn is a repository of any information that could siphon the fun out of our day.

"The Seven Cities of Cibola are in a little hut in the middle of the Ramble," William announces.

"What?"

"There's this little thing called a rustic shelter in the middle of the Ramble. I saw it in that book you gave me. That's the Seven Cities."

"Or one of them. You know, I think I sat in that hut once, a couple of years ago. It was neat, because it was summer, and it felt really cool inside. I think it's much colder inside that hut than outside in the rest of the park."

"It's full of gold."

"I remember that. It was totally full of gold. Heaps of gold, everywhere. The only reason I didn't take any was because I was wearing a sundress and didn't have any pockets."

"Let's go!" William says.

We march into the Ramble, keeping far to the west of the area where I saw the homeless man. We climb a flight of stairs and cross one of the many small bridges over the stream that curves through the Ramble. There is a small field below us, and William holds on to a tree and leans out over the edge of the rocky path.

"What're those?" he says. He points his stick at a cluster of what appear to be plastic milk containers hanging from the tree branches, decorated with Frisbees.

"I haven't the faintest idea. Bird feeders, maybe?"

He frowns, suspiciously, and we continue walking.

"I can smell gold," he says. "We must be close to the hut. Are we close to the hut, do you think?"

"I don't really know. I can't remember what part of the Ramble it was in. We'll find it if we keep wandering around."

He stomps his foot into an icy puddle. "It's cold."

"If we pick up our pace a little, we'll warm up."

We cross a small, high bridge between two bluffs of schist.

William hangs over the rail for a moment, and I move closer to him, ready to snatch him if he loses his balance. He coughs loudly, gathering mucus from his throat. Then he spits over the side. We watch his clot of saliva travel to the icy stream.

I say, "Excellent aim."

He stands up and we continue walking. A few minutes later we somehow arrive on the same bridge; the path has switched back and led us in a circle.

William clicks his tongue impatiently. "Why don't we just go to the Dairy and buy a map?"

"Because that would be cheating. We have to explore until we find it. Did Coronada have a map?"

"Coronad*o*. Not Coronada." He has stopped walking. His stick is leaning on the toe of his boot. "I want to get a map."

"We can't."

"Why not?"

"Because."

"Because why?"

"Just because. Come on. Pretend we're in uncharted territory, and there are no maps."

We walk on for a while longer, getting colder and colder. Soon I begin to realize that while it might have been fun to be explorers who *find* a little wooden hut in the Ramble, it is no fun at all to play at being failed explorers. It's no fun stumbling around the Azalea Pond when there are no azaleas and the pond is frozen, and it is no fun worrying about homeless men hiding under rocks. When I twist my ankle on a root I decide that Coronado was an idiot and it served him right not to find the Seven Cities of Cibola. I look at my watch.

"Maybe being explorers isn't such a great idea," I say.

"The Ramble is boring."

"Okay, what about if we do something totally different. What about if we go to the very northern-most part of the park."

"And do what?"

I waggle my eyebrows mysteriously and lead the way out of the Ramble. Unfortunately, this takes a while, because I am completely lost. Finally, through sheer luck and the force of my determination, we somehow end up on the far eastern side of the park. I spot the statue of the panther, crouching over East Drive.

"Aha!" I shout, and grab William's hand. We run up behind the statue. It is high above the road atop a slab of rock, much too high for us to jump down, but a little ways past the statue the hill slopes gently enough for us to scramble to the street.

"That was an adventure," I say.

"We went off the path."

"I know. How cool is that!"

"My mother would be so mad, Emilia."

"So don't tell her."

While he is considering adding this to our litany of secrets, I drag him across the Glade to the exit at Seventy-ninth Street.

I instruct our cabdriver to take us to the Conservatory Garden, near 105th Street. If I were on my own I would have walked, but I cannot imagine forcing a little boy to march nearly thirty blocks.

I have not spent much time in the garden. It is a little formal for my tastes, the north end particularly, with its geometric rings of shrubs and its fountains. The south end is actually my favorite, an English perennial garden, but there is not much to see there in the winter; most of it is dried and shriveled, cut back and hibernating in anticipation of a glorious spring and summer. I will bring William back here in late April or early May, when the crab-apple allées carpet the paths with pink petals. It's ridiculously beautiful here in the spring.

William, his mood salvaged by the warm cab ride and a soft pretzel, likes the garden. He asks at least four hundred and sixty questions about species of flowers. Even if it were the height of spring, even if the air was filled with swirling petals, I would not be able to identify enough subspecies of flora for William. I tell him that there are twenty thousand tulip bulbs planted in the garden and that we can return in May to see them bloom, and somehow the magnitude of this number appeases his curiosity, even though there is nothing to see of the slumbering flowers.

When we come across the Secret Garden Fountain stuck in the frozen water-lily pool in the South Garden, William claims not to know who Frances Hodgson Burnett is, nor to have read the book.

"That is appalling," I say. "That is an appalling hole in your education that I am going to have to remedy immediately."

"*The Secret Garden* is a girl's book," William says, aghast at the very idea of reading such a thing.

Only when I inform him that it is probably much too difficult for him does he instruct me to purchase him a copy immediately.

The hellebores fascinate William. I had hoped we would be able to see their drooping white, pink, green, and dark purple flowers but it is still too early. They will bloom next month, I suppose.

"They're poisonous," I say in a very dramatic, Creature Feature voice. "If you eat a blossom or leaf you'll die. Shall we take some to slip in someone's tea?"

"We'll be arrested," he says.

"Only if you tell."

He ponders this. "Who should we kill?"

I consider his question. He knows too many of the people on my list.

"Let's walk back up to the North Garden," I say, instead.

We meander to the fountain of the Three Dancing Maidens. The fountain is turned off, of course, because of the cold. We look at it for a moment. "It's prettier with the water running," I say.

"Hey," William says, "look at that." He points to the far side of the concentric rings of low shrubs surrounding the fountain. "They're making a movie."

Across the bank of flowers is a little huddle of people, two men and a woman. For a moment, I think the men might be identical twins. They are both bald, with tiny soul patches under their lower lips, and thick-rimmed glasses. They are wearing complementary puffy down jackets, one black with orange piping, the other orange with a black racing stripe. The woman is neither bald nor bearded, but also seems to be part of their fashion family, in her red acrylic ski cap, torn hip-hugger jeans over heavy boots, and rhinestone cat's-eye glasses. There was a time when I tried to affect a version of this hip-hop East Village chic, although the digital movie camera, beat-up leather cases, and light meters heaped around the ankles of this trio lend them an air of artistic authenticity I always lacked in my club-hopping days. Somehow I usually ended up looking like what I was: a girl from New Jersey, with an unfortunately tenuous grasp on what constituted style.

I say, "My favorite movie of all time, *Where's Poppa?*, was shot in the park. George Segal puts on a gorilla suit so he can run across the park at night. I love that movie because George Segal's mother pulls down his pants and kisses him right on the butt."

William has been leaning over to break a dried twig off one of the hedges, but he is halted in mid-bend. "That is so gross, Emilia."

"Haven't your parents ever kissed you on the butt?"

"No!"

"Remind me to tell your dad to kiss you on the butt today."

"No way!"

"Or maybe I should kiss you on the butt right now." I lunge in his direction and he shrieks, tearing around an ice-frosted, low-clipped shrub. I chase him and then catch him in my arms, scooping him up in the air. I make loud kissing noises in the direction of his rear end and he shrieks, laughing so hard that he can barely breathe. I am laughing, too, almost as hysterically as he is.

The movie-making team desultorily swings the camera around, as if distracted from their work by our boisterous games.

I set him on the ground and William tries to divert my attention from his unprotected rear end. "Tell me some other movies that were filmed in the park," he says.

"Let's see. *Hair*. And *Marathon Man* with Dustin Hoffman jogging around the Reservoir. Don't see that one if you ever want to go to the dentist again."

"I like my dentist. He's a friend of my mother's."

"You *like* your dentist? That figures."

He ponders this for a moment. "My dentist is my mother's special friend."

"Her special friend?" I repeat.

"You know. Her *boy*friend."

"Oh."

"Any more?"

"Any more what?" I say.

"Movies. In the park."

I force myself to dismiss Carolyn and her special impregnating dentist from my mind. "Well, *When Harry Met Sally*. Oh, I know one you must have seen. *Ghostbusters*. You've seen *Ghostbusters*, right?"

"No."

"I'll rent it for you. Next time your father lets us get a DVD."

"I wonder what movie those guys are making," William says.

"Why don't we go ask them?"

"Really?"

"Sure."

We cross the garden. One of the twins is busy removing the camera from the tripod and packing it away in its case. The other is folding up a round, white reflecting screen.

"Excuse me," I say.

The woman in the red stocking cap looks up.

"We were wondering if you were making a movie."

"We're scouting shots for a film."

"What film?" I say.

"*Lyle, Lyle, Crocodile.*"

William gasps. "*Lyle, Lyle, Crocodile*, like the book *Lyle, Lyle, Crocodile*?" he says.

The woman laughs. "Supposed to be. We'll see."

William is so excited that he is bouncing on his tiptoes. "I love that book. My mom read it to me, and then I read it to myself. I love it. I love Lyle."

One of the bald men says, "The first Thursday in March we're going to be shooting crowd scenes at the Children's Zoo. For the scene where Mr. Grumps sends Lyle to live at the zoo."

"I love that part," William breathes.

"You should come," the woman says. "They'll need plenty of extras. Check-in is at around two PM."

"Can we, Emilia, can we please?"

"I don't know, William. I'll have to talk to your mom. Thursdays you're at your mom's."

"Switch with her. Just switch with her! Please! I love *Lyle, Lyle, Crocodile*. It's my favorite book. It's the best book I've ever read in my whole life."

There is no chance that Carolyn will let me have him on a Thursday. She will say no, but somehow contrive things so that I end up looking like the wicked stepmother for promising something I cannot deliver.

I say, "First of all, *The Amber Spyglass* is your favorite book. I've never even heard you talk about Lyle. And I would remember, William, because *The House on East 88th Street* was one of my favorite books when I was a little girl. *My* father used to read it to *me* all the time. You even have it on your bookshelf, and I swear I'm the only person who's ever opened it." When my father would read me the Lyle stories he would do all the voices, including that of Hector P. Valenti, Lyle's former owner and dance partner. My father does a terrible South American accent.

William shakes his head. "*The Amber Spyglass* is my this year's favorite book. You just don't know me very well, Emilia. If you knew me you'd know that *Lyle, Lyle, Crocodile* is my very favorite book of all time. It's better than *The House on East 88th Street*. Much better. I just haven't read it *recently*, Emilia, because I'm reading other things. But that doesn't mean it isn't my favorite. It is." And then he gets an idea. He pastes a winning smile to his face. A large, crocodilian grin. "And since it's your favorite, too, don't you want to be in the movie?"

"We'll talk about it," I say. "Let's go over to the Harlem Meer now. We can fish. They have fishing poles at the discovery center that they let people borrow."

"I don't want to go fishing. I want to be in the movie. Please, Emilia. Promise me you'll take me."

"I said we'll talk about it. Come on, let's go to the Meer."

"But . . ."

"We'll talk about it, William," I say.

He grudgingly follows me out the garden gates and around the Meer. The Dana Discovery Center on the far side is beautifully renovated, a tiny brick jewel at the farthest north point of the park. The contrast from the time I visited here with my father when I was only a few years older than William could not be starker. However, when we arrive, the dour-faced park employee is incredulous at our request. Why would anyone want to fish in February?

"The Meer is full of ice," she says.

"But the fish are still there," I point out to her. "It's not like you removed them."

She will not indulge such foolishness. Neither William nor I is particularly interested in her alternative suggestion of exploring the ecology exhibits in the discovery center.

"Well, we can always go look for fish," I say. "Who needs to catch them anyway?" I want so desperately to resume our high spirits, but the cheer in my voice is plainly false and William isn't having any of it.

"It's too bad we don't have any of those hellebores," I say. "We could drop them in the Meer and poison us some fish."

He doesn't laugh.

It has started to drizzle when we walk out the door of the discovery center. Once again I have left the house without an umbrella.

"It's raining," William says.

"Only a little. Let's go *pretend* to kill some fish."

"I think we'd better go home. It's cold, and I don't want to get wet."

"Do you know what Meer means? It means 'lake' in Dutch."

"I don't care." He is sulking now.

"Oh come on, William. We came all the way uptown, we can't leave without seeing the Meer up close." I grab his hand and start running toward the water. The raindrops are cold on my face but I am trying to have fun. I can see us in my mind's eye, how we must look to an observer, a mother and her young son, laughing and running through the rain. Except only I am laughing. William is slow and when I try to speed up he resists. When we get close to the water's edge he jerks his hand, trying to wrench free. I slip and fling my arms forward to keep from falling. I am still holding William's hand, though, and with a splat, he falls to the ground, his feet and legs splayed before him. His butt is planted firmly on the muddy curb at the water's edge, but his feet and legs crash right through the brittle membrane of ice into the freezing water.

"Oh shit," I say. "Shit, shit, shit." I pull him to his feet. "Are you okay? I'm so sorry, William."

"You threw me in the lake! You threw me in the lake!"

"I did not."

"Yes, you did. This is the second time you made me fall down.

Once ice-skating and now you threw me in the lake. I'm soaking wet again, and my jeans are all dirty and muddy. My mom is going to be so mad at you, Emilia! She is going to kill you!"

"It was an accident, William. I slipped. I'm sorry."

"I want to go home now," he says. "I hate this place. It's dirty and cold and I hate it. I hate it."

"Okay, just calm down. We'll go home right now. Come on."

William does not even look up as we pass under the Duke Ellington Memorial. I try to point out the columns with the nine nude caryatid figures representing the muses. I say, "Look, Sir Duke is just standing there on top next to his grand piano. He's not even playing."

William stumbles along next to me, refusing to lift his face.

"It's twenty-five feet tall," I say, desperately.

William is silent.

"Stevie Wonder made up the nickname Sir Duke. I think he might be the only one who called him that. You know who Stevie Wonder is, don't you?" I try to do a Stevie Wonder imitation, waggling my head back and forth and plonking on imaginary piano keys while I sing, but the only song I can think of is "Ebony and Ivory."

William makes a sound like an angry cat, half hiss and half snarl. I shut up and stare at the hideous memorial. The columns reach between the muses' legs into their pubic clefts like massive phalluses. What have poor Duke Ellington and Harlem done to deserve such an ugly memorial?

There are, of course, no taxis to be had and soon I am almost as frantic as William. I cannot believe I'm getting this kid wet again. I cannot believe I have no umbrella. I cannot believe this is all happening one more time. Finally, when we are soaked through, our hair plastered to our heads, I wave down a gypsy cab. William balks but I push him into the backseat. There are no shoulder belts but the car is clean and dry.

"Central Park West and Eighty-first," I say to the driver.

We ride in silence for a while, then I say, "William, I think maybe this should be another secret."

William says, "No way."

Chapter 22

When we arrive at our building we find Jack standing in the lobby, talking baseball with the new weekend doorman.

"Sometimes, Mr. Woolf, I get a little jealous of those Yankee fans. I hate to admit it, but—"

"You're killing me, Rodrigo."

"I could only admit it to you."

Jack shakes his head. "I'm losing respect for you very quickly, here."

"Daddy!" William calls from the front door. He spreads his arms wide, but not in an invitation to an embrace, rather to exhibit his befouled little self.

"Hey Will! What happened to you? You're a mud ball."

"Emilia threw me in the lake. She threw me right in the freezing lake."

I do not stop. I simply shake my head, walk by, and punch the call button for the elevator.

"Em?" Jack calls after me. "What's going on?"

I shake my head again.

"Emilia!"

Rodrigo is nowhere to be seen. He has melted away into the bowels of the building or disappeared out the front door to huddle under the awning in the rain until we are done making an exhibition of ourselves.

"Can we do this upstairs?" I say.

The ride up in the elevator is silent, punctuated only by the rattle of William's sniffles, mucus sucked through his nose and throat with dramatic intensity.

Once we are inside our apartment Jack says again, "What happened?"

William says, "Emilia threw me in the lake," and then he bursts into tears.

"Don't be ridiculous," I snap. Then I explain briefly what happened, how we slipped and he fell into the Meer. How it was an accident. "We were having so much fun," I say, wincing at the pathetic, pleading tone in my voice. "We were actually having a good time."

Jack turns away from me and bends down to William. He uses his thumbs to wipe the boy's tears away. "Let's get you out of these wet clothes and into a hot bubble bath." He picks William up and is immediately wrapped in the clutch of the boy's octopus legs and arms.

"I'm so wet, Daddy," William says, piteously.

I say, "This is ridiculous!"

Jack says nothing. They are halfway down the hallway when I call out, "Just a minute."

Jack pauses in the doorway to William's room.

"What?" he says. His voice is taut, stretched close to breaking.

"Aren't you going to tell him that he's *overreacting*? Explain that he shouldn't get so crazy over a little mud and water? We were having *fun*, Jack! Aren't you going to say something to him?"

Jack narrows his lips into a thin line and his nostrils flare as he inhales. His face is pale, white with anger, especially around his eyes. "You want me to say something, Emilia?" he bites off each word and spits it out like a bitter morsel. "You really want me to say something?"

Don't say anything. Don't release the words that I can see swirling in your mouth, even across this dark and lonely room.

"It was an accident!" I insist. "We tripped. We were running, and we fell."

"You don't even *give* a shit. He's cold, and scared, and you couldn't care less."

"I do so care. But he wasn't scared. You know William, Jack. You know he's just being dramatic. It's like he can't bear the fact that he had fun with me. Like it's a betrayal of Carolyn or something. But that's just silly. You need to tell him that's just silly."

Jack gently puts William down, propels him through the door, and then pulls it closed. He leans toward me and says in a low voice, "You have no idea what your face is like when you look at him, Emilia. You are so cold. You are colder than the fucking frozen Harlem Meer."

He jerks William's door open and walks through it, slamming it shut behind him. I was not cold before. Before, I was warming to his son. I was. But now his words and those unsaid that have spilled over me like liquid hydrogen. It is his words that have frozen me, made me brittle and immovable. Colder than even Jack knows.

I am white with cold and for some reason I think of this moment's polar opposite, so long ago. When I felt like someone had opened a small door in the top of my head and poured sunlight into my body, filling me from the tips of my toes and fingers up through the filaments of hair on my scalp. That moment was all the more precious because of what had led up to it. All day long, and for at least a week before, I had been convinced, had known the way I know my own telephone number, the way I know now what Jack is not saying, that he was going to break up with me once again.

Since Carolyn had thrown Jack out three months earlier, we had been dating, like a regular couple, like normal people. We had gone out to dinner, seen movies. We had gone to a play, to the opera, even twice to the ballet before I confessed my loathing for it. We had gone to three Mets games, and to Yankee Stadium once, but only because Jack had a friend with season tickets right behind home plate, and because they were playing the Red Sox and ever since college I have been partial to the Red Sox. We were having an office romance, surreptitious only in the way those always are. We no longer slipped out for long lunches, snacking on room service and one another's bodies while pretending no more than a passing acquaintance in front of other people at work. Not that we were obvious. We refrained from heavy petting in the firm cafeteria, but we allowed ourselves to arrive at the same time in the morning, even to stand side by side in line for our coffee at the Italian bakery in the lobby of the building. We made love at night, always in Jack's new apartment on the Upper West Side, on the mattress and box spring that lay on the floor of his bedroom. Jack never came to my apartment. I slept over at his place three or four nights a week, never more, sometimes less. But I kept none of my things there. Instead, I carried a large purse with extra panties, a toothbrush, and a makeup bag. I kept two or three suits and a few blouses hanging in dry cleaning bags on the back of my office door and six or seven pair of shoes lined up under my desk.

I was never at Jack's apartment when William stayed over; I was never there unless we had a prearranged date the evening before. That we would spend our nights together was not taken for granted. If Jack called during the day and asked me to dinner, then I knew we would sleep together. If I asked him on a Tuesday to go to a concert that Saturday, then we would make love on Saturday night. Sometimes, when we were both working late, Jack would call and ask if I wanted to come over to his place for a late dinner or to watch a movie. There was always a pretext for the evenings Jack and I spent in each other's company. Never would one of us suggest simply going home from work in order to be together, to make love, to sleep. We were dating, which meant we had to do something, even if that something was as simple as watching a DVD.

But in the week before the perfect moment, Jack had called only once, to cancel a date we had with Simon and his boyfriend to go to an opening of an art show in Chelsea. We had planned to meet at seven, to take a quick whirl through the pieces—the artist did something with pulleys and string—and then go to dinner at Man Ray. Jack begged off on account of work, unmoved even by my pleas that without him I would not have the strength to face a pretentious art show and a pretentious meal in the company of the pretentious lover of my best friend. Then the artist, the newly coronated darling of the West Chelsea gallery district, put the moves on Simon's boyfriend and Simon and I ended up alone at the Red Cat, sharing a plate of fried sardines and bemoaning the perfidy of men.

Jack and I ate only one meal together that week, dinner at his desk. I decided to surprise him one night, and ordered in and billed both meals to the client I was working for, figuring that the waste management company could afford the extra tempura udon. Jack's office was empty, but I found him in the conference room down the hall, eating a slice of pizza with the team of associates he was keeping busy working long hours on a petition for certiorari that would be denied later in the month. He saw the white paper bag in my hand and put his half-eaten slice of pizza on a paper plate.

"Take your time," he said to the young lawyers. "I'll be back in a bit."

We were about halfway down the hall when we heard the room break up into a quickly hushed burst of laughter.

"Well, that was humiliating," I said as I followed him into his office. "Sorry."

"No, it's fine," he said.

We ate quickly. I could tell right away that the piece of pizza Jack left behind had not been his first. He sipped at his soup, taking only a few mouthfuls of noodles before laying his chopsticks across the top of the bowl. After I was done eating, Jack went back to work and I went home to my own apartment. By Saturday morning it had been five days since we'd slept in the same bed, and six since we'd made love. I waited for Jack to call, hovering over my telephone like a character in a Dorothy Parker short story. I forced myself to go to the deli for coffee and a doughnut, but lacked the fortitude to leave my cell phone behind. I put it in my pocket, with the ringer on both high and vibrate. By two in the afternoon I was terrified that Jack was planning on leaving me, and by four I knew that he already had. At that point, with nothing left to lose, I went to Jack's apartment. Those were the days before I took cabs so readily, when I was still paying off student loans and had more patience for changing trains. I sat on the subway and stared at my fellow miscreants, the rest of the city's rabble who, like me, had no place to escape even on a holiday weekend. No one looked particularly pathetic, except for a crippled man working the Times Square Shuttle. He slid from car to car on an upholstered cart, his wizened legs origamied beneath him. I gave him five dollars, as a reward for being more miserable than I was.

Ivan, working on a rare Saturday, let me wait for Jack on the divan in the lobby, the one on which I have never since seen anyone sit. I think mine may be the only buttocks to have creased the floral silk upholstery. If that's true, and if the purple ladies from the other floors find out, they will not be happy. I have never, after all, been approved by the co-op board.

Ivan gave me a *Time* magazine and a shortbread cookie. I felt like a small child, little Miss Greenleaf waiting in the lobby. When Jack arrived, carrying his squash racquet and a gym bag, I had just declined, for the third time, a Dixie cup of Diet Coke.

Jack looked neither happy nor surprised to see me. He held the elevator door open with his arm and, once we were out of Ivan's view, bussed me lightly on the lips. We walked into his empty apartment—despite having lived there for three months, Jack had not furnished it with more than a kitchen table and chairs, the mattress and box springs on the floor of his bedroom, and an ugly highboy foisted on him by an aggressive antique dealer. The only room in the house that was fully furnished was William's. Jack had allowed William to decorate his own room, and the resulting design was a combination dinosaur hatchery and pirate's lair. They had found a bed and matching dresser at a furniture store out in New Jersey that had a vaguely seafaring air to it, with loops of rope across the faces of the drawers instead of pulls. William had distributed his collection of two-foot dinosaurs on top of the dresser and along the floor in front of the built-in bookcase. He had dozens of these rubberized plastic dinosaurs, every species the Museum of Natural History had to offer, even ones I'd never heard of like Maiasaurus and Hypsilophodon. Jack had done his best to replicate exactly the contents of the bookcase William had at Carolyn's house, and there was something heartbreaking about the rows of hardback books—*Ferdinand the Bull*; the famous *House on East 88th Street*; *Mike Mulligan and His Steam Shovel*; *Dinosaur Bob*—jackets bright and shiny, bindings firm and unbent, pages bearing none of the smudges left by years of a child's eager fingers.

Jack propped his racquet in a corner of the empty living room. "Do you want something to drink? A glass of wine or a beer? Some water?"

I shook my head.

"I think I'll have a beer. It's so incredibly hot out there," he said.

I followed him into the kitchen and watched while he opened the fridge and took a bottle from the cardboard six-pack on the shelf. Except for the beer, Jack's fridge was stocked for a lactose-intolerant three-year-old, with packages of tortellini, grapes and baby carrots, and a dozen containers of soy milk.

I watched him lift the bottle to his lips and tilt his head back. His Adam's apple was sharp in his throat, a perfect triangle shifting up and down with his swallow.

"I think I should move in here with you," I said.

Jack set the bottle down on his kitchen table and looked at me with his velvet eyes, soft and dark as navy blue ink.

Here is what we did not say:

I did not say, I know you are planning to leave me. Don't. Don't leave me.

He did not say, I'm sorry, Emilia. I can't do this. I can't move so quickly into another relationship. My marriage has barely ended. I'm not in any shape to start over again with someone new.

But you love me, I didn't say.

That doesn't matter, he didn't reply. I just can't right now. I'm confused. I'm in pain. I need room to figure out how to be without Carolyn and William before I can figure out how to be with someone else.

Here is something else we didn't say:

I did not say, You are mine. You cannot leave me because you are mine.

He didn't reply, I cannot bear how much you want me. I cannot stand the force of your desire. It has burned through my family, separated me from my son. I cannot be with you because I am afraid you will burn through me, too. You will set me on fire and there will be nothing left of me that isn't black and smoldering.

I did not say, You love me, too. You want me that way, too. I didn't burn your house down by myself. You are your own arsonist.

He did not say, That may be true, but that's even more reason for you to go away. Arson, fire. Who needs this shit? Take your thermal haze and get the hell out of here.

And here is yet more we didn't say:

He did not say, My son does not love you.

I did not say, It doesn't matter. I love you so much that it will spill over you like golden light. My love will fill your ink blue eyes and blind you to what I don't feel for your son.

This is what was said:

Jack said, "Can you live without furniture?"

Chapter 23

Since Sunday night Jack and I have spoken in modulated voices, treating each conversation as if it is an outing over cracking ice too thin to bear the weight of our remorse. We do not discuss William, or the Meer, or how close we came to uttering unthinkable words. We just tiptoe around each other, taking such exaggerated care with every comment, every gesture that it feels like we are a couple of lunatics trapped in a very pretty three-bedroom asylum. Even the refusal of a second cup of coffee is suddenly so fraught that breakfast is exhausting enough to force me back to my bed for two hours of restorative napping after Jack has left for work. One of the blessings of Jack's being a partner in a law firm is that he can arrive home at ten or eleven o'clock at night without having to make even the excuse of an unusually heavy workload, so at least we are spared achingly courteous takeout dinners.

This morning Jack wakes early and stands over me, elegant and handsome in his dark gray suit and pink shirt, his hair wet from the shower, his fresh-shaved cheek fragrant from the astringent lotion I buy him.

"Are you awake?"

"Yes."

"Did you sleep well?"

"Yes, very well."

"I have a deposition this afternoon so I can't pick up William after school."

"That's fine."

"Would you prefer it if I called Carolyn and asked her to have Sonia stay with him until I finish work?"

"No, I'll get him."

"Are you sure?"

"Yes."

"Because it's no problem."

"I said, I'll get him." My voice is harsh. I have violated our rule of polite discourse and I cringe.

Jack leans over and wipes a speck of invisible lint off the toe of his shiny black loafer. To his shoe he says, "What are you going to do with him?"

"I don't know, I thought I'd pitch him into the model boat pond. Unless it's frozen over, in which case I'll try the Lake."

He stands up, his face grim, unsmiling.

"I'll bring him home," I say. "I'll give him a nondairy snack, and we'll play Lego or dinosaurs until you get home."

"You could rent a DVD."

"I don't need to rent a DVD. He's not allowed to watch TV, remember? We'll be fine."

"If you're sure."

"I'm sure. It will be fine."

Jack nods. He buttons his suit jacket, and then unbuttons it. "I've been thinking about that thing in the park. That Walk to Remember."

"You have?" I haven't. I have not thought about it at all.

"Do you still want to go?" he asks. He does not give me time to answer. "I think we should go. All three of us. I think it'll be good for us. We should do it together."

"Okay," I say.

He leans over the bed, stopping with his lips a few inches from mine. I lift my face and close the distance between us. It is the first time we've kissed since before the incident at the Meer, since our fight. It's a plain kiss, not particularly soft or tender, but it is familiar and firm.

"I'll see you tonight," he says.

"Don't worry. William and I will be fine."

We aren't, of course. When William sees me waiting for him outside the Red Room, he frowns. He cocks his head to one side, seems to be considering his possibilities, evaluating the situation. Then he walks over.

"I'm not going with you," he says.

"It's Wednesday, William. On Wednesdays you come to our house."

"Not today."

"Yes, today. Today is Wednesday."

"No, Emilia." William shakes his head firmly. "I'm not going with you. Not anymore. You threw me in a lake. In Harlem."

"It was the Harlem *Meer*. And I did not throw you in. You slipped. We slipped. It was an accident. Accidents happen. Get your coat on."

"No!" William yells.

Sharlene pops her head out of the Red Room, her attention attracted by the vehemence of his cry. "Use your inside voice, William," she says.

"Tell Emilia I'm not going with her," he says and runs to the door. He ducks under Sharlene's arm and into the classroom.

"Oh for God's sake," I mutter, following him. One or two of the nannies give me sympathetic smiles. They've been there; they know what it's like to deal with a recalcitrant child whom you are not permitted to discipline but for whose behavior you are responsible. The mothers, on the other hand, shake their heads or cast disapproving scowls my way. Who am I to impose my adulterous presence on a little boy who wants only his mother, his real mother, the one who should never have been usurped in the first place?

"I'm sorry about this," I say to Sharlene when I walk into the classroom. "Come on William. We've got to go."

"William is having a hard day, Emilia," Sharlene says. "He's been having a difficult time processing what happened in the park this past weekend."

I no longer love and admire Sharlene. Sharlene is an idiot. Sharlene should not be allowed to teach small children.

"There's not a whole lot to process. He slipped and fell. His feet got wet. It's no big deal."

"I think it was a big deal to William. I think he's having a hard time feeling safe with you right now. Safety and security is a big issue for children, particularly for those whose sense of stability in the world has been compromised by divorce or other trauma."

Sharlene is sitting next to William in the book nook. He has taken out an oversized dinosaur reference book and is reading it, licking his forefinger and ostentatiously turning the pages. I stand over them, shifting from foot to foot. I am hot in my winter coat.

"William," I say. "I'm sorry about the Meer. I'm sorry you got wet. I'm sorry about all of it. I just wanted to show you that part of

Central Park. The Harlem Meer is one of my favorite places and I wanted to show it to you. I had hoped you would like it as much as I do."

William squints and leans closer to his book.

"William," I say. "If you come right now I'll take you to buy a copy of *The Secret Garden*. You can prove to me that it's not too hard for you. And we can get the other Lyle books, too. All you've got at our house is *The House on East 88th Street*."

Sharlene takes her hand and lays it gently over the page. "William, are you ready to go home with Emilia?"

"No," he says.

"Do you think you might be ready soon?"

"No."

She removes her hand. "I think we should call Jack or Carolyn," she says. "I don't like to force him, not when he's feeling so fragile."

William is about as fragile as the outcroppings of schist on the bluffs above the Meer.

"Fine," I say. "I'll call Jack." Jack, however, is not at the office. Jack is not reachable on his cell phone. Jack, according to Marilyn, is in a hearing and will not be free before five o'clock.

"William isn't registered for any afternoon programs," Sharlene says.

"We're going home, William," I say.

"No!" William bellows.

"I'm afraid I don't think we have a choice," Sharlene says. "I'm going to have to call Carolyn."

"Of course you are," I say. "Why not? Things haven't quite deteriorated to a complete shambles. I still have one or two tiny shreds of dignity. You'd better call Carolyn so we can lay waste to what's left."

"Emilia, this isn't about you. It's about William."

"Tell me about it," I say.

I wait for Carolyn. Not because I am a masochist, not because I believe I deserve the laceration she is bound to give me, but because today is Wednesday and Wednesday is Jack's day with William. I can't just leave and deliver him into the hands of the enemy with nary a peep. I want Jack to know I went down kicking and screaming.

Carolyn swoops into the Red Room like an avenging angel, like a mother hawk come to rescue her fluffy chick. She is smooth and sleek, smooth hair, smooth skin, smooth lips, long sleek legs, long sleek cashmere coat. I can actually feel myself growing shorter and more rotund. In a few minutes I will be a hobbit.

She gathers William to her narrow, stingy bosom and says, "William, darling. Are you all right? My poor darling. Are you frightened?"

Sharlene seems embarrassed by this lavish display of inappropriate maternal concern. "He's fine, Carolyn. He's just having some difficulty with the schedule this week, that's all."

Sure, be sensible now, traitor, I say silently.

"William, darling, there's no need for you to go to your father's house," Carolyn says. "Sonia is waiting in the lobby. You're coming home."

"It's Wednesday," I say, as if that is the problem. As if William is confused about what day it is. As if William has not been reciting the days of the week, in order, since he was fifteen months old.

Carolyn shoots me a malevolent look. She hustles William to his feet and out the door. I follow. On my way out I pass the clothesline drooping with family drawings. I spot William's right away; it is the only one taped down the middle. I peer at it, trying to discern the features of the lightly drawn angel baby. She has curly hair, and she is smiling. Her wings are very elaborate, decorated with curlicues, hearts, and, for some reason, dollar signs. Isabel makes a pretty angel. William has done a beautiful job.

"Isn't it lovely?" Sharlene says.

"Yes," I say, and leave the classroom.

When the door to my elevator opens to the lobby, I see Carolyn and William just stepping out of theirs. I curse the notoriously unreliable 92nd Street Y elevators, steel myself, and follow them. Carolyn hands Sonia the booster seat and grips William's mittened paw.

"Hello, Sonia," I say.

Sonia nods. "Hello, Emilia."

"You really take the cake," Carolyn says to me.

"What?"

"You have some goddamn nerve. Trying to force yourself on my son after what you did to him. It's sick. You're a sick person, you know that?"

The lobby of the 92nd Street Y is full of people heading up to the gym, old women on their way to the senior citizens' center, parents of preschool children, older children attending after-school programs. Carolyn's voice is low but it carries. We are putting on a little show.

"I didn't do anything to William. It was an accident. We slipped, and his feet got wet. It was water, for heaven's sake, not hydrochloric acid."

"How dare you?" Carolyn steps up to me and pushes her pretty face close to mine. The irises of her eyes are pale blue. Even the whites of her eyes are blue-tinged, like skim milk.

"How dare I what?" I say, backing away slightly.

"You took him to Harlem!" she hisses. "And don't think I don't know about the skating. You sent him out on the ice without a helmet. You're lucky he wasn't killed."

I sigh. William ratted me out.

"You have some objection to your child visiting Harlem?" The woman who has interrupted our conversation is about four and a half feet tall, no more. She has a dowager's hump and wields her walker like a weapon. Her voice is deep and raspy; it holds too much gravel to come from such a brittle, bird-boned frame. "You say Harlem like it's so terrible. You should be ashamed, young lady."

Carolyn steps away from me, and looks down at my defending crone, her mouth agape.

The old woman continues, her face raised to us like a wrinkled moon. "Many a night I danced in Harlem, listened to music, ate dinner. All alone or with my girlfriends. We had no carfare, we walked home. All the way. No one laid a finger on us. So you should maybe think again before you make such criticisms of Harlem. And let me ask you this." She raises a gnarled finger and shakes it at Carolyn. She is so small that she is shaking it not in Carolyn's face but at her belt. "Do you pay her social security taxes, this young girl you're yelling at? Do you put money into a pension plan for her? What about overtime? Do you pay time and a half? Maybe instead of criticizing your nanny for showing your child the city in all its beauty you should be thinking about behaving less like an overprivileged fat cat!"

"She is not my nanny," Carolyn says. "She is my husband's wife. And I'd kindly ask you to mind your own damn business."

"It is my business, my friend. It takes a village to raise a child. You should read the book. Hillary Clinton. It's wonderful. I'm your village, my dear, whether you like it or not." The old woman humps her walker away, toddling along behind it.

"I'm not just Jack's wife," I say. "I'm also William's stepmother."

"And what does *that* mean?" Carolyn says. "I'll tell you what. Nothing. It means nothing. You have no rights to my child. None. None, do you understand me? If you ever cause him harm again, if you ever throw him into a lake, or take him to Harlem, or take him skating, or even into Central Park, so help me God, I will have you arrested for child abuse."

Carolyn has not, I notice, mentioned ice cream. Clearly there are some secrets William is still happy to keep.

Carolyn leans her face so close to mine that one of her long, fine, brown hairs, lifted by the static electricity of the forced heat of the room and her rage, hovers between us and attaches itself lightly to my lip. "Stay away from my son," she says, a mist of saliva spraying my face with every sibilant *S*.

"Carolyn," Sonia says, very softly. "Dr. Soule. Carolyn." She tugs gently on Carolyn's arm, pulling her away from me. "Not in front of the boy." She points to William who is standing, his hand still clasped by his mother's, but his whole body leaning away, like a water-skier pulling back on the bar. His face is turned to the floor, almost parallel to it, and as we stare at him a tear splashes down, then another. He is crying silently, motionlessly, his body not wracked by sobs, not trembling with weeping, just taut like wire strung against the restraining hand of his mother, tears dripping onto the dirty stone slabs of the lobby floor.

Sonia slips an arm around her employer, easing her away from me. Then she loosens Carolyn's grip on William's hand and substitutes her own. Strangely, Carolyn allows herself to be led, succumbing to the temperate authority of this young woman. She backs off and then whirls away, storming across the lobby and out the front door, leaving Sonia, William, and me standing in a stunned little clot in the middle of the room.

"Thank you," I say.

Sonia nods, picks up the booster seat that Carolyn has left lying on the floor, and leads William out the door. I follow them, and watch as they dodge around the cement planters to where Carolyn is waiting impatiently, one hand on her hip. I stay near the exit, as far from them as I can be, as Carolyn waves down a cab with a snap of her fingers. She has more luck than I do, even with the dreaded booster seat. She opens the door and holds it for Sonia, who gets in and installs the seat. William climbs in and Sonia buckles him, testing the straps to make sure they are tight. Carolyn leans inside and says something to the driver. Then she slams the door and lifts her arm to hail a second cab.

Chapter 24

When the driver of my taxi asks me where I am going, I hesitate, unable to bear the idea of going back to our apartment where I will have nothing to do but wait for Jack to come home so I can confess what has happened. Instead I say, "Le Pain Quotidien, on Madison and Eighty-fifth."

I sit once again at the community table, and while there are no babies, there is a little boy, a few years younger than William. He is eating a chocolate cupcake and I wonder if it is dairy free. I order my latte, and am about to order a strawberry cupcake with which to soothe the ache knotting my stomach from my horrible encounter with William's mother, when instead I ask for a vanilla cupcake with chocolate frosting, dairy free like the one William gets.

"Did you want soy milk in that latte?" the waitress asks.

"No," I say.

She looks confused for a moment and then shrugs, as if she has already spent too much time puzzling the intricate eating disorders of neurotic East Side matrons and has vowed not to squander any more.

When the cupcake comes I lick the frosting and then take a bite of the cake. It's surprisingly tasty, light and fluffy, with little of the oily texture I would have expected from butter-free pastry. Still, William is right, it isn't as good as the strawberry cupcake. I lick the frosting thoughtfully, swirling my tongue through the chocolate.

I would not have expected William to cry like that. He is too young to be embarrassed by a scene, and it must have been, after all, what he wanted. He had all but insisted that Carolyn come and rescue him from me. And yet, when she bore down with her righteous and bilious indignation, he had cried.

I wave to the waitress.

"Is the pastry chef here?" I ask.

"There is no pastry chef," she says. "We have everything made at a production facility in Long Island City."

"What about the owner?"

"It's a chain. Why, is there something wrong?"

"No, no. Nothing. Everything's great. It's just . . . I sort of have a suggestion."

She sighs. "I'll get the manager," she says.

When he comes the manager is extraordinarily polite, but firm, as if he has become accustomed, by virtue of the restaurant's address, to dealing with a certain kind of patron, one who views complaint as not merely a right but an obligation, one who does not hesitate to write scathing letters to corporate directors and throw shrill and costly tantrums in crowded restaurants.

"What can I do for you, madam? Is there some problem I can help you with?" he says in an accent of undefined European origin.

"No, not at all. There's no problem at all. It's just. My stepson is allergic to dairy. Sort of. Anyway, he thinks he is, and his mother never lets him eat dairy. He loves the dairy-free cupcakes here. But you only make them with chocolate and vanilla frosting. I was wondering if you might consider adding pink frosting to the menu."

"Ah," he says.

"Because he had some of my pink cupcake, and he loved it."

"He is allergic to dairy but he ate the regular cupcake?" The manager is perturbed, as if he can already imagine the cupcake litigation; he can see in his mind's eye the depositions, the discovery requests demanding release of secret recipes, the expert witnesses—scientists with multiple degrees in lactose intolerance and the digestion of dairy enzymes.

"He's not really allergic. He just thinks he is."

"But you want him to have dairy-free cupcakes nonetheless?"

Well, no, I don't want to indulge this insanity, but his mother insists on it. "Yes."

"Ah."

"So I just thought you might consider making dairy-free strawberry cupcakes."

"I will present your suggestion to Claudio, the head of our production facility."

"Thank you. Thank you so much."

"Not at all, madam. Please, enjoy your cupcake. You are eating now the dairy free, I see."

"Yes. Just to try it."

"Ah."

"To see if it's as good. As the regular cupcake."

"And is it?"

"No."

"Ah."

"It's very good. Really. Delicious. It's just, you know. Not *as* good."

The manager leaves me to finish my cupcake and think how happy William will be if Claudio takes my suggestion seriously and adds pink to his dairy-free repertoire. Perhaps William will be so pleased that he will forget what happened in the lobby of his school. He will forget how his mother and I made him feel. He will be overcome by the bliss of a strawberry cupcake and he will forget the rage in his mother's face when she looked at me. I wish there was a cupcake that delicious.

What will it take for me to forget, I wonder?

"Where's William?"

These are the first words out of Jack's mouth, before he even hangs his coat up in the hall closet, while his umbrella is still dripping water down the sides of the tall, galvanized bucket in the hallway outside our front door.

"At his mother's."

Standing in the front hall, I explain what happened, and I can see Jack begin to shrink. His long black raincoat loosens, hangs lower toward the floor, the shoulders droop, the cuffs hide his hand. He is contracting and shriveling before my eyes. Telescoping into his despair. He shucks his coat and it puddles onto the floor. He drops his briefcase on top of it. He walks by me, trailing raindrops from the wet cuffs of his pants. I follow him down the long hall into our bedroom.

"It will be all right," I say hopefully. I am hovering close to him, but not touching. I am afraid to touch him. It is as if we are poles of like magnets and between us is a palpable field of energy, pushing us apart. Or, rather, pushing me away from him. I sit down on the bed. My feet are flat on the floor, my back is straight, my knees are pressed primly together. I look like a schoolgirl awaiting a scolding.

Jack says, "Oh *shit*." He looks at his watch, and then at the clock on the nightstand as if verifying that it really is 6:17. "Shit."

I say, "Do you think we should go get him? I mean, you. You should go get him. Should you go get him?"

"I don't know."

I must figure out a way to change the ringer on our telephone. Something less malevolent. Something that doesn't scream "Carolyn" quite so loudly.

"Shit," Jack says. His "hello" is so wary it is nearly comical. So is his relief. "It's your mom," he says, passing me the phone after an obligatory moment of stilted conversation.

"Hi," I say. I have not spoken to my mother since I abandoned her on that suburban main street, and I gear myself up to apologize.

"What's wrong?" she says.

"Nothing. Nothing's wrong. Wait, do you mean now? Or like, because of the other night?"

She clucks her tongue. "Forget about the other night. The other night doesn't matter. I just wanted to make sure we're still on for that memorial walk."

"Yes. I mean, I think so." I cover the mouthpiece with my hand. "She wants to make sure we're still going to the Walk to Remember."

Jack is standing in the middle of the bedroom, holding the lapels of his suit jacket as if trying to decide whether to take it off. "Why?"

"She wants to come."

"Oh. I guess so. I mean, sure."

"Mom?" I say. "Meet us at four at Strawberry Fields."

"Let me write that down," she says, and just then the call waiting beeps.

"Hold on a second," I say and press the flash button. Now it is, of course, Carolyn.

"I'd like to speak to Jack, please."

"Hello, Carolyn." I am impressed with how cool my voice is, given the knot in my stomach. It must be the lawyer in me. I am not my father's daughter for nothing. "One moment," I say. I click back over to my mother. "It's Carolyn."

"Do you have to go?" my mother says.

"Yup. I'll see you at the thing, okay?"

"Yes. Um, honey?"

"I really have to go."

"Okay. I love you, sweetheart."

"I love you, too, Mom."

I hand over the phone. Poor Jack. I toss his son into the Harlem Meer and get into a fight with his ex-wife, but it is he who must stand in his stocking feet with her voice boring a hole in his eardrum. I am impressed with the job he does defending me, although it is true that I've given him all the ammunition; he simply uses the phrases I coined when defending myself against *his* opprobrium.

"It was an accident."

"They tripped and fell."

"It's only a little water and mud."

I feel especially gratified when he tells her that she is overreacting. Jack improves on me significantly by telling Carolyn that he fears she has become hydrophobic. That's a very good word. I wait for him to suggest aversion therapy or flooding—I'm ready to volunteer to dump the woman into the Meer myself—but he is not so sarcastic as that. Alas, by the end of the conversation, he is apologizing. And then he says, "Well, thank you. Thank you for that. I do appreciate it."

"Thank you?" I say, horrified. "For what? Thank you for what?"

He waves his hand, silencing me. A moment later he hangs up the phone.

"What the hell were you *thanking* her for?"

"She said she hadn't intended to say anything about the incident. She was apparently just going to let it go, but when William got so upset, she didn't feel like she had a choice."

"The *incident*." I laugh bitterly. "You thanked her for changing her mind and yelling at you after all?"

"I thanked her for being willing to let it go. I'm just *managing* her, Emilia. Don't you see that? Don't you understand that that's what I have to do? I have to *manage* her. Jesus, you'd think you of all people would understand that."

"Why? Because you have to manage me, too?"

"I didn't say that."

"But that's what you meant."

"Can we just stop this, Emilia?" He yanks off his jacket and throws it on the little armchair. His tie quickly follows. He unbuttons the top button of his shirt and sits down heavily on the bed next to me. He rubs his hands roughly across his face. "I'm just so tired of all this."

I grab his hand and hold it in both of mine. "I'm sorry. I'm sorry. I can't believe I even said that. This whole thing is totally my fault." I kiss his palm. "I'm sorry Jack."

"I know."

I pull his palm to my cheek and rest my face on it. It's smooth against my skin. "Do you think William can still come with us to the walk?" I say.

"What?"

"You know, the Walk to Remember. What my mom was just calling about. It's next Sunday afternoon. The 29th. Leap day. Or whatever you call it. The last day of February."

Jack lets his hand stay against my face but he does not cup my cheek like I want him to. "Do you still *want* him to come?" he says.

"I *need* him to come." And I do. I need all of us to be there together, even William, *especially* William, so that I can show him that I am trying to put things back together, to become the kind of stepmother who doesn't drop you into icy water. The kind whom you can trust to change your soiled pants. If William joins us on the walk through the park, I can begin the reconstruction of my life and our family.

I tell this to Jack and though he seems unconvinced, he says, "He'll be there."

"But Carolyn said I couldn't take him to the park anymore."

"It's not Carolyn's decision."

Chapter 25

In the late afternoon of Sunday, February 29th, Jack, William, and I make our way downtown in the direction of Strawberry Fields and the black-and-white, circular Imagine mosaic where the Walk to Remember will begin. Ever conscientious and rule abiding, I made sure to register online, even though doing so required me to fill in a blank for the name and birthday of my "precious baby." I paid the $20 fee, the very top of the sliding scale, but declined to order a commemorative Walk to Remember T-shirt or sweatshirt from RTS Bereavement Services.

I have no idea how many people to expect at this event. As we walk down Central Park West toward Seventy-second Street, I keep eyeing the passersby, on the lookout for others who might be headed to the walk. A melancholy woman pushing her sadness in front of her like an empty stroller seems certain to be one of us, but when she drags herself up the front steps under the marquee of the elegant Langham, into the warm glow of the lobby, I remind myself that there are reasons for dejection besides my own. We follow two blond women in ski parkas into the park. Despite their vocal cheer and their very tall cups of coffee, they are walkers and rememberers.

"This is your gate, Emilia," William says.

"What do you mean?"

"It's Women's Gate. That's the name. West Seventy-second Street is the Women's Gate."

I cannot enjoy William's chatter about the park. I appreciate the fact that he has learned so much about this place that I love, but I am far too anxious this afternoon to participate in his pleasure.

Strawberry Fields is overrun with dead-baby people. There are far too many to fit comfortably in the area of the mosaic; they spill out over the pathways onto the area behind the benches that in summer is a grassy meadow and now, in winter, is nothing but a bank of hard-packed earth. Some are even gathering as far away as the gnarled and naked wisteria arbors. In the center of the mosaic stands a woman with a clipboard, checking people in. A long line snakes around her and the two women scrambling through a large cardboard box at her feet.

"I'll go sign in," I say to Jack.

By the time I have worked my way to the front of the line I am regretting my decision to come this afternoon. It is cold and uncomfortable here in Strawberry Fields. People are smiling too kindly at one another, and there are women wearing oversized Walk to Remember T-shirts on top of their coats. They are circulating through the crowd waving boxes of tissue. Most people are wearing large white stars pinned to their coats. The stars have names printed on them, and I wonder if I'm the only one who thinks they are uncomfortably reminiscent of the yellow stars of Nazi Germany. While we wait in line I read the names on the stars pinned to the coats of the people around me. "Jacob 12/16/03," "Tallulah Lee 3/3/01." Some women have more than one name printed on their stars, and I wonder what bad luck has poisoned their lives. I am startled by a woman wearing a hot-pink coat and turquoise Ugg boots, whose star has three names on it. I peer at it more closely. Two of the names are only three months apart and the third is six months later. I realize, with a vertigo that almost knocks me off my feet, that this woman has named her miscarriages. Henry Marcus, Jackson Felipe, and Lucy Julianne. How, I wonder, did she determine their gender? Surely in at least one case it was too early for ultrasound to detect a sex.

I know it is unfair to feel disgust for this pink-clad, perky blonde. After all, at the very least she has had a terrible time maintaining a pregnancy. I know how much grief there is in that. I've seen how wretched it has made Mindy to lose one pregnancy after another. This woman looks like she would be a perfect mother, a mother who would insist on moving to Westchester or New Jersey so that her children would not have to ride their bikes in small circles in front of the doorman, a mother who would be an active participant on UrbanBaby.com, sharing her goodwill and knowledge, a mother who would pack attractive and well-balanced lunches complete with a cold pack to keep the turkey breast fresh, a mother who would use a melon baller so that her children would eat papaya and cantaloupe for breakfast. I have no right to condemn her just because she has given her miscarriages middle names.

I have a sudden, sickening thought. Has Mindy named her miscarriages, too? I hope not. I hope she is one of the women with a list of dates on her star and nothing else. That is bad enough.

"What's your angel's name?"

"Excuse me?" I say.

"Your little star? Your baby?" The woman with the clipboard is making a sad-clown face with her head cocked to one side and her eyebrows bunched together. It is disturbingly like the one Simon sometimes makes. Still, her voice is very nice. Melodic. Soothing.

"Isabel. Isabel Woolf."

She flips to a back page and makes a check mark. Then she points to the women with the box. "They have your stars. There's one to wear, and one made out of cellulose to float in the pond at the end of the walk."

I am about to get my star when I notice the one pinned on her heavy pea coat. It has only one name. William 7/19/98.

"Oh," I say.

Her hand flutters to her star. "I've been doing these walks for a long time," she says.

"No, it's not that. It's just . . . that's my stepson's name."

She smiles. "It's a nice name."

"It is."

She strokes the star, like it is her child's soft, downy hair. "It was my grandfather's name. Billy was named after him. We called him Billy, though. William seems like such a grown-up name for a little boy."

"How did . . . never mind, that's none of my business."

"No, no. It's fine to ask. People here like to talk about their babies. For most of us it's the only time we get to talk about them. SIDS. Billy died of SIDS."

"Isabel, too. That's how Isabel died."

She leans closer to me, bends her head so that our murmuring cannot be overheard. "It's a terrible way to lose them. However it happens is bad, but SIDS is the worst. I mean, of course I'd think that, but I know I'm right. It's the mystery of it. Never knowing why it happened."

I back away from her secretive and seductive confidence. In a normal, conversational tone, I ask, "Do you have other kids?"

I can tell that she is hurt by my refusal to accept her intimacy. Still she says, "Of course. Billy was our second, and we've had two more since he passed away. I've got four. Four with Billy. Three living. And now I'd better finish with this line. We're going to start the walk soon. Don't forget to take a candle for every member of your party."

I hold the cardboard star with Isabel's name and date of birth. Her name looks so odd without the surname. Just Isabel Greenleaf. As though Jack were not part of her life at all. When we gave her my last name as a middle name it never occurred to either of us that she would ever be known by just the first two parts of her name. I don't want to pin this star on my lapel.

"Emilia," Jack says, appearing at my elbow. "I found your mom and dad."

"My mom and *dad*?"

There, standing in the gray afternoon light, holding William's hand tightly in his own, is my father, a proud, shy smile on his face. Look, his smile says. Look what a fine and understanding man I am. I have picked up my ex-wife and driven across the George Washington Bridge in order to show my grandfatherly support. My father is a mild-looking man, he looks like Clark Kent ought to have looked, had he really wanted to retain his anonymity. He is about five foot six, of middling weight, although after the divorce he acquired a paunch borne of restaurant meals and breakfasts of Krispy Kremes. His hair is gray, almost white, and floats over his freckled, pink scalp as if it is waiting for a heavy wind to blow it away once and for all. When he is running for president of the bar association, or when he is meeting a friend of one of his children for the first time, he gives the impression of joviality. He is prone to bursts of high spirits and optimism and to occasional deep black moods, flashes of inexplicable rage.

"I'm so sorry we're late," my mother said. "You wouldn't think there would be traffic going in this direction on a Sunday in the middle of winter. And then parking. You know your father, he'll never just put the car in a lot. We kept circling and circling. I was afraid we'd miss the whole thing." She is talking rapidly, giving me time to overcome my surprise at seeing my father here, at seeing them together.

"How did you know about the walk?" I ask him.

"I told him," William says, matter-of-factly. He is swinging my father's arm back and forth and over, like a jump rope. I used to do that when I was a little girl.

"*You* told him?"

My father says, "I called the other day, didn't William give you the message? You two were on your way to explore the pinetum."

I say, "We weren't going to the pinetum. You were the one who said we should go to the pinetum. We went to the Ramble. And to the Conservatory Garden."

"And to the Harlem Meer," William says ominously. Then he laughs and slips under my father's arm, like a square dancer.

My father tugs William back and spins him out a few times. They are the only people giggling and dancing at the Walk to Remember and I wish they would stop.

"Young William told me about this event, and when I found out your mother was going, I thought to myself, Old Man Greenleaf, you should do this with your family. After all, how long has it been since you've seen the luminaires all lit up?"

"That's what *I* said!" William crows. "I said I wanted to come because I wanted to see the luminaires!"

"Aren't you going to put on your star, honey?" my mother asks.

I look down at the cardboard star in my hand. I have been clutching it too tightly and one point is crumpled. I try to smooth it out, but the crease remains. I pin the star to my chest and the bent point sticks out at an angle.

"I only have four candles," I say.

"I'll get another one," Jack says. In a moment he returns and we busy ourselves adjusting the wax-paper cones to protect them from the wind.

A few minutes later there is a rustle through the crowd, an expectant buzz. The woman with the clipboard, the mother of the William who slipped away in the middle of the night, like Isabel, calls out in her clear bell of a voice, "Welcome to this special leap year Walk to Remember. We're going to set out in a moment. We'll be walking east to Bethesda Fountain, and then cutting north. If you lose the group for any reason, you'll be able to find us at our final destination, the model boat pond, by the Hans Christian Andersen statue. I'd like to remind you that we try to observe silence on the walk, until the end when we'll have the traditional poetry reading and ceremony."

The crowd slowly unwinds, making its way along the path. My father holds William's hand, and the two of them occasionally whisper to each other. William's whisper is louder than a Shakespearian actor's. It is a stage whisper meant to be heard at the very back of the balcony. A hawk-nosed man in a well-tailored coat glances censoriously our way a few times. Finally, the man's wife puts her hand on his sleeve and together they quicken their pace, moving away from us and our bad behavior.

"Shh," I hiss at my father.

"This child doesn't know who Daniel Webster was!" my father whispers. We are passing the tall bronze sculpture of the frowning orator. William imitates his pose, shoving his hand in the lapel of his jacket, and my father laughs. My father is a Daniel Webster fan. He collects the biographies of dead lawyers: Clarence Darrow, Oliver Wendell Holmes, Louis Nizer.

"Sheldon," my mother whispers to my father. "Shelly be quiet. You're bothering the other people."

Jack puts his arm around my shoulders and hugs me close, laying a soft kiss on my temple. He keeps me moving toward the Angel of the Waters.

By now it is getting dark and the art nouveau luminaires are glowing orange. There is a scrim of ice on the long gentle flight of stairs leading down to Bethesda Terrace and the fountain and we step in the footprints of the walkers who have gone before us, treading carefully so as not to slip. I turn and look for my mother, who is walking behind us. She is wearing winter boots with thick rubber soles and steps more confidently than I.

The walk has paused at the fountain, and people are circling the round pool, their flickering candles reflected in the water. The huge bronze statue rises in the middle, a winged woman held up by four cherubs, curly haired children like the ones we don't have. I stand between Jack and my mother and wait to be moved, wait to be overcome by a transformative, epiphanous healing. I stamp my feet against the cold and my candle goes out.

"Damn it," I mutter.

Jack bends his candle to mine and marries the wicks.

I turn back to the fountain. Across the pool I see the helpers in T-shirts busy distributing their tissues. There are lots of tear-streaked faces. Even some audible sobbing. It takes me a minute to find my father and William. They are standing at the edge of the Lake, throwing rocks into the water. People have begun to drift away, to continue on the walk. I concentrate, desperate to feel something, quickly, before it is too late. This is the time for me to liberate myself from the guilt that lodges like a stone in my gullet. I try to picture Isabel's face, but it is just a baby face, soft and unformed, too much like other babies for me to focus on with any clarity. Instead I think of Emma Stebbins, who designed this sculpture, they say to honor her lover, the actress Charlotte Cushman, who was dying of breast cancer. I've even heard that that's why the angel has such a great rack, because Charlotte did, too, before she underwent the horrors of nineteenth-century mastectomy. But Charlotte Cushman's breasts and Emma Stebbins's overwrought sculpture are not what I am supposed to be contemplating right now.

"Let's keep going," Jack murmurs into my ear. Ever solicitous, he leads us on, my mother and me, a hand for each of us. As we cross the terrace and head north along the path I look back to see if my father and William are following. I can't find them anywhere.

"Where are they?" I say.

Jack looks over at the Lake and then up the terrace.

"What is it?" my mother says. She is still whispering, even though by now the rest of the walkers have passed us and are on their way up the meandering path to the model boat pond.

"Daddy!" I call. "Daddy! William!"

"Stay right here," Jack says. He takes off at a run up the terrace calling William's name. It does not take long. A few moments, only. They had not actually intended to hide and have not gone far. The two of them are in the Arcade, in the tunnel underneath the stairs leading to the terrace.

"Nono is going to come with me to be in the Lyle movie," William says. He stomps his feet up and down, kicking his knees high. "We're practicing our dance steps."

"Do you remember how you and I used to dance like Lyle and Signor Valenti when you were little?" my father says.

"Let's try to catch up to the rest of the group," Jack says.

"Sorry," my father says. "I guess young William and I got a little carried away." It is much darker under the Arcade and all of our candles have gone out.

I can feel it rise in me, the poisonous shame I've been running from for so long. I turn it on him, because he, too, has reasons to be ashamed. "What are you doing here?" I say.

"We didn't want to interrupt the solemn occasion with our high jinks," my father says. "We thought it would be better to practice here, in the Arcade."

"No. Why are you here at all? Why did you bother coming?"

Jack, who has been herding my mother and William in the direction of the terrace, stops. He stands very still, like a soldier whose job it is to diffuse land mines. Slowly, very slowly, he reaches out his hand. I duck away from his grasp.

"Why did you bother coming?" I repeat, my voice louder.

My father looks from me to Jack and then over at my mother. It is too dark to make out his expression. "You know why I came," he says finally. "As a show of support, to you and to Jack."

"You came to play in the park at night."

He laughs uncomfortably. "Now don't be silly, honey. I'm here for you. For you two, and for Isabel."

"Don't you *dare*," I scream. "Don't even say her name!"

Jack moves quickly now. He grabs my upper arm roughly and half leads, half drags me out of the Arcade and onto the terrace. "Let's go," he says. "William!" he calls over his shoulder. "You walk with me now." Out on the terrace Jack pauses, and I know he is trying to decide whether to attempt to catch up to the distant line of tiny glittering candles or just turn back and go home. It is that moment of indecision that allows my father to reach us.

"Emilia!" my father blusters. His hat is askew and he is breathing heavily from his short pursuit. "I will not allow you to speak to me that way."

Fury expands my chest and lifts my chin. Right before I explode I catch my mother's eye. She has run up behind my father and even in the yellow light of Central Park at dusk I can see what she feels. She is so used to this, so used to submitting to the power of my fury. What else, after all, has she been doing all her life but subsuming her happiness, even her hope of happiness, to the whims of everyone else around her, most especially to those of her daughter? So reconciled is she to the havoc I will wreck on the complicated love she has worked out with this man, that she does not even think to ask what right I have to destroy what I can't possibly understand. She is resigned to the inevitable demolition of any contentment she might have rebuilt.

I see this, I know this, but it is too late.

"You won't allow me to speak to you that way?" I snarl at my father.

"I will not."

"You know what I won't allow? I won't allow you near my kid. I won't allow you to touch William, or even to talk to him. I don't want him exposed to any diseases you might have picked up from your stripper."

In the half-light I watch my father's face cave in like a coal mine after an ill-positioned dynamite explosion. First his mouth collapses inward, then his eyes sink. His wrinkles deepen until his face looks like a closed fist.

"Emilia," Jack says. "What are you doing?"

I spin around to my husband. "You know why my parents got divorced? Because my father was spending thousands of dollars a month on a Russian stripper. Sheldon Greenleaf, president of the New Jersey Bar Association and sex addict. Who knows, maybe he was doing that the whole time he was married to my mother. Maybe whenever he'd take his little girls into the city for a day playing in the park and climbing on the Balto statue, he was really looking to get laid."

We are a frozen tableau, silent but for the horrified intake of breath of each one. Then Jack leans down and hoists William into his arms. His strides are long; in moments he is across the terrace and up the steps, taking them two at a time. He is a black smudge against the lamplight. Then he is gone.

"Come Shelly," my mother says. "We'll flag down a cab to take us back to the car." She slips her hand into the crook of my father's arm and they walk slowly away, suddenly much older even than my father's sixty-five years. At the foot of the steps my mother turns back to me. "Catch up to the others," she calls. "It's almost dark and you shouldn't be on your own in the park at night."

And then I am alone. I slip my hands into my pockets and find the second Isabel star, the one I am supposed to float in the water in the model boat pond. Although it is too late for healing, although I cursed and shouted away whatever reparative and rejuvenative dreams I had for this memory walk, I take off after the dead-baby people at a run. There is a tangle of paths leading from the Bethesda Fountain along East Drive to the model boat pond and I'm not sure which one they have taken. I can no longer see the dim line of candles, so I just head up the road and cut over where I think the Hans Christian Andersen statue is. Even though I know this part of the park well, it all changes shape in the dark, reforms and reconstructs itself into a new and strange topography, and until I see the Trefoil Arch I am not entirely sure where I am going. I run down the stairs into the dark hole of the arch, my steps echoing loudly. It is black and terrifying and I am very alone. I burst into the gray light and run up the hill, off the path now, running through mud and dead grass until I see the back of the bronze man seated with his book and his duck.

The crowd is gathered around the water, and I come up in time to hear the last lines of a poem read in a trembling, weeping voice by someone whom I cannot see.

"Your memory is sweet in my heart. A gentle teardrop, a tug in my womb. Forever mine, forever part. A snowdrop, a lily, always in bloom."

I wince. An irreparable rift with my parents, and bad poetry. This is indeed a walk to remember.

In small groups, couples and families, or just women on their own, people approach the model boat pond, bend down, say the name of their babies aloud, and send their cellulose stars out into the icy water. The water is partially frozen but the rain has done its work and left enough liquid to dissolve the stars. I watch for a little while.

Most people are crying now, the couples holding on to each other, the men supporting their wives, keeping them on their feet. The tissue women are very busy, slipping back and forth with their boxes and their condoling embraces. I envy the ease of their grief. I finger the star in my pocket. There is no point in bringing this one home. I already have the bent one pinned to my coat, and what, after all, will I do with that?

Kneeling on the edge of the pond, I take off my glove and push up the sleeve of my coat and my sweater. Then, holding the star in my hand, I bend over the pond and plunge my hand through the ice into the freezing water. The shock of the cold scalds my hand, a freezing burn, but I grit my teeth and keep my fist in the water. My fingers quickly grow numb, but I can just barely feel the cellulose of the star soften and melt. I ball it up and hold a fistful of dissolving Isabel star for a few more seconds, then it is gone. I open my fist and slide my fingers through the bitter water, but I cannot tolerate it for much longer. When I pull my hand out, it feels anesthetized, like a dead limb hanging from my sleeve.

"Kleenex?" a woman in a Walk to Remember T-shirt says.

"No, thank you," I say, drying my hand and forearm on my coat. I stuff my now tingling fingers back into my glove.

"We're asking people to leave the park in a group at East Seventy-second Street," she said. "When you're ready."

"I think I'll just walk back across," I say. "I live on the West Side."

"No, don't do that. It's much too dangerous to be in the park on your own at night."

She's wrong. It is safe now in Central Park, even at night. It is no longer what it was, the place where the first murder occurred in the same year construction was completed. As I make my way through the empty darkness, I think about William's namesake. In 1870, a man named William Kane was mistaken for Catholic and stabbed and shot to death by a group of the Protestant Orangemen. When William is older I will tell him this story. It features Orangemen, violence, and a man named William. I will have to find out where, exactly, this earlier William was killed. There might even be a secret memorial of which I'm not aware. Perhaps William and I will make a pilgrimage to the spot, create our own memorial. It's too bad he's too young now for a tale of murder and carnage. It would have been the perfect way to distract him from this terrible, unfortunate evening.

It does not take me long to cross the park. I leave the park at Seventy-seventh Street, reminding myself, as William would, that this is Explorer's Gate. I am home soon enough, but I am chilled through, my hands and feet numb with cold, especially the hand I immersed in the model boat pond. I am awkward with my keys, and I make a lot of noise coming into the apartment. Still, although I know they are home—I can see their coats and boots in the entryway—Jack and William do not greet me. They don't even respond to my tentative call.

I find William in the living room, engaged in the unthinkable.

"What are you watching?" I ask.

"*Walking with Prehistoric Beasts.*"

"Is it any good?"

He shrugs, not taking his eyes off the dinosaurs battling onscreen.

"I'm sorry about what happened before, at the park. I guess I kind of lost it."

He shrugs again.

"I'm just kind of . . . you know . . . mad at my father. At Nono."

"I can't hear the movie when you're talking."

"Oh. Okay. Sorry."

I check in Jack's study, but he is not there. Our bedroom door is closed, and for a moment I hover outside, feeling almost like I should knock.

Jack is lying on the bed, his feet crossed neatly at the ankles, his arms folded behind his head. His eyes are closed and his eyelids look translucent in the bright light from the bedside lamp; they glow pink with a faint blue hue lent by the delicate tracery of veins. His skin, in the summer nut brown, a perfect canvas for his brilliant inky eyes, is now winter pale. He is so handsome, compacted into a small and perfect package, sized for me.

"I'm sorry," I say.

He opens his eyes. "I can't do this any more."

"I'm sorry I lost it. The whole thing just freaked me out. The cardboard stars. The ectopic pregnancies with names. Everything."

"It's not a get-out-of-jail-free card, Emilia. Isabel's death doesn't entitle you to do and say whatever the hell you want, to hurt whomever you want."

"I know that."

"No, you don't."

I am standing at the end of the bed, gripping the footboard. I hold it tightly, because I cannot hold him. He will not let me near him, I can tell. He has been so patient, this kind man, such an old-fashioned gentleman of a husband, that I am taken by surprise. My intuition, my prescience, my precognition of all things to do with Jack Woolf fails me. I am entirely unprepared for how angry he is, for how many words he has saved up in these months of supportive silence.

"I have been such a fool," Jack says. "I can't believe I allowed myself to be deluded into thinking I was the great love of your life." He makes the phrase hollow and trite, italicizes it with irony.

"You are. You are the great love of my life." I try to restore the rightful grandeur to what I know I feel, but for some reason my words ring as false as his.

"Do you even understand why you fell in love with me?" he asks. His face flushes and the red contrasts sharply with the blue of his unshaved stubble.

"What do you mean? You're my *bashert*. I fell in love with you the first time I saw you."

"Stop it!" he barks. My head jerks back on the stem of my neck, and my shoulders snap. I feel like the dry twigs in the park sound when they break under my feet.

"Just stop it with that nonsense. All I'm asking is that you think clearly for one minute. Just a single moment of your life, Emilia. Try it this once, okay?"

"Okay," I whisper.

"You've always been your father's girl, haven't you?"

I don't bother to answer because this question is so obviously rhetorical.

To Jack, however, nothing begs the question today. "Haven't you?" he says.

"Yes."

"You became a lawyer just like him."

"Yes."

"You love the park because he does."

"Yes."

"And then, when he destroyed your mother and their marriage, you set out to prove that you were just like him."

I step away from the bed and back up, all the way to the little armchair in the corner of the room. I don't sit in it, but I feel it pushing up against the back of my calves.

"Answer me," Jack says. He swings his legs off the bed so he is sitting on the edge.

"You're cross-examining me."

"No, I'm not."

"Yes, you are. You're asking me leading questions. You're treating me like a witness for the opposition."

"You're avoiding my questions. You're refusing to confront the truth. Your father cheated on your mother and your response was to get involved with a married man. Your response was to show that you were just as bad as he was."

"It was not," I say. I am breathing hard, through my nose, and my jaw aches from being clenched tight.

"Your whole life has been spent trying to prove that you're like your father, not a doormat like your mother. So when he did what he did, you had to do the equivalent."

"No."

"You behave like *you're* the victim. You behave like when he slept with that stripper he didn't betray your mother, he betrayed *you*. You're jealous."

"I am not!"

"Think about it."

And when I do, I realize that of course he is right. I am furious with my father. I have been furious ever since my mother told me what he did, not because he betrayed her but because he betrayed me. By being this cheap and disgusting kind of a man, he threw in my face the sticky and lascivious truth of his sexuality, forever begriming the innocent romance of our relationship. I will never again be able to slip my hand into his and walk along the paths of the Ravine, or enjoy a picnic lunch on a blanket in the clearing beneath the historic red oaks, or sit opposite him in a restaurant smiling over glasses of wine, because unlike other daughters I know where my father's hands have been. I can far too easily imagine them slipped between the thighs of a girl ten years younger than I. I think that in every close father-daughter relationship there is a whisper of romance. What keeps the evil at bay is the vigilant suspension of even the remotest hint of the sexual. That barrier is gone for us now and with it the possibility of innocent intimacy. My father stole that from us when he tucked his dollar bills into Oksana's G-string. My mother stole it when she told me.

I collapse onto the soft armchair, the armchair Jack bought me and carried home on his back because it would not fit in the cab and I loved it so much I could not wait five days for it to be delivered. I sink into the soft down cushion and press my tremulous fingers into the threadbare fabric of the armrests.

"That's not true," I lie, finally, when I can trust my voice.

"It is. Look who you picked to marry." He laughs bitterly. "You picked a short, Jewish lawyer from New York. Jesus Christ, I'm just a slightly younger version of your father. Old Man Woolf."

"No, you're not. You're not like my father at all."

"Oh, is that the problem, Emilia? I'm not enough like your father? Maybe you'd be happier if I was off fucking Russian lap dancers in New Jersey."

"How can you say that? Are you out of your mind?"

"Am *I* out of my mind? What about you, Emilia?"

He stands up suddenly and starts pacing back and forth, pushing his hands through his hair.

"I can't believe I did this to my son," he says. "I can't believe I ruined my son's life for this. For *this*!" He jerks to a stop in the middle of the bedroom and flings his arms around, taking the entire room into the circle of his disgust. "I subjected my son to you for nothing. For nothing."

"How can you say that?" I stand up. I am finally as angry as he is. "What do you mean *subjected* him to me? What the fuck does that mean? You've had some brilliant Freudian epiphany. So what? Everybody's got a fucked up reason for being with who they're with. You like woman with big butts; you think that's *pure*? Have you ever noticed the size of your mother's ass? You can't negate the value of your emotional decisions, just because you think you've decoded their psychological origins."

Jack says, "I forced William to be with someone who doesn't appreciate him. I forced him to live with someone who doesn't love him." His voice is low, so that William will not hear what he is saying, but his face is now beet red.

"You have no idea what I feel about William! You have no idea!"

"Then say it! If you love him then say it."

"That's bullshit, Jack. It doesn't mean anything if I say it just because you tell me to."

"Say it! Say you love him."

"Fuck you! I won't. I won't say it just because you tell me to say it!"

He spins around. Next to the bedroom door, there is a little metal garbage can printed with a Toulouse-Lautrec cancan dancer in a ruffled red petticoat. Jack kicks the garbage pail, sending it smashing into the wall. He kicks it again and again, until it is crumpled, bent over on itself, and his foot is stuck in the pleat. He shakes his foot free and sits heavily on the floor, his head in his hands. His shoulders shake.

I sit back down in my pretty little armchair. "Yes," I say.

"Yes? Yes, what?" he says, without lifting his face.

"Yes, I am completely out of my mind."

For a moment he does not answer. Then he says, "Go to hell, Emilia."

"I'm already there."

"Oh, for God's sake."

"I've been in hell since Isabel died."

"This isn't about Isabel."

"Yes, it is. Yes, it is."

He crawls across the floor. He grabs my chin and forces me to look into his face. "Emilia, if you are in hell it is only because you put yourself there. You put all of us there. You are not the first woman to have lost a child. Losing Isabel broke my heart, too, but it is not the end of the world. Life isn't over. We have to keep on living. We lost our *baby*, Emilia. Not our lives."

"I didn't *lose* our baby."

"What?"

Our faces are inches apart. His hand is on my chin, keeping my eyes locked on his. I can feel his breath on my lips. I can smell the coffee he drank today, the onion from his lunch, the cinnamon gum he chewed.

"I didn't *lose* Isabel. I *killed* her."

So I tell him of my real crime, the crime that makes what I have felt or not felt about my father pale by comparison. I take us back to that night, November 17, 2003. I lay in our bed, our child in my arms. She was nursing at last, grunting, noisily sucking. I tell Jack how tired I was, worn out by hours of crying and panicking. My eyelids felt sticky and my head heavy. With the two middle fingers of my left hand I pulled my heavy flesh away from Isabel's tiny nostrils. I had to hold my left elbow high to do this, and my arm ached. The pose was so awkward, so uncomfortable, that it should have kept me awake, it should have kept me with her. But I was so tired. As I slipped into sleep my arm fell to my side. Once I woke, and reminded myself to pull the skin back, to keep her nose clear, to make sure she could breathe. Then I drifted off again, and again my elbow dropped to my side and my fingers loosened their grip. I woke again and listened to the gulping and clicking of her steady feeding. And that's when I did the unforgivable. I was so tired, I stopped taking care. I told myself I could go to sleep, because if she couldn't breathe, she would pull away. She would know to do that. It was a reflex, an animal instinct. I tucked her tightly against me with my right arm and drifted off, holding her head in place, keeping her still, her tiny nose and mouth sealed tightly against my warm, round, milk-laden breast.

As I tell Jack this story, I watch him creep slowly back and away from me. When I am done Jack stares at me. He is a foot away, more even. The air between us is dead, everything sucked out of it.

"No," he says.

"Yes."

"You did not smother her. The autopsy report said she died of natural causes. It said she died of SIDS."

"It said they found no cause of death. The medical examiner said she stopped breathing. And the reason she stopped breathing, Jack, was because she *couldn't* breathe. Because my breast was in the way, and she couldn't get any air."

"She wasn't crushed. The autopsy report said specifically that she wasn't crushed."

"I didn't say that I crushed her. I didn't crush her. I smothered her."

Jack sits on his knees, his ink eyes wide and staring and I see that he believes me. And I am surprised. Because I realize now that when I told him, when I made my confession, I was hoping he would save me. Jack is, after all, a litigator. He is an expert in the fine arts of cross-examination, of oral argument, of shaping words and making pictures, of creating a story from a series of facts. He twists and twirls, he convinces. He is a magician. Just as he could cross-examine me about my feelings for my father and confront me with a truth I did not see until he showed it to me, I want him to convince me that I am wrong, that my memory is flawed by grief and sorrow, that I have no way of knowing that Isabel died struggling to pull her face from the moon of my breast.

But he doesn't say anything. He sits on his knees, stares at me, and believes. And whatever last scrap of hope I might have clung to curls up and blows away.

He opens his mouth, and closes it again.

"No," I say. "It's your apartment, and William's. All his stuff is here. It's ridiculous for you to be the one who leaves."

I am impressed by how steady I am, considering that my heart has been ripped from my chest and my bones have all melted. I am not even crying. Yet. I am even able to make a sensible decision about luggage. The rolling suitcase, not the pretty Kate Spade overnight bag, because I can fit more in the larger case. Cell phone charger and tampons, deodorant and extra contact lenses. I am a paragon of practicality. By the time I realize that I have packed no pants—no jeans or skirts or even a dress—I am bent over in the elevator, my fist in my mouth.

Chapter 26

There really is no way to overstate the cheerlessness of the Port Authority bus terminal. The urine-stenched grimness of it is so complete, so absolute, that it is almost a parody of itself. Does anywhere else have cafés so depressing, with Formica tables of such putrid colors, with such derelict patrons hunched over such sour coffee recalling and bemoaning such wretched and wasted lives? Even in the middle of the week, the lawyers and secretaries, the bankers and commercial real estate brokers on their way home to Bergenfield and Mahwah seem to assume a brief morose dejection as they cross the threshold into Port Authority. Today, on Sunday, it's unbearable.

I stand in the main lobby wrinkling my nose against the stink and imagine the scene that awaits me at my mother's house. How often lately have I skulked back to hide under my mother's skirts. Who else will I find there tonight? Who else will await my apology? The thought of coming upon my parents cavorting in some lascivious lap-dance reenactment is stomach-turning. Worse is the thought that they seem to be managing to salvage a relationship, one that should have been irrevocably poisoned by unforgivable betrayal. And my marriage, my beautiful marriage, the marriage for which I was willing to do anything, spend anything, waste anything, destroy anything, is an unsalvageable wreck.

Dragging my suitcase behind me, I head back out to the street. For no reason other than the inherent drama of self-pity, I decide to walk to Simon's rather than take a cab. He lives in London Terrace, in an apartment I found for him when I finally got sick of having him sleep on my couch in Stuyvesant Town.

It is almost twenty blocks to London Terrace from Port Authority, and by the time I arrive I am chilled through, but at least I do not look like I have been hysterically crying, like a woman who has left her husband. Still, Simon's doorman does not want to let me up, even though I have a key. I am arguing with him when Simon walks in.

"Good work, Francisco," Simon says. "This woman is a menace. God knows what she would have done to my apartment."

I say, "Jack and I broke up. And I forgot my pants." Then I burst into tears.

Simon swoops down on me, all long limbs and expensive coat. He pulls me into his arms and I bury my head in the wool of his chest, shuddering and weeping, crying as hard as I did in the elevator of my building. I am crying so hard I barely notice that we are walking, crab-like, toward the mailboxes and away from the middle of the lobby.

"Why aren't you wearing any pants?" Simon whispers, once my sobs have subsided.

"I'm *wearing* pants, you idiot. I just forgot to pack any others."

He hugs me again. "We'll go shopping tomorrow," he murmurs, as he leads me to the elevator.

And of course we do, because Simon is my dear, dear friend, and he once again puts me ahead of his work, this time banishing four sexually harassed gay members of the Plumbers and Pipefitters Local 217 to the back of his mind in order to help me riffle through the piles of jeans on the eighth floor of Barneys. I am feeling oddly well rested, because I prophylactically took an extra sleeping pill last night, and another when I found myself awake and panicking at five this morning. I am also stuffed, because Simon and I went out for breakfast. I had pancakes, bacon, and the half of his oatmeal that he did not want to finish. A woman whose marriage has collapsed is supposed to be listless and wan, with dark smudges under her eyes. I have powdered sugar on my chin and more nervous energy than a skittish greyhound moments before a race.

"Try these," Simon says, holding up a pair of flared jeans in a dark indigo.

"They're, like, six feet long."

"So you'll get them hemmed."

I take them.

"Those won't work for you," a young woman says.

"Excuse me?"

She puts her hands on her bony hips and leans forward, appraising the size and shape of my ass. Hers is smaller than William's.

"They'll be too small. And they don't have any stretch. Try the Sevens. They give really nicely, and the pockets are a little higher so they'll make your butt look smaller."

Fifteen minutes later I am standing outside the dressing room with two pairs of jeans that fit me perfectly in the hips and rear, although they flap ludicrously around my feet. It feels good to surrender myself to the competent and bossy care of this knowledgeable young jeans-girl. She is brusque but not unpleasant, informing me that with my loose belly I do not want to wear tight jeans.

"You think they make you look thinner, but they don't. You need to have the waist sit right here at your hip," she places her hand at my hips. "If you bulge out over the top it just looks nasty. But if it sits right, like this, you look hot."

I look in the mirror. It has been a long time since I stared at myself like this. I realize that when Simon and I were first taking pairs of pants off the stacks, I was reaching for my original size, the size that would have fit me before Isabel pulled my body all out of shape. I look different now. I am thicker around the middle, softer. My hips have an extra curve to them, and my belly protrudes where it didn't use to. I still have a waist where I always did, but below it, things seem looser. I wonder if this is a permanent disfigurement, if my body will always reflect her brief tenancy.

"Can you hem these for her, because I don't know if you've noticed, but they're a tad on the long side," Simon says.

"Sure," our salesgirl says. "I'll have one of the seamstresses come right up. It usually takes a week, but I can put in a rush order and have them for you by Thursday or Friday."

Because I cannot wear this same pair of pants for the next week, Simon spends another half hour with me, choosing a long suede skirt, one that, although it is on sale, is far more expensive than I have any reason to allow myself, especially since it has been a very long time since I paid my own credit card bill. As I sign the slip I imagine Jack's face when he opens the bill. Will he wonder how I could be indulging in a shopping spree on the very morning after I have packed my bags and left our home? Perhaps he will decide that I was just trying to comfort myself in some small way. Perhaps he will even be pleased at this evidence of my desperate search for consolation. In that case, I should probably buy a pair of boots to match the skirt.

I walk Simon to work after we leave Barneys, and then I head back downtown on the subway. Somehow, when my idleness took place in my own home, and could be classified under the caption of "grief," I did not seem quite so indolent. It was not this embarrassing to be wandering the city in the middle of the day. I think about calling Mindy, but pregnancy lies between us, the proverbial elephant in the room about whose HCG levels we do not speak. I can't face that. Instead of calling her or of going back to Simon's house and watching television, I take the train down to the Village to the little corner bookstore where Simon and I used to go before I moved uptown.

I choose a Russian novel thick enough to bury myself in its pages. The upside of the loneliness of my life now is that I will no longer need to lie about having read the classics. I find a Modern Library edition of *The Secret Garden* for William and a Lyle book that I don't think he owns. Then I search out the parenting section.

My mother's bookshelves groaned with well-thumbed volumes on stepparenting. Every time a new one was published she would rush to buy it, sure that this one would contain the keys to creating a relationship with Allison and Lucy. She read them hungrily, but no book ever told her how to make my sisters love her.

I have never once bought a book on being a stepmother. I have refused, perversely. Now I pull them out, one after the other. There are so many.

Step Lightly: Advice for the Stepmother; *Step by Stepmotherhood*; *Stepmotherhood: How not to be wicked*; even, humiliatingly, *Warm and Wonderful Stepmothers of Famous People*.

I leaf through them one by one, trying to decide which is the best, which will give me the answers I seek. Then, impulsively, I pile them all in my arms.

The sales clerk asks if I would like to have my purchases wrapped, and for a moment I can't decide. I don't know when I will give William his gifts, and I am afraid that the forced joviality of festive paper will make an occasion where none exists. But they have morphologically accurate dinosaur-themed wrapping paper that I know he will love. I tell the clerk to wrap just the copy of *The Secret Garden*. Then I head to a nearby café.

I bring my coffee to a small table, take off my coat, and settle myself in for a comfortable read. The café is remarkably full for a Monday early afternoon. This place is blessedly devoid of the stroller-pushing crowd. Some of the denizens might be students, but most are merely as slothful as I. Don't any of these people have jobs? There are people clicking away on laptops, and newspaper readers, and one or two just sipping their coffee and staring dreamily into space. I reach into my bookstore bag, but instead of pulling out my self-assigned Russian novel, I choose *Lovable Lyle* to read. It's about a series of hate notes that Lyle receives and is a little grim, until the end where Lyle saves the day. I don't recall this installment in Lyle's saga from my childhood. I'm not sure that my father read me any Lyle books beyond the first one or two. I can remember quite clearly being read to by my father, how he would sit next to me, the book angled toward my bedside lamp. I remember the voices he adopted for different characters in different books. I don't remember when he stopped the bedtime stories, however. At some point I learned to read to myself and then that was that. Even though William is such a precocious reader, Jack still reads to him. They read reference books together, or a chapter of whatever novel William is reading. He is a lucky little boy.

I put the book back in my bag and take out my Gogol. I am diligently leafing past the introduction when someone says, "Do you mind if I take this chair?"

I look up. He is my age, I think. Early thirties, with a barely tamed head of tight curls and chestnut-colored skin.

"Go ahead."

He lifts the chair easily with one long-fingered hand and glances down at my book.

He says, "I had to read that in college. It's really funny. Bleak, but funny."

"Were you an English major?"

He shakes his head. "No. I took a Russian literature class. What about you?"

"What was my major?" I ask archly, raising my eyebrows. It takes me a moment to realize that I am flirting.

He laughs. "Sure. And do you want to see my etchings?"

I wonder for a moment what my future would be like if I made space at my café table for the man with the caramel-sweet eyes. Would I turn into someone else? Would my eyes then be able to skate over the women with the Bugaboo strollers, unmoved, unshattered by their presence because my life would be so full of other things? Would I suddenly stop missing Jack and Isabel and William?

I glance down at the circle of hammered gold around the fourth finger of my left hand. The gaze of the handsome man holding the chair follows mine.

"Enjoy your book," he says.

I nod, but put the Russian novel back in my bag. Instead I take out the stepmothering guides and pile them in a tall, rickety tower on my café table. My coffee grows cold and sour in its cup as I read. Every book writes about the stepmother's turmoil and stress. Every book describes the stepmother's mistaken expectations. Every book urges me to confront the truth of the complicated nature of the stepfamily's feelings. And I gobble them up. I read voraciously, just like my mother did when I was a child. I realize now that she read not for answers but for company. Those well-thumbed reference tomes were her solace, not her salvation. These books cannot teach me how to be a better stepmother, but they can give me the tremendous consolation of knowing that I am not alone.

My favorite book is the unlikely *Warm and Wonderful Stepmothers of Famous People*. This book is much more fun than one would expect, and worth the gymnastics required to hide its embarrassing title from my coffee-drinking neighbors. I particularly enjoy the story of the wretched little royal tart Elizabeth I, who slept with her pregnant stepmother's husband, when the woman had been so loyal and kind to her, and the story of John James Audubon, the illegitimate child of a sea captain and his mistress, who was raised by an indulgent and long-suffering stepmother. I like these self-abnegating stepmothers, even if they are a bit hyperbolic in their devotion. Self-abnegation is certainly a trait no one could accuse me of. I could use a good role model.

Chapter 27

On Thursday, after Simon has gone to work, I clean his immaculate apartment, vacuuming the gray carpet, straightening the gray pillows on the gray couch. For some reason I cannot bring myself to go pick up my jeans, and I wonder if it is because doing so will mean that I need these new clothes, that I have really left home and cannot return. I tell myself that I'm being foolish. If Jack and I were finished, wouldn't he pack my things and send them to me, making shopping for new clothes unnecessary? So new jeans, therefore, rather than symbolizing the permanence of our separation, are actually a sign of the possibility of reunion. Or maybe I don't want to pick them up because they are a size thirty-one waist and I cannot believe I still haven't gotten myself back into a twenty-nine.

By early afternoon I have cleaned as much of the apartment as I can stand, reread two of the stepmothering guides, skimmed two chapters of my Russian novel, and am starving. The food in Simon's fridge is as gray as his furniture.

I am halfway down the block to the Greek diner on the corner when I finally realize that today is the first Thursday of March. I stand in the middle of the block, indecisive. I am hungry and I have left my home and my marriage, but I made a promise. Finally, I take out my phone and scroll through the address book until I find Sonia's number. She answers right away, but there is so much noise in the background that I can barely hear her.

"This is Emilia," I shout.

"Emilia?"

"Yes." I try to explain about today, how it is the first Thursday of the month and they are filming the zoo scene of *Lyle, Lyle, Crocodile*, but she keeps saying, "What?" over and over again.

Finally, she says, "I'm sorry, I can't hear. There are too many people here. They are making a movie and there are men with loud microphones."

"You're at the filming? In Central Park?"

"I'm sorry, I can't hear you." And then she hangs up.

In the middle of the day it is much faster to take the train, and because I know this, I make it to the park in twenty minutes. What is more amazing, miraculous even, is that I find them, standing beneath the Delacorte Clock. I arrive on the strike of two. The animals begin their dance with a jerk, the bronze monkeys banging their hammers on the bell, the bear playing his tambourine, the penguin drumming, the hippo fiddling, the kangaroo tooting his horn, the goat playing the pipes, and my favorite, the elephant, jamming on the concertina. It is to the tune of "Mary Had a Little Lamb" that I begin to cry again. I am crying because William is jumping up and down, excited to see the animals revolve in their circle, and I can remember the very first time that we met, right here, in this zoo, in the park. He was so small, up on his father's shoulders, and so sad. In the intervening two years what have I brought to this child's life but more of the same misery?

First I destroyed his family—and however flawed, however complicated by lovelessness, misunderstanding, and pain, it was a family. Then I refused to participate in the creation of the right kind of new family, an alternative where he might somehow reinvent the life I had taken from him. And now, I have rent, shattered even, the illusion of our false family, torn it asunder once and for all.

When she sees me Sonia says, "Emilia, today is not your day. You cannot come on this day. I think Dr. Soule is very angry that you are here today."

"It'll be okay," I say, as if I have some confidence that this is true.

"I think you go home now, Emilia," Sonia says. "Today is not your day, and they don't want crying in the movie. I take William to be in the movie. You go home."

I want to tell Sonia that I can't go home because Jack has left me, although I am the one gone. But I can see that she is so tired of all this. She is sick to death of these Americans and their self-important histrionics. She is tired of the weeping and the screaming. She is tired of the self-aggrandizement and the self-flagellation, the latter really a kind of variation on the former. She wishes we had some real problems, problems like an economy so bad that teenage girls sell themselves into prostitution to escape it, or an environment laid waste by decades of nuclear mismanagement. Or maybe what Sonia is really sick of is me.

It makes a dismal kind of sense that here, under the animal dance of the Delacorte Clock, which has never been able to bring him the joy it was designed to produce, I will have to tell William that only now, when I don't know if I will be able to see him again, do I realize how much it matters.

When the clock is done striking the hour I crouch down. William has pulled off his hat and his sandy hair crackles with static electricity.

Something about his eyes looks different and I peer at his face. They are darker, softer, more like ink or velvet.

"William," I say. My eyes and nose are running and I wipe angrily at my tears.

"Why are you crying?" he says, calm and curious.

"Let me just say this, okay? Whatever's happening between your dad and me . . ."

"I can't understand you. Maybe you should blow your nose."

"William, will you just be quiet for a second, so I can say this? I'm trying to tell that you that I think you're a great kid. And no matter what happens, I'm always going to think that."

But William is not listening. He is looking over my shoulder. "Nono!" he shouts. "Emilia is here, too! Did you put mustard on my pretzel?"

My father has taken off his glove and balances three pretzels on his outstretched fingers. The smile he gives me is tentative, pleading. It softens his face and pleats his cheeks and eyes with deep wrinkles. He looks so old.

"Hi, honey," he says.

"Hi."

Before I can ask him what he is doing here he says, "William and I made plans to be in this movie together, remember? Jack said it would be all right if I called his mother."

"Carolyn said you could bring him here?"

"Yes."

"Really?"

He cocks his head to one side and frowns a little sorrowfully, as if asking what I take him for, do I really think he would have lied? Then he distributes a pretzel to William and one to Sonia. He tears the third in half. "Here," he says, handing me the larger half. I take it. It's hot and soft, the mustard is tangy against my tongue. I am starving, and this is the most delicious pretzel I've ever eaten in my life.

"Thank you," I say with my mouth full.

"You're welcome. You have mustard on your lip." He gives me a napkin.

"Extras who have not yet signed releases, please meet in the zoo in front of the penguin pool," a voice blares over the loudspeaker. "Extras with signed releases, please proceed to the caiman tank in the children's zoo."

"Come on!" William shouts. He grabs my father's hand. "Let's go!"

Sonia frowns, looking at me.

"It's okay, Sonia," my father says. "I'm sure Carolyn won't mind."

She ponders this for a moment and then seems to give in to his authority as she never has to mine. We allow William to lead us under the clock to the Children's Zoo, where the cameras are set up around the caiman tank. I think I recognize one of the young men from the Conservatory Garden, but most of the people wearing headsets and busily shifting the crowd from place to place seem to be clones of that trio and I'm not really sure.

"Where are the crocodiles?" I ask William.

"There are no crocodiles in the Central Park Zoo," he explains.

"Well, doesn't that strike you as something of a problem? The book is called *Lyle, Lyle, Crocodile* not *Kyle, Kyle, Caiman*. Are they going to change the title?"

He shakes his head in exasperation. "They'll use special effects. Haven't you ever heard of CGI?"

For the next couple of hours we walk back and forth in front of the caiman tank. William frustrates the extras wrangler to no end by ostentatiously exclaiming in awe over the empty area where he assumes the computer-generated image of Lyle will be doing his handstands and crocodile soft-shoe. Sonia, my father, and I don't talk much. We do a pretty good impression of a group of New Yorkers out for an afternoon at the zoo with their child, parading in relatively blank-faced silence past the cages and exhibits.

After two hours, even William seems to have had enough, and when Sonia suggests that it might be time for the two of them to be heading home, he is only too eager to acquiesce.

"Can we stop at Le Pain Quotidien?" he says.

She considers for a moment, and then nods her head.

"Ask about the strawberry cupcakes," I say. "See if they've finally started doing them dairy free."

"Would you like to join us?" Sonia invites, although it is clear that she hopes we will not accept.

"No, thank you," my father says. "I'd better be getting back across the bridge."

We watch them as they walk off down the path in the waning light. When we can no longer see them I turn. Across the park lies my apartment—Jack's apartment. And in between a vast expanse of gray and green, Ramble and schist, lawns and gardens. Fanciful wooden, stone, and iron bridges. Raptors and woodpeckers, eastern kingbirds, warblers, ducks, and the ever-present pigeons. Pine-tree nurseries and numbered lampposts. The park. My park.

My father says, "Would you like to take a walk?"

"Okay."

We head north, walking silently side by side until we reach the statue of Balto the heroic sled dog. We pause in front of the bronze malamute and I wonder if my words from Sunday night are ringing in my father's ears as they are in mine. We continue on, walking in silence through the underground arch. Then my father says, "Jack told me you left home."

In place of a reply I kick a pebble with my foot.

"When I called about taking William to the filming, he told me."

I still don't say anything.

We wander past the statues of the writers: Shakespeare, Sir Walter Scott. In front of Robert Burns, my father says, "Don't make the same mistake I did, Emilia."

"Which mistake was that?"

He sighs.

"Sorry," I say, and because I can't bear to look at my father, I say it to the drunken, philandering Scottish poet cast in bronze.

My father says, "Jack's a good man."

"I know."

We start walking again, along the southern path of Sheep Meadow.

"They had sheep in the meadow all the way until the 1930s," my father tells me, as he has a hundred times before. "By the time they were taken away, they were completely inbred."

"Freak sheep." I've said this a hundred times, too.

"They sent the shepherd to work in the lion house at the zoo, poor guy. Wonder what he made of that. Probably ended up feeding his old charges to his new. What do you say we get a drink?"

"Where?"

He points to the festive white lights of Tavern on the Green.

"Really?" I ask. He has taught me that only tourists and dowagers frequent Tavern on the Green.

"Just a drink," he says.

We walk up to the restaurant. I have never been inside, and it is a monstrous chocolate box of Tiffany glass, gilded mirrors, and Victoriana. At once, I understand the hulking topiary out in the garden, the gorilla and the reindeer. It's all of a piece with this lantern-lit insanity. My father orders a Glenfiddich and soda, something I've never seen him drink before. Perhaps he's been inspired by Burns. I want something more suitable to our surroundings, something ridiculous and fancy. Something with absinthe. I settle for a kir royal.

We sip our drinks. My father and I have not gone this long without talking in all our lives, I think. We are normally loquacious companions. We chat about the law, politics, my sisters. Even after I knew about what he had done, our facile conversations carried on. His continued ease masked any stiffness on my part.

The bubbles in my champagne tickle the roof of my mouth and the kir is sweet. I take a very large swallow, gearing myself up to speak. Before I can my father says, "I wasn't a very good husband."

He rushes on before I agree. "I don't mean because of what caused the divorce." And this is as close as we will get to referring to what, specifically, he has done. "I wasn't there for your mother in other ways. With Lucy and Allison, especially."

I take another sip of my drink. "You don't have to tell me this, Daddy."

He shrugs. "Right, you were there."

"No, I mean, you don't owe me an explanation. I had no right to say what I did. I have no right be so angry with you. This is between Mom and you. It has nothing to do with me. It's none of my business."

He frowns and twirls his straw between his fingers. "That's partly true. Part of it is just between your mother and me. But part of it affects you. What happened to us affects you. It's still affecting you."

I am finished with my drink now, my head buzzing from the alcohol. "I'm sorry, Daddy. I'm sorry I was so mean to you the other night. In front of Jack and William. I'm so sorry."

"It's all right, honey." We are sitting side by side and he puts his arm around me. "You're my girl."

I lay my head on his shoulder. He pats my hair and says, sadly, "You try so hard to be like me, daughter."

I sit up. I want to tell him that I am nothing like him, but we both know the truth. When my father betrayed my mother, when he humiliated her in the most degrading, horrible way he could have, and in a moment of terrible weakness, she confided in me, I set out to prove our similarity. What was my response when my mother shared her aching shame and curdled the love I felt for my father? I ensnared and entrapped a man like him, who looked like him, who did the same work he did, who loved his child as my father loved his. I dug my claws into Jack, ruined his marriage and his family, turned him and myself into traitors. Just like my father.

And then I was punished. I was punished and I punished.

Oh Isabel. Oh Jack. Oh William. What have I done to you all?

My father says, "You're hopelessly unrealistic about love. You're as foolish as I am, just in a different way."

"What does that mean?" I am fighting tears now, so my voice sounds more hostile than I intend.

"Your fantasy is as unrealistic as mine, and it's going to end up with the same end result."

"*My* fantasy?"

"That old wives' tale of your grandmother's, that *bashert* story." My father's voice takes on a gentle mocking tone. "You fell in love with Jack at first sight. He's your soul mate, your intended. You two were meant to be. How many times have I heard you tell the story of how you first saw him, Emilia? On his knees in the hallway of Friedman Taft? Love at first sight, love at first sight. Do you really think that that's what love is all about?"

"Yes," I whisper.

"No," he says, firmly. He grasps both my shoulders and gives me a small but firm shake. "No. That's a fantasy, honey. Love and marriage are about work and compromise. They're about seeing someone for what he is, being disappointed, and deciding to stick around anyway. They're about commitment and comfort, not some kind of sudden, hysterical recognition."

"That's not what I want. Disappointment and comfort is not what I want."

"Why not? Because you expect it to be magical and mystical? Because you don't want to work?"

"Why can't it be magical? Why can't it be mystical?"

"Because if you count on magic and mysticism, Emilia, then as soon as shit happens, as soon as life interferes, as soon as your stepson treats you badly, or your husband's ex-wife has a fit about something, or your baby dies, as soon as *life* happens, the magic will disappear and you'll be left with nothing. You can't count on magic, Emilia. Trust me, I know. Sweetheart, little girl, you can't count on magic."

Fortunately, my father is good at managing scenes. He would have to be, wouldn't he? My sisters and I have been throwing public tantrums since we were two years old. When I lose control of my tears and my sobbing grows loud, he holds out his capacious handkerchief and brandishes it in front of my face like a toreador with a recalcitrant bull. The bartender and waiters shy away from our small table and the other drinkers avert their eyes until I have managed to lift my head and catch my breath. After a while I am still crying, but I no longer need to cover my mouth to keep my sobs from shaking the windows in their frames and breaking the crystal goblets lined up along the back of the bar.

"I'm so sorry, sweetheart," my father says.

"It's okay, Daddy," I manage to say around my tears. "I just . . . I do love him. I do."

"Of course you do. I'm not saying you don't. And he loves you, too."

"I've screwed this up so badly."

"That's okay. You haven't got a patch on me, kiddo. If that makes you feel any better."

I wipe my eyes. "Not a whole lot, to be perfectly honest."

He pauses for a moment, and then he laughs. "I guess not."

"I love you, Daddy," I say.

"I love you too, my girl."

Chapter 28

"Oh *will* you please give me a fucking *break*?" I say. I am sitting in the toilet stall in the restaurant, my new suede skirt hitched up around my waist.

"Excuse me?" The woman in the next stall is unperturbed, as though used to being sworn at in public restrooms.

I wonder if I should ask her how she would respond to the following: Oh, lady in the next stall, having confronted and confessed your darkest secret to your husband, that you are responsible for the death of your child, and having your husband not only believe you but shrink from you, finally recognizing you for the malignant evil you are, and thus all but ask you leave his house, and having yourself come to the conclusion that your marriage is a farce, born of a kind of proto-Freudian reenactment of your father's infidelity, and having realized, altogether too late, that the worst crimes you've committed in all this mess are directed at the one person who is truly a victim of circumstance, who you've all but tried to kill by feeding him things he's allergic to, sending him to play in dangerous and unprotected circumstances, and pitching him into freezing water, if only accidentally, and doesn't Freud say there are no accidents, having dealt with all this, lady in the next stall over, how would you deal with the nightmare flashing on your caller ID?

I should have known this was coming. I should have realized that the only misery missing from my life was a nice, quick evisceration, courtesy of the miracle of fiber optics.

"It's nothing," I say to the lady in the next stall, and "Hello, Carolyn," I say into the phone.

"I need to see you."

"Is that so." Why not? I mean, really, why not?

"Come to my office. Can you make it this evening? I only have a few more patients. I'm at . . ."

"I know where you are." What does she think? That in the months I was waiting for Jack to forget that he was married, I didn't look up her address? That I didn't cast telepathic hexes in her direction, complete with nine-digit zip codes?

"Try not to be late. I have an operating room booked for seven tomorrow morning and I'd like to get home at a decent hour."

Why would I be late to my own execution?

The waiting room of Carolyn's office looks just like I imagined, complete with two pregnant women sitting on the sleek leather couch. One of them is reading *Parenting* magazine with a more tortured expression than an article on baby names should inspire in anyone, no matter how influenced by the vagaries of hormonal ebb and flow. The other has a beatific glow about her that I find loathsome. I realize that this is the first time I have been in an obstetrician's office since before Isabel was born. I pretended to forget my six-week follow-up appointment with Dr. Brewster and ignored the messages from his office calling to reschedule. It is not as difficult to be here as I would have expected; I'm not so angered by the presence of pregnant women. I don't like the smug Madonna woman, but the other, the worried one, does not bother me overmuch. Perhaps the prospect of my conversation with Carolyn makes everything else pale by comparison.

"Don't worry, it will happen," the smug woman says suddenly.

"Excuse me?"

"Your baby. You'll have one. It took me six years and now I'm pregnant with twins. I can always tell when someone else is going through it. Dr. Soule is the best. And the reproductive endocrinologist she works with is amazing. It'll happen for you. I know it."

This violation of the unwritten rule of conception and infant-loss protocol stuns me. Just as you never, never ask a fat woman if she's pregnant, isn't it true that you never assume a fucked-up-looking woman in an obstetrician's office is trying to get pregnant? Isn't that something that simply isn't done?

"Six years, one baby with hydrocephalus that we lost at nineteen weeks, four miscarriages, and three IVFs. And now Finn and Emmet are due on June nineteenth. So you see, it's only a matter of time. It always works out. Dr. Soule will make it happen. She's a miracle worker."

"Ms. Greenleaf?" a nurse in lavender scrubs dotted with violets says from the doorway. "Right this way."

"Congratulations," I tell the woman, who suddenly seems to be entitled to her complacency. On my way out the door I touch my toe to the doorjamb and surreptitiously tap it three times. I no longer approve of naming children before they are born. It is too tempting of the evil eye to make such assumptions about a baby. Who knows whether a child whose life is so counted on will even take his first breath? Still not even I am superstitious enough to believe that I could have protected Isabel from my own negligence by referring to her forever as "she."

I imagine for a moment being asked to strip and don a paper robe for this consultation, this dressing-down, and although I know it is absurd, I am relieved when the nurse leads me into Carolyn's office and not into an examining room. It takes me a moment to figure out what disturbs me about this office, why it is at once familiar and strange. Then I realize what it is: the furnishings are identical to those in the office Carolyn decorated for Jack at Friedman Taft. There is the black walnut desk, polished to a high shine. There is the bookcase with the minimal scrollwork, there are the two visitors' chairs upholstered in an elegant interlocking geometry, there is the photograph of toddler William on the beach in Nantucket, sand stippling his skinny legs, his diaper sagging around his bottom. There, heaven help me, are the credenza and the Aeron chair.

"I wish I had known that you intended to join your father and William at the filming of the movie in the park," Carolyn says. She strides through the doorway and across the room as though she owns it, as of course she does. She is elegant in a long, slim black skirt, with boots and a high-collared sweater, also black. Her belly swells like a small ball underneath the fine wool. I have bought outfits like this, expensive ones, too, but no matter how much of her husband's money I spend, I never look like Carolyn Soule. She is right. In marrying me, Jack did slink back to his middle-class roots. I am not sophisticated, like William and his mother.

She is sitting now behind her desk, rocked back in the chair. Her fingers are interlaced in front of her, the pads of her thumbs and pinkies pressed against one another. Her nails are as clean and well kept as I imagined they would be.

She says, "Jack told me that you left him. He told me what happened the night Isabel died."

For a moment I am stunned. Then I accept it as inevitable. When he was faced with my ultimate betrayal, he did what would hurt me the most.

"Quite frankly, I've never heard Jack like this, Emilia. He was absolutely distraught. He was crying."

"When did you talk to him?" My voice is a croak, unfamiliar to me.

"On Monday night. William was very upset when he saw you leave with your suitcase, and I called to speak to Jack about it. Jack told me what you believe about what happened on the night your daughter died. And he asked me if it was possible. He asked if you could really have smothered the baby against your breast."

"He asked *you*?"

"Jack knows to trust my judgment. My medical judgment, if nothing else."

"What did you tell him?"

Her composure cracks just the littlest bit. She presses her pinkies together so hard they bend and whiten. She purses her narrow lips and the wrinkles stand out like the tines of a fork. "I told him it was possible. I said, yes, you could have accidentally killed Isabel. And I said you probably had, because any woman who could be so casual with William's safety could just as easily fall sleep and smother her own child."

Carolyn's manner, the clinical detachment of a physician combined with the suppressed yet still-pulsating anger of a wife and mother betrayed, lends a sure confidence to her words. My own confidence in the accuracy of her indictment stems from no such detachment and no such anger. I have not been betrayed, and I am no clinician. I just know that she is right.

"Don't," Carolyn says.

Don't what? I wonder.

She pushes a box of tissues across the wide desk to me. I wipe my finger across my cheek and am surprised to find that I am crying again.

"That's not why I asked you to come here today. I'm not proud of what I said. It was a terrible thing to say, and I'm ashamed of myself. What I'm most ashamed of is that it took William to point that out to me."

"William? William knows?"

She nods. "He overheard the conversation. I'm sorry. My apartment is quite small."

It is a prewar seven on Fifth Avenue. How loud was she yelling?

Underneath Carolyn's smooth porcelain cheek, a faint, pink flush begins to spread. I have seen her enraged but I have never seen her embarrassed. "He was standing there when I hung up the phone, holding his *Giganotosaurus* and a book. He was waiting for me to read to him."

"What book?"

She knits her beautifully shaped eyebrows. "Excuse me?"

"What book?"

This is not the part of the story she expected me to latch on to. "*Lyle, Lyle, Crocodile*," she says.

I smile.

"He's a very loyal boy, Emilia," she says.

She doesn't need to tell me that. For more than two years I've watched him be her most loyal accolyte.

She says, "He was very angry with me for saying that about you. He told me that you loved Isabel, and that you could not have killed her."

I am flabbergasted. The loyalty about which Carolyn spoke was to *me*? William defended *me*? And to his mother, no less?

"What did you say?" I ask.

She pauses, and I can almost see her deciding whether or not to tell me the truth. "I told him that I hadn't said you killed the baby. I told him that you might have accidentally smothered her. The way you accidentally threw him in the Lake."

"Oh."

"He corrected me."

"What?"

"He reminded me that it was the Harlem Meer. Not the Lake. He said that the Lake is much farther south, below the Reservoir. And then he informed me that the word 'meer' means lake in Dutch."

And then something amazing happens. Something that has never happened in all the time that I have been a stepmother to this woman's son. We share a smile of rueful impatience, tinged with pride. He is so smart, we say, wordlessly. And such a little know-it-all.

Carolyn pulls the tissues out of the box herself, since I am incapable of actually taking them. She pushes them into my hand. "He asked me to help you. He said that since I was a doctor I could find out what really happened to Isabel."

I blow my nose.

"Your pediatrician was sent a copy of Isabel's autopsy report. I had his office fax it to me yesterday, and I reviewed it with a medical school classmate of mine who is at Stanford. She's a pathologist and is something of a specialist in neonatal cases. She's testified at criminal trials. She confirmed the coroner's conclusion. She said there is absolutely no evidence to indicate that Isabel was smothered. Smothering always leaves traces—a torn upper lip frenulum, signs of positional asphyxia, dots of blood in the lungs. In Isabel's case there were no physical indications of smothering. You can't have smothered her; you did not kill her. Isabel died of SIDS." Carolyn's voice softens, almost imperceptibly. "You just had the terrible misfortune to be holding her when she died."

"Your friend is a pathologist?"

"Yes."

"A perinatal specialist?"

"Yes."

"And she reviewed the autopsy report?"

"Yes."

"And she said . . ." my voice trails away. I need her to repeat it. I need to hear it again, and for some reason Carolyn understands this.

Very slowly she says, "My friend the pathologist said that she is confident from the autopsy report that Isabel's death was not due to smothering. She said that while without an exhumation she cannot make a final determination, she does not recommend that you and Jack take that step. She said that she feels secure in her conclusion that Isabel died of SIDS. She also said that she would be willing to tell you this herself, if you'd rather hear it directly from her, or if you have any other questions."

I now understand why the women on the UrbanBaby.com Web

site like Dr. Carolyn Soule so much, why they so confidently put themselves in her competent and compassionate hands. My husband's ex-wife repeated herself, slowly and clearly, gently and patiently, for as long as it took for me to stop crying and start believing that my daughter was dead not because I was so careless and wretched that I left a swath of ruin in my path but because sometimes babies die, sometimes they just slip away, the electric pulses of their brain turning off, shutting down, shorting out, for some mysterious reason, for no reason at all.

Chapter 29

I *leave* Carolyn's office stunned—I feel a lightening that I know must be joy but feels more like relief. I can go home now. I *must* go home and tell Jack what I know, what I've learned today, what his ex-wife and my father have taught me. I am also happy because as I was leaving her office Carolyn announced to me that she is getting married.

"Congratulations," I said. "When is the wedding?"

"We're not having a real wedding. My fiancé's brother is a judge and he'll do a simple ceremony in his chambers. And then we'll have a small dinner at our favorite bistro. A week from Friday."

"That's so soon!" I said.

She smiled and patted the small drum of her belly.

Before I leave the warmth of the lobby of Carolyn's building, I call Jack's cell phone.

His greeting is muted.

"It's me," I say, unnecessarily.

"How are you?"

"Good. I need to talk to you. Where are you? Are you still at work?"

"Yes."

"Can you leave? Are you busy?"

We are faced, suddenly, with the dilemma of where to meet. I do not want to have this conversation in Jack's office, with Marilyn so close by. Going home is too fraught with symbolism. It is still early, but we decide to meet for dinner on the East Side, not far from Jack's office. I have time to stop at Barneys on Madison and pick up my jeans, but I don't. I don't want them, even though they fit me perfectly. Even though I paid for them. I have so many pairs of jeans in my closet at home. I won't need these new ones because I'll be going home now. Won't I? Won't I be going home?

I arrive at the restaurant before Jack and am seated at a small table along the wall where I can see the door and a bit of the sidewalk through the narrow-paned windows. There are few diners at this early hour, and I have an unobstructed view. When I see Jack I feel an instant of vertigo, like in a dream of falling when you suddenly awake. His dark overcoat flaps open behind him, the ends of his scarf trailing. Even through the window I can see that his cheeks are reddened by the cold air. He is like Snow White: ruby lips, raven hair, rosy cheeks, blue, blue eyes.

He strides across the restaurant and brushes my cheek with his lips. This embrace is too swift and I cling for an awkward moment before letting him unwind his scarf and take off his coat. He hands them to the hovering waiter and orders a drink.

"Since when do you drink vodka martinis?" I ask.

"I don't," he says. "It's just the first thing that came to mind. Do you want something?"

You. I want you back. "Just water. No. A glass of red wine. Anything. Whatever they have by the glass."

The waiter is good and he does not ask any questions about what kind of wine I want, he just melts away.

"I saw Carolyn today," I blurt before we can begin making small talk. "And my father. I saw them both. My father and Carolyn."

"What?"

"Not at the same time. First I saw my father, and then Carolyn. She called me, Jack. Carolyn called me."

I am having such a hard time figuring out what he is feeling. Usually it is easy to tell, his emotions dance across his face, scream themselves out to me, even when they are only whispering to him. But now it is like he has learned a foreign language, one that I do not speak. Instead of trying to discern what is going on under the indecipherable mask, I just plow forward. I tell him about Carolyn's friend the pathologist, about the physical evidence that does not exist. I explain how his ex-wife has exonerated me.

"I didn't do it," I say, finally. "It wasn't my fault."

"I know," he says. He isn't looking at me. He stares instead at the edge of the table, or at the heavy silverware, or at the napkin folded in the shape of a swan.

"What do you mean, you know? How do you know? Did Carolyn call you?"

At this moment the waiter arrives with our drinks and we sit silently while he sets them before us.

"Did she call you?" I ask again, once he is gone.

Jack takes a sip of his drink and makes a face. He pulls out the olive and puts it into his mouth. "No, I haven't spoken to Carolyn in days."

"So how did you know?"

He sighs, and spits the pit discreetly into his palm. "I never thought you killed her, Emilia."

"Yes, you did."

"No, I didn't." He pauses and swirls his drink in his glass. "When you first told me, I thought it might have been possible. You seemed so sure. But then when I talked to Carolyn . . ."

At that moment the waiter arrives to take our order, and it is a long minute of rare or medium, sautéed or grilled, before I know what he means. Once the waiter has left with our menus and Jack's empty glass I say, "But Carolyn told you I did it. She told you anyone who was so bad at taking care of William could easily have killed her own baby."

He shrugs.

"I don't understand," I say.

"Carolyn had the reaction I would have expected her to have if I'd been thinking clearly. She's angry, and her anger makes her irrational. Hearing her say what she did made me realize how ridiculous and impossible it was. What surprises me is that she had the grace to call you afterward. That surprises me."

"Aren't you relieved?"

"I'm relieved that you feel absolved. I'm relieved that you no longer feel the terrible guilt that's been crippling you for the past few months. So, yes, I guess you could say I'm relieved. But I never really believed you were responsible for Isabel's death. I never needed proof that you weren't."

I am not sure what to feel right now. I am grateful to him for his faith and his faithfulness, but at the same time, I almost wish he had thought me the murderer of his child. Because if he had, then now I could be forgiven.

I am terrified of the self-contained coolness I see on the other side of the table and I wish there were some way I could push it aside, some way I could just make this stop right now.

"I apologized to my father," I say.

"That's good."

"We talked about a lot of things. I think you're right about the way I've dealt with him and my mom, and about how that's affected how I look at relationships." I'm about to launch into a speech about my misplaced search for perfection, and how that has polluted our relationship, and how I am determined to be fairer from here on to Jack and to myself, when he holds up his hand.

"Emilia, don't."

"But . . ."

"None of this matters."

"What?"

"I am so sorry, and I love you, Emilia. I do. But I can't be with you anymore. I can't do this to William anymore."

I feel like I have been sucker punched. My gut is twisting, my throat constricts, and I cannot breathe. Or I am breathing too fast. I can't tell. Why does this man always do this to me in restaurants? I should have known better than to meet him here. I should have insisted on hot dogs from a street vender.

I realize suddenly that Jack is talking.

"What?" I whisper.

"I said, it's not fair to him. He's my child. He has to come first in my life. Everything else, what I want, what makes me happy, all that has to come second. I need to do what's best for William."

I find my voice now. "And why does that mean leaving me?"

Jack pushes his chair in, leans across the table, and takes my hand in his. His face assumes an avuncular expression: fond, gentle, condescending. "Emilia, you're thirty-two years old. You don't want an instant family. A school-age kid. An old husband. It's ridiculous. You're too young."

"You don't think it's maybe a little late for you to have this epiphany?"

"It was a mistake. We made a mistake."

"You said you love me."

He reaches his palm out to cup my cheek. "I do love you. You're lovely."

At this I prove my immaturity by jerking away and snorting in disgust at the precise moment the waiter is placing my halibut in front of me. He startles and tips the plate, but deftly catches the slosh of beurre blanc with the edge of his linen napkin.

"Madame?" he says.

"I'm fine," I say. "Thank you."

When the waiter has set Jack's roasted lamb before him and disappeared I say, "We did not make a mistake."

Jack is holding his knife and fork, but he has not taken a bite of his meat.

I say it again. "We didn't make a mistake. I didn't make a mistake. You're my family and I want to be with you."

He lays his silverware down. "William is my family," he says gently.

"And me. William and me."

"You don't . . ."

"I do Jack. I do love William. I do." Even as I hear the words I know how false they sound, how desperate. I know that Jack thinks I am saying them just so that he will not end our marriage. I know that he thinks I am lying.

But the maddening irony is that the words are true. It is only now when it is too late that I understand that somehow that irritatingly precocious, selfish boy, with his dinosaurs and his daemons, his bicycle helmets and his lactose allergies, has wormed his way into my heart. And more than that. He has given me back my baby by forcing his mother, *his mother* of all unlikely people, to release me from my festering shame and guilt. Without ever intending to, he even gave me back my father. And yet, I can't help but think it's sort of typical of William to make me fall in love with him only when doing so does me no good at all.

I say, "Give me another chance."

Jack says, "I'm sorry."

"Give me another chance."

"I can't."

"What does that mean? Of course you can. Yes, you can."

He shakes his head, and I see all of a sudden that his eyes are damp.

"Don't," I say, or not. I'm not sure if I have spoken.

"I don't trust you, Emilia. I don't trust you anymore."

And then what do you do? Because you still have to pay the check. You have to wait for them to clear your plates and bring you your coats. You have to stand out in front of the restaurant side by side and flag down your cabs. You have to decide whether to give a kiss good-bye and if so, what kind (brief, formal, on the cheek). It would have been so much easier just to disappear.

I have a geographical crisis in the cab. My cabbie and I are conveniently stuck behind a truck in crosstown traffic so there is plenty of time for me to hesitate between a dozen alternative destinations. There are so many places in this city, but only one place I want to be, only one man I want to be with. One man, and one boy.

I refuse to accept banishment. I will not be exiled. Not now, not when I have finally realized what it is that I will lose. I must somehow prove to Jack that he and his son are my family, and I am theirs. We belong together.

But until then I have nothing to wear so I'm going to go pick up my goddamn jeans.

"Just take me to Barneys," I say. "Madison and Sixty-first."

Chapter 30

It is a long week and Simon's house has never been so sparkling clean. Every morning I tackle something new: cleaning the moldings on the windows and doors, scrubbing the tile grout in the bathroom, polishing the marble tiles in the kitchenette, vacuuming up the dust bunnies behind the books in the built-in bookcases. This last project leads me to Simon's collection of pornographic DVDs and I spend most of one morning eating microwave popcorn and watching men do things to one another that seem geometrically unlikely if not impossible. I feel it has been a learning experience, and I think that if I ever manage to convince Jack to take me back, he will not be sorry.

Afternoons I spend reading my stepmother books, taking copious notes. When I can no longer stand it, I leave the house and wander around downtown. Once or twice I consider heading north toward the park, but I cannot seem to make the trip. Instead of earth and grass, I walk concrete, and instead of trees and monuments, I look at store windows. There are things down here I want to buy for William and for Jack, but I don't allow myself this indulgence. It would seem craven, and though I know William would not care, that he would be perfectly happy to assemble his Chasmosaurus skull model without worrying whether I was trying to purchase his affection, I don't buy it or the mulberry cashmere socks, the last pair in men's size small, perfect for Jack's well-formed feet.

I eat a lot. More than a lot. I drink coffee and eat muffins and morning buns, hamburgers and large plates of Vietnamese noodles. I order enough for two in a filthy Chinatown restaurant with bright orange waterfowl hanging in the window and finish everything on my plate. I buy hot dogs from street venders at ten in the morning, before the water in their carts has grown cloudy with hot-dog sweat. I eat at a terrible tourist trap in Little Italy, ordering a plate of pasta smothered in scalding hot cheese and cornstarch-thickened white sauce. This is the only meal I leave unfinished, but I soothe my empty stomach with slices of fresh mozzarella from Joe's Dairy. Simon's scale is the only thing in his apartment that I do not clean, because I am afraid to get close to it, even with a duster or a sponge. I don't want to accidentally fall on top of it and discover I have gained thirteen pounds while in exile in lower Manhattan waiting to figure out a way to make my husband take me back.

On Thursday night, after a day spent wandering the streets, sitting in cafés, and highlighting sections of my stepmothering books like some kind of crazed fairy-tale bag lady, I cook an elaborate dinner for Simon. He comes home to find his table set with rose-patterned china and linen napkins, a saffron-infused fish soup simmering on the back burner of his stove. I am pounding garlic and parsley into a paste on his kitchen countertop.

"What are you doing?" he says.

"Don't worry, it's granite. It won't break. I made garlic mayonnaise. I didn't have time to bake bread, so I got an olive loaf from Dean & DeLuca. Can you rinse the salad leaves?"

"Wow," he says, taking off his necktie. "What's with all this industry?"

"I have a phone call to make."

He raises one eyebrow.

"I've been procrastinating."

While Simon rinses arugula and blots it with wads of paper toweling, I find my cell phone and dial the number that I decided to call in the early afternoon but have been avoiding ever since then. Every one of my stepmother reference volumes suggests therapy as an option for the stepmother, and family therapy for the beleaguered relationship. Two even encourage the stepmother to speak individually to the stepchild's therapist. Apparently all the children have them. I have never spoken to William's therapist, the noted child psychologist Dr. Bartholomew Allerton. In fact, I have never spoken *about* Dr. Allerton except in the most derisive of tones. But I know William trusts this man. I know that every week, when William sits in that office on what I imagine is a tiny little couch, the two of them must do more than just play endless games of Stratego, even though that is all William will say about his visits with Dr. Allerton. Dr. Allerton surely possesses insight into this convoluted and fucked-up situation of ours. If Dr. Allerton will see me, he will help me figure out how to save my family.

After the voice mail beeps I begin, "Dr. Allerton, this is Emilia Greenleaf. Emilia Woolf Greenleaf. Jack Woolf's wife. William Woolf's stepmother." I recite my phone number into the telephone. Twice. Then I continue. "I'm calling because, as you probably know, things haven't been going so well with us and I was wondering, I was hoping, that you might consider talking to me, or giving me an appointment. You see the thing is, I really want to, I mean I think I'm ready to." My pause is too long. "Or I could . . . if Jack would let me . . ." Again I pause for too long and there is another beep and I am cut off.

"Goddamn it," I say. I dial again. "Hi, Dr. Allerton, this is Emilia Greenleaf again. William Woolf's stepmother. It's just that I really do want to learn how to be . . . better . . . with William and do the kind of things he needs. Or at least not hurt him. I guess. It's just that I think if I could talk to you, I might get some more insight into William and what he's feeling, maybe. Or something . . ." My voice trails away, the voice mail beeps and I'm once again cut off.

"Fuck." I dial again. "Hi, Emilia Greenleaf again. I feel really awkward about this, because you probably know that Jack and I are sort of separated, and I'm not trying to go behind Jack's back or anything, but I was thinking maybe you could help me figure out if there's a way to maybe fix things. Because I want things to work out with Jack and with William, and I know . . ." Beep.

"Emilia?" Simon says.

"What?" I hold the receiver in one hand while I dial again with the other.

"Can you spell 'restraining order'?"

I pause, the phone receiver halfway to my ear. "Too much?"

"Uh, you could say that."

"Shit."

My cell phone rings.

"Shit," I say again.

"Answer it," Simon says.

I look at the caller ID. "It's the doctor."

"Answer it!"

"No. He probably thinks I'm a psycho."

"Will you please stop *acting* like a psycho and answer the goddamn phone?"

Dr. Allerton's offices are lush and impeccably decorated, with only the most discerning disturbed children in mind. The couch and chairs in the waiting room are of some stain-resistant yet luxurious fabric and the toys all look new. The plastic boxes of Legos are full to the brim, the hair on the dolls is still glossy and unmatted, the cardboard boxes of games and puzzles are not dented or torn. Either the noted child psychologist replenishes the shelves of his waiting room on a weekly basis,. or the children who wait here are so demoralized and depressed that they have no energy to play.

It is a few minutes before seven in the morning, and I am his very first appointment of the day. He is squeezing me in, he said last night on the phone, because he is concerned. I sounded "distraught" and "confused" in my messages. I tried to explain to the doctor that I am not confused. I have finally achieved some clarity and it is for this reason that I want to see him, in order to seek his assistance, but after a rather, well, confusing few minutes of discussion, we decided it was better for me to come in and try to explain in person what it is that I am looking for.

At precisely seven o'clock, the door at the far end of the office opens and a small man pokes his very large head into the waiting room. His head is covered by a pelt of black curls, tight and shiny like a Persian lamb Cossack hat, and his gray beard crawls down his throat into the open neck of his shirt, joining up with his chest hair. I am surprised that William has never mentioned that his therapist is so hairy.

"Ms. Greenleaf?" he says. "Come in."

Dr. Allerton points me toward the couch and sits down on a dark brown leather Eames chair. I sit down and shuck my coat. My scarf I leave on, wrapped loosely around my neck. I duck my chin inside the folds of soft wool.

"So," the doctor says, "what can I do for you?"

I launch into a longer version of what I said into his answering machine, that I am hoping he will help me to understand William better, to be a better stepmother. I tell him that my relationship with Jack is in crisis, that unless I can figure out a way to solve this problem, our marriage will be over.

"Hmm," the doctor says when I have finally wound down.

This is the insight for which I woke up at six in the morning?

"Hmm," he says again. Then he scratches his beard.

I look over his shoulder at the bookshelf where the games and toys are arrayed. There is the famous Stratego that has consumed so many of William's weekly therapeutic hours. I look back at Dr. Allerton. Now he is scratching his head.

"Emilia," he says. "May I call you Emilia?"

"Yes."

"Emilia, do you want to be a better stepmother because you think you ought to be for William's sake, and for your own, or do you want to be a better stepmother because you are afraid that otherwise your husband will leave you?"

It's cold in this office and I bury my chin in my scarf.

He waits.

"Both reasons," I say.

He nods. "I can give you some general guidelines about being a stepmother. I can direct you to some very fine books on the topic or to the Stepfamily Foundation. I can even give you a few recommendations of counselors with expertise in the area. However, my concern is that you have come to me in order to prove something to Jack, rather than out of a real desire to improve the situation."

I think about Jack and about how much I want him. I know that I am here because I am trying to prove to him that I can be what he needs me to be, what William needs me to be. But is that the only reason? I think of William, of his narrow face, his earnest tone, his blue eyes. I see him gliding across the ice of Wohlman rink, his wobbly ankles barely supporting his weight, his determined expression as he pushed forward despite his fear.

"Emilia, being a stepmother is a terribly difficult job. It's normal to feel resentment toward your stepson, it's normal to feel anger. It's normal even to feel, occasionally, that you dislike him. You can't expect to be immune to these feelings, nor should your husband expect you to be. You can't control your feelings, nor can you control anyone else's. The only thing you can control is your own behavior, your own response to the inevitable stress. That is, if you want to."

"I do. I do want to. I just . . ."

"What?"

"I just don't know if William . . . how William . . ." I tuck my chin into my scarf again, hiding from the furry shrink.

Dr. Allerton sighs. "Are you asking me how William feels about you? Is that why you're here?"

"No. No, of course not. Not really. I mean. Does he talk about me?"

"What do *you* think he feels," the doctor asks.

I think of the risk William took in coming to my defense before his mother, the gift of absolution he has given me. I see him standing before her, a tattered copy of *Lyle, Lyle, Crocodile* in one hand, a two-foot-tall *Giganotosaurus* in the other.

"I don't know," I lie.

On Friday I am wandering Canal Street, trying to decide whether my afternoon snack will be cuchifrito or mofongo, neither of which means anything to me, but both of which sound enticing in their own way, when my cell phone rings. I see it is Jack on my caller ID and I am so happy that I rush out of the tiny Dominican restaurant without ordering anything.

"Jack!"

"I need your help."

Jack is in a Lincoln Town Car circling the federal courthouse. William is with him, throwing a world-class hissy fit. For some reason, surely because he is confident that it is the one request that is guaranteed to queer the works, he has insisted on seeing me. God bless that boy.

Today is Carolyn's wedding day, and William is not happy. His misery was made manifest in the morning when he threw a tantrum on the way to school, at school when he bit one of his classmates and tried to fling a chair off the roof playground—a fairly pointless gesture as the whole thing is fenced in, but it's the intent that counts, not the result, which was less dramatic and more frustrating than he would have liked—and after school when he kicked Sonia so hard he managed to crack her composure if not her shin. That, quite frankly, astonishes me like nothing else does.

Once he is home he refused to dress and could not be bullied into his nice clothes. He insisted on telephoning his father. I can only imagine what it cost Carolyn to give in to this demand. Jack tells me that William wanted to speak to him and that Carolyn allowed him to call, and then requested Jack's assistance in convincing William to ready himself for the ceremony. I'm willing to bet she did so through gritted teeth. I feel for her, honestly I do, and not merely because she has recently been the source of some salvation for me. It must be terribly aggravating to have to request your ex-husband's aid in talking your son off a cliff so that your wedding can go forward peacefully.

Jack was not successful. Or at least, not entirely. William wept, but would not explain the reason for his tears. He said he wanted his daddy, he refused to go to the wedding ceremony, he begged Jack to come get him. He agreed, finally, to get dressed, but only if Jack would ferry him downtown. Once they'd reached the courthouse, however, he'd refused to exit the car. Jack had tried to pry him loose, but had realized that dragging a screaming child into the judge's chambers was not what Carolyn had meant when she had asked for his help in managing William. Through his tears William had suddenly announced that if Jack could produce *me*, and if we could talk, then William would go to the wedding.

"Put him on the phone," I say.

"He wants to see you."

"How much time do you have?"

"The ceremony is due to start at five."

I look at my watch. "We've got plenty of time, it's only one subway stop."

Everything is on my side. My train arrives in the station as I pass through the turnstile, and I slip through the door just before it closes. I have barely enough time in the moments it takes to travel to the next station to consider why William is asking for me now, when it is least convenient for his parents, when it will upset Carolyn's plans the most. Surely that's *why* he has asked for me because he knows how much this will irk his mother, still, it's funny. He has never accommodated me in this way, and now he needs me so much, precisely when I need him.

I exit the subway station to see the Town Car waiting for me. I yank open the car door. William is sitting on his father's lap, his face smudged with tears and mucus. Jack's coat and suit jacket are balled up on the seat next to him and the top button of his shirt is undone, his tie askew. He looks beautiful.

"Hey guys," I say. "What's up?"

Jack gives me a this-is-no-time-for-jokes look. William, forgetting that he is the reason I am here, looks shocked to see me, and begins to sniffle.

"Shove over," I say as I climb in the car.

The driver looks in the rearview mirror and says, "Once more around, Mr. Woolf?"

"Yes, Henry, if you don't mind."

I lean back against the black leather upholstery and angle myself so that I can look at Jack and William. "Dude!" I say. "Score! No booster seat."

"It was the last thing on our minds," Jack says.

"Nice," I say to William, nodding my head knowingly, as if I am the only person who realizes that this whole afternoon has been designed as a ploy to leave the booster at home. William's mouth begins to twist into a smile, but he clamps his lips.

"So, what's up, William? Why did you want to see me?"

He shrugs.

"Seriously. I don't mind, or anything, but any minute the cops are going to decide that poor Henry's a terrorist casing the federal building and pull us over, and your mom's inside having who knows what kind of conniption fit. It's definitely time for you to start talking."

He rubs his crusted nose with his fist and then wipes his hand on the leg of his expensive gray slacks. I hope if I manage to get him into the wedding his mother will forgive me for the snot.

"You don't want your mother to marry your dentist," I say.

He shakes his head and whispers, "No."

"Well, honestly, who would? I mean, a dentist." I shudder. "But you're not like most people, William. You're weird, remember? You like the guy. Didn't you tell me that? Didn't you tell me that you like your dentist?"

"Yeah."

"Did you change your mind?"

"No."

Jack has leaned his head back against the headrest and closed his eyes, as if he can't bear to watch the hash I am making of this.

"So, what gives?"

"I don't know."

"I do."

Now William finally stops whispering. "You do?" he says, aloud.

"If your mommy gets married to your dentist, and your daddy is married to me, then that's it, right? They're never going to get back together ever again. Your family will never go back to being the way it used to be. Your dad and your mom and you."

He tears up again, and rubs his eyes. I am sad that it's started already, this manly pushing away of tears. For all that he's crying so readily, this small boy, something is telling him that he shouldn't be, that it's better not to cry, that he is shaming himself. I can tell that, now at least, he is trying not to give in to the seductive pleasure.

William says, "When I was a baby I used to think that when you and Daddy were done being married that then Daddy and my mom could stop being divorced."

"You did?"

"Yeah. I used to think that when the divorce was finished then my dad would come home."

"Do you remember a lot of things about when your dad lived with you and your mom?"

He screws up his face, wrinkling his brow and thinking hard. "Some things. I remember my dad coming to Nantucket with us one summer. I remember stuff like that. But I don't remember a lot of stuff."

"You were pretty little when they got divorced."

He leans against Jack, pressing his small back against his father's firm chest.

"William, did you think when I left last week that your dad would move back in with your mom?"

I can see Jack stiffen, and I know William must feel the tension against his back. Jack and I are both waiting for William's response.

First he shrugs, then whispers, "Sort of."

"And is that why you're so angry today? Because your mom's getting married to your dentist instead of to your dad?"

He nods.

I lean forward and take one of his sticky little hands in mine. "So, kiddo, why did you want to see me? I don't get it. I would have thought I'd be the *last* person you'd want to see."

William falls awkwardly off his father's lap and sprawls across my legs. He starts crying again, and pushes his head into my knees. "I don't know," he says. "I don't know."

I pull him up onto my legs, shifting him around. I've never held him on my lap before. He all knobby knees and dangling limbs and it takes me a moment to get him situated so we're not ridiculously uncomfortable. I smooth his hair and rock gently. "It's okay, William. It's okay," I murmur.

"It's just, you know. All *bad* now," he wails. "Everything is messed up. Just put it all back. Put it all back." He is nearly hyperventilating, his whole body shaking with his tears. I wrap my arms as tightly around him as I can.

"I'm sorry, William," I say, rocking him. "I can't."

"Why don't you live with us anymore?" William says.

I hold my breath, waiting, I'm not sure what for. Jack says, "Emilia and I are just trying to figure things out, William. I know it's hard to understand."

No kidding.

I say, "You know, it's like Lyle. Should he live in the house on East Eighty-eighth Street, should he live in the zoo with all the other crocodiles? That kind of thing. We're working it out."

William sits up, shifting off my lap and onto the seat between his father and me. "That is so stupid, Emilia," he says vehemently. "You know very well that Mr. Grumps *makes* Lyle go to the zoo. Lyle doesn't belong there. He belongs with his family on East Eighty-eighth Street."

"Yeah, well, but that's fiction. In real life crocodiles don't have families. Not human ones. They live with the other crocodiles in the Central Park Zoo."

"There are no crocodiles in the Central Park Zoo, only caimans."

"It's a *metaphor,* William. I'm trying to say that maybe I'm like Lyle. Maybe I don't belong with you and your daddy because I'm not like you. My teeth are too sharp and . . . and my tail's too long." That last part didn't work, but he gets it. At least I hope he gets it. I'm doing Jack's work for him here, and I'm not going to be able to do it much longer. I'm doing my best not to cry, but I'm not going to last.

"Lyle does *so* belong with his family, Emilia. They love him even though he's a crocodile."

I stare at him. I cannot tell if he has said what I think he has. Has he told me that he loves me, or is five years old too young to speak metaphorically? Is he just talking about a silly children's book? I don't care, I hug him anyway. And then Jack is there, too, and we are all bundled together in the suddenly too-small backseat of the Lincoln Town Car.

"Another circle, Mr. Woolf?" Henry says.

"No," I say. "We're ready to get out."

William lifts his face, shocked. He starts to shake his head.

"Come on, sweetie," I say. "It's late, and your mom's getting married with or without us. Let's not ruin her day."

I rummage around in my purse until I find a tissue that looks only slightly worse for wear. I clean him up as best I can, and then I straighten Jack's tie. We take the steps to the federal courthouse at a jog.

Carolyn is waiting in front of the metal detectors in a small knot of similarly agitated people. This time, I see, she is not making the mistake of marrying a small Jew. Her dentist is tall and blond and decidedly Nordic. He is a polar bear next to Jack's koala. I'm partial to the smaller breeds, myself.

Our arrival is greeted with some surprise, but with general relief.

"Thank God," Carolyn says, snatching William's hand from mine. "What happened? Emilia, what are you . . . oh never mind. Let's go. We were due in Judge Doty's chambers at five."

I look at my watch. It is eleven minutes past the hour.

Carolyn, her Scandinavian or Icelandic dentist, and the few members of their retinue rush through the metal detectors. With the hand that is not grasped by his mother, William gives us a resigned wave. When the group disappears into an elevator, Jack and I sag against each other with relief.

"Let's get out of here," Jack says.

Chapter 31

Henry takes us uptown, to Carolyn's building, to pick up the suitcase Sonia has packed for William and left for us in the lobby. We have not spoken about where we are going afterward, so I ask Henry to stop at Seventy-sixth Street. The names of the entrances to the park are so rarely used, and it is only because William has told me so that I know that, like Women's Gate, this particular break in the stone wall is one of the only ones not named for a profession or a calling, like Scholars' Gate, or Mariner's Gate, or Inventor's, Engineers', Woodsman's, or Artist's. It is called Children's Gate.

When we get out of the car I pull my scarf down. It is cold and blustery and I stamp my feet a few times to warm them up.

"Where do you want to go?" Jack asks.

"Let's just walk."

"Do you want to go to that little hut in the Ramble?"

"We can't go to the hut because I can't *find* the fucking hut. William and I tromped around for ages. If I couldn't find it in the middle of the day I sure as hell won't be able to find it when the sun's about to set."

"I know where it is."

"What? How can you possibly know where it is?"

Jack is looking into the park, and his back is to me, neat and smooth in his dark coat. His slate blue plaid scarf is untied and one end eddies around his waist in the wind. As I cross toward him, my steps are quiet, but not silent; there are twigs and dried leaves on the sidewalk and they crack and break under my feet. I know he hears me but he doesn't turn. When I reach him, I slip my arms around his waist, lay my cheek against the rough wool of his back, and match my breath to his. "How do you know where it is?" I say to his back.

"William and I went looking for it on Wednesday afternoon."

"And you found it? How did you find it?"

"I bought a map at the Dairy."

"Oh. A map. Well. If you're going to cheat." I suppose if I had stopped at the Dairy, if I had bought a map like Jack did, then William and I would have found this little hut in the Ramble as easily. We would have found it, and then we might never have gone up to the Meer. We would have avoided that debacle, but if we had we might have avoided it all, including what inspired Carolyn to tell me about Isabel's death, and what inspired William to call for me when he needed someone's help today.

The wind buffets us as we walk along the winding paths under the creaking trees. It is at our backs and propels us like a couple of ungainly kites over the cracked cement walks. As we walk north, looking for a path that will cut west to the Ramble and the bridge, the sound of children's voices begins to grow louder. There is a playground here, at Seventy-seventh Street. It is like the other playgrounds in Central Park, full of bundled children and their mothers, cocoa-skinned nannies, babies batting mittened hands at toys dangling from the hoods of the carriages. As we pass the playground, Jack shoots me a glance, evaluating my response. I look inside the gates. There is a little boy, four or five years old, too small to see over the handle of the stroller he is pushing. The baby in the stroller screams with excitement, laughs wildly at the thrill of being humped along by her big brother. Their mother walks next to them, a protective hand occasionally adjusting their direction keeping the stroller from rolling into harm's way.

I think of William, and of Isabel. I imagine how he might have wheeled her in her denim Bugaboo. I think of the baby Carolyn will have, the little brother or sister he will have a chance to know. And before my mind wanders further, I take Jack's hand and we continue walking west, toward the Ramble.

We don't speak while we walk, just watch our breath mist in the air as we climb. It takes only ten or fifteen minutes to reach the hut. My problem was that I was trying to come from the wrong side. All I needed to do was take the Lake path and cut north. It's a straight shot from there.

It is a little wooden structure, a kind of pergola with arched sides and a shake roof. The walls are made of odd-shaped logs hewn from the trunks of narrow trees. It is very hut-like and disappointingly unsecluded, with paths running into it from all sides.

"I can't believe this is right here," I say.

"I can't believe you couldn't find it."

Jack reaches over and tugs together the sides of my coat. It is much colder here inside the hut than it was outside.

We sit down on one of the rustic little benches. I extend my legs out toward the center of the cobblestone starburst that makes up the floor. Jack also puts his feet out and they go much farther than mine. As small as he is, he is taller than me. We are a nice pair, a good matched set. But are we a magical unit? The story I have always told Jack about the way we fell in love was a kabalistic tale of *bashert*, of magic and meant to be, of angels flying through lifetimes.

I'm afraid my father is right; I spun a dream web no more real than the fantasy he himself chased.

I mystified and mysticized our love to excuse the damage we did. The miraculous tale made it possible to ignore promises made and oaths sworn, children born and trust laid. Jack and I were *bashert*, and thus we had no choice but to rain nuclear fire on those who stood between us. We were meant to be, not by choice but by destiny. Because we were powerless in the face of fate, we were also blameless.

But Jack was a father first, before I became a mother, and thus he believed less readily than I. The gravitational pull of his paternal guilt was strong, and I was forced to be an aeronaut, constantly tending gas fires and lines, filling the balloon with hot air so that our tiny basket would stay aloft. When the silk tore and my skills failed, we crashed hard, breaking bones and crushing limbs in our race to the earth.

Now I see we are not a chapter from an ancient mystical text, ordained by God. We do not love with magic. We love each other like a man and a woman are supposed to love each other. With hard work and fear. With effort and misunderstanding. With moments of ease. And finally, necessarily, with trust.

I open my mouth to explain this to Jack, to tell him the way our love is and must be, to plead my case and show my heart, but he speaks first.

"I like your new jeans," he says. "They make your ass look great."

"You had time to notice my ass during all this?"

"Always."

I smile, and put my leg on top of his. He slips his arm around me, cupping that ass he admires so.

There is much to say, many apologies, many promises. We say nothing. The sky grows dark, this corner of the park lit only by the luminaires and the glow of the buildings surrounding the park on all sides.

After a long time Jack says, "Let's go home. It's freezing out here."

Chapter 32

I *am* waiting for William. It is hot for September and I am sweating as I stand outside the door of the kindergarten class at the Ethical Culture School. I am aloof from the crowd of waiting mothers, partly because the kindergarten mothers don't trust second wives any more than nursery school mothers did, but mostly because I do not want anyone to jostle and crush what I have brought. It is delicate, and I don't trust five-year-olds.

"Hey, it's not Wednesday," William says when he sees me.

"But it *is* your lucky day."

"Why aren't you working?"

"I took the day off." Allison has gotten me a job in the appellate division of Legal Aid. I write briefs for a living now. When my brother-in-law and his colleagues are unsuccessful in convincing juries to release their young clients to continue roaming the hopeless streets, I urge appellate judges to do so instead. I like the work very much, and I think I'm good at it. Brief writing, after all, is the part of lawyering I'm best at.

"Where's Sonia?"

"She took the day off, too."

"What's that?"

"A fried egg."

"Seriously."

"What does it look like?"

"A boat. A remote control boat."

"Bingo." I dip the boat down where he can see it more clearly. It is a miniature tall ship, with cloth sails and a wooden mast. There is a very small pirate at the helm. He wears a tiny patch on his eye. The boat cost almost $200 and was not the most expensive in the store. Not even close.

"It's a pirate ship!"

"Indeed. Come on, let's go."

"Where are we going?"

"Duh," I say.

"Model boat pond?"

"Bingo."

"Okay," William says. "Let me get my backpack and my lunch box."

"The model boat pond is actually called the Conservatory Water," William says as we launch the boat into the stagnant green water. "Most people don't know that."

He is a natural on the remote control. I stand back and look around the pond. Up the path I can see the small boys and girls clamber over the Alice in Wonderland statue, giving chase to the pigeons that befoul her shoulders with white-and-black goo.

"This is excellent," William says. He buzzes the ship along the shore and then takes it out to the middle of the pond.

"Avast there, matey," I say.

"Ahoy. Not Avast."

"Ahoy there, matey."

William gives me a turn and I do my best, but my circles are not as tight as his and we are both worried that I will capsize the ship.

"You have a fine ship, Emilia," William says.

"I bought it for you, dude."

"No kidding? For me! That is so excellent." William attempts a risky figure eight.

"It's your birthday present."

"My birthday is next month, in October." He frowns. "Does this mean you won't be giving me a present on my actual birthday?"

"It's not for *your* birthday. It's your present, and it's for a birthday, but it's not for your birthday. Get it?"

"No."

"Think." I sit down on the concrete shoulder of the pond, my back to the water. I cross my eyes at him.

"Blair," he says at last.

"You got it."

Carolyn called Jack this morning on her way to the hospital. She is in labor, and so William will be staying with us for a few days, until after she has had a day or two alone at home with the baby.

"He was born today, while I was at school?"

"He's being born right now. Or will be soon. Your dentist will call Daddy as soon as the baby makes his appearance."

William says, "The baby's name is going to be Blair Soule Doty.

The first. That's a Roman numeral. And I'm William Soule Woolf I. We have the same middle name, and we are both firsts."

"I know. You've told me that about six hundred times. It's a great name. They're both great names."

"I'll have to draw a family portrait with Blair in it." He executes another tight turn. "You never saw the family picture I drew in nursery school."

"I saw it." I cross my legs in front of me and hold my face up to the sun. It is warm against my cheeks. We are having a brilliant September Indian summer. I close my eyes. "It was beautiful."

"I made Isabel as an angel."

I open my eyes. "I know."

"That was for you."

"What do you mean?"

"The angel was for you. I don't actually believe in angels. I don't think there is a heaven where people go when they die. But I thought it would make you feel good to think of Isabel like that, like a little angel with wings, flying over your head."

I reach my hand out and stroke William's hair. He tolerates my touch for a moment before he returns to the ship. I say, "It did. It did make me feel good."

"What do you think happens when you die? Do you believe in angels?"

I think of Isabel, an angel with luminous wings, fluttering over my head. "No, I don't think so."

"Jews don't. Especially not Orthodox Jews. I mean, they don't believe in the heaven kind of angels. Remember when I said I was an Orthodox Jew?"

"I do."

"Only I'm not really an Orthodox Jew."

"I know, William."

"Episcopalians believe in angels and in heaven, but I don't think I'm an Episcopalian either."

"No?"

"No. I think I might be Buddhist. Buddhists believe in reincarnation. That means that you get to come back as someone else. Or as an animal. Do you believe in that? Do you think Isabel might come back as an animal? A fish in the model boat pond, maybe? Or a penguin in the Central Park Zoo? Or maybe she'll come back as Blair. Then she'll be my brother, instead of my sister."

This stops me. Would Isabel want so much to live that she would come back as another mother's child? As Carolyn's child? Perhaps as mine, the child I will have one day. I wish for William's kindergarten-Buddhist certainty. "I don't know, William. I guess I don't really believe in reincarnation."

William swoops his ship down on a stray leaf. Then he careens it around the edge of the pond, his turn so tight the mast is nearly at a forty-five degree angle.

"Well," he says. "What do you think happened to Isabel when she died?"

"I guess I think that Isabel is just gone, that whatever she was, whatever made her different from everybody else, disappeared when she did."

"So you believe in nothing." He says it as if he has heard about believing in nothing before. Believing in nothing is a concept he understands.

"I don't know, William. I just don't know."

William spins the dial on his remote control and the ship turns crazily, tipping on its side, nearly capsizing before it rights itself again. "Well, I'm a Buddhist."

"Go for it," I say.

"I'll let you know if I find Isabel."

"You do that. It makes me feel good knowing you're doing that." I watch him at the controls. He is so confident. "It's time to bring the boat in now."

"One more circle."

William circles the boat around the pond, very slowly, dragging out his time. When he brings the boat in to dock, I pull it out of the water and shake it off.

William holds his arms out for his boat. It is too big for him to carry, but I let him take it. I put the remote control in my purse.

"I love my boat, Emilia. Thank you for the birthday present."

"You're welcome, William Soule Woolf the first. Happy Blair's birthday. I love you."

And I do love him. I am in love with this scrawny know-it-all of a boy, with his irritating precocity and his embarrassingly cloistered and self-centered view of the world. I have fallen in love with him, not with the mad hysterical rush of instantaneous, spontaneous passion I felt for his father, but slowly, jolting and creaking along, like a three-wheeled cart on a rutted dirt road. I did not tumble down a precipice into this love, I climbed up the side of a rocky crag of Manhattan schist, my fingernails breaking against the rock, my knees scraped and torn, spread-eagled as I searched for toeholds and fingerholds.

This love was so hard to recognize, but I have finally been able to see it for what it is—grace. Grace is when something is more beautiful than we deserve, more elegant and lovely than it should be. Grace is like Central Park. Carved from schist and swamp, boulders and undergrowth, by a vast construction project of thousands of surveyors, dirt carters, blasting teams, roadbuilders, stonemasons, blacksmiths, and bricklayers, Central Park is, in this city of steel and glass, marble and asphalt, brick and stone, 843 acres of grace. It is far more lovely, more bedecked with weeping willows trailing into moss-filled ponds, gentle arching bridges, blue-gray gnatcatchers, than any Nasdaq-obsessed stock trader, any taxi driver with a law degree from the University of Karachi, any Upper West Side mother of twins, or any of us eight million different kinds of New Yorkers deserves. The citizens of other cities are surely no less wonderful than we are, no less special, no less worthy of sanctuary. Yet we have our grace, and most other cities but a modicum of theirs.

When I saw William, outside the zoo, his legs dangling from his father's shoulders, I saw in him the impediment to the fulfillment of the angel's plan. But I was wrong. The gorgeousness of life comes in accidental beauty; it comes in inexplicable grace. Grace, like when a child brings to your life an unplanned magic.

William Soule Wolfe, my unsought, my fortuitous grace.

Acknowledgments

This book was written in large part at the MacDowell Colony, and I am forever grateful for the gift of time and space that marvelous institution provides. The generosity of the Stanford Calderwood Foundation made my fellowship there possible.

The following people gave me insights and assistance: Andrew of Le Pain Quotidien, Hillery Borton, Sylvia Brownrigg, Alicia Costelloe, Carmen Dario, Elizabeth Gaffney, Andy Greer, Daniel Handler, Rick Karr, Kristina Larsen, Micheline Marcom, Devin McIntyre, Daniel Mendelsohn, Peggy Orenstein, Susanne Pari, Lis Petkevich, Elissa Schappell, Nancy Schulman and Alix Friedman of the 92 Street Y Preschool, Mona Simpson, Carla Sinz, Joshua Tager, Sedge Thomson, Vendela Vida, and Ires Wilbanks. And, of course, Michael Chabon.

For championing this book I am indebted to Maggie Doyle, Karen Glass, Marc Platt and Abby Wolf-Weiss, Sylvie Rabineau, and Marianne Velmanns. And the champion of them all, Mary Evans.

Most of all I am grateful to the incomparable Phyllis Grann.

Questions for Discussion

A Note to the Reader

If you have not finished *Love and Other Impossible Pursuits*, we respectfully suggest that you may want to wait before reviewing this guide.

1. What were your initial impressions of Emilia? In what way did your image of her change as you learned more about her? As she narrates, is she always honest with us and with herself? How does she balance humor and intensity when describing what it's like to be a woman on the edge?

2. Discuss the many forms of love described in the novel. Is love ever a truly impossible pursuit? What factors make it seem that way to Emilia?

3. How does Emilia cope with being a pariah among the other preschool parents? What are the criteria within this community for determining whether a woman is a good mother? What purpose does their competitive attitude serve? What does Sonia seem to think about the culture of American mommyhood?

4. What does Emilia's own mother teach her about being a parent? How does Emilia's mom compare to Jack's mother from Syria?

5. Discuss the author's choice of New York, and Central Park in particular, as the backdrop for much of the novel. How does Emilia perceive the wonders and dangers of this locale? What fragments of her childhood can she revive in the park?

6. Is the tension between Jack and Emilia solely related to the loss of Isabel and the presence of a testy ex-wife? How might the

early months of their marriage have gone in the absence of such agonies? Did their relationship change very much as they went from being lovers to being spouses?

7. What seems to account for the vast differences between Emilia and her sister Allison? Out of the many parenting styles presented in the novel, which seems to be the ideal? In what way are parenting styles reflective of an adult's overall outlook on life, as much as his or her concern for a child? How do you personally determine when a level of caution has become irrational and unrealistic?

8. What do you make of William's seemingly nonchalant response to tragedy, such as loudly announcing the absence of the Twin Towers while crossing the Brooklyn Bridge? What do children see (or not see) compared to adults? What did you make of his attempts to draw a family picture and his depiction of Isabel as an angel?

9. Do you agree with Jack's assertion that Emilia married him because she was trying to become her father? Do you believe his statement that he married Carolyn because he loved her? Do you agree with his friends who believe that age had everything to do with his attraction to Emilia? What ultimately is the basis for deep romantic attraction?

10. What keeps Emilia from experiencing the Walk to Remember in the same way that the other families experience it? Does the walk nonetheless have healing results for her?

11. After her blowout argument with Jack, Emilia takes refuge in her best friend, Simon, and a jaunt to Barneys. What makes her

friendship with Simon such a lasting one? Why is she in some ways more comfortable with him than with Mindy? Why is Simon the ideal person to accompany her as she faces her new waistline while shopping?

12. How significant is Judaism to Emilia's identity? How do she and William contend with issues of spiritual traditions? What other elements shape Emilia's sense of self?

13. How would you characterize Emilia's father? Do you empathize with his ex-wife's desire to rekindle a romance with him?

14. Do Emilia and William share any common personality traits? Is she genuinely reckless or insensitive to his needs? Why is it so easy for Jack to believe the accusations that Emilia is not fit to care for his son?

15. What motivates Carolyn to provide Emilia with pathological evidence that Isabel's cause of death was Sudden Infant Death Syndrome? Were you happy to see Carolyn achieve happiness in the end with a man who seems suited to her and a baby on the way?

16. Emilia gets her hands on numerous guides to stepparenting and even pays a visit to William's therapist. What wisdom does *Love and Other Impossible Pursuits* offer stepparents?

17. At the end of the novel, Emilia confirms her father's advice about rational thinking; she says that mystical ideas and hopes interfered with her marriage to Jack. Do you agree with her? Is the concept of *bashert*, the notion of meant-to-be, unrealistic?

Find out more about the author at www.ayeletwaldman.com